continued . . .

DEATH INSTINCT

Bentley Little

WRITING AS PHILLIP EMMONS

A SIGNET BOOK

SIGNET
Published by New American Library, a division of
Penguin Group (USA) Inc., 375 Hudson Street,
New York, New York 10014, USA
Penguin Group (Canada), 90 Eglinton Avenue East, Suite 700, Toronto,
Ontario M4P 2Y3, Canada (a division of Pearson Penguin Canada Inc.)
Penguin Books Ltd., 80 Strand, London WC2R 0RL, England
Penguin Ireland, 25 St. Stephen's Green, Dublin 2,
Ireland (a division of Penguin Books Ltd.)
Penguin Group (Australia), 250 Camberwell Road, Camberwell, Victoria 3124,
Australia (a division of Pearson Australia Group Pty. Ltd.)
Penguin Books India Pvt. Ltd., 11 Community Centre, Panchsheel Park,
New Delhi - 110 017, India
Penguin Group (NZ), cnr Airborne and Rosedale Roads, Albany,
Auckland 1310, New Zealand (a division of Pearson New Zealand Ltd.)
Penguin Books (South Africa) (Pty.) Ltd., 24 Sturdee Avenue,
Rosebank, Johannesburg 2196, South Africa

Penguin Books Ltd., Registered Offices:
80 Strand, London WC2R 0RL, England

Published by Signet, an imprint of New American Library, a division of Penguin Group (USA) Inc. *Death Instinct* was first published in a Signet edition under the name Phillip Emmons

First Printing (Emmons Edition), July 1992
First Printing (Little Edition), December 2006
10 9 8 7 6 5 4 3 2 1

Copyright © Bentley Little, 1992
All rights reserved

 REGISTERED TRADEMARK—MARCA REGISTRADA

For Wai Sau, with love

Evil deeds from evil causes spring.

—*Aristophanes*

Acknowledgments

Thanks to my agent, Dominick Abel, for his expert handling of my fledgling career.

Thanks to Keith Neilson, for his suggestion of a mid-course correction.

Thanks to my parents, for allowing me to grow up strange.

Prologue

Cathy sat in David's darkened room, nervous, though she wasn't quite sure why. Their parents were gone for the afternoon, and David had closed the drapes, throwing the room into a daytime approximation of night. Next to her on the narrow bed sat Billy and, next to Billy, David's friend Rodney. Rodney kept looking at her, trying to catch her eye, though he was ostensibly talking to her brother. She purposely ignored him, staring instead at the closed closet door.

What was David up to?

Her hands pulled nervously on the hem of her skirt, just below her knee. The back of her head itched, and she scratched it. The room seemed darker than it had when she'd first come in, though she could see a thin beam of light streaming through a crack in the drapes to form a wedge of brightness on the closed closet door.

Loud thumping noises sounded from inside the closet, and there was a soft persistent shuffling.

Rodney giggled. "What's he doing in there?"

Cathy wondered herself. She was already sorry she'd come—she knew she wasn't going to like whatever David had planned—but it was too late to back out now. She looked from the closed door of the closet to the closed door of the bedroom and wondered why. she'd agreed to take part in this at all. She knew how David's plans inevitably turned out. But she hadn't been doing anything important, only rereading her favorite parts of *One Hundred and One Dalmations,* her favorite book, and when Billy had burst in on her, inviting her to David's room, telling her that David had something planned, she hadn't been able to resist.

She looked away from the door and her eyes accidentally met Rodney's.

Caught!

He smiled at her and cleared his throat. "So," he said. "What grade are you in this year?"

He knew perfectly well that she was in the seventh grade this year; she had told him the last time he'd been over. She knew that he was only trying to make conversation, trying to talk to her, but she didn't really think they had anything to say to each other. She was still nervously pulling on the hem of her skirt, and she realized with sudden horror that she had pulled it far above her knee, exposing the lower portion of her thigh. She dropped it, blushing, feeling the hot redness creep up her face, and she looked away, certain that Rodney had seen.

"You're still going to St. Catherine's, huh? Don't you hate wearing those uniforms?"

He *had* seen!

Cathy reddened even more, a flush of embarrassment spreading across her skin, but she was determined not to let him gain the upper hand. "I like St. Catherine's," she said evenly.

"Really?" He sounded surprised.

"I don't," Billy announced. "I hate it."

Rodney continued to stare at Cathy. "Have you thought about where you're going to go to high school?"

Cathy didn't want to answer him, but she had brought this on herself. She should never have given him such an opening. "St. Mary's," she said. "I'm thinking of going to St. Mary's."

"But that's an all-girls' school!"

She had shocked him, thrown him off balance. Cathy smiled, feeling as though she had finally gotten the upper hand. "Yes," she said.

There was a look of puzzlement on his face. "Why?"

She shrugged noncommitally.

He stared at her. "Don't you like boys?"

She colored again, embarrassed, and turned away, refusing to answer him.

There was a loud knock from the inside of the closet and all three of them became suddenly silent, turning to face the closed door where David was about to make his entrance. From inside the closet came the muffled imitation of a brass fanfare, half-hummed, half-sung. There was a second of weighty expectant silence, then the closet door was kicked open from the inside, the brass doorknob slamming against the wall as the door swung all the way out. "IT'S TIME," David announced, "FOR NAKED CIRCUS!"

He was sitting astride Billy's old hobbyhorse—a plastic riding horse supported by large springs attached to a metal frame—and he came bounding out of the closet into the room, forcing the horse forward through sheer weight and will in a lurching, jerking jump.

He was completely naked.

Cathy stared, unmoving, rigid with shock and embarrassment, wishing that she could sink into the floor and disappear, wishing that she could hide, wishing that she had never come. But she did not look away. She stared. She couldn't help herself. She and David used to take baths together when they were little, but she hadn't seen him naked in years. Now she stared at the hard stiff organ that rose up from between his legs and at the wiry black hair that had started to grow around it.

David was bounding toward the bed on his horse, laughing and discordantly humming the tune to some circus song. His *thing* bounced up and down with each jog of the horse.

Cathy looked away.

Both Billy and Rodney were laughing uproariously, falling back on the bed, and she was acutely aware that she was the only girl in the room. The air was stuffy, and her skin felt hot and sweaty. She was ashamed, ashamed of David, but she wasn't sure if she was ashamed because she was seeing this or because Rodney was seeing this.

David moved further into the room, jerking his horse forward. "Come one, come all!" he announced. "Come to Naked Circus!"

She found herself, almost against her will, staring once again at his stiff straight erection. His penis was long and thick. She looked away, and her eyes met Rodney's. He was still laughing hard, and his eyes held hers for a moment. She saw something in them that she didn't understand . . . and didn't quite like.

David and his horse jumped a little closer and she stood up, running across the room, flinging open the door, and rushing down the hall to her own safe bedroom.

She closed her door, locked it, and sat on the bed, breathing heavily, her heart pounding. Her hand found *One Hundred and One Dalmatians* and held it. She looked around her room at the reassuring pink walls, at the cluster of stuffed animals in the corner.

Down the hall, David and Rodney and Billy were still laughing.

It sounded as though they were laughing at her.

One

"Someone's moving into the Lauter house!" Little Jimmy Goldstein pointed across the street to where a large yellow moving van was backing into the driveway of the empty residence, coming to a stop a few feet in front of the garage door.

Cathy nodded, turning off the hose and draping the nozzle over the metal pipe next to the rosebushes. "Have you seen the people yet?" she asked him.

Jimmy shook his head. "No." He sat down on his Big Wheel and looked up at her. "I hope they have kids," he said.

Cathy smiled. She hoped they had kids, too. Jimmy needed someone his own age to play with. It wasn't good for him to be hanging around her all the time. When she and David and Billy had been little, the neighborhood had been full of children. But these days the children had all grown up and moved out, leaving the street to their parents, and poor Jimmy was all alone, the only child on a childless block.

She turned to look across the street. Two uniformed men emerged from the van's cab and walked around to the rear of the truck, where they talked for a moment. One mover, looking down at a sheet of paper in his hands, walked to the front door of the house and, pulling a key from his pocket, let himself in. The other mover slid open the rear door of the truck.

Cathy turned back toward Jimmy. "I'm sorry," she said, "but I've got to go. I'm cooking dinner in there, and I've got to check on it."

"Can I come with you?" he asked.

She shook her head. "Not today. Besides, it must be almost your dinnertime, too. Shouldn't you be getting home?"

He shrugged. "My dad doesn't get back 'til late tonight. There's nothing for me to do at home."

Cathy looked at the boy and felt the anger building up inside her. She could never understand why or how Mr. Goldstein had gotten custody of Jimmy. The man was a terrible father, negligent and uncaring. He thought only of himself and treated Jimmy as though he were a pet and not a son, paying attention to him only at mealtimes—and sometimes not even then. Mrs. Goldstein may have been somewhat flighty, but there was no way she could have been as bad a parent as her ex-husband. She might not have been able to provide for the boy as well, but at least she cared about him, at least she could have given him a decent home life.

Jimmy turned his Big Wheel around so it was facing back up the street. "See you," he said.

"Wait." Cathy reached down and put a hand on his bony shoulder, stopping him. "You want to have dinner with us tonight?"

He looked toward the closed drapes of the house. "Is your father there?"

She nodded.

"I guess not. Anyway, I have to feed Dusty. And my dad might call. I'd get my butt kicked if I wasn't home." He pushed his Big Wheel off and waved over his shoulder. "Later!" He began pedaling furiously up the street, and she watched as he skidded into his driveway.

Poor kid.

She wiped her muddy sneakers on the mat and stepped into the house, walking through the living room to the kitchen, where she checked the meat loaf in the oven. She used a fork to poke into the center. Another ten minutes or so. She opened the lid on the peas, not yet boiling on top of the stove, and turned the gas up a little higher. Setting the small timer on the counter for ten minutes, she walked down the hall to the den.

Her father was sitting in the darkened room in his favorite chair, watching the local news. Cathy flipped on the light as she walked into the room. "You're going to ruin your eyes, sitting in the dark all the time."

"I like the dark."

Cathy ignored him and adjusted the vertical hold on the television. There was a black band across the top of the screen, and she could tell that the set was about to start acting up again. She crossed the room and sat down on the couch next to her father's chair. They really needed a new TV, but they couldn't afford it. Not on her salary.

Her father cleared his throat loudly. "What are we having tonight? Not meat loaf, I hope."

She stared at him. Last night, after dinner, he had specifically told her that it had been a long time since he'd had meat loaf and that it sounded good to him. "You know we are," she said. "That's what you wanted."

"Well, I changed my mind."

"It's kind of late for that."

He glared at her. "I'm not eating it."

She met his eyes, held his gaze for a few seconds, then looked away, shrugging her shoulders. "Okay, I'll freeze it and we'll have it some other day."

"Then what are we having tonight?"

"What do you want?"

"I don't know."

They both sat in silence for a few moments, watching the TV. "Someone's moving in across the street,"

Cathy said, deliberately changing the subject. She hoped that if she could get him talking about something else, he'd forget about the meat loaf. She could tell he was just looking for something to fight about this evening.

"So what?" he said. "You think I care?"

"There's a moving van in front of the Lauter house."

"Who gives a damn?"

Cathy stood up. "I have to check on dinner," she said shortly.

"I'm not eating meat loaf!" he called after her.

She held her breath as she walked down the hall, her hands clenched into fists, resisting the temptation to pick up his crutches and smash them against the wall. Sometimes he made her so damn angry.

No, not sometimes.

Most of the time.

She walked across the tile floor of the kitchen and grabbed hold of the edge of the sink. She held on tightly, until her knuckles were white, staring out the kitchen window at the darkening side yard. The shadows were black against the reddish light of the sunset. She watched as they lengthened, grew, charting the progress of the rapidly dying day. It was her fault, too, she knew. She shouldn't let him make her so mad. He was only trying to get a rise out of her. And it encouraged him when he saw that he could still get her goat.

She took a deep breath and closed her eyes, forcing herself to calm down. She should try to get along with him better. After all, he was her father, no matter how childishly he acted or how rude he became. And he didn't have that much longer to live. It was her responsibility to see that his last years on earth were happy ones.

But he was so damned infuriating.

She moved over to the oven and shut off the heat, using two worn potholders to remove the pan from the oven. She emptied the meat loaf onto a dish, covering the dish with tin foil and placing it in the refrigerator. Turning off the gas on the stove, she moved the pot of peas onto a cold burner. She rummaged through the cupboards, moving cans, peering past boxes, but she could find nothing suitable for dinner. She hadn't been to the store in over a week, and they were desperately short of supplies. The only thing in the freezer was a frozen pizza, and her father hated pizza.

She walked back into the den. The *NBC Nightly News* was on, and her father was raptly watching a segment on a late cold spell the East Coast was experiencing. He looked up at her as she entered and chuckled. "I bet Billy's freezing his ass off," he said, pointing toward the screen.

Cathy watched a snowplow trying to maneuver through a street of sleet.

The old man chuckled again. "Serves him right for moving."

She sighed, sitting down on the couch. "What do you want for dinner?"

"I don't care." He shrugged. "Meat loaf, anything."

She stared at him in disbelief, then angrily got up to take the food out of the refrigerator before it became too cold.

After dinner, Cathy drove her father to the club, where she helped him get settled at one of the poker tables, next to his friends. She leaned his crutches against the table, within easy reach, and asked him when he'd like her to pick him up.

"I don't want you to pick me up. Just get the hell out of here and leave me alone."

Geoff Roland looked at her sympathetically. "Don't worry," he said. "I'll drive him home."

She smiled at him. "Thanks."

She left without saying good-bye, striding out of the club and across the parking lot without looking back, and she immediately felt bad. What if he suffered a fatal stroke while playing cards and keeled over on the table, dead? What if Geoff, not one of the world's greatest drivers, got into an accident on the way home and both of them were killed? She put her key in the ignition and was about to start the car, then thought better of it and hurried back into the club.

Her father looked up at her, annoyed. "What's the matter? Forget your keys?"

"No," she said. "I just wanted to say good-bye."

He was silent for a moment as he looked at her, and his expression softened.

"I'll see you later," he said. "I'll be home early."

She walked out to the car feeling better. She'd broken his mood. Things would probably be pleasant for awhile now. At least for a few days. She smiled to herself, feeling almost happy. She got in the car, revved the engine, and drove toward home. On the way, she decided to give herself a treat and stopped off at Baskin-Robbins for an ice cream cone.

The house was dark as she pulled into the driveway, and when she cut the headlights she could see the streetlamp reflected in the front windows. She got out of the car and looked across the street at the Lauter place. The moving van had gone, and sheets had been put up over the inside of the windows. From behind the sheets came a soft glow.

Someone's in there, she thought.

The idea of someone actually living in the Lauter house made her shiver, and she pinched the collar of her blouse closed with two fingers, pressing her hand against her throat. It seemed strange for people to be there, wrong almost.

She found herself staring at the house. She had only been six when Keith Lauter had killed both himself and his wife, but she remembered the events as clearly as if they'd happened yesterday. It had been early morning, and she'd been playing outside with David, helping him attach playing cards to the spokes of his bicycle wheels, when she heard the first shot.

And the scream.

"What's that?" David said, his eyes wide.

There was another shot. And another. And another.

The sounds echoed around the neighborhood like thunder, louder than the loudest sonic boom, and people came out of their houses to see what was happening. It was a Saturday, and most of the fathers were home. Her own father stepped onto the porch in his bathrobe, and Mr. Donaldson from next door came over to see if anyone knew what was going on.

There was yet another shot—a single shot—and it echoed into the blue skies with a grim finality.

Her mother hurried out, spoke quickly to her father in low hushed tones, and immediately grabbed both Cathy and David by the arm. "Come on," she said firmly. "I want you inside for the rest of the day."

They were banished to David's room at the back of the house, away from windows that faced the street, but David sneaked into the den on the pretext of looking for a lost Tonka truck, and he convinced her to go with him. Peeking through the windows, they saw the two bodies loaded onto the ambulance. The bodies were covered with sheets, but the sheets had soaked through with blood, and they could clearly see the wet red mounds of Mrs. Lauter's breasts as her stretcher was put into the ambulance.

One of Mr. Lauter's hands fell out from underneath his sheet, and before the attendant had put it back onto his chest, a thin stream of blood had dribbled onto the asphalt.

The blood had been scrubbed from the pavement that afternoon, but David said later that they never had erased all of the stains from the floor of the house. He had entered the house through the broken back door once, on a truth-or-dare, and he said that traces of the blood were everywhere, staining the walls as well as the floors.

The house had remained vacant for nearly three years after that, and though several renters had lived there during the intervening years, none of them had stayed very long, and the neighborhood children had long since decided that the house was haunted.

Cathy looked at the glowing sheets over the windows of the house and felt a field of goosebumps pop up on her arm. She was twenty-five, no longer a child, but the house still scared her. She found herself wondering if the realtor had told the new tenants or owners the history of the house. Probably not, she decided. It had happened a long time ago, and while events like that might remain fresh and alive within a neighborhood, to outsiders they quickly became ancient history.

She turned away, trying to find the house key on her ring, and thought she saw the corner of one of the front sheets move slightly. She looked up, toward the Lauter house, but now there was no sign of movement.

Shivering, she opened the front door and stepped inside, turning on all of the lights.

Two

A Magritte morning. Ocean blue with bone-white clouds of fluff. The trees outside the window: tall and perfectly even, brown and green. A rider going by, one could almost see the lips. A Magritte morning. A Dali day.

Surreal.

Allan took a sip from the warm can of Diet Coke on his desk. He tended to think in terms of painters, to categorize days by artist. It was only logical. Words were such formal things, such imperfect symbols; the descriptions of even the world's greatest writers were invariably lacking. Words were too stiff and distanced. They could never do justice to anything. Too literal, too factual. Music, on the other hand, was beautiful, but it existed in a world of its own. It bore no resemblance to reality, did not reflect what was happening in the visual universe. But art . . . Ah, art! Painting! Here was something able to do justice to the flowers, the forests, the sky, the day, everything. Real but not literal. Complementing reality. Capturing the essence if not the actual.

And today was the work of the surrealists.

He looked out his window at the park, unsure exactly why he had put such a label on this day. In the adjoining office Lieutenant Thomasson was typing up his report on the prostitution sting, and Allan could hear the staggered clacking of keys as he worked his one-fingered way through the alphabet jungle. He'd felt strange ever since he woke up this morning, and though the feeling was unsettling, it was also perversely enjoyable. There was nothing concrete, nothing he could put his finger on, but for some reason everything seemed slightly off kilter, subtly altered, and this mild feeling of disassociation from his surroundings had a not unpleasant effect on him.

He was still staring out the window, idly tracing circles around the rim of the Diet Coke can with his finger, when the intercom on his desk buzzed twice. He pushed the button for line one and picked up the receiver. "Lieutenant Grant."

The captain wasted no time with pleasantries or salutations. "Get your shit together as fast as you can, Grant." His gruff voice was short and to the point. "There's been a murder in your district. We'd better get over there right away."

"We?"

The captain paused. "It's a bad one. I'm coming with you."

"I'll be right out." Allan dropped the receiver in its cradle; grabbed a notebook, pen, and cassette recorder from the messy pile on top of his desk; and hurried out the door. He strode quickly down the long hallway to the captain's office at the end. Captain Pynchon had strapped on a shoulder holster and was pulling on his coat. "There's a car waiting out front," he said. "We already have patrolmen on the scene." He looked up at Allan, his Brezhnev brows beetled into a worried frown. "Natalie just took the call five minutes ago."

"What happened?"

The captain pushed his way past Allan into the hall. "An old man," he said. "He's been skinned alive."

Grayson Street was fairly close to the police station, and they were at the scene in less than eight minutes. Two patrol cars were parked in front of the one-story tract house, and four uniformed officers were busily cordoning off the area with yellow tape. A crowd had already gathered, older people and housewives primarily, and the onlookers were huddled into small groups, speculating amongst themselves as to what had happened.

The captain was out of the car before it had come to a complete stop. Allan followed him as he ducked under the barrier tape and stepped over to one of the uniforms. He nodded a curt greeting to the patrolman. "Any witnesses?" he asked.

The officer shook his head.

"Who called it in?"

"Woman over there." He pointed toward a middle-aged Hispanic woman sitting in the open backseat of one of the patrol cars. Her hands were clasped together in her lap, and her faraway gaze was blank with shock. "The victim was apparently an invalid, and he hired her to cook, clean, and do chores he couldn't do himself. She found him first thing this morning." He was silent for a moment and he looked from the captain to Allan. "I've never seen anything like it."

Another car pulled up in front of the house—the photographer—and Captain Pynchon stepped back outside the border tape to meet him. Allan looked again at the stunned woman in back of the patrol car, then turned toward the house. All of the drapes were drawn, but the door was wide open. Inside, the entryway was dark. The front of the house looked like a face. Behind him, like the low hum of some monstrous machine, he could hear the rhythmic babble of gossiping spectators.

Surreal.

"I'm going in!" he announced. The captain, conferring with the photographer, raised his hand in acknowledgement, and Allan walked past a guarding patrolman, up the front porch into the house.

The smell hit him the second he stepped through the doorway. He gagged, holding a hand over his nose. The stench was horrible, a sickening combination of heavy copper and hot bile. Blood. He backed up and took a deep breath of the relatively fresh air outside, closing his eyes tightly, trying not to vomit. He opened his eyes, giving them a moment to adjust before venturing into the front room. He walked past a wood-framed Norman Rockwell print and stood under the squared archway of the family room entrance, looking around. There was no sign of violence. The glassware in the china cabinet against the far wall was untouched, the furniture in the room had not been disturbed. The gray carpet was spotless.

He moved toward the kitchen, and the smell of death became stronger. He pinched his nose closed, breathing entirely through his mouth. His eyes scanned the narrow room. Pink Frigidaire. White tile counter. Grease-spattered electric stove. Dripping faucet. Red and white linoleum floor.

No, not a red and white linoleum floor.

A white linoleum floor dissected with rivulets of drying blood.

Heart pounding in his chest, Allan walked slowly forward. He had seen a lot of dead bodies in his seven years on the force, quite a few of them homicides, but it never got any easier. It was always horrible, always a shock. On television, in the movies, policemen became jaded, cynical, immune to the sight of death. But in real life it was different. The bodies had a sensory dimension that could not be experienced secondhand. The blood had a nauseatingly vivid quality that did not translate to representational media.

Violent death was always a difficult thing to face.

Allan neared the corner of the kitchen where the

blood had come from. Slowly, tentatively, bracing himself, he peeked around the corner into the darkened dining room.

The old man's body was spread out on top of the dining room table, fingers and toes splayed and affixed to the wood with sharp kitchen utensils. He had indeed been skinned, and his skin lay in a slimy red and brown heap near the head of the table. Allan could see that the skin had been peeled off in even, rectangular strips. The dead man's eyes were wide open and staring, the pupils strangely white and round against the exposed red flesh of his face. The visible muscles of his body were frozen in concrete patterns of strain, and his mouth was open wide in what had apparently been his final scream.

Scream? Then how come the neighbors hadn't heard anything?

Allan bent closer. A large hole had been torn open in the man's throat, from which his larynx hung limply out.

There was a sharp flash of sudden bright light, and Allan jumped. He whirled around to see Captain Pynchon and the photographer standing behind him, staring at the corpse. He had been so involved in his thoughts that he had not heard them approach. The photographer snapped another picture, then moved around to get a side view. The captain shook his head, his eyes riveted on the body. "Jesus," he said. He, too, was holding a hand over his nose to keep from throwing up.

The photographer snapped another picture. He looked up at Allan. He was an old man, bald with a bushy white mustache, but his face bore the frightened expression of a sixteen-year-old boy. "I've seen a lot of bad bodies in my time," he said, his voice low. "But I've never seen nothing like this." He stared at the drying stalactites of blood dripping from the edge of the table. "I can't believe someone could do something like this."

The captain looked at Allan. "Don't go running to the papers," he said. "I want to keep this away from them for as long as we can."

"Running to the papers?"

"Just don't be as cooperative with the press as you usually are, okay? They don't need to know every little detail."

Allan looked back at the body, at the knives, forks, and icepicks shoved through the old man's fingers and toes. The white round eyes bored lifelessly into his own as the silent mouth screamed. "It's going to be hard to keep this one a secret," he said.

The pathologist and his men arrived soon after to collect the body, and while the photographer took his final pictures, Allan and two of the uniforms searched the house. There seemed to be no sign of a struggle; nothing was overturned, nothing was out of place. Aside from the dining room, the house seemed to be undisturbed.

Allan peeked out the front window of one of the bedrooms. The crowd outside was larger now, and enquiring neighbors were pressing close to the barrier tape, hungry for a better view. A group of curious onlookers had gathered around the rear of the ambulance. He let the drapes fall shut and turned to Bob Whitehead, the officer nearest him. "I want you to dust for prints," he said. "Cover the front, back, and side doors, and everything in the dining room. Leave the knives and the other utensils. I'll take those back with me to the lab."

Whitehead nodded silently. He licked lips. "Do you really think we're going to find anything?"

"No." Allan shook his head. "Anyone who could pull off something like that wouldn't leave any prints. But we have to check."

He led the way back out to the dining room. The kitchen utensils had already been removed from the body and had been placed in a sealed plastic bag on the floor. Two white-suited men, each of them wearing gloves and thin paper masks, were gingerly shifting the corpse into a body bag. The pathologist himself was crouched on the floor, using a pair of plastic tongs to place the pieces of peeled skin into a metal container. Whitehead and Jim Williams, the other uniformed officer, went outside to retrieve the fingerprinting kit. Allan sidled next to the captain. He grimaced as he watched a red-muscled arm flop out of the open body bag, fingers dripping thickly with newly released blood. "The guy sure knew what he was doing, didn't he?"

Pynchon nodded, watching an attendant zip the bag closed. His thick eyebrows furrowed in thought. "I want you to run this through the computer when you get back," he said. "Maybe I'm getting senile, but I think something similar to this happened up in northern California a few years back."

Allan stared at him. "Similar to *this*?"

"I think it was a cult or something. I can't really remember." He shook his head as the body was carried out, the clear bag growing increasingly red as the plastic settled on the body. "I wish to Christ this had happened in someone else's jurisdiction." He started toward the kitchen, then turned around. "I'm heading back. You want me to send a car for you in an hour or so?"

Allan shook his head. "I'll be here for awhile. I don't know how long it'll take. I want to interview this cleaning woman, some of the immediate neighbors, run a vacuum, go over everything in the house thoroughly. I'll catch a ride back."

"All right." The captain walked through the kitchen toward the front of the house, stepping over the red streaks on the linoleum. A moment later, there was a clamor of voices, and Allan heard the captain gruffly call out. "No comment! I said, no comment!"

Allan smiled. The reporters had already found out.

"Excuse me." The pathologist pushed past him, his arms clutching the metal container. Allan watched him round the corner in the kitchen. He turned back toward the dining room table. A bloody outline of the body was clearly visible on the finished wood.

He looked around the room. Not Magritte, he thought. Not Dali.

Bosch.

A vision of hell.

He went through the kitchen to oversee the print dusting.

Three

Jimmy Goldstein stood alone next to the monkey bars, glancing every so often out of the corner of his eye at the two bullies huddled next to the tetherball court. Above him, several happily playing children climbed the bars or slid down the center pole, laughing and talking excitedly. He looked up as one of the more active kids swung from the top bar and landed feet first in the sand below. Casually, he allowed his gaze to wander over to the tetherball court.

Both Tim Halback and Dan Samson were staring at him and smiling.

He looked quickly away, his heart pounding. He grabbed the bar above his head and began climbing, as if he had been playing all the while and had just happened to glance over in their direction. He climbed to the top of the monkey bars, resisting the temptation to see where they were now or what they were doing. He wasn't fooling them, he knew. They were well aware of the fact that he had seen them. Against his better judgment, he hazarded another glance in their direction.

They were still staring.

Jimmy's skin felt suddenly cold. They were after

him. There was no doubt about it now. If they didn't get him at lunch or at afternoon recess, they'd wait for him after school. He was doomed. His ass was grass.

"Jimmy!"

He looked down to see Paul Butler crawling up the bars behind him. Paul was smiling, his silver tooth glinting in the mid-morning sunlight. He climbed next to Jimmy. "It wasn't anything," he said. "I just forgot my lunch."

Paul had been called to the principal's office just before recess, and Jimmy hadn't expected to see him until after class had begun again. He looked over at his friend. "I thought you were in trouble."

Paul grinned. "So did I. Especially when I saw my mom waiting there in the office for me. But she just came by to drop my lunch off."

Jimmy looked down, through the geometric tangle of bars, at the top of a girl's blonde head. He swallowed and took a deep breath. "Halback and Samson are after me," he said.

"Really?" Paul's eyes widened.

He nodded, pointing toward the tetherball court with a surreptitious finger. Paul's eyes darted in that direction. "They've been staring at me all recess."

"What did you do to them?"

"Nothing."

"You must've done something. They can't be after you for no reason."

Jimmy thought for a moment. "Well, a few days ago, on the way home, Dalton rode by and called me something, and I called him a weenie."

"You said that to *Dalton*? He's practically Samson's best friend!" He glanced toward the tetherball court. Both of the bullies were looking in their direction. Halback was grinding a fist into his palm, an expression of gleeful malice on his face. Paul shivered. "What are you going to do during lunch?"

"Stay close to the lunch monitors. They won't try anything with them around."

The bell rang, and students began dropping off the

sides of the monkey bars. A rush of converging kids from the swings, slides, field, bathrooms, and four-square and tetherball courts moved in staggered waves toward the classrooms. Jimmy watched the two bullies follow the crowd toward their classes before jumping off the monkey bars. Paul landed on the sand next to him, dusting his hands off on his pants. "What about after school? Is your dad going to pick you up?"

Jimmy shook his head. "I don't know what I'm going to do."

The two boys walked slowly back toward class, giving Halback and Samson plenty of time to pull ahead of them. "Maybe you should talk to the principal," Paul suggested. "Tell him what's going on."

"Are you kidding? They'd really kill me then."

Paul thought for a moment. "You could get sick, go home early."

Jimmy shook his head. "They'd just get me tomorrow. I can't be sick every day."

"What are you going to do, then?"

"I don't know," Jimmy said tiredly. "I need some time to think about it."

"You don't have much time." Paul glanced from side to side. They had reached the classroom area, and a lot of people were around them. He lowered his voice. "You heard about Samson's brother, didn't you?"

"I heard he was in jail."

"Did you hear why?"

Jimmy looked at him. "Why?"

"He cut off a baby's dick."

Jimmy felt the cold grip of fear settle around the pit of his stomach. He shook his head incredulously. "I don't believe it."

"It's true. Him and his gang were at Safeway and they walked into the bathroom, and there was this baby sitting on the toilet. His father was standing there watching him, and two of the guys hit the father over the head and knocked him out. Then Samson's brother took out his switchblade and cut the kid's dick clean off."

"I don't believe it," Jimmy repeated, but the fear in his stomach grew. He thought of the cold dark bathroom in that grocery store, thought of the baby screaming there on the toilet with his penis cut off, blood gushing from between his chubby thighs, and he knew he would never go in that bathroom again.

Paul looked at him seriously, stopping just outside the door of their classroom. "Those guys are mean," he said. "If I were you, I'd get sick and go home early."

The day went by slowly. Jimmy could concentrate on neither math nor history after recess. As the teacher droned on, he found himself thinking about the two older boys and what they would do if they caught him. In his mind, he plotted the safest route home. During lunch, he stayed close to the lunch monitors, as planned, but he needn't have bothered. Halback and Samson were nowhere in sight. They were there at afternoon recess, however, looking for him, and he stayed close to the classrooms, hiding.

He didn't know how he was going to make it home.

They were waiting for him after school, just outside the playground gates. Jimmy was talking loudly to Paul as they walked, trying to pretend that nothing was going on, hoping that by ignoring the problem he would make it go away. But when he saw the two of them standing on the other side of the chain-link fence, he stopped cold, the fear welling up inside him. His legs suddenly felt weak.

Samson grinned at him, his lips thin, his smile cruel. "C'mere, kid. We want to talk to you."

Although Tim Halback and Dan Samson were in fifth grade, only two grades ahead of him, they both looked much older. Halback was thin, with long blond hair and a hard angular face. He seldom wore anything save Levi's and rock T-shirts, and his arms were brown with a combination of suntan and dirt. Samson was taller and stockier. His eyes were blue and unflinchingly icy, and his mouth curved naturally into an unattractive sneer. He had been suspended three times this year alone for fighting, and Jimmy had been witness to one of the fights, watching as Samson repeatedly shoved his opponent's head into a tree trunk. By the time one of the teachers had broken up the fight, the other boy's face had been battered and bleeding. He had lost two teeth. Samson had not even been hurt.

"Come here, kid."

"Go to the principal's office," Paul whispered. "You can get away."

Jimmy backed up.

"You're going to have to leave school sometime," Halback said. "We'll just wait here until you do."

Samson looked at him coldly. He spat. "Pussy," he said.

Jimmy turned around and started walking toward the office, moving purposely, without hesitation. Paul stood rooted for a second, unsure of what to do, then hurried to follow his friend.

"Where are you going?" Halback demanded.

"To the principal's office," Jimmy announced loudly.

"We haven't touched you." Jimmy was gratified to hear the worry in Halback's voice. He kept walking, not turning around, not saying anything.

"You're dead," Samson said. His voice was low and even, without fear, and he said the words as if he were stating a fact. "You're dead, kid."

"They're leaving!" Paul whispered, walking next to him with a sideways gait. "You scared them."

Jimmy stopped and turned around. His mouth was dry, and his hands were shaking. His heart was pumping a mile a minute, pounding loudly in his chest, the blood thumping in his head. The two older boys had started home, walking slowly along the fence toward Oak Street. Periodically, they glanced back at him, and even from this far away he could see the expressions of hatred in their faces.

"Let's keep walking toward the principal's office," Jimmy said. "Just in case." He smiled at Paul, pretending to be brave, pretending he had just won the war though he knew it had only begun. He wondered how he was going to make it home safely.

He had the feeling they would be waiting for him somewhere along the way.

Four

"I heard about the murder this morning," Ann Turner said. She put the sealed box she had been carrying next to Cathy's register and knelt on one knee to rummage through the miscellaneous junk on the shelf beneath the counter for an X-Acto knife. "Gruesome."

Cathy looked at her blankly. "What murder?"

"You didn't hear?"

Cathy shook her head.

"That's right. You've been here all day. You had to open this morning." Ann found the knife she had been looking for and stood up. She sliced open the box, threw the X-Acto back under the counter, and pulled out a stack of *People* magazines, placing them on the other side of the register. She brushed a strand out of her eyes and used a rubber band to tie her long brown hair back into a ponytail. "It's all over the radio. They found this old man murdered in his house. He'd been skinned."

"What were they going to do? Stuff him and mount him on the wall?" Jeff Martin peeked out from behind the bookstore's Occult aisle, where he was shelving new releases. He grinned. His ever-changing hair was black and slicked back today. Yesterday, it had been orange and spiked. As always, he wore an old black dinner jacket with multicolored buttons arranged strategically on its skinny lapels.

Ann ignored him. "It was right in your neighborhood," she told Cathy. "Maybe two or three streets down from you."

"He was skinned?"

Ann nodded. "Completely." She used a finger to push her slipping glasses up the bridge of her nose.

"Are you sure it was my neighborhood?"

Ann withdrew a pile of *Newsweek* magazines from the box. "Grayson Street. That's just a few blocks down from you, right?"

"Two," Cathy admitted. She shook her head slowly in disbelief. "What kind of person could do something like that?"

Jeff peeked his head around the corner of the bookshelf. "Your dad?" he said. Cathy had to laugh.

Ann frowned at him. "Just get to work." She sidled close to Cathy, lowering her voice to a whisper, an expression of disapproval on her face. "I don't know why Barry hired that asshole."

"I heard that!" Jeff called out. He emerged from the aisle and was about to make a cutting reply when a customer walked through the door—a trim middle-aged man wearing a dark gray business suit. All three of them smiled pleasantly at the man, who nodded in return. Jeff silently went back to his shelving, and Ann continued to unload the box.

"Is there anything I can help you with?" Cathy asked.

The customer shook his head and smiled at her. "I'm just looking." He glanced at the magazine rack opposite the front counter before moving slowly back toward the best-sellers at the rear of the store.

With nothing to do while the customer browsed, Cathy watched Ann as she finished taking the magazines out of the box. The other girl's mouth was set in an expression of concentration that lent a look of intelligence to her already pretty face. She wore very little makeup, but the shadow and lipstick she did have on expertly highlighted her natural assets. Her thick brown hair, now tied in a ponytail for convenience, usually curled softly around her shoulders in a seductive wave and looked good no matter what she did with it. Cathy felt the vague stirrings of jealousy within her. Although Ann was nearly three years younger than herself and still in college, she was much more attractive, and she had about her an aura of confident sophistication that Cathy knew she would never possess.

Cathy liked Ann. In fact, when it came down to it, Ann was probably the closest thing she had to a real friend. But she couldn't help feeling slightly envious, and the unpleasant feelings of jealousy she periodically experienced only led to even more unpleasant feelings of guilt.

Ann took the empty box off the counter and put it down on the floor by her feet. She picked up a *Playgirl* from the pile and idly thumbed through it, stopping every so often to look at one of the pictures. Over the younger girl's shoulder, Cathy saw the naked form of a brown-haired man leaning against a rock by the seashore, and she turned away, blushing in embarrassment.

The customer emerged from the back of the store and smiled politely at them. Ann quickly closed her magazine, putting it back in the pile. "Did you find what you were looking for?" she asked.

"Yes, but I'll have to come back for it later. I'm a little short of cash right now."

Ann smiled at him. "We'll still be here," she said.

The man waved good-bye to them and walked out the door. Ann stood for a moment, staring at the pile of periodicals before her, then started separating the magazines by subject. Cathy decided to help her. The rest of the afternoon would be slow until the schools let out at three, and there was really nothing for her to do right now. She hated just standing by the register when there were no customers. She picked up a pile of *Time* magazines and took them over to the rack, replacing last week's copies.

"You don't have to do that," Ann told her.

Cathy smiled. "There's nothing else to do."

Jeff walked up to the front counter, adjusting his skinny black rep tie. "So," he said, "were they big ones?"

Ann glared at him. "What?"

"I saw what you were looking at." He picked up a *Playgirl* and opened it. "I heard they only picked guys with big huge ones." He grinned at Cathy and raised his eyebrows in an absurd parody of a lecherous leer. She turned away, her cheeks reddening.

"Shut up," Ann said.

He laughed and put the magazine down. He loosened his tie. "I'm going on break," he said.

Cathy nodded, and he walked out the door, already digging in his pocket for change. He ran across the busy street to the Circle K.

Ann shook her head and pushed her glasses up the bridge of her nose. "I don't know why Barry hired that asshole."

Cathy drove home feeling tired. It had been a long day, and Jeff had skipped out an hour before his shift was scheduled to end, claiming that his allergies were bothering him. She had stayed a half hour longer than she was supposed to in order to help Ann with the rush.

She signaled automatically and turned left onto Lincoln. Right now she just wanted to relax and take a hot bath.

She approached Grayson and found herself slowing the car to look down the street. Halfway up the block, two police cars and several civilian vehicles were parked in front of a nondescript house fenced in by what looked like yellow ribbon. A small crowd of onlookers stood across the street.

Skinned.

Cathy shivered and drove past the street, speeding

up. Once, long ago, she had had a friend, Pam Rice, who lived on Grayson, and she and David and Billy had often gone over there to play. It scared her now to think of the butchery that had happened within walking distance of Pam's old place, and she wondered how she would have reacted to it as a child. No doubt she would have had nightmares for months.

She flipped on the radio, turning it to the all-news station, hoping to hear something about the murder, but the announcer was in the middle of a business report, and she switched the radio off. She'd catch the story on the TV news later.

As she pulled into the driveway, Jimmy Goldstein was waiting for her, seated on the curb in front of her house, using a small stick to divert currents in the stream of dirty water that ran through the gutter. He stood up as she pulled to a stop in front of the closed garage door, dropping his stick into the miniature rapids and wiping his hands on his jeans. Cathy smiled at him as she got out of the car. "How's it going today?"

He looked at the ground and shook his head. "Not so good." He kicked at a tuft of grass growing through a crack in the sidewalk with his sneakered foot.

She walked around the back of the car and approached him. He looked up at her, his eyes filled with a glum resignation. "What's wrong?" she asked.

"Two guys are going to pug my mug."

"Pug your mug?"

"You know, beat me up." He sighed. "I don't know what I'm going to do. Maybe I'll transfer to another school."

Cathy suppressed a smile. "It can't be that bad."

He stared at her, and she saw an animated desperation in his features, a fervent belief in the hopelessness of his situation reflected in his face. "It *is* that bad. You don't know these guys. They're big. And they're mean."

"They'll forget about you in a couple days," she said reassuringly.

"They won't forget. They won't give up until they

get me." His skinny arms were rigid, his hands balled into fists. "I wish I knew karate or something, so I could fight back."

Cathy laughed. She couldn't help it. "I'm sorry!" she said immediately. "I'm sorry!" She held up her hands in an expression of apology, shaking her head as if to deny her laughter, but she started laughing even more, unable to stop.

Jimmy looked up at her, obviously trying to maintain the feelings of self-pitying dejection he'd been cultivating all afternoon, but he soon found himself smiling as well. He looked down at his thin unathletic body and tried to imagine himself using karate to beat up Halback and Samson. "I guess it is kind of funny," he admitted, his grin widening.

Cathy giggled. "I'm not laughing at you," she said.

"Yes, you are."

"No, I'm not. Really." She shouldered her purse, wiping tears from the corners of her eyes, her fit of laughter spent. She smiled at him. "It's just that you were so serious. To be honest, you reminded me of me."

"You?"

She nodded. "When I was about your age, maybe a little older, this new girl came to our school. Beth Dotson. She was big and tough and mean and could beat up anyone in our class, boys included. One day, I accidentally bumped into her while standing in line. 'You're dead,' she told me. And I believed her. For a month after that, I invented reasons to stay after school so I would be able to get home safely. Once, I even purposely got in trouble so I would have to stay after. When I said my prayers each night, I prayed that Beth Dotson wouldn't beat me up the next day."

"Did she ever get you?" Jimmy asked.

Cathy shook her head, smiling. "She forgot about it. Sooner than I did, probably."

Jimmy's face clouded over. "But these guys won't forget. They're serious. They want to kill me."

"When you're my age, you'll look back on this and laugh."

"I don't think so."

Overhead, there was the sound of a sonic boom as a jet, glinting orange as it sped away from the setting sun, charted a path across the skies of Phoenix toward the Air Force base in Gilbert. Cathy looked up, following the jet's progress as it disappeared into the east. Her gaze returned to Jimmy, and she was silent for a moment as she studied the young boy's face. He really did look scared. "Are you going to tell your dad?" she asked finally.

"I don't think so. He'd just go down to the school and tell the principal, and then they'd really be after me."

"So what's your plan?"

"Hide," he said. "I'll just have to hide the rest of the year and stay out of their way. If I can make it to the summer, I'll probably be safe. I figure they'll forget about me over the summer." He looked at her, the corners of his mouth turning up despite himself. "They're not real smart."

She smiled at him encouragingly. "They'll probably forget even before then." She put a hand on his shoulder. "Don't worry. Things'll work out." She looked at her watch. "It's getting late. I have to go in and cook dinner."

"Can I come in with you?"

She felt a rush of pity for the small boy. The way Jimmy looked up at her made him seem like a small lost puppy. She experienced a renewed feeling of anger toward his father. She glanced away from his pleading eyes and saw that across the street, at the Lauter house, light green curtains had been hung in the front windows. The multilighted form of a chandelier was visible through the translucent material. The old house was already starting to acquire a lived-in look. She turned back toward Jimmy. "Do you know who's moved in there yet?"

He shook his head. "I haven't seen anybody."

"I'll have to go over there sometime and meet them. I'll bring them a cake. Or some brownies."

"Can I go too?"

"Yeah, you can go. Who knows? Maybe they have a boy your age."

"I doubt it. If there was, he probably would've come out by now."

He had a point. Cathy took her keys out of her purse. "What time does your father get home tonight?" she asked, already knowing the answer.

"Late. He left me a pizza to heat up in the microwave."

"Okay," she said. "You can come in with me. You can even stay to dinner, if you want. I'm not sure what we're having yet, but I'm sure I can find something you like."

"I have to feed Dusty."

"Dusty can wait. She'll just have to eat a little later tonight. That's all."

Jimmy's eyes darted toward the closed curtains of the living room window, and Cathy knew that he was thinking about her father. She saw the look of indecision on his face.

"You can eat with me in the kitchen," she said softly. "I think my father is going to eat in front of the TV in the den."

He looked up at her gratefully. "Thanks."

"Come on." She led the way around the row of flower boxes up the steps of the front porch. "Let's eat."

Five

Allan leaned back in the broken swivel chair, massaging his temples with his fingertips. He had turned off the overheads in his office, and the only illumination came from the streetlamps outside the police station. Across the way, the park was dark, a rounded natural black mass against the artificially lighted geometric backdrop of the city. On the sidewalk, a Navajo family walked slowly by.

Allan closed his eyes. He had planned a quiet evening at home tonight. The Suns were playing Los Angeles, and he'd hoped to sit in front of the tube with a couple of beers and a bowl of popcorn and watch the Lakers get the crap beaten out of them, but that plan had gone straight down the toilet. He thought for some reason of Jack Nicholson, who had Lakers season tickets and was in the front row of every home game, and wished that he had the time to use season tickets. Or the money to buy them.

You picked the wrong profession, he told himself.

There was a low buzzing on his intercom, and he opened his eyes, pushing his chair back down. He picked up the receiver. "Lieutenant Grant," he said tiredly.

"Computer check's coming through." Adamson's voice did not sound overly enthusiastic. "I don't think it's what you're looking for."

"I'll be right down." Allan hung up the receiver and opened his office door, moving quickly down the hall. He cut through Dispatching and arrived in the computer room just as Adamson was pulling the printout. He took the sheet of perforated paper from the other man's hand. A quick glance told him all he needed to know. The captain had been right. Two men connected with the Ramreesh cult had been found murdered in northern California in the late seventies. The skin on their arms and legs had been peeled. Three other cult members had been tried and convicted of the crime, sentenced to life imprisonment.

All three were still incarcerated in a maximum-security prison.

"Damn," Allan swore softly. "I was afraid of this." He reread the information, then folded the printout and put it in the pocket of his jacket. He nodded at the technician. "Thanks, Jack."

"Sorry it wasn't what you were looking for."

"It's not your fault."

Adamson smiled. "I never thought it was." He turned off the printer. "What are you going to do now?"

"What I should've done hours ago—go home." He nodded to the technician. "Later." Walking out of the computer room, he stepped through the short corridor between Dispatching and Administration and turned down the first hallway. He glanced down the hall at Captain Pynchon's office, but the captain's door was closed. He'd gone home hours ago.

Allan shuffled back to his office, flipped on the light, and took the printout from his pocket, throwing it on top of the cluttered mess of papers on his desk. He rubbed his burning eyes. This was going to be one mother of a case. The house had been free of all fingerprints save for those of Morrison and his maid, and the kitchen implements that had been used to nail him to the table had been equally clean. The maid herself had told him next to nothing, and Forensics hadn't turned up anything worth mentioning. Thus far, there had been no notes, phone calls, or other warnings. None of the usual sickos had even called up to take credit for the murder.

They were up shit creek.

Allan picked his keys up off his desk, patted his jacket to make sure he had his wallet, and made a quick spot check of the office to see if there was anything he'd forgotten.

They were following the usual police procedures. Descriptions of the victim and the murderer's M.O. had been telexed earlier to police and sheriffs' offices throughout the state, and anything any of Morrison's neighbors could recall was being diligently followed up. Policemen were even canvasing the surrounding neighborhoods. But there was really nothing they could do at this point to catch whoever had committed the savage crime.

Allan closed the door to his office and locked it. He stood there for a moment, listening to the unfamiliar night sounds of the police station. This was the worst part of an investigation, the bad time—when there were no leads to go on and a murderer was still free to do as he pleased. This was when guilt and frustration set in, when a cop felt the most helpless. With only one murder, a killer's pattern could not be established. And until a pattern was established or a significant lead was found, there was no way to protect potential victims.

The only thing they could do was wait until he struck again.

Allan swallowed. His mouth was dry, and he could taste the tired foulness of his breath. He needed a drink. His stomach rumbled noisily. And he needed food. He hadn't had anything to eat all day save a piece of toast for breakfast and half a bag of McDonald's fries around lunchtime.

He walked down the hall, through the lobby, and waved good night to the desk sergeant and the two other officers on duty before stepping out the automatic double doors that opened onto the side yard. He walked past the rows of patrol cars and impounded vehicles to his own battered white Bronco. He thought of what he had at home. There was a pint of unopened scotch in his liquor cabinet, left over from his apartment-warming party last September, but there was no food in his cupboards. He hadn't had time to go shopping this week. He unlocked the door and got into the Bronco. He didn't feel much like cooking tonight, anyway. Maybe he'd just grab some junk food and take it back with him. There was a Taco Bell on the way, a Burger King, a Pizza Hut, a Jack in the Box. He could find something to eat.

He pulled out of the yard and onto the street. The traffic was heavy, particularly for this time of evening, and he couldn't make it into the left lane fast enough to get to Taco Bell, so on the next block he pulled into Jack in the Box, which was on the right-hand side of the road. He ordered a Jumbo Jack, large fries, and an apple turnover. Deciding that scotch didn't really wash well with hamburger, he amended his order to include an extra-large Diet Coke.

The fries were gone by the time he reached his apartment complex, and by the time he'd made it up the stairs to his landing, the bag containing his hamburger and apple turnover was cold. Balancing his drink and his bag of food in one hand, he opened the door with the other. The apartment was dark, and he flipped on the lights. Recessed bulbs in the white ceiling illuminated the front room, shedding warm light on the beige shag carpet and the modern furnishings. A row of track lights lit from above the framed art prints on the wall above the sofa. He put his Diet

Coke down on a low coffee table and took his hamburger into the kitchen to microwave it. He brought both the now-steaming Jumbo Jack and the apple turnover back into the front room, turning on the television set and sitting down on the floor next to the coffee table.

He glanced through the TV guide as he ate, but there was nothing but crap on the networks. The game was over, and he'd already missed the first forty-five minutes of a movie on cable, so he got up and changed the channel to an early local newscast. He settled back on the carpet, leaning against the sofa, to eat his dessert. On the news, there was a story on renewed hostilities in the Middle East and a quick recap of the day's events in Washington.

The top local story was Morrison's murder, and he quickly turned up the volume. There was a still photograph of the old man taken last year, and footage of the covered body being put into the ambulance this morning. The reporter covering the story said that the body had been skinned, that the instrument of torture had not yet been determined and that the police were "currently following all available leads."

Allan smiled at that one.

Before signing off, the reporter noted the similarity between this killing and two murders that had occurred in northern California several years ago. Allan shook his head. It always amazed him how fast reporters latched onto information. He finished the last bite of his apple turnover. Maybe he should assign a few reporters to the case instead of policemen.

He had already thrown away his bag and cup and was about to go into the bathroom and take a relaxing shower when the phone rang.

He jumped, startled.

No, he thought, closing his eyes. *Don't let it be that.*

But he knew before picking up the receiver who was on the other end. He saw again in his mind the red exposed muscles of the old man, the pile of greasy skin near the head of the dining room table, the congealed pools of blood. He smelled the nauseous odor of violence. The phone rang once more, and he answered it. "Hello?"

His heart sank as he heard Pynchon's gruff voice. "There's been another one."

Six

"Is that little bastard gone yet?"

Cathy put down the glass she had been rinsing and turned to face her father. He was leaning on one crutch, his free hand grasping the edge of the kitchen door. His short gray hair looked bristled and asymmetrical, as if he had been sleeping on it, and the corners of his mouth were turned down in a disapproving scowl. She wiped her hands on a dry dish towel and forced herself to regard him calmly. "Jimmy has left," she said.

"Good thing." He pulled himself into the kitchen, using one hand to steady himself against the wall and the other to hold the metal crutch. "I hate that kid."

"You could at least treat him decently. He's scared to death of you."

"And well he should be."

"I don't know why you dislike him so much."

"And I don't know why you like him." Using his crutch to steady himself, he lowered his body into a chair. His voice took on a nasty suggestive tone. "It's not natural for a grown woman to be playing around with little boys."

She ignored him, not even bothering to dignify his

filthy insinuation with an answer. She turned back to the sink and began putting the dirty dishes she had been rinsing into the empty dishwasher.

"Why don't you ever go out with men your own age?"

Cathy concentrated on the dishes in her hand, her face muscles clenching involuntarily. She hated this conversation. Though the subject had long since been beaten to death, her father constantly and consistently brought it up, insisting on talking about her lack of an active social life though he knew how painful it was for her. He claimed to be interested in her welfare, concerned about her future, but his remarks were always viciously delivered criticism thinly disguised as helpful hints, and she knew that he secretly gloated over the fact that she spent most of her nights alone with him. She pushed in the bottom rack of the dishwasher, finished with the large items, and pulled out the top rack, saying nothing.

"Huh?" His voice was insistent, almost belligerent.

"Huh what?" She did not even bother to turn around.

"Why don't you ever go out?"

"We've been over this a million times. I don't really feel like discussing it right now." She finished loading the dishwasher and took a box of Cascade out from under the sink, pouring the detergent into the plastic indentation on the inside of the dishwasher door. She closed the door and pushed the button for Full Cycle.

"Why don't you ever go out?"

She put the detergent back under the sink. "Look, I don't want to talk about it, okay?"

"You can't blame everything on David, you know."

Cathy swiveled toward him. He was sitting at the kitchen table, pretending to examine his fingernails, but there was an expression of smug satisfaction on his lined face. "I'm not blaming David," she said evenly.

"Are you waiting for him to turn up somewhere? Are you waiting for him to come back?"

"You're sick."

"Then why don't you ever go out?" His eyes met hers, and she saw in them a look she did not recognize. The half-smile on his lips was cold and cruel.

She flinched, shocked by her father's almost passionate animosity. She had never seen him this way before. He was often mean, often cruel, often thoughtless, but he had never before seemed filled with such deliberate malice. "I go out," she said defensively.

"When?"

"Sometimes."

"Not in the past five years."

She shook her head. "It hasn't been that long. I went out with George Wright. And Campbell Haught, that friend of Ann's brother."

He snorted. "I mean out on dates. Real dates."

"Those were dates."

"The hell they were!" He glared at her, and she reached behind her to grasp the edge of the sink for support. His eyes bored into hers. "Why didn't you go out with them again?"

"Look," she said. "I don't really have much time to go out. I have to work. I have to take care of you. I have to—"

"Did they try to get in your pants?"

"Go to hell!" she said, throwing the dish towel at him. She strode out of the kitchen and walked purposefully down the hall, her heart pounding. She had never sworn at her father before. She had never dared to stand up to him that way. He had often sworn at her, and she had frequently argued with him, but though she'd wanted to tell him to go to hell many times, she had never been able to muster the courage. She had always backed down, given in, and tried to placate him. This time, however, he had gone too far.

Cathy stormed into her room and slammed the door. She was about to throw herself on the bed when she thought the better of it and turned around to lock the door. She didn't want him walking in on her. She didn't want him in her room at all.

From the front of the house, she heard the familiar

syncopated shuffling rhythm of her father maneuvering across the hardwood floor on his crutches. He was leaving the kitchen, going into the den to watch TV. She heard the soft thump of his padded crutch ends on the floor, and she was filled with rage. She had grown to hate the sounds associated with his infirmity, just as she had grown to hate the sweet cloying smells of his medication. Whatever pity she had once felt for him had long since dissipated. Her feelings toward him now were closer to loathing and disgust than anything else.

Cathy sat down on her bed for a moment and closed her eyes. Slowly, the pounding of her heart relaxed into a more natural rhythm and her breathing became normal again. She stood up and walked across her room to the bookcase, where she turned on her small black-and-white TV. She found an old movie, a comedy with Cary Grant, and moved back to the bed, lying down.

She didn't hate her father. Not really. But it was getting harder and harder to love him. He was increasingly bitter, increasingly thoughtless and self-centered, and she had to think back to the past, remember what he once was, in order to generate any feelings for him at all. The things she had once done out of kindness and love, she realized, she did now out of duty. She felt bad that she had sworn at him the way she had, but she did not feel guilty. He had deserved it. He had probably deserved more.

On the television, Cary Grant was lying on a couch inside his advertising office, trying to meet a deadline. He snapped his fingers as he thought of ideas, bouncing his thoughts off a secretary.

Cathy watched the picture. She might go out more often, she thought, if there were more men like Cary Grant. It was an idiotic thought, and she knew she was edging well into Harlequin territory, but it would be nice to find someone charming, suave, and sophisticated. Someone romantic, instead of some gutter-minded philistine.

Did they try to get in your pants?

She thought of her last two aborted dates, more than a year ago. She recalled the crude moves, the almost begging insistence, and her own growing panic and fear.

She forced herself to concentrate on the movie. From the den, she heard her father yelling for her. He had given her the standard fifteen minutes to get over whatever was bothering her, and now he wanted her to return to the routine, to do something for him, to be his servant, to brew him a cup of coffee, to get him a beer. "Cathy!"

She ignored him. This time she was not giving in. This time she would demand an apology. She lay on her bed and watched the movie, tuning out his cries. Several minutes later, he stopped calling.

After the movie, she switched the channel to a local prime-time newscast. The murder was the top story. She sat up in bed, leaning her back against the headboard, watching with interest as they showed a photograph of an old man that segued into a shot of his dead body being loaded onto an ambulance. Even from this angle, she could see the spattered blood on the inside of the plastic body bag.

"According to the police," the reporter said, "Morrison had been skinned alive. The murder weapon has not yet been determined, and police are following all available leads."

There was another shot of the front of the house surrounded by yellow police ribbon, and Cathy felt goosebumps pop up on her arms as she recognized the familiar house and trees on the street. *What kind of person would commit a murder like that?* she wondered. *And why?*

She found herself thinking of David.

And the jackrabbit.

She shivered and tried to recall whether she had locked and deadbolted the front door after letting Jimmy out earlier, but could not remember. She knew her father would not bother to check.

Cathy watched the rest of the news and a rerun of a syndicated sitcom, then heard her father use both crutches to navigate down the hall to his bedroom. She heard his door close, then gave him an extra few minutes to settle in. Slowly, she opened her own door. The hall light was still on, as was the light in the kitchen. He had not even bothered to turn off the TV in the den—she could hear the sounds of canned laughter coming from the room.

Moving quietly, she made her way down the hall, checked the kitchen door to make sure it was locked, and turned off the light. She switched off the TV in the den and went to the front door. It was unlocked, and she pushed in the deadbolt and turned the lock, glad she'd decided to check. Peeking through one of the front windows next to the door, she saw that lights were still on in the Lauter house, and behind the sheer green drapes she saw a small dark figure pressed against the glass. It looked like a child. She stepped away from the window, feeling suddenly chilled.

She moved back down the hall toward the bedroom. She'd go over there sometime in the next few days and meet her new neighbors. They were probably perfectly nice, normal people, and she was sure that meeting them face to face would cure her of irrational jitters she felt each time she looked at their house.

She wouldn't mention the Lauters.

She went into her room and turned down the blankets. Before putting on her pajamas, she closed and locked the bedroom door behind her.

Seven

Though it was late and a weekend, Tucker Avenue was crowded and ablaze with light. The entire street had been cordoned off, and police cars, both marked and unmarked, were parked catty-corner across the roadway. The front doors to most of the houses were open and men, women, and children stood on their front lawns in various stages of dress and undress. Though the block was crowded and filled with movement, the atmosphere was by no means festive, and Allan felt the oppressiveness bear down upon him the instant he stepped out of the Bronco.

Pynchon had already arrived and was standing in the center of the street, coordinating police efforts and barking out orders. His voice was harsher and more curt than usual, and when he saw Allan pushing his way through the crowd on the sidewalk, he gestured him over with a quick jerk of his hand. "Get your ass over here!"

Allan slid by a young woman in a terrycloth bathrobe who was holding tightly to her two excited boys, trying to keep them from getting a glimpse of the corpse. Walking between two police cars parked head to head, he shouldered his way through the line of uniformed officers blocking the body.

The dead woman was lying in the middle of the road, the sheet that had been covering her now bunched up around her feet. Allan stared, his heart racing, a wave of cold passing over him. After the insane gruesomeness of Morrison's murder this morning, he had thought he'd known what to expect and had prepared himself for something horrific.

But he was not ready for the sight that greeted him now.

The woman on the asphalt was naked, her lithe body intentionally twisted and contorted into an impossibly pretzeled position. Her backbone and spinal cord had obviously been broken, and her torso was bent at a right angle, her head lying backward between her knees, as though she had been snapped in half. The joints where her legs met her crotch and her arms met her shoulders had been pulled out expertly, and rounded ridges of clearly defined bone protruded from the sockets, almost, but not quite, breaking the skin. Her jagged broken ribs formed a tiny mountainous chain down the center of her chest. On her blank staring face, bony protuberances, perfectly outlined beneath the taut skin, almost obscured her eyes and mouth. Her nose had been pushed into her skull.

But there was no blood.

All the damage had been done below the surface of the skin.

"Jesus," Allan breathed. He turned to the captain. "What the hell happened?"

Pynchon nodded toward a black-and-silver Cadillac smashed into a tree across the street. "Talk to the driver. He's in the back of the van."

Allan frowned. "That woman wasn't hit by a car."

"Talk to the driver."

Allan walked around the twisted naked body, past the photographer and the two waiting paramedics who were holding the gurney, to where the police van was parked. Williams was standing outside the open back

door of the vehicle, taking down the statement of a
man seated on the van's floor. He looked up and nodded in tired recognition. "Lieutenant."

Allan nodded back, glancing over at the witness.
The man was probably somewhere between forty-five
and fifty, but tonight he looked much older. His face
was pale and there were dark bags under his bloodshot eyes. His hands, large and red, were clenching
and unclenching tensely as he held them between his
knees. He looked up as Allan approached, and his
gaze was blurred and unfocused, as though he had
been drinking.

"No alcohol," Williams said, as if reading his
thoughts. His voice was modulated and controlled, but
there was a hint of fear in it.

Allan met the eyes of the uniformed officer, and
the look he saw there was troubled. "What happened?" he asked softly.

"Mr. Hodges"—Williams pointed toward the man
in the back of the van—"was driving home from the
grocery store. He decided to take a shortcut down
Tucker and was halfway down the street when he
saw her."

"I didn't see her until the last minute," the man
said. There was a flatness to his voice, a monotonic
quality that made it sound as though he were reading
the statement from a cue card or repeating it by rote.
"There was nothing I could do. I had to swerve into
the tree."

Allan nodded understandingly. "It's hard to see objects in the road at night."

"She wasn't in the road," the man said. "She was
just coming off the sidewalk."

"What?" Allan blinked. A chill passed through him
and he looked back toward the dead woman, lying on
the asphalt. He could see only one strangely ridged
leg between the feet of the crowding policemen. "You
mean she was still alive?"

"She was moving. She was . . . sort of crawling, only
her arms and legs weren't working right. They were

all twisted and bunched up. I . . . I saw her for an instant in my headlights, and I didn't know what she was. She was all white and . . . and I didn't even know if she was human or animal or what. I turned the car to miss her, and I hit the tree." He licked his lips. "Someone must have already called you guys, because a police car was there almost before I got out of the car. I rushed over to look at her, and she was . . . she looked all deformed, like she'd been snapped in half backwards, like her bones had all been moved to the wrong place, like . . . I don't know . . ."

"Did she say anything?" Allan asked. "Did you hear her speak at all?"

"She was already dead. She'd just collapsed there in the middle of the street, and she was . . ." He made a twisting motion with his hand, unable to complete the sentence.

Allan looked toward Williams, now reading over his notes. "Who called it in?" he asked.

The uniformed officer shook his head. "Anonymous. It was a woman, but she didn't dial 911 and we didn't have a chance to trace the line. Montoya, Lee, Dobrinin, and Whitehead are canvasing the street right now. Even if we don't find the caller, there's a good chance that someone saw something. Hopefully, we'll be able to pick up some kind of lead." He was silent for a moment, thinking. "Lieutenant?" he asked.

"Yes?"

"You think this is connected to Morrison's murder?"

"We don't know yet whether this *is* a murder. Even if it is, the M.O.'s nothing like that of Morrison's killer."

"But you think they're connected."

Allan nodded slowly. "I think they're connected." He sighed, his gaze focused on the crowd of neighbors pressing against the police barricade, trying to catch a glimpse of the body. "This scares the hell out of me," he admitted. "You know that? We're not dealing here with your average sicko, or run-of-the-mill serial killer. If the same guy did this, and I think he did, he's not only unpredictable in his choice of victims, he's unpredictable in his choice of murder methods. He knows exactly what he's doing, and he's done a damn good job of making sure he leaves no trace."

Captain Pynchon, still bellowing orders at a group of policemen and paramedics surrounding the body, walked around the van and moved next to Allan. "No I.D. yet," he said. "I have two men searching the area for the woman's clothes. We're checking missing persons, and I'll have the computer run her picture once it's developed." His thick black eyebrows were furrowed into a single line of anger. "We've got to get this fucker as soon as possible. I don't want a panic on our hands here."

Allan nodded.

"Any leads, any ideas, anything to go on?"

Allan shook his head. "I haven't gone over everything yet, but offhand I'd say the only thing these murders have in common is their complete dissimilarity. Someone's gone to a lot of trouble to make these look unconnected."

"Does he think we're stupid? Two crazy murders on the same day in the same district and he doesn't think we'll put two and two together?" Pynchon spat onto the ground, muttering under his breath. He looked up at Williams, who was watching him attentively. "Don't just stand there! If you've finished taking the man's statement, start knocking on doors."

Williams closed his notebook. "Yes, sir." He moved next to Mr. Hodges, still sitting stunned on the floor of the van. He started explaining the department's policy regarding murder witnesses.

"Shit howdy," Pynchon said. He massaged his temples, as if he had a headache. "You think you can handle this circus, Grant?"

"Yes, sir," Allan said.

"Keep the goddamn newsmen away from the body, you got it? I don't want any pictures of this thing in the paper tomorrow. I'll make an official statement to the press in the morning. You can tell them that, if you have to. That should shut them up." He spit again, grimacing. "Right now, I want to go home and get some sleep. I don't know why I came out here in the first place. I should let you handle this crap."

Allan nodded. "Go on home," he said. "I'll take care of everything."

"No screwups. Keep a man with the body at all times. I don't want the coroner doing any grandstands this time and pulling one of his little stunts. And for God's sake, keep those rubbernecks away. We have work to do around here."

"Will do." Allan felt a yawn coming on and tried to stifle it, but was unsuccessful. Pynchon glared at him, and he shrugged. "I'm working double shift."

"Clean this up and get home to bed, then. I need you clearheaded tomorrow."

A white-suited paramedic came around the side of the van and turned to face the captain. "Sir? They're ready to take the body."

"Come on." The captain walked to the front of the van, roughly pushed aside two men from the coroner's office who were blocking his way. Allan, following immediately behind, saw the lumpy unnatural form under the plastic covering. If he had not known better, he would not have guessed that the figure in the bag was human. Pynchon gave the high sign, and two attendants loaded the body into the ambulance.

The photographer stepped forward. He nodded to Allan, then turned toward the captain. "How many prints do you want?" he asked.

Pynchon jerked his thumb tiredly toward Allan. "He's in charge of this investigation. I'm going home."

"I want a print for each man on the investigation team," Allan said. "That'll be five. I also want a half-tone to run through the computer and something we can release to the press. And a poster print."

The photographer nodded. "You got it." His eyes

followed the ambulance pulling slowly through the crowd. "You guys have anything to go on yet?"

"I have to get to work," Allan said, pushing past the man. He watched Pynchon get into his car and drive away. He started giving orders.

Eight

Before going home, Al Goldstein stopped off at Benny's, as he had every evening for the past two weeks. He parked his oversized Oldsmobile in the rutted and only partially paved lot at the side of the rundown building and stepped into the dark smoke-filled bar. On the wall, a cascading waterfall fell in a perpetually shimmering stream of light, an advertisement for Olympia that half lit two of Benny's four booths. A red and white Bud Light sign above the counter was reflected in the dark mirror above the cash register and offered the only other illumination in the room.

Al sat down on an empty stool close to the door and put a twenty-dollar bill on the counter. "Set 'em up," he said.

Jimbo Gleason, the bar's sole owner and proprietor since Benny Coleman had died, smiled and nodded. "Sure thing, Mr. Goldstein." He poured a shot of Johnnie Walker Red and set it down on the counter, swapping it for the twenty. "You want me to keep 'em coming 'til this runs out?"

"You got it." Al watched as Jimbo put the twenty in the register and grabbed a wet rag to wipe off the top of the counter. At the other end of the bar, three old men were arguing loudly over who had been the most dishonest president. In one of the booths, a man and woman were giggling softly.

Al hated the bar. It was dirty and depressing and it always made him feel like shit. But it was better than going home. At least here he wasn't continually confronted with the proof of his own failure. At least here the past intruded only when he allowed it to. At home, he would be forced to face his past head on.

He would be forced to face his son.

He downed the shot of Johnnie Walker and tapped the bar for another. It was a horrible thing to admit, but he did not like his son, and he found himself spending more and more time away from home these days, just trying to get away from him, although he did not really know why. He was not a bad father. He did not beat Jimmy. He did not abuse him in any way. But he was well aware of the fact that he was not the kind of father he should be. And that only made him resent the boy more.

Had he ever loved his son? Had he ever even liked him? He could not honestly recall. He was sure he must have, once, but by the time he and Shirley had gotten the divorce, Jimmy had been little more than a bargaining chip to him, a way to hurt the bitch as much as she had hurt him.

And he had hurt her all right. He had hurt her a lot.

Jimbo came by with the bottle, filling up the glass, and Al downed the shot instantly, gesturing for more. The bartender gave him a strange half-concealed glance that was about to turn into a comment, but then someone else walked into the bar, demanding a beer, and Jimbo hurried to pour the order.

Al looked up at the smoky mirror above the cash register, and he saw his own dark reflection, small in the emptiness of the large room. He looked even worse than he felt, if that was possible. His thin hair was greasy and disheveled, and the circles under his eyes made him look almost clownish.

He finished the third shot. It probably wouldn't be

so bad if the boy didn't look so damn much like her. But every time he looked at his son—*her* son—he saw Shirley's dark complexion, Shirley's thin tapered nose, Shirley's big brown eyes. He knew his response was childish, he knew that he was being stupid and irrational, but though he understood this intellectually, emotionally he could not help feeling a strong dislike for the boy.

He closed his eyes, feeling suddenly hot, the way he always did when he drank too much too fast. He wondered where Shirley was now. He wondered who the slut was spreading her legs for tonight. He was sure she wasn't still with the claims adjuster she'd taken up with. Hell, she'd probably fucked half a dozen guys since then.

"Last shot," Jimbo said, coming back to his end of the bar. "You sure you can handle it? Or would you rather have your change?"

Al looked up at him and tried to smile. "Pour it."

The bartender nodded, saying nothing. He filled up the small glass and put the bottle away before getting out his rag again. He wiped the top of the counter, then grabbed a small towel. He started cleaning the glasses that had stacked up near the tap. Glancing over at Al, he cleared his throat. "So, Mr. Goldstein, how's life treating you?"

"Like shit."

"I wasn't going to say anything, but you do look a little down in the dumps. What is it? Work? Kid? Old lady?"

Al nodded. "Yeah."

The bartender polished a glass, trying to think of what to say next. At the far end of the bar, one of the old men loudly declared Richard Nixon to be the most dishonest president ever to hold office. "And I *voted* for him!" he said. "I voted for the slimy, shifty-eyed son of a bitch!"

Jimmy was already home, Al knew. He'd probably heated up his pizza in the microwave and was now doing his homework or watching TV. He was a good kid, really, and Al felt guilty when he thought of him spending so much of his time alone in an empty house. He felt sorry for the boy. But it was a disinterested sorry, a hypocritical form of pity, and he did not feel bad enough to go home. He would probably not go home until after Jimmy had gone to bed.

"You'll get over it," Jimbo said.

Al blinked. "What?"

"Whatever it is that's bothering you—you'll get over it." The bartender put down his towel and glass and moved forward, leaning against the counter. "I remember when my wife and I split up. I thought it was the end of the world. I didn't eat, didn't sleep, didn't do shit. Hell, I didn't even bathe for a fuckin' week. She'd been boffing someone else, and I found out about it. Then she turned it around, tried to make it seem like it was my fault. I threw her and all her stuff out the door. I didn't know what to do. I'm telling you, man, I was fucking lost. I kind of felt the way you look. I thought of killing her, I thought of killing myself." He shook his head. "But you know what? It wasn't the end of the world. I got through it, I got over it, I put it past me. Now I look back on those days, I can't believe what an idiot I was."

"You calling me an idiot?"

Jimbo looked flustered. "No, that's not what I meant at all. I was just—"

Al forced himself to laugh. "I know. I know what you're saying. Everything comes to an end, everything passes, I'll get over it."

"Exactly."

Al stood up and downed his last shot. He nodded at the bartender. "Thanks for the drinks and the pep talk," he said.

Jimbo looked surprised. "Going so soon?"

Yeah, so I don't have to listen to any more of your stupid simplistic bullshit, Al thought. But he smiled and said, "Yeah, I'd better be going."

"Drive carefully."

After the dark interior of the bar, the evening out-

side seemed almost bright. Though there were few
lights on in this part of Phoenix, there was a full moon,
and the resulting illumination dimmed all but the
brightest stars. Al walked across the tiny parking lot,
which seemed even rougher and more rutted than
usual, and got into his car. He sat behind the wheel
for a moment, unmoving, staring at the graffiti-
covered wall before him. He should go home, he
thought. He was drunker than usual, and it was probably dangerous for him to drive. Besides, Jimmy was
all alone, for the third night in a row, and he should
really make an effort to be some sort of father to the
boy, take an interest in his schoolwork, in his life.

He started the car, put it into reverse, and pulled
onto the street. He drove down Central toward home
but was stopped by a red light at Washington. Glancing over at the car next to him, a black Thunderbird,
he saw two teenagers sitting next to each other on the
seat, the boy's arm draped protectively around the
girl's shoulder, her head resting comfortably against
his neck.

Al looked away. He had been in that boy's place
before, in earlier, better days. He too had driven end-
lessly around the Valley, his arm around Shirley, making skypie plans for the future as the radio played
their songs in the background.

The light turned green, the car next to him took
off, and Al no longer felt like going home. He had no
place else to go, but tonight he didn't want to be a
father. He didn't want to be an ex-husband. He just
wanted to be plain old Al Goldstein.

He drove aimlessly toward the open desert, not paying attention to where he was going, not caring. The
more he thought, the darker his thoughts grew, and
somewhere along the way he thought of a place he
could go, something he could do.

When he finally got home, well after midnight,
Jimmy was fast asleep.

Nine

Breakfast was tense.

Cathy awoke early, showered, dressed, and went into the kitchen to make oatmeal, pretending that nothing was wrong. She walked outside, picked up the newspaper, which had been thrown into the flowerbed by an overeager paperboy, and placed the paper on the table in front of her father's chair, next to his coffee and orange juice. He walked in a few moments later, leaning heavily on his crutches, his face a mask of pain, and she could tell it was going to be one of his bad days. He lowered himself into his chair, set his crutches against the table, and unfolded the newspaper. Cathy, standing by the stove, cleared her throat timidly. "I'm sorry," she said. The only sound in the kitchen was the muffled scrape of metal on metal as she stirred the oatmeal in the pot. "About last night."

He continued to read the paper, not bothering to reply.

"Father?" she said.

He took a sip of orange juice, then opened up the paper to read the second page, using the newsprint as a wall to hide his face.

Cathy spooned the oatmeal into two bowls and put

one of the bowls on the table before him. "I said I'm sorry."

He ignored her, loudly turning to the next page of his newspaper.

She stared at him for a moment, then put her own bowl on the table and sat down. "Fine, then."

After that they were both silent, the only noise in the brightly lit kitchen the light clink of silverware and pewter as they ate their oatmeal, and the occasional sound of birdsong from the honeysuckle outside the window. The prolonged silence made Cathy nervous, edgy, and halfway through her cereal she got up and flipped on the radio, tuning it to the all-news station. The sound of the newsman's authoritarian voice, backed by the constant clacking of a canned teletype, seemed somehow soothing, and she sat back down at the table, relaxing a little.

She found her eyes focused on the collection of antique cheese graters displayed on a shelf above the refrigerator rather than on the front page of the newspaper directly opposite her, and she realized that she was deliberately avoiding looking in her father's direction. She was angry at herself, angry for falling into his trap, angry for still being afraid of him, but the feeling soon passed, replaced by a dull melancholy that settled into its place.

It was going to be a long day, she knew. Saturdays were always long. She didn't work and didn't really have any friends with whom she could go places, so she usually ended up spending the day doing household chores and grocery shopping. She hazarded a glance in her father's direction, but he was still hidden behind the paper. She hoped to God he'd go somewhere today. Sometimes he spent the day at the club with Geoff or Don or Rob, but more often than not he stayed home, harrassing her as she did her work, criticizing her as she cleaned the house, spying on her as she worked in the yard. She didn't want to go through that. Not today. If he was going to spend the day at home, she'd just have to go somewhere to get away from him. Maybe she'd go to Metro Center and buy some clothes or go to Fifth Avenue in Scottsdale and do some window shopping.

She picked up her bowl and orange juice glass and carried them to the sink.

"Top local story," the radio announcer said. "Another murder, the second in two days, occurred late last night in north Phoenix. According to police, the body of Susan Welmers, a thirty-year-old legal assistant, was found beaten to death on Tucker Avenue—"

Tucker Avenue! Cathy put down her dishes and stared at the black plastic radio. That was the next street over.

It's coming closer.

Her gaze automatically shifted toward her father, but he seemed not to have heard or not to have been listening. He was pushing his chair back from the table and reaching for his crutches. One of the crutches was slightly beyond his reach, and she watched him struggle as he tried to grab it. He could have asked her to help him, the way he usually did, but he refused to give her the satisfaction of acknowledging her presence. She watched his fingers clutch in vain for the cross-handle of the crutch, and she forgot about the murder. She strode over to the table, grabbed the crutch, and handed it to him. "Here," she said.

He accepted the crutch silently, not looking at her.

She held onto her end. "What are your plans for today?" she asked, taking advantage of the contact.

He turned to stare at her. His eyes were cold, unreadable. "You were sleepwalking last night."

She blinked. "What?"

"You heard me."

Sleepwalking. She looked at her father, hoping he was joking, knowing he was not, feeling frightened. She could not remember the last time she'd been sleepwalking. "No, I wasn't."

"I heard you." He shifted his weight on the crutches. "I thought you stopped all that a long time ago."

She said nothing, but moved back to the sink.

"Maybe you should go back to a shrink."

She turned on him. "What is it with you? Why are you always trying to pick a fight with me?"

"I'm concerned about your mental health."

"Knock it off."

The phone rang, and he glared silently at her until she went to answer it. It was Geoff, asking what time her father wanted to be picked up. There was a big poker tournament at the club, Geoff said, and he wanted to get there early. She turned around to ask her father what time he wanted to leave, but he grabbed the phone from her hand and spoke into the receiver himself, turning his back on her.

She left him alone and went back into the kitchen to wash the dishes.

After her father left, Cathy went outside, anxious to escape the claustrophobic atmosphere of the house. The air was warm and dry, the sky a deep dark blue. Jimmy was on his Big Wheel, riding along the sidewalk from one corner to the other, the only sign of life on the empty street. She waved to him as she uncurled the hose and turned on the sprinkler. When she had been his age, both sides of the street had been bustling with activity on Saturday mornings. Kids played, fathers mowed lawns, mothers pulled weeds. Now the yardwork was done by hired gardeners on weekdays and invariably the only people outside on weekend mornings were Jimmy and herself.

He rode over, skidding to a stop in the driveway, spinning around in a 180-degree turn. He grinned up at her, pushing the hair back from his eyes. "Hi."

"Hi."

"I saw your dad leave this morning."

Cathy couldn't help smiling. "Did you wave at him?"

"Yeah," Jimmy said. "But I don't think he saw me."

"He'll be gone all day," she told him, and was pleased to see a look of relief cross his face. She placed the sprinkler in the middle of the lawn and turned on the water, adjusting it so the spray would cover the grass but not wet the sidewalk.

Her eyes fell on the Lauter house across the street. In the bright light of morning, the house did not seem threatening at all. Indeed, the light green curtains hanging in the front windows and the two potted cacti that flanked the porch steps made it appear almost cheerful. Through the kitchen window of the house, she could see a woman busying herself at the sink. She looked down at Jimmy, rocking absently back and forth on his Big Wheel. "Let's meet our new neighbors," she said.

His eyes lit up. "Okay."

"You can help me bake a cake. We'll give it to them as a housewarming gift."

He jumped off his Big Wheel. "All right!"

Laughing at his enthusiasm, she led the way through the garage to the kitchen. She was grateful that Jimmy was coming with her. She would probably not have had the nerve to go over there otherwise. Not because she was scared of the house—though that might have been a factor at night—but because she really had no idea what to say to her new neighbors. Her social skills were not up to something like this. She could introduce herself, say hello, perhaps talk briefly about the neighborhood, or about Arizona if they were from out of state, but she certainly wasn't adept enough to hold an extended conversation with absolute strangers.

Still, she had grown up here on this street, had known her neighbors all her life, and she felt a certain obligation to welcome these new people into the fold. She could also sympathize with the newcomers. She, too, knew what it was like to be on the outside looking in.

She was glad Jimmy would be tagging along, though. Always talkative, he could be counted on to rescue the conversation if it started to die. She could even use his presence as an excuse to leave early if she had to. She looked down at him, smiling happily up at her, and she felt a little guilty about using him this way, but she pushed the thought out of her mind. "We'll make a chocolate one," she said. "You can lick the bowl when we're done."

It was after noon before the cake was baked, and Cathy made them both tuna sandwiches for lunch while they waited. She would have made peanut butter and jelly, but she thought Jimmy probably got enough of that at home. He needed to eat something healthy.

After they finished their meal, she wrapped the cake in cellophane and tied the package with a red ribbon. She let Jimmy carry it across the street.

It seemed strange, walking up the driveway of the Lauter house. In her entire life, she had never been this close to the house before, and even now she felt as though she were doing something forbidden. From the expression on Jimmy's face, he felt the same way. They looked at each other and laughed, sharing the joke, and the spell was broken.

Cathy examined the front of the house. Seen from this perspective, there was nothing remotely sinister or frightening about the place. It was a typical tract home, nearly identical to her own. Once again, she wondered what type of people had bought the house. She hoped they were young. And she hoped they liked her; it would be nice to have a friend in the neighborhood rather than just another acquaintance.

They walked up the porch steps and Cathy pressed the doorbell. There was no ring, no sound, but she still waited a moment before knocking. She knocked twice, but there was no answer. She looked at Jimmy and knocked again.

"I'm coming," said a tired voice from inside.

The woman who answered the door looked prematurely aged, old beyond her years. She was wearing a faded floral housedress, a pair of worn once-red slippers, and her mousy brown hair was pulled back in a careless frazzled bun. Although she needed it desperately, she was wearing no makeup. Her skin, neither a healthy brown tan nor an exotic albino white, was the gray and pasty color of someone who spent most of her time indoors. Deep lines were etched around her mouth and eyes, and Cathy could tell from the direction of the creases that they were not laugh lines.

Cathy felt disappointed as she looked at the woman, but she tried to keep the feeling from showing on her face. She put on her most cheerful smile and took the cake from Jimmy, thrusting it awkwardly forward. "Hello," she said. "My name's Cathy Riley. I'm your neighbor right across the street." She put a hand on Jimmy's head. "This Jimmy Goldstein. He lives three doors down from me in that brown brick house with the cactus in the yard."

The woman stared at her blankly, accepting the cake.

"I thought we'd welcome you to the neighborhood." Her voice remained bright, friendly, but Cathy sensed that her welcome-wagon routine was failing miserably, and she felt a hot flush creep up her cheeks. She was acutely aware of Jimmy standing beside her, watching this performance, and she noticed that the woman's eyes remained fixed on the boy. Cathy forced a smile. "What's your name?" she asked.

The woman's gaze moved from Jimmy to Cathy, and her eyes became more focused. She shook her head, as if to clear it. Cathy noticed that the woman was sweating heavily. "I'm sorry," the woman said. "My name's Mrs. West. Katrina West. You can call me Katrina." She opened the door wider and stepped to one side, motioning them in. "Won't you come inside?"

Katrina, Cathy thought. It was an incongruously attractive name for such a purposefully dowdy woman. She stepped into the entryway, Jimmy following.

Inside, the Lauter house looked like any other home on the block. The ceiling was low stucco; a central fireplace separated the living room and family room. Although the walls had obviously not been painted in some time, they were not spattered with dried blood. The linoleum floor shone cleanly with recent waxing.

"I'm sorry for all the boxes," Katrina said, gesturing toward a hill of sealed cartons and crates in the family room. "We're still not finished unpacking."

Cathy nodded in acknowledgement. "Do you and your husband live here alone?"

"My husband's dead. I live here with my son."

"I'm sorry," Cathy said. She cleared her throat. "I mean, I'm sorry your husband's dead," she amended. "I'm not sorry you live here with your son." She looked around, as if searching for a way out of the verbal hole into which she had dug herself. "Uh, how old is your son?"

"He's nine."

"Oh, he's around Jimmy's age!" She smiled at Jimmy, who was peeking around the corner into the dining room. "It'll be nice for him to have someone to play with around here. This neighborhood's kind of dead for young kids."

"My son's retarded."

The bluntness of the statement caught Cathy off guard. She didn't know what to say. She didn't know how she was supposed to take that statement, how it was intended, what it was supposed to mean. She licked her lips, pretending to concentrate on the view through the family room window. She could see her own house through the recently washed glass, and she wished that she'd stayed there, not started on this fool's errand. "Well, I'm sure your son would still like someone his own age to play with," she said lamely.

"My son doesn't play with other children."

We should not have come over here, Cathy thought. *It was a mistake.* The woman continued to look at Jimmy, who was now staring at his shoes, swinging one foot nervously. *Retarded?* It seemed like a cruel word, unnecessarily harsh, and Cathy wondered what type of life the poor boy led. She thought she'd heard an undercurrent of resentment in Katrina's voice when she'd mentioned her son, and even from this short and superficial contact, she could tell that the woman kept her son tightly reined. Cathy's eyes met Jimmy's, and

he inclined his head slightly toward the door in a not-
so-subtle hint. She tried to think of a simple, tactful
way to get them out of here quickly.

"Do you want to meet my son?" Katrina asked. She
tried to smile, but there was no warmth or humor in
the gesture, and her eyes remained hard, grim. It was
as though the muscles of her mouth worked indepen-
dently of the rest of her face, in opposition to their
setting. The smile seemed painted on, Cathy thought,
not part of the woman, and the overall effect was
almost spooky. "Do you want to meet Randy?"

Cathy forced herself to nod enthusiastically. "Yes,"
she said, shooting an apologetic look at Jimmy. "We'd
love to."

"He's in his room." Katrina led the way down the
hall, still holding the cake, warning them not to trip
over the boxes and sacks spaced along the floor. Cathy
walked slowly. The three doors they passed were
closed and the hallway was dark, unnaturally so. Katrina knocked on the door at the far end of the hall
before using a key to unlock it. She opened the door
and walked inside. Cathy followed, placing an arm
protectively around Jimmy's shoulder.

The room they entered was even darker than the
hallway. The lights were off and the heavy red curtains
drawn, and it took Cathy's eyes a moment to adjust.
She squinted, peering into the gloom.

Randy was sitting on the edge of an unmade bed,
staring dully across the room at a framed picture of a
collie in a snowstorm. Above his head was a reproduction of a Renaissance painting of the crucified Jesus.
The rest of the walls were gray and empty, devoid of
decoration. The only furniture in the room was the
bed. Three or four small toys littered the carpeted
floor. The open closet was empty save for a box of
clothes.

Cathy stared at the boy, feeling strangely nervous.
The pity she had expected to feel for the child had
not materialized, and she experienced only a tense
sense of unease as she looked at him. Slack-jawed, a

thick tongue protruding slightly from his open mouth, his chin glistening with a thin patina of saliva, he looked at her, his dark brown eyes unreadable. His features had the faintly Oriental cast universal to those suffering from Down's Syndrome, but there was a subtly shifting element in it, something strange and undefined that Cathy did not like. She found herself glancing away from his face, concentrating instead on his hands. His fingers, thick and overly large, kneaded a white soccer ball in his lap, and she watched the ball turn over and over.

"Randy!" the mother called.

Instantly, the boy's blank expression transformed into a look of simplistic happiness. He started bouncing up and down on the bed. "HA!" he screamed. "HA MA MA MA MA MA MA MA MA MA!"

"Randy, I want you to meet some new friends." Katrina spoke slowly and clearly but without condescension, as if talking to an adult who was slightly deaf. "This is Cathy."

Cathy nodded politely.

"And this is Jimmy."

Cathy glanced at her young companion. Jimmy smiled awkwardly at the boy on the bed, feigning a friendliness he obviously did not feel. She could tell that he was nervous, too. She squeezed his shoulder—a silent promise that they would leave as soon as possible.

"BA!" Randy yelled. He suddenly threw the soccer ball at Jimmy, who caught it in midair. "BA!" he yelled again. "BA BA BA BA BA BA BA!"

Confused, Jimmy looked at the boy's mother. "What should I do?" he asked.

"Throw it back to him."

Jimmy tossed the ball, a slow underhanded lob. Randy caught it, hugging it to him and screaming incoherently. He threw the ball again, hard, and Jimmy barely had time to put up his hands and block the throw. Randy bounced up and down on the bed, laughing and clapping.

"I think he likes you," Katrina said. She turned

toward Cathy, and though her features were still grim, filled with a natural, inherent resignation, her expression seemed a trifle lighter, more relaxed. "Maybe it would be good for him to have someone to play with."

Again Jimmy returned the ball, and this time Randy threw it back immediately. The ball whizzed through the air and hit Jimmy full in the face. He screamed in pain and turned away, the ball bouncing harmlessly to a stop on the carpet. Randy leaped out of bed to grab it, an eager expression on his face, but his mother pointed an accusing finger at him.

"Stop!" she ordered. "Now!"

The boy backtracked to the bed and sat down glumly. He grabbed the pillow and held it over his face as if he were embarrassed.

Katrina moved next to Jimmy. "Are you all right?" she asked. Her voice was flat. There was no concern in it, no interest; she was asking only out of obligation.

Jimmy nodded, but his eyes were teary and the skin on his right cheek was bright red where the ball had hit.

"I think you'd better go."

Cathy cleared her throat.

"Now," Katrina said coldly.

"It was just an accident," Cathy said. "I'm sure—"

The woman's faded blue eyes were fixed in a hard glare. "Please don't tell me how to run my house," she said. Her eyes bored into Cathy's, making her look away. She silently forced the two of them out of the bedroom, closing the door behind them, and pressuring them down the hall into the entryway.

Beneath her hands, Cathy could feel Jimmy's shoulders shaking, and she knew that he was trying his hardest to be brave. Although he wasn't crying aloud, he continued to surreptitiously wipe his eyes, catching tears before they could escape down his cheeks. She felt guilty for even bringing him here.

Katrina opened the front door. "Get out," she said. "You've done enough." All civility was gone from her voice.

They stepped outside. Cathy turned around. "I'm glad I met you—" she began.

The door slammed shut.

Cathy and Jimmy stared at each other for a long moment, saying nothing. Then Cathy smiled, and Jimmy smiled, and by the time they had reached the end of the driveway they were both laughing.

Ten

The alarm woke Allan long before his body was ready to be awakened, the incessant electronic beeping forcing him rudely into consciousness. He still felt the fatigue from last night's vigil, and he tried to open his eyes, but they stung as if they were coated with sand, and he shut them instantly. He reached over and tried to push the snooze button on the alarm to give himself another ten minutes, but he seemed to have temporarily lost all small muscle coordination; his fingers simply weren't up to such delicate work. He sat up groggily, leaning against the headboard, and willed his eyes open. Unhappily, he turned off the alarm.

His mind was still swimming with unconnected images from a half-remembered dream as he staggered out of bed toward the bathroom. He recalled a woman with skinned breasts nursing a dead infant; a department store mannequin with hideously bloated fish lips working in a knife shop, selling weapons; Captain Pynchon, running like hell from something big and black with foul-smelling slime skin. Allan shook his head. This was not like him. He seldom dreamed, and he could not remember the last time he'd had an honest-to-God nightmare. This thing must have really gotten to him.

He turned on the shower, then sat passively for a moment on the covered lid of the toilet, waiting for the water to warm up.

At least he hadn't had to tell the woman's family what had happened. He'd felt like a shit, but by the time they'd discovered her identity it had been nearly two-thirty and he'd been dead on his feet, so he'd pulled a Pynchon and pawned that duty off on Williams.

Reaching over, he stuck his fingers in the shower to check the temperature. The water was fine, and he stripped off his underwear and got in. The warm spray on his face made his mind more alert, but his eyes still hurt like hell. He adjusted the shower head, moving it lower, and grabbed the washcloth and a bar of soap. He washed his arms and legs, and some of the feeling returned to his tired muscles.

The phone was ringing when he stepped out of the shower, but he didn't bother to answer it. He used a towel to dry himself off, then put his clothes on and took the shaving cream out of the medicine cabinet. The phone was still ringing, and he let it ring. He knew it was someone from the station, but he didn't feel like answering right now. He'd be in soon enough.

Twenty minutes later, he was in his office at the station. He hadn't had time to make breakfast, so he'd just grabbed an Egg McMuffin and some juice at McDonald's.

Jesus, he thought, looking at the sandwich, *I'm going to die from eating all this junk food.*

But that went with the territory, he knew. Cops seldom ate regular meals.

He finished off the McMuffin and threw the paper container into the wastebasket.

"Allan?"

He looked up, his mouth still full. "Mmmm?"

Thomasson grinned tiredly. "Captain wants to see you."

"All right." Allan grabbed his notebook from the desk and headed down the hall to Pynchon's office. As he walked, he looked down at the notes he'd scribbled last night, trying to make out what he'd written, but he'd been tired and the light had been bad and the notes were almost indecipherable.

The captain's door was closed when he reached it, and he knocked loudly.

"Come in!" Pynchon's voice was hoarse but still loud and commanding. Allan pushed open the door and stepped into the cluttered office. The captain was standing next to the window, facing the yard outside. He turned when Allan entered the room and nodded brusquely toward a straight-backed chair. "Sit down," he said.

Allan sat.

Pynchon moved away from the window and settled into a swivel seat behind his desk. "Where's Whitehead?" he asked.

Allan frowned. "Whitehead? I'm sorry, sir. I don't know what you mean."

"You don't know what I mean?" The captain pounded on the desk with a thick fist. "Jesus Christ! Don't you even communicate with your own damn team?"

"I'm sorry, sir. I just got in about five minutes ago—"

"That's no excuse!" The captain coughed loudly, holding a fist in front of his mouth. "Shit." He glared at Allan. "It's your responsibility to know exactly what's going on in this investigation, Lieutenant. You have to delegate authority, make all assignments and decisions, and keep track of what everyone is doing. If you're not going to be able to handle it, I'll yank your ass right off this case."

Allan remembered the ringing phone and mentally kicked himself. "I—"

"I don't want to hear any excuses."

"What about Whitehead?"

"He's missing."

Allan stood up. He felt a cold knot of dread in the pit of his stomach. He had sent Whitehead, Lee, and Dobrinin out to search the woman's street last night after they'd discovered her identity, in the hopes that they'd be able to learn something about what had happened. They were his three best men, and he knew that if they couldn't dig something up, no one could. His mouth felt suddenly dry. He took a deep breath. "Since when?" he asked.

"He never reported back. Dobrinin and Lee checked in several hours ago, and neither of them knew what happened to Whitehead. They'd assumed he'd already returned."

"Maybe he just went home without checking in. It was late, he was tired, he'd probably been up since—"

"We're not completely dense." Pynchon coughed. "Kelly called his house several times, but there was no answer. I sent a man down there myself to check about fifteen minutes ago." His eyes met Allan's. "I was hoping you'd be able to tell me what happened."

Allan shook his head helplessly.

"I'm hoping he just went to a bar or something. God knows, that . . . thing I saw yesterday sure as hell made me want to throw down a few belts." He coughed into his hand and hawked loudly. "This wouldn't be the first time miscommunication almost started a panic, so we'll wait another hour or so before we start worrying. Or at least until we find out whether he went home last night. In the meantime, I want you to get busy on these investigations. We're assuming they're connected, aren't we?"

"Yes, sir. There's nothing to connect them but their bizarreness and a complete lack of evidence, but we're assuming they're connected."

"Good." The captain nodded. "Now I want you to set up a meeting for ten o'clock this morning between you and me and everyone else on the investigative team. Whitehead, too, if we can find him. I want to hash over what we have, what we don't have, what we know, what we suspect, and see if we can come up with any ideas."

"All right."

"As you can tell, my voice is going, so you'll have to do most of the talking."

Allan nodded, saying nothing. Hoarse voice or no hoarse voice, he knew that when Pynchon was in the room he did almost all of the talking. It was hard for anyone else to get a word in edgewise.

"All right, then. Get off your dead ass and get to work. The heat's going to come down on this one, and if my butt gets even a little warm, yours is going to fry. You understand me?"

"I understand. My ass is going to fry."

Pynchon smiled shortly, but the smile was interrupted almost instantly by a cough. He waved Allan away. "Get the hell out of here."

Allan walked down the hall quickly, the tension in his muscles growing. He had a bad feeling about Whitehead, though he could not say why. God, he hated this job sometimes.

He strode into Dispatching and clapped a hand on Yvonne's shoulder. "Hey, beautiful." She jerked around. "Patch me into Bob Whitehead's home line."

The angry expression on her face disappeared when she saw it was him. "There's no answer," she said. "I've been trying all morning."

"Try again."

She punched a set of numbers into her console. Allan grabbed a headset and pressed the tiny headphone next to his ear. The line rang once, twice, three times, and then someone picked up the phone. "Hello!" Allan said. "Whitehead? This is Lieutenant Grant."

The voice on the other end was flat, official, unemotional. "This is not Whitehead. This is Cannon. Whitehead's door was unlocked, so, I made the decision to enter his apartment." There was a pause. "He's not here, Lieutenant. He didn't come home at all last night."

Eleven

Bob Whitehead did not know where he was. One minute he had been crawling through a series of bushes at the side of a house in north Phoenix, and the next he had awakened . . . where?

He was lying down, and he tried to sit up, but his limbs had no power, no energy. He lay unmoving on his back. He was not restrained in any way, but he literally could not move a muscle. Around him, it was dark. The deepest dark he'd ever known. He could not distinguish even shadowy forms; there were no gradations in the blackness that surrounded him. His world consisted entirely of an inky monochromatic jet. His head was pounding strangely, and he sensed rather than felt that blood was dripping down his face.

But he experienced nothing. There was no pain. There was no feeling whatsoever. He tried to touch the top of his head to see if he was injured, but he could not get his arms to respond.

He must have lost a lot of blood to be this weak.

He tried to call out, to yell for help, but found that he had no voice. He was not even sure his lips were moving; he couldn't feel them.

Where was he?

He tried to think over everything that had happened, everything he remembered. He recalled walking down the left side of Cherry Street, trying to retrace a hypothetical path taken by the woman, Susan Welmers, while Lee and Dobrinin combed the right side of the street. They had seen no evidence at Welmers' house that what had happened to her had occurred there, and they were working from the assumption that she had left the house and had been attacked outside somewhere, either mutilated in the open or abducted into one of the neighboring houses and tortured, eventually finding her way over to Tucker Avenue. Her husband, shell-shocked and dazed, had been absolutely no help at all, and they'd decided they'd better look for a trail while a trail still existed. They'd split up, Lee and Dobrinin taking the side of the street closest to Tucker, while he stayed on the same side of the street as the Welmers' residence. He was halfway down the block when he thought he heard a noise—a low rustling in the bushes at the side of a darkened house. He looked around for his two companions, but the other side of the street appeared completely empty.

He heard the noise again.

It could be a dog, he thought. Or a cat.

But as the noise came again, he knew it was neither.

There was no time to find Dobrinin or Lee, so he drew his gun and crouched low, trying to peer under the bottom branches of a neatly trimmed bush. He saw nothing, detected no movement. "This is Officer Whitehead," he said loudly. "Please step forward and identify yourself."

There was a sudden rustle, as if something was trying to escape in the opposite direction. He dropped to his knees, quickly checking his pistol to make sure the safety catch was on, and started crawling along the side of the house.

And he'd awakened here.

Wherever here was.

He heard a noise from somewhere. In this darkness

and in his state, it was impossible for him to judge the direction from which it had come. It was a strange high-pitched cackling sound, like the cawing of a bird, and its utter incongruity sent a chill down Whitehead's spine. Again he tried to sit up, but again he could not, and he realized that he was completely helpless. He could not move, could not defend himself, could not even cry out.

And it was certain that no one knew where he was. There would be no one to save him.

The immediacy of the danger he faced suddenly came home to him, and Whitehead willed himself to roll, to wiggle, to somehow move. Nothing worked. The panic flared within him, now very close to the surface. Did he still have his gun? he wondered. Or had that been taken from him?

The cawing cackle was very close. It exploded somewhere nearby, and if he had been able to he would have jumped. He heard a low heavy sound, as of something being dragged across a floor, and—

—and then there was light.

After the total darkness, the light was blindingly white, and to his burning pupils it seemed as though he was staring directly into the heart of the sun. One second, all was blackness, the next, all was white.

He would have closed his eyes had he been able to do so.

WHO ARE YOU? he wanted to shout. WHERE THE HELL AM I? WHAT'S HAPPENING? WHAT ARE YOU GOING TO DO TO ME? but his mind and mouth could not seem to connect.

And then the light faded. Blinding whiteness faded into yellow and the furnishings of a room became visible through the glare as his eyes adjusted. There was a standing lamp and an overstuffed armchair covered in plastic. A table piled high with several chairs. Old trunks, one on top of another. He was in an attic, he realized. Or a basement.

His vision adjusted even more, and Whitehead saw that the light that had seemed so bright and all encompassing was actually coming from a single low-wattage bulb suspended from a wooden ceiling by a braided wire. As he stared upward, a long mirror inserted itself between his eyes and the ceiling, guided by unseen hands.

And then he knew why he could neither move nor speak nor blink.

He stared at himself in the mirror. He was completely naked, and his normally tan body was red with wet, smeared blood. From his broken skin protruded hundreds, perhaps thousands, of tiny pins and sewing needles. He looked like an exaggerated parody of an acupuncture body diagram, and he realized that the needles had been expertly placed in the junctures of muscles and nerves, that all of his functional nerve fibers had been severed. He was completely helpless, unable to move or respond physically in any way. He could not even scream, and tears were rolling down from his eyes in compensation. The severing of the nerves had successfully blocked off all pain, but the sight of his bleeding and tortured body caused his already overloaded brain to fill in the gaps. He suddenly felt each and every needle puncturing his skin.

He wanted to close his eyes, but his eyelids had been pinned open.

The cawing sounded right next to his ear, and it was a cry of triumph.

Twelve

He was sitting on the stoop of his house, staring at her.

Cathy put her lunch in the car and looked across the street at Randy West. Even from this far away, she could see his open slack mouth and the tired slump of his thick awkward body. She waved, smiling, but he ignored her, continuing to stare, and she turned away. He made her nervous, she realized, and instantly she felt guilty for having such a thought. She had always considered herself sympathetic and understanding, not one to judge on surface appearances, but now she wondered if she had been fooling herself. Was it possible that she disliked the boy merely because he was retarded? Could she really be that shallow?

She recalled her uncomfortable feelings in his room, remembered the strangeness of the scene and the almost violent way the boy had behaved toward Jimmy.

No. It wasn't because he was retarded. There was something else about Randy West that she didn't like.

She walked around the car and turned on the hose, giving the flowers in front of the house a quick watering before she left for work. It was going to be a hot day, and they needed the extra protection. As she sprinkled the plants, she had the unsettling feeling that

Randy's eyes were studying her every move. She could almost feel his gaze on her back, and she suddenly felt hot and itchy. She continued watering long after the flowers were wet, and she realized that she was afraid to turn around. She saw in her mind his almond-shaped eyes, bright and alert in his broad face. That's stupid, she told herself. The boy was retarded. He could not possibly be *studying* her. And his eyes were dull, unfocused, not perceptive in any way.

So why did she feel as though his eyes were purposefully focused on her?

She turned off the hose and forced herself to look across the street.

He was still staring.

As she watched, the front door of the house opened and Katrina stepped out. She was dressed in a loose-fitting blue robe that she held closed at the neck, and her mousy hair was tangled in disarray. "No!" she said. "Not again!"

Sound carried far in the early morning, and even from across the street Cathy could hear the note of fear in the woman's voice.

"How did you get out?" she demanded. "I told you never to go outside!"

"BA!" Randy screamed. "BA! BA! BA! BABABA-BABABABABA!" He pointed across the street toward Cathy.

Katrina saw Cathy for the first time, and Cathy reddened, embarrassed at being caught snooping. She waved hello in an attempt to save face, but the older woman ignored her. Placing both hands under her son's armpits, Katrina lifted him into a standing position. He obviously weighed a lot, and it was a considerable effort for her to pull him to his feet. Randy made no attempt to help her. His body remained limp, and he dragged his feet, still screaming, as she pulled him into the open front door of the house.

"BABABABABABA!"

And then the screaming was abruptly cut off.

Shaking her head, Cathy got into her car. She was

not sure what she'd just witnessed, but she didn't like it at all.

The morning went by slowly. Jeff was not scheduled to work today, and Ann had classes until one and so would not be in until two. Cathy had the store to herself, and though she usually resented working alone, today she was glad. She had a sharp migraine, the effects of which even aspirin did not seem to be able to lessen, and she was glad she didn't have to deal with conversation as well as her store duties.

She spent the first few hours straightening the mess from last night, rearranging the paperbacks, filling in the empty spaces on the shelves. She glanced at the blurbs on the covers of the paperbacks as she worked, looking for something interesting to read. She'd just finished the last John Barth book and was looking for something lightweight to occupy her mind for the next week or so. After some searching, she found a trashy Hollywood novel and bought it for herself from herself, ringing up the sale and putting the money in the cash register.

She stood for a moment behind the counter after buying the book, closing her eyes against the painful pounding in her head. The headache's intensity had remained constant but bearable during the past hour, but now it had grown to nearly intolerable proportions. Although she wasn't supposed to take another aspirin for two more hours, she reached under the counter for the small plastic bottle and popped two of the pills in her mouth, swallowing them quickly and without water. She hadn't had a headache this bad since . . . well, since she'd stopped seeing Dr. Magnusen.

She leaned against the counter, waiting for the aspirin to take effect, and found herself thinking about the psychiatrist. He was without a doubt the most understanding, sympathetic person she had ever met, and while she knew that was part of his job, she felt that his affinity for people went deeper than mere training and that he really and truly had cared about her and her problems. Sometimes even now she missed being able to talk to him. He'd said there was nothing wrong with her, had convinced her of it, in fact, and had helped her readjust to normal life after the accident. But he had also told her that whenever she felt under pressure, whenever she needed someone to talk with, he would be there for her; she could visit him any time. She had never gone back, preferring to put that part of her past behind her, but she had thought of returning several times. There were unanswered questions she wanted to ask, some loose ends she wanted tied up, but somehow she could never bring herself to return to his office. Now it had been so long that she was not sure the offer would still be open. She wasn't even sure he'd remember her; after all, he'd probably had hundreds of patients since then.

The headache disappeared as quickly as it had come, without a trace, leaving her head clear and uncluttered, and the irregularity of its departure disturbed her as much as the intensity of its presence.

Sleepwalking and headaches.

She pushed the thought from her mind and returned to shelving.

There was a rush at noon, employees from nearby shops and offices hurrying over on their lunch hours to do some browsing, and Cathy was kept busy. Most of them staked out the periodical section, reading the latest magazines, but there were a lot of questions to be answered. A new Stephen King book was out in paperback and quite a few people bought copies. The hour flew by. The crowd dwindled to a handful by one and had disappeared entirely by one-thirty.

Fifteen minutes later, Ann came in, smiling and waving hello to Cathy as she dropped her backpack behind the counter. "Tough day," she said, shaking her head. She walked over to the Classics aisle and stood in front of the Penguin paperbacks, her finger following along the shelf as she silently mouthed the titles. She peeked her head around the bookcase, pushing her glasses up the bridge of her nose. "You went to ASU, didn't you?" she asked.

Cathy nodded.

"Did you ever have Dr. Varton for English?"

"No. I heard nothing but bad things about him, so I didn't take his class. I took Smith instead."

"Wise move."

"What do you have him for? American Lit?"

"Yeah." Ann shook her head. "We're supposed to have *The Sound and the Fury* read and analyzed by Wednesday. He's going to test us on it. God, I hate that class."

Cathy laughed. "Get the CliffsNotes."

"I might." Ann reached out and grabbed a book off the shelf. She sighed. "I read this in high school, but I only remember the basic plot. Knowing Varton, he's going to test us on the fifth speech by the fourth character in the third chapter, or ask us the exact number of hours over which the novel takes place."

Cathy smiled. "You could start reading now," she said, looking around the empty store. "The place is pretty dead."

"No. I need a rest. I'll read it tonight." She walked behind the counter and zipped open her backpack, tossing in the book. "Charge it to my account," she said.

Cathy found the price of the book and wrote it on the piece of paper used to keep track of employee purchases that was attached to the side of the cash register. Ann walked into the stockroom at the back of the store to sign in. She emerged a few moments later drinking a Sprite she'd taken from the refrigerator. She moved behind the front counter, where Cathy was idly doodling on a scrap of paper.

Cathy looked up. "So have you decided what you're going to do after you graduate?" she asked. "Are you going to go on and get your Master's?"

"I still don't know yet. To be honest, I'm pretty sick of school. Even if I do decide to get a Master's, I think I'll take a year off and just have fun. Maybe I'll see what kind of job I can get with a B.A." She was silent for a moment, and Cathy knew what she was thinking. "Why haven't you tried to get a better job?" she asked finally. "You know you can do better than this."

Cathy shrugged. "Too lazy, I guess. I'm used to it here. It's not that bad."

"But the pay's shit."

Cathy laughed. "Yeah, I do wish I earned more money. Between my salary and my father's disability, we just barely squeak by."

"Why don't you look around?"

"There's not a whole lot you can do with a degree in Liberal Studies."

"You could teach."

"I don't want to teach."

Ann ran a hand through her hair. "You really are exasperating sometimes." She looked Cathy in the eye. "I'm only saying this because I think you're capable of being more than a clerk in a bookstore for the rest of your life."

"I like working in a bookstore," Cathy said defensively. "It's—"

"Rationalizing," Ann said. "You're making excuses."

"You're right."

"I just think—"

"Let's talk about something else, okay?"

Ann sighed. "You're impossible."

"Let's talk about you for once."

"Me? Okay." Ann picked up a bookmark from the counter, examining it. "I have a date tomorrow," she said.

"Who?"

"Someone new."

"Really? Where did you meet him? One of your classes?"

"Right here," Ann said. "In the store."

Cathy was surprised. "Here?"

Ann smiled. "Believe it or not, it's a good place to meet people. A lot better than school. If I go out with some guy from my class and things don't work out, I still have to see him three times a week. If this doesn't work out, he can do his book shopping at B. Dalton and I never have to see him again."

"That's true," Cathy acknowledged.

They were silent for a moment.

"You really should try to meet more people, you know." Ann's voice was kind, but serious, concerned.

Cathy reddened. "What is this?" she said lightly, trying to turn it into a joke. "Pick on Cathy day?"

"I'm telling you this as a friend."

Cathy sighed, nodding. "I know. It's just that . . ."

" 'Just that' what?"

"I don't know, it seems so hard for me to meet people. I never know what to say."

"It's not that hard."

"That's easy for you to say."

Ann cleared her throat nervously. "What if I set you up on a blind date?"

Cathy laughed. "Another one? Thanks, but no thanks."

"We could make it a double date. It might be fun."

"I know—he has a great personality." She smiled. "I appreciate your concern, but I'm not that desperate." She paused. "Not yet."

They both laughed.

"Come on," Cathy said, changing the subject. "We got a big shipment in yesterday, and I need you to help me cart the box out front."

"All right."

She took the small bell from under the counter, putting it next to the "Ring bell for service" sign, as they both went into the back stockroom.

Thirteen

Allan had gone over the statistics until his head hurt, but he could find nothing relevant to the murders at all. He looked at the printouts and reports spread on the desk in front of him. There were lists of recent escapees and parolees from prisons in Arizona and the entire Southwest, lists of violent patients released from mental institutions within the same geographic area and lists of murders committed within the past six months in all states west of the Mississippi. He had cross-indexed and referenced each of the lists but could find no correlations and, even worse, nothing remotely similar to what was occurring here in Phoenix.

He rubbed his aching forehead. He would use the computer to check statistics for the past year, maybe the past two years, but he didn't have much confidence in finding anything. He had the feeling that they were dealing with someone new here, someone not recorded on the files of America's law-enforcement agencies, and it was not a thought that made him feel happy. They were narrowing down their investigative options, ruling out possibilities, and would soon be flying blind, relying on nothing but chance and luck.

Technology was still not an efficient weapon against a psychotic mind.

Sighing, he took the bottle of Tylenol out of his desk and popped two of the small white caplets into his mouth, downing them with cold coffee. He looked at the white plastic container before returning it to the drawer. After that Tylenol scare a few years back, he now felt a twinge of apprehension each time he took one of the pills, as if he were doing something daring, and he'd thought before that that might be one reason why he continued to use the product.

But he certainly didn't need any extra excitement now.

He buzzed Pynchon on the intercom, telling the captain that he was going out for some fieldwork, though he was actually going out for some fresh air and a bite to eat. He was hungry and feeling claustrophobic, and he thought that getting out of his cooped-up office, if only for ten minutes, might help keep him from going stir-crazy.

Outside, the air was hot and dry, the Arizona sky blue and cloudless. Not quite summer weather, but damn close. Allan walked across the asphalt, the heat soaking through the rubber soles of his tennis shoes. In another month, the asphalt would be softened, pliable, and the ground of the parking lot would give with each step he took.

Sometimes he wished he worked in a more temperate area.

Getting into the Bronco, he turned on the air conditioner and backed out of the lot onto the street.

He was at the tail end of the drive-through line at Taco Bell when his beeper went off. Allan looked at the square menu just one car length in front of him, his eyes focusing on the small black intercom near the top, tantalizingly close. "Shit," he muttered. He threw the car into reverse and backed up, pulling into one of the marked parking stalls at the side of the fast-food restaurant. He knew he should have taken a city vehicle. His Bronco wasn't equipped with a radio, and when he went out in it he always had to rely on the damned beeper, which invariably went off at the most inopportune moments.

A dented white pickup truck pulled into the drive-through line, usurping his place.

Ordinarily, he would have waited until after ordering and eating his food before calling the station. But this was not an ordinary situation. His stomach growling, Allan strode into the tan stucco building and walked up to the closest cashier, a blonde high school-age girl wearing too much makeup. "Excuse me," he said. "May I use your phone?"

"There's a pay phone next door at the liquor store," she said.

Allan reached into his back pocket and pulled out his wallet, flashing the badge. "I'm a police officer. I need to use your phone."

The girl looked confused. "We're not supposed to let people use our phone," she said. "But I . . . Wait a minute. Let me get the manager."

"Forget it." Allan hurried outside and crossed the parking lot to the liquor store. He didn't have time to deal with airheads this afternoon.

There were two pay phones flanking the double doors of the liquor store, encased in half-squares of tinted plastic. He grabbed the first one, dropping in a quarter and dialing the station.

"Hello, Phoenix Police Department—"

"Yvonne," Allan said. "It's me, Allan. What's up?"

"They've found Whitehead, sir."

"Is he—?"

"They found his body in an empty house on Center."

"Jesus." Allan closed his eyes, swallowing hard. He felt suddenly cold. "What happened?"

"It's bad, sir."

"What happened?"

"It's bad."

Allan drove straight to Center, his hunger forgotten. The street intersected Tucker Avenue a block north of the spot where they'd found Susan Welmers' body. At least that was something, he thought. The murderer was obviously staying within a small geographic area.

This time there was no crowd of spectators or fleet of police cars. There were only three unmarked vehicles parked on either side of the residence. The ambulance had not yet arrived. Allan stepped out of the Bronco, looking at the house. It was atypical for the area, a clapboard home from the early forties, two stories with a basement. The yard was overgrown with dying weeds, and the white paint was peeling, showing yellow underneath. Next to the sidewalk was a "For Sale" sign from a local real-estate firm.

He strode up the walk, his eyes on the empty windows of the house. They were black and blank, looking uncomfortably like the staring eyes of a malevolent house he'd seen once in a surrealist painting. This had no doubt been the first home in the area and the land had probably been built up around it. There were several such homes throughout the Valley, old farmhouses and ranch estates whose surrounding land was sold to developers, leaving the original residence an interesting anachronism in a sea of crackerbox conformity.

He opened the front door. "Lieutenant Grant!" he called out.

"In here!"

He followed Williams's voice into the kitchen where he, Lee, Dobrinin, and two other officers were seated on a dining room table, the only piece of furniture on the entire first floor. Leaning against the opposite wall, looking pale and shaken, was a man wearing the red coat and nametag of a real-estate agent.

"Give it to me," Allan said. "What happened?"

Williams stood up. He licked his lips nervously, and it was obvious that he was pretty shaken as well. "Mr. Ansley there was showing the house to a couple of prospective buyers." He nodded toward the pale man. "They found Bob in the attic."

"The body's still undisturbed?"

"We didn't do anything. We waited until you arrived."

"Does the captain know?"

Williams nodded. "He said he'd notify Whitehead's parents. He said you'd take over the on-site."

"Where's the ambulance?"

"Out back." Williams pointed toward a weathered wooden fence visible through the clouded glass of the kitchen window, a red light protruding above its top. "There's an alley that runs behind these homes, and the captain told the ambulance to come through there, siren off. He didn't want any publicity."

Allan nodded. "Photographer? Forensics?"

"They should be here any second."

Allan looked at the real-estate agent, then back toward the policemen. "Someone take him down to the station and get a statement. He doesn't have to be here."

Lee stood up. "Yes, sir."

"Thank you," the man said.

Allan nodded curtly. "Let's go upstairs."

Williams led the way up the wooden steps to the second floor. They walked down a dusty hallway to another stairwell, this one much narrower, steeper, and shorter. Even from here, Allan could smell the blood, the violence, and a wave of nausea welled within him. He forced the feelings down, aware that his heart was thundering in his chest. Williams was looking up at the top of the stairway, a few feet above his head. Instead of walking up he hesitated a moment, and Allan put a hand on his shoulder, sliding past him. "I'll go first," he said softly.

The next few steps were the longest he'd ever taken, and he found himself wondering how long the steps to the gallows, the gas chamber, the electric chair must seem to a condemned man. He wondered if they could be worse than this. He forced himself to put one foot in front of another. Above him was not a faceless victim, not an unknown body, but Bob Whitehead, a man he had known and worked with for the past three years. For the first time in his life, he was not a disinterested third party, able to view the victim as merely a corpse, as the evidence of a crime for which someone must be punished. He had known Bob Whitehead as a living, breathing human being, as a man with thoughts and feelings. He'd known Bob's taste in movies, in music, in clothes, in cars, in women. He'd known his likes and dislikes, his hopes, his fears, his dreams.

He moved up another step, and another, the hideous stench of death growing ever stronger. Now he could see the floor of the attic, the old furniture that had for some reason been left here though the rest of the house was empty. Another step, and another, and then he was at the top, Williams and the others behind him. He pulled a handkerchief from his pocket, holding it over his nose.

"He's behind that cabinet," Williams said. "Past the light."

Allan walked slowly forward, his muscles tightening. He moved past a tangle of chairs and an old steamer trunk. On the dusty floor before him, he saw a wide trail where Whitehead's body had obviously been dragged to its final destination. He pointed toward the trail and to the chaotic outlines of several surrounding footsteps. "Did any of you think to isolate a set of footprints before you clomped around up here?"

"We stayed within the path made by . . . Bob's body," Dobrinin said. "Those other prints are from Mr. Ansley and the people he was showing the house to."

"Where are those people?"

"They were gone before we got here," Williams said. "But Ansley has their names. It should be fairly easy to get a matching set of prints from the shoes they were wearing today. If there's a fourth pair here we'll find them."

"Right," Allan said. He walked along the dusted

trail of floor around the cabinet to which Williams had pointed, steeling himself for the worst.

Again, he was not prepared.

Whitehead's naked body was flat on the floor and had obviously been dead for some time. The smeared blood had dried to a brownish rust. He was lying on his back, open eyes staring upward at the ceiling. So many needles and pins had been embedded in his skin, and so closely together, that he seemed almost to be wearing some type of metallic bodysuit. As he drew closer, Allan could see that the pins and needles had been arranged in patterns. There was a tic-tac-toe field on Whitehead's upper thigh, a checkerboard of squares on his chest. Lines of pins ran lengthwise down each arm. Needles outlined eyes, nose, and lips. Still others, pushed all the way in, were placed randomly over his naked form.

His penis and testicles were completely covered with tightly packed pins.

"God," Allan breathed.

Williams nodded, sucking in breath.

From outside came the sound of a car parking, the high-pitched whine of old brakes squealing. Dobrinin moved over to the attic window and looked out. "Photographer," he said.

"Go downstairs and meet him," Allan ordered. "Tell him where to walk. We don't want anyone destroying these footprints. They may be the only clue we have."

He looked again at Whitehead's desecrated body. The policeman had obviously been tortured and had died hideously in unbelievable pain. Unable to look away, Allan stared at Whitehead's face, the face that had been alive and expressive two days ago, the mirror of the man's thoughts and emotions, now frozen into an aspect of agony, pinned into place.

"We're going to get that bastard," Allan said quietly. "And we're going to hang his twisted ass out to dry."

Fourteen

Jimmy took his burrito out of the microwave, unwrapped the plastic, and dropped the food onto his plate. He poured himself some milk and took his dinner out into the living room. It was his second dinner, really. He had made himself a hot dog earlier, but it hadn't been enough and he'd soon found that he was hungry again. He glanced at the clock on top of the television as he sat down on the couch. Nine o'clock. It was late even for his dad.

He wondered what his father had been doing after work lately. Jimmy knew his dad usually stopped off for a few drinks before coming home—he could always smell the alcohol on his old man's breath—but for the past few weeks his dad had been coming home *much* later than usual, often not returning until after he himself had gone to bed.

He would have thought that his father would make an effort to come home earlier than usual because of the murders. Paul's parents, he knew, now kept much closer tabs on their son and were reluctant to leave him home alone at all. The parents of most of the kids at school seemed to be taking extra precautions because of the killings.

But not his dad.

Jimmy bit into the burrito, but it was still too hot and burned the roof of his mouth. He quickly took a swig of milk to quench the fire, putting his plate down on the low coffee table. He looked at the television. He could not concentrate with noise, so he had turned off the sound on the set in order to do his homework. Now he watched as a sitcom family chased each other, laughing, around a living room couch.

He wondered what his mom was doing right now. He wondered if she was thinking about him.

Sometimes he wished his mom had taken him instead of his dad.

That wasn't fair, he knew. He loved his father. And he understood that his dad had a lot of worries and responsibilities. But sometimes . . . well, sometimes he wished he lived with his mother and saw his father on special occasions, instead of the other way round.

From outside came the sound of a scream. A high-pitched cry.

Jimmy jumped. He stood up and quickly checked both the front and back doors, making sure that both were locked. The scream hadn't sounded malevolent. It hadn't even sounded that serious. More likely than not, it was the response to a fall or a hurt finger. Sound traveled far at this time of night. But he couldn't afford to take chances. Not with those murders occurring so close by.

Not with Halback and Samson after him.

That was stupid. They wouldn't stake out his house. They wouldn't go to those lengths to get him.

But maybe they would. Maybe they knew he was alone. Maybe they knew his dad wouldn't come back until late.

The side window, next to the ottoman, was open, and he walked over to close it, suddenly aware of how vulnerable he was in the empty house.

The scream came again, a woman's scream, and he realized as a field of goosebumps cascaded down his arms that it had come from the Lauter house.

He quickly shut the window and ran to the TV, turning up the sound, grateful for the laugh track.

The woman Al Goldstein met at Benny's looked a hell of a lot like Shirley. Tall, brunette, white even teeth, dark tan skin. She was prettier than Shirley, though, with clear green eyes, full lips, and a perfect aquiline nose.

And her tits were huge.

She was drunker than a skunk, and Al knew that that was the only reason she had even given him the time of day. She could obviously do a lot better. But it was she who had approached him, who had initiated the conversation, and who was he to turn down a good thing?

Her name was Joanne. She said she was a career woman, with no time for a relationship, and she hinted broadly in the way that only a drunk woman can, that she was looking for a good time. Al saw her gold wedding ring, and he was fairly certain that if he opened her purse and looked in her wallet he'd see photos of children, but he said nothing. It wasn't every day that fortune smiled upon him, and he was grateful for the little crumbs that came his way.

He was careful not to drink too much, to stay sober enough to drive, and, sure enough, she eventually suggested that they retire to his place. He readily agreed, and though he felt a small twinge of guilt when he thought about Jimmy, the guilt disappeared as they walked across the parking lot out to the car and she slid a hand into his back pocket.

Jimmy was sitting on the floor of the living room, next to Dusty, watching TV when they walked in. Al tried to smile, though the expression felt stiff and false on his face. "Jimmy," he said. "Could you go into your room? Joanne and I have some business to discuss."

The boy nodded understandingly. "Sure, Dad." He turned off the TV, patted Dusty's head, and went down the hall to his bedroom.

"Don't forget to take a bath!" Al called out.

"I already did!"

Joanne giggled drunkenly, her left breast pressing against the side of Al's arm. "That leaves the bathtub free for us."

Al put a finger to his lips. "We have to be quiet." He pointed toward Jimmy's closed door. "Don't want to corrupt the youth."

Dusty stood, yawned, stretched, and padded over to Al, wagging her tail happily.

Al gave Joanne a quick kiss on the lips. "Wait a minute," he said. "I have to throw this damn dog out." He grabbed Dusty's collar and yanked, forcing the animal to follow him through the kitchen to the back door. "Get out of here!" he told Dusty, pushing her outside.

He closed and locked the door.

"Cute dog," Joanne said when he returned.

"If you like dogs."

"You don't?"

"Hate 'em."

She laughed, and he led her down the hall into the bedroom. He looked at the double bed, aware of the fact that this was the first woman who'd been here since Shirley left. From somewhere in the back of his mind came the thought that he was betraying Shirley, but he pushed that thought away. The bitch had dumped him, ran off to fuck some other guy. He had a perfect right to bed whomever he pleased.

He closed the door behind them and moved over to the bed, pulling down the covers. "Welcome to my boudoir," he said, and Joanne giggled.

He put a finger to his lips, telling her to keep the noise down, but as she pulled off her top, revealing large round breasts with erect brown nipples, he realized that he didn't care whether Jimmy heard them or not.

Fifteen

The day was not cold and overcast as it should have been. No dark clouds threatened rain, no untamed wind whipped over the cemetery. It was a typical May day in Phoenix, sunny and hot, the deep blue sky devoid of clouds. The plants and grass and trees all shone a clean technicolor green. Many of the mourners were wearing sunglasses, and Allan would not have been surprised had some of the younger men been wearing bathing trunks under their dark three-piece suits so they could go straight to the river after the funeral instead of stopping by their houses.

The scene was entirely too cheerful, and that only served to trivialize the ceremony, to somehow diminish the impact of Bob Whitehead's death. Several of the people standing near the rear of the crowd were talking amongst themselves and smiling.

Smiling!

This was wrong, Allan thought. It was all wrong. A funeral was not supposed to be merely another item on the agenda, something sandwiched in between breakfast and tennis. It was supposed to be important, goddamn it, it was supposed to mean something.

But he had no control over the weather and could not manipulate the scene into turning out the way it should. He was no painter, this was no painting, and he had no jurisdiction over the elements of composition.

It was a good turnout, though. At least he could say that much. Not only had Whitehead's close friends on the force shown up, his real friends, but nearly all of his coworkers had put in an appearance. Even Pynchon had come, although the captain had been ill enough to have been out for the past two days.

There were also friends from real life, from outside the force, and that made Allan feel good. It was always nice when a man's social life wasn't confined solely to a circle of policemen.

The minister finished speaking, and the mourners bowed their heads in prayer. He knew he'd probably seen too many movies, but Allan could not help scanning the assembled guests for an unfamiliar face. It was not likely that a killer brilliant enough and sophisticated enough to carry out such technically perfect murders and leave no trace would pull such a trite and clichéd routine as visiting the funeral of a victim, but it could not hurt to look. And who could tell? The murderer was obviously a genius, but he was obviously also very sick. Such a blatantly cinematic ploy might appeal to whatever warped sense of amusement he possessed.

There was no one at the cemetery, however, whom Allan had not seen before. Many of the mourners' names were unknown to him, but none of their faces were entirely unfamiliar.

The minister finished his prayer, and at his bidding all heads looked to the left, where a police unit performed its makeshift ten-gun salute, the rifle reports echoing across the still air of the flat cemetery. The salute was ragged and rough, a last-minute idea, unrehearsed, but it was something that Allan knew Bob would have appreciated. Whitehead had never been one for smooth and well-run affairs. Once, on his birthday, given the choice between dinner at an expensive French restaurant or homemade hamburgers, he'd chosen the hamburgers.

But his choosing days were over.

As the last report echoed, faded, and disappeared, Allan thought of Whitehead's motto: "Life is a boner caked with shit and shoved down your throat." Whitehead had had the saying carved into a block of wood he kept on his desk, and while the other officers had always found it funny as hell, Bob never gave an indication that the motto was anything but serious. He had never been one to look on the bright side of life. He'd looked at what he called the "realistic" side. "Every silver lining has a cloud," he always said.

Life was a boner caked with shit and shoved down your throat.

The closed casket was lowered into the grave, and there was a soft snuffling of running noses, a sudden outbreak of handkerchiefs. Allan looked down at the ground. It seemed to him that the sun had just become much brighter or that there was a sudden infusion of smog into the atmosphere, because his eyes were hurting. They were teary and watering, and though he'd thought he was more angry than sad, he realized that he was crying. Around him, several other men looked down at their feet or wiped their eyes.

Allan looked up. As quickly as they had come, his tears fled, sadness replaced by fear. A cold hand ran down his spine, playing his vertebrae like piano keys. Standing next to Williams and his wife in the line of mourners, he suddenly felt as though he were being watched. He turned quickly around, and although he saw nothing unusual in the cemetery or beyond the gates, no mysterious lurking strangers, he could not shake the sensation that a pair of unwelcome eyes were trained on his back. He moved forward with the other mourners, paying his last respects as handfuls of dirt were thrown ceremoniously onto the coffin. He forgot about being watched for the few moments he was next to the open grave, but the sensation returned immediately afterward.

The feeling followed him all the way back to the car.

It did not disappear until he was off cemetery property and on the open road.

Sixteen

On the playground, life was hell. Halback and Samson were everywhere, sneaking through crowds to pop up near the swings, suddenly appearing by the lunch tables. Jimmy stayed close to the teachers during recess, became the lunch monitors' constant companion during lunch, and hovered around the door of the principal's office after school, but he knew that this sanctuary in the outer fringes of the adult world was temporary—sooner or later, he would be forced to face the two bullies, to deal with his problem head on. So far he had been safe, but the two were starting to close in. The web was tightening. Bob Wade, one of his friends from class, had been pantsed on the way home from school yesterday, in front of the girls, and had been made to kiss the ground. Halback and Samson had chased Paul but had not caught him. And the word "die" had been penciled in large block letters on the door of Jimmy's classroom each morning before school started.

It was only a matter of time.

They were not forgetting about him, as Cathy had predicted and as he had secretly hoped. They were intensifying their efforts—he was becoming an obsession with them. He knew that if they caught him now the punishment would be much worse, much more severe, much more brutal, than if he had let them beat him up that first day. He had eluded them for quite a while, and it was making them crazy. They wanted him badly, and when they finally caught him they would not stop with just making him kiss the ground.

They cut his dick clean off.

Paul's story had never been very far from his mind, and his thoughts kept returning to the terrifying image of the baby sitting on the toilet, screaming in agony as blood gushed from the bloody stump that had been his penis. True, it had been Samson's brother who had done the dirty deed, but Jimmy had no difficulty in imagining Samson doing exactly the same thing.

While Halback handed him the blade and grinned.

Cut his dick clean off.

It was no wonder that his schoolwork had suffered tremendously the past week. How was he supposed to concentrate on math and spelling and social studies when two guys wanted him dead?

Now, hiding behind a brick pillar under the covering of the walkway next to the principal's office, Jimmy spied on Halback and Samson as they waited for him by the playground gate. They did not know where he was—he had waited until they were off the school grounds before daring to venture forth even to this hiding place—but they were pretty sure that he had not gone home. They clamped rough fingers through chain-link fence, staring menacingly into the playground, scaring other kids into leaving school by an alternate route. Gradually, the threatening looks were replaced by expressions of boredom, and the two threw stones at a junky car across the street, skirmished a bit between themselves, then headed for home, believing that Jimmy had either taken off early and thus escaped them or had eluded them by somehow sneaking around their ambush.

Either way, they'd be plenty mad tomorrow.

Walking down the empty street a half hour later,

Jimmy found himself checking behind every tree and bush, afraid to turn each corner for fear of seeing the two bullies waiting for him. This was stupid, he knew. Halback and Samson were home already. He had watched them leave school at three-fifteen and had given them an extra half hour before starting home himself. But still the fear was there, no matter how hard he tried to reason himself out of it, no matter how much he tried to convince himself that he was acting like a baby.

He walked slowly down the street toward his house. Summer was close; already it felt as though it had arrived. The sky was swimming-pool blue, lit by a hot and powerful sun that had burned off even the smallest wisp of cloud, and several of the yards on the street had been flooded for irrigation, the short grass stalks buried under water. He could hear the gentle hum of air conditioners in the still afternoon air, a prelude to the music of June, July, and August. He knew he should feel happy that summer was approaching, but he felt only an unfamiliar sense of unease, a feeling that was almost like dread. Something must be wrong with him. He wasn't looking forward to the end of school, even though it would probably put an end to his problem with Halback and Samson. He wasn't excited that summer was approaching and he would be free for three full months. He felt only a dull apprehension and an emptiness that was not quite depression.

This was not something he could blame on the two older boys. This was entirely different.

From the next street over came the yells and squeals of a group of preschoolers playing in the sun. This far away, their words were muffled, only the shrill tones carrying to his ears. He listened as he bent down to pick a penny up off the sidewalk. Their screams reminded him of the screams last night. The screams of his father's friend.

"Oh God, Al!! Oh God!!!"

He did not know exactly what had gone on last night, but he had a pretty good idea. He was not stupid. And though neither his father nor mother nor any of his teachers had ever sat him down to explain the facts of life, he had been able to get a rough idea of what happened during sex from keeping his ears open on the playground and from watching movies on TV.

"Oh God!!"

He had not liked the words the woman said or the noises that she made: the breathless yelps, the staccato moans. And he'd liked even less the low grunting that sounded as though it had come from the throat of his father. He had put the pillow over his head to block out the noise, and when that had not worked, he'd used his fingers to plug his ears.

She had been gone by morning.

Maybe that was why this day seemed so strange, why he felt nothing but emptiness inside.

He wished his mother were still living with them.

"BA!"

Jimmy looked up at the sound, recognizing immediately the distorted voice of Randy West. Sure enough, the retarded boy was standing across the street in front of his house, clutching what looked like a ball to his stomach.

Jimmy waved, trying to smile, though he felt no friendliness toward the boy. He remembered all too clearly the way Randy had thrown the ball at him the last time, not in a playful way, but viciously, as hard as he could. Part of him felt sorry for Randy—it was not his fault he was retarded. He had been born that way and there was nothing he could do about it. But another part of him knew that being retarded did not absolve him from everything. He had seen Randy's face as he'd thrown the ball. The boy had wanted to hurt him.

Now Randy's face was blank, completely devoid of expression. He stared dully at Jimmy as though he didn't recognize him. Jimmy slowly put his arm down, his wave tapering off to nothing. Shaking his head, he started walking toward home.

Suddenly, Randy ran across the street. He did not bother to look for cars but sped over the asphalt, his thick legs pumping, making a beeline for Jimmy.

"Hey!" Jimmy yelled, startled.

"AAAAAAAA!" Randy screamed. Still running, he threw the ball as hard as he could. It smashed into Jimmy's mouth, forcing his lips back against his teeth and cracking the lower lip open. Jimmy tasted the sickening saltiness of blood as he staggered backward, holding the palm of his hand against his streaming mouth.

"What—?" he began through split lips. But the retarded boy had the ball in hand and instantly threw it again. This time it caught Jimmy full in the eye, and he fell to the ground. The pain was unbelievably intense, and even as he blinked back tears he could feel his face beginning to swell. He scrambled to his feet but was knocked down with the force of a throw to the back of his head.

"BA BA BA BA BA!" Randy screamed. Jimmy crawled as quickly as he could across the thin strip of grass next to the sidewalk, tensing himself for the expected blow. "Help!" he screamed at the top of his lungs. "Help!"

The ball hit hard the small of his back and bounced off. He felt around for it, his vision blurry. The eye that had been hit was already swelling shut, and the other eye was watering painfully. His fingers found the ball and closed around it, pulling the round object to his chest.

"MA BA! MA BA! MA BA!" Randy's thick fingers closed around his own, yanking the ball free.

"Randy!"

It was the voice of Mrs. West from across the street, loud and clear and filled with unconcealed rage.

"Ba!" Randy said, but his voice was quieter, more

submissive, devoid of the manic fury that had propelled it only seconds before.

"You get in here right now!" Her voice was getting closer. "I told you a million times, you are not to go out of the yard. Do you understand me?"

Jimmy looked up to see Mrs. West grab the ball out of her son's hand and slap him hard across the upper arm. She looked down at Jimmy. "Sorry," she said. "Randy didn't mean anything by it. He can't help himself."

She walked back across the street, the retarded boy firmly in tow. Jimmy stood up, watching as she pulled him into the house, slamming the door shut behind him.

Sorry?

Blood was streaming from his lips. He could feel it on his chin. Through his blurred vision, he could see it on his clothes and on the sidewalk. The entire right side of his face was swollen. *Sorry?* That's the best she could do? He glanced up and down the street, looking for a witness, someone who might have seen what had occurred, but there was no one there. Everyone was inside. From the next street over came the sounds of the playing children.

Limping from the pain in his back, holding a hand against his mouth to stem the bleeding, Jimmy walked down the block toward home.

Seventeen

Fieldwork.

He used to like doing fieldwork. Paperwork had been something he'd had to put up with, but fieldwork he had enjoyed.

He wasn't sure he enjoyed it so much any more.

Allan signaled and turned left on Seventh. He still liked the technical aspects of homicide investigation, still enjoyed conducting crime scene analysis, still received satisfaction applying deductive reasoning to evidence obtained through scientific methods, but some of the other tasks that had once energized him now just left him feeling empty and drained.

Mostly he hated dealing with victims. And survivors. Living people. Bodies were bad, but they had no feelings, no reactions. He didn't have to concern himself with their emotional responses, he didn't have to hide his own responses from them. But with victims and survivors he was expected to remain aloof, objective, and impartial, to play the impassive robot to their emotional human.

And that was becoming harder and harder to do.

He'd just finished interviewing, for the second time, Susan Welmers' husband. He did not think that the murder had been committed by the woman's family or by anyone the woman had known, but a second interview was SOP. Hunches and intuition might be tools used in an investigation, but it was not possible to build a case on such intangibles and the process of elimination required that before a possibility was eliminated it be thoroughly investigated and disproved.

Ray Welmers, understandably, was still devastated by the loss of his wife, but the extent of his grief had been painful for Allan to see. The inside of the Welmers' house looked as though it had not been cleaned for days, and dirty dishes and half-filled cups littered every table and countertop. Ray had smelled of sweat and alcohol and had been wearing mismatched socks with no shoes. His face had been red, his eyes swollen and puffy.

Allan had wanted to comfort the man, though he knew that nothing he could ever say could mitigate or lessen the impact of his tragedy. But he had been constrained by his role as investigating officer and, despite his personal feelings, he had been forced to reask painful questions that the husband had already answered definitively on the night of the murder.

Ray had been cooperative, had at first answered the questions without complaint. Allan had been disconcerted, however, when the man answered two questions in a row as though his wife were merely missing, not dead. It had been even worse when Ray told him to wait a minute and had gone into the bedroom to retrieve his wife's nightgown. "Maybe the dogs can find her scent on here and track her," he said hopefully.

Allan had reminded Ray gently that his wife was murdered, not missing, and had sat impassively on the couch while the man broke down, crying nonstop for a full five minutes. After the interview, he had given Ray a card with the phone number of Maricopa County Mental Health Services.

Now he was on his way back to the station to talk

to a woman who had been a victim of an attempted kidnapping in Glendale this morning. The Glendale PD believed that the kidnapping attempt might have been an abduction effort by the murderer and had brought the woman to Phoenix so that Allan and his team could determine whether there was any connection.

Dobrinin had already set up the video camera and was waiting with the woman, Martha Brenner, in one of the interrogation rooms when Allan arrived. Allan wasted no time but sat down, apologized for being late, scanned the Glendale report, and started immediately on the questions.

Martha Brenner, twenty-eight, was a waitress at Bob's and had been getting off the night shift at six when she'd been jumped by a man hiding behind the dumpster at the side of the restaurant. The man had had no weapon and had not been particularly strong, but the attack had been a surprise, and before Martha knew what was happening she was being dragged toward the man's car. She'd kicked and fought, had bit the hand attempting to gag her mouth, and with one lucky backward kick to the man's crotch had managed to escape. She'd run, screaming, back into the restaurant and the man had hopped in his car and driven away.

"What kind of car was it?" Allan asked.

"A big car. An Oldsmobile, I think. Maybe a Buick. I'm not sure. It was white, though."

"Do you remember any numbers or letters of the license plate?"

Martha shook her head.

"Can you think of any reason, any reason at all, why anyone would want to abduct you?"

"No." She ran a tired hand through her hair. "Look, I already told all this to Lieutenant Hopper in Glendale. How many times do I have to go over it? I want to help you out, I want you to catch this guy, but I'm tired, and I don't really have anything to tell

you. I don't know what happened or why, I just . . .
I don't know."

Allan looked down at the report in front of him.
The Glendale PD had already provided them with a
composite sketch, but he wanted to try it again with
Ralph Sable, their own artist.

"I know, and I'm sorry, but if you could just bear
with me for a little while longer, we'll get this over
with and it'll save you another trip down here
tomorrow."

Martha gave him a weary nod. "All right."

He went over everything again, point by point, hoping to jog her memory, hoping to uncover something
that had eluded the Glendale police but her story remained unchanged, indeed showed signs of cementing
into rote recitation, and at that point Allan decided
to give the questioning a rest.

"Do you think you could do me one last favor?"
he asked.

She nodded.

"We have some books of photographs I'd like you
to go through. Mug shots of previous offenders. I'd
like you to look through these books and see if any
of the pictures resemble the man you saw. Do you
think you could do that for me?"

"I'll try."

Allan gave her an encouraging smile. "Thanks." He
led her out of the interrogation room and to a table
in the tech library, stopping first to get her a Diet Dr.
Pepper from the machine, and set a pile of books in
front of her. He urged her to take her time, to rest
when she felt tired and the faces started to blur, to
inform Detective Dobrinin if she came across a man
who looked like her attacker. He remained patient,
helpful, as he explained this to her, but was inwardly
convinced that the attempted kidnapper bore no rela-
tion to the murderer for whom they were searching.
A killer capable of flawlessly carrying out such grue-
somely original murders was not the type of person

to leap out from behind a trash bin in a crowded parking lot in a failed kidnapping attempt.

"Stay with her," he told Dobrinin.

The other policeman nodded. "Will do."

Allan bade Martha Brenner good-bye and tried not to let his discouragement show as he headed down the hall to the break room for a late machine lunch.

Eighteen

Jimmy was sitting on the curb in front of his house as Cathy drove down the street. He jumped up as she approached, waving his arms, and even from this far away she could see the dark stains of dried blood on his shirt. She pulled over to where he stood, and now she could see the dark bruises on his face, the redness of his split lips. One side of his face was badly swollen.

She stopped the car and threw open the door, rushing over to him. "Jesus! What happened?" Her first thought was that the bullies had beat him up, and she immediately felt guilty for having tried to trivialize their threat. "Are you all right?"

He nodded and tried to smile. The effort was not a success, and she could see the pain in his features. "The retard," he said.

"Randy?" Cathy was confused. "He did this?"

"I was just walking home from school, and he attacked me. With his ball. Then his mom came and took him inside."

"She just left you there? Like this?"

He nodded. Anger flared within her, and she looked toward the Wests' house. The curtains were shut, the front door closed. She turned back to Jimmy. "What are you doing out here? Why aren't you inside? Did you call your father and tell him what happened?"

He looked embarrassed. "I can't find my key."

"You've been sitting out here all this time?" Cathy was shocked. "Why didn't you go over to the Boykins' or Mrs. Maltin's?"

Jimmy shrugged, saying nothing.

"Come on, get in the car." Cathy walked around the front of the Volkswagen and got in, starting the engine. Opening the passenger door, Jimmy hopped into the seat beside her. She drove the three doors down to her house and pulled into the driveway. "I have some Bactine in here for your cuts," she said, leading him through the front door into the house. "I want you to call your father and tell him what happened, then we'll go back to your place and wait for him."

"I don't know where my key is. I can't get in."

"I have an extra key in the kitchen, remember? Your father gave it to me in case of an emergency."

"Oh, yeah."

The TV was on in the den, and she knew her father was home, but she did not stop by to say hello or to tell him that she was back. Holding Jimmy by the arm, she brought him into the back bathroom and sat him down on the covered toilet as she pulled Bactine and Band-Aids out of the medicine cabinet. His lower lip looked bad, and as she cleaned the wound, dabbing at it with a cotton ball soaked in Bactine, she wondered if he would need stitches. There was clearly a long cut across the lip, and it appeared wide enough that it might not grow back together. The bleeding did not resume after cleansing, however, and she decided to let Jimmy's father make any medical decisions.

After assisting Jimmy with his cuts, she took him into the kitchen and opened the freezer, taking out two ice cubes and wrapping them in a clean washcloth. "Here," she said, handing him the icepack. "Hold this on the side of your face until the swelling goes down a little." She walked across the kitchen to the phone and picked up the receiver, handing it to him. "And call your father."

"I don't know his number," Jimmy admitted. "It's at home."

She shook her head, smiling. "This just isn't your day, is it?"

Jimmy smiled back. "No."

"Come on, then." Cathy went into the hall and grabbed her ring of extra keys from the small desk near the entryway. "We'll go to your house."

They went out the side door, walking past the garage to the sidewalk. She looked down at him, at his bloodstained shirt. "He just attacked you for no reason? You didn't do anything to provoke him?"

"Provoke him?" He looked at her, not understanding the word.

"Make him mad."

Jimmy shook his head emphatically. "I was just walking home from school, and he ran across the street and heaved the ball at my head. Hard. It hit me in the face, and he kept throwing it at me until his mom took him away."

They'd reached Jimmy's house by this time, and they moved up the front walk to the door. It took Cathy a moment to find the right key among the tangle of unfamiliar metal, but Jimmy pointed it out to her, and she inserted it into the keyhole. She turned the knob and opened the door.

And screamed.

On the floor, next to the small knickknack table in the entryway, was the bloody body of a dog.

Instinctively, she grabbed Jimmy's head and turned it away from the sight, jerking her own gaze away as well. She hadn't gotten a good look, but in the brief glance she'd had, she knew it was Dusty, Jimmy's dog. She closed her eyes, willing herself not to throw up, holding Jimmy's head tightly against her stomach.

"What is it?" he demanded. "What happened?"

Unable to speak, she shook her head, though she

knew he couldn't see the gesture. Her heart was pounding wildly; she could feel the adrenaline pulsing of blood through her wrists and in her head. She prayed that this wasn't happening, but she knew from the revulsion in her guts that it was. Her mouth was suddenly dry.

She thought of David.

The jackrabbit.

She staggered away from the porch, dragging Jimmy with her. Imprinted on her mind, even as she stared at the street ahead, was the sight of the bloody body.

"What is it?"

She reached down and grabbed his shoulders. "Dusty," she said.

He stared up at her, eyes wide with unwanted understanding. "Dusty?"

"Run over to my house and call the police. Now."

"I want to—"

"Now!" She met his eyes. "She's been killed. Whoever did it might still be in your house."

"What are you going to do?"

"Stay here. Watch and see if anyone comes out. If I see anyone, I'll try to get their license plate or something." She gave him a push. "Call them. Fast."

"But your dad's home—"

"Go!" she yelled.

He took off, feet flying, tennis shoes flapping rhythmically on the sidewalk. The street was silent now, and the sky in the east was already turning a dull yellowish blue in preparation for sundown. She stood on the sidewalk in front of Jimmy's house, staring at the open windows and the open door, looking for some sign of movement, but the house was quiet, dead.

Dead.

With the sun behind it, the inside of Jimmy's house was dark, and she could not see into the entryway though the door was more than half open. She could not see Dusty's body. Part of her wanted to rush quickly back up the porch and take a peek inside, to

make sure she'd seen what she thought she'd seen.
But that was stupid, and possibly dangerous. Besides,
as unbelievable and impossible as it seemed, she knew
exactly what was waiting there within the house. She
needed no confirmation. She felt cold, freezing, and
thought she might never be warm again. She could
still see the image, imprinted on her mind—Dusty,
turned inside out, facing the door as if waiting for her
master to come home, her lipless red dog mouth dripping with blood and forced into an unnatural smile.

The patrol car pulled up in front of the house less
than ten minutes later. Jimmy had returned and was
seated on the edge of the curb, staring into the gutter,
his face pale and lifeless. Cathy stood on the curb next
to him. She had seen no one come out of the house,
there had been no discernable movement inside, but
she had not allowed him to see Dusty and had insisted
that both of them wait on the curb until the police
arrived. Looking at the homes across the street, her
back to the half-open doorway, her horror had dissipated somewhat, replaced with a feeling of pity for
Jimmy and a sense of anger at his negligent father.
But with the arrival of the police car, the tentative
bubble of normalcy burst, and she felt again the fear.
She turned furtively to look at the house. In her mind,
she saw Dusty's head, skin reversed, grinning a bloody
dog-mouth smile.

She closed her eyes, forcing down the image.

The police car pulled to a stop, and Jimmy stood
up, walking forward to meet the officer emerging from
the car. Cathy realized that her hands were sweaty,
and she wiped them on her jeans. Dealing with figures
of authority, particularly those in uniform, always
made her nervous.

Miss Riley?

Keep calm, she told herself.

The police officer was younger than she expected,
and not as intimidating. She had been expecting a big
burly crew-cut man with iron features and a Jack

Webb demeanor, but the man walking toward her was only a few years older than herself and had black hair with a mustache. Although the look on his face was serious, his expression was kind, his eyes understanding, and that made her feel much more at ease. "Hello," she said, holding out her hand.

The policeman's strong fingers closed around her palm. "I'm Officer McClure," he said.

"Cathy Riley."

McClure looked at Jimmy. "You're Jimmy Goldstein?"

Jimmy nodded. His movements were slow and tired. "My dog's been killed."

"Where is the dog?" McClure's tone was sympathetic.

"She's in the house," Cathy told him. "I . . . I didn't want Jimmy to see her."

The officer took a small notebook and pen from his shirt pocket. "I know this is hard, but could you tell me exactly what happened?"

She looked at Jimmy's pale lifeless face, then turned away, finding it easier to face McClure. "Dusty's right by the door. She . . . she's been . . ." Cathy took a deep breath. "It looks like she's been turned inside out."

McClure stared at her. "Inside out?"

Cathy nodded.

"Let me see the dog." The officer's voice became brisker, more official. His eyes, bright now, betrayed his increased interest.

With a look at Jimmy that told him to remain where he was, Cathy led the policeman up the walk to the front door. She put a hand on the brass doorknob and stood unmoving for a moment, staring at the wooden rectangle before her, suddenly unable to push the door all the way open. She realized that her hand was shaking. She took her hand from the knob and looked at McClure apologetically. "In there," she said. "Just inside the entryway."

The policeman nodded understandingly and opened the door.

She did not look at the mutilated dog, but she saw a reflection of the scene in the visible reaction of McClure's face. His eyes took in the entryway, scanning from left to right, and the color drained from his face. His mouth settled into a grim line. Still staring at the dog, he pulled the door shut. "I think I'd better call Lieutenant Grant," he said.

Two cars arrived simultaneously—a patrol car and a white Bronco. The patrol car arrived with lights and siren off, but the presence of two police cars and another unfamiliar vehicle in front of Jimmy's house was more than enough to attract the attention of the neighborhood. Within seconds, neighbors from up and down the block moved onto their porches or lawns, craning their necks to see what was happening. A few of the closer neighbors—Mrs. Maltin and Mr. Green among them—walked up the sidewalk to see what was happening for themselves. They looked quizzically at Cathy, hoping she'd provide them with answers, but she shook her head, signaling that she couldn't talk, and followed McClure as he walked purposefully toward the Bronco.

The man who met them was wearing street clothes, but even in a uniform he would not have looked like a cop. He was tall and trim, almost slight, and his straight brown hair hung just below his collar. His eyes, big and brown, looked both compassionate and intelligent—the eyes of an artist, not a cop. The grim expression on his face contrasted sharply with his features and seemed jarringly out of place, as if it belonged to someone else and had mistakenly settled on the wrong person. He nodded curtly at McClure.

"Lieutenant," McClure said.

"Let's see it." The lieutenant's voice was cold and without humor, and it seemed to issue unnaturally from his lips, as though he was not used to using such a tone of voice.

"This is Cathy Riley and Jimmy Goldstein," McClure said, gesturing toward them. "They found the, uh, animal." His voice lowered politely so they wouldn't be able to hear, but Cathy heard every word, and she was sure Jimmy did, too. "It—she—was Jimmy's pet."

The lieutenant looked at Jimmy, and for a moment all the disparate elements of his face came together in an expression of honest empathy. His voice lost its cold edge and took on a more welcome human quality. "What was her name, Jimmy?"

"Dusty," he said, and the first tears spilled from his eyes. He wiped them angrily off his cheek with the back of his hand. "Her name is . . ." He looked up at Cathy, and she saw the hurt etched on his features. ". . . *was* Dusty." She put an arm around his shoulder, holding onto him tightly.

"Let's see the dog," the lieutenant said.

The next hour was a blur. Cathy stood outside with Jimmy as the policemen examined the inside of the house, dusting for fingerprints, hand vacuuming the floor, looking for clues. McClure stayed with them for the most part, keeping them out of the way of the investigation and protecting them from the insensitive questions of the ever-growing crowd. Most of the neighbors, the people Cathy knew, went inside after the first rush of curiosity, but other people from other blocks took their place, pressing eagerly against the yellow border ribbon, trying to get a glimpse of what was going on. Vans from two of the four local news stations were parked on the street, and reporters whom Cathy had only seen on TV were now clamoring for an interview.

Eventually, the police took Dusty's body out of the house and loaded it into what appeared to be some type of specially equipped ambulance.

McClure had finished writing down what Cathy had told him and was taking down Jimmy's statement when Jimmy's father arrived. He honked his horn several times and tried to pull into the driveway but was stopped by a uniformed police officer. Jumping out of the car, he ran under the barricade before anyone could stop him. His face was red and florid, and he had obviously been drinking. "What happened?" he demanded. "Where's Jimmy? Where's my boy? Did something happen to him?"

"Dad!" Jimmy cried. He ran across the lawn to his father, throwing his arms around him and burying his face in his stomach.

"That's Mr. Goldstein," Cathy explained to Mc-Clure, although she was sure he had figured that out for himself.

McClure signaled to the three policemen outside the barricade that the man was to be let through and left alone.

His eyes glazed, confused, Al Goldstein made his way across the lawn with Jimmy to where Cathy and McClure stood like an island of calm amidst the frenetic activity around them. A moment later, the lieutenant walked across the lawn toward them. He nodded, introduced himself to Jimmy's father, gave him a brief rundown of what had occurred, asked a few perfunctory questions, then went back into the house to supervise the investigation.

"Why's there so many people here?" Mr. Goldstein asked.

McClure stared at him as if he had asked a profoundly stupid question. "You've heard about the murders the past few weeks?"

Jimmy's father nodded.

"The murderer just killed your dog."

Al Goldstein was silent. It seemed to take his alcohol-fogged brain a moment to voice the question in his head, but when he spoke his voice was neither outraged nor surprised. "Why would he kill a dog?"

McClure smiled grimly. "If we knew answers to questions like that, we probably would have caught him by now."

Forty-five minutes later the ambulance and most of the policemen had left. Lieutenant Grant, looking tired and discouraged, approached Cathy. "I'd like to call it a day here," he said. "But I was wondering if you and Jimmy could come by the station tomorrow for some further questioning. Nothing serious. It's just that after a good night's sleep, people sometimes recall things they don't remember seeing at first." He looked from Cathy to Jimmy to Jimmy's father. "It'll just take a few minutes. I'd really appreciate it."

"Sure," Cathy said. "I don't work until the afternoon tomorrow. I can drive Jimmy over in the morning. If it's okay with you, Mr. Goldstein."

Al Goldstein nodded, squeezing his son's hand.

Cathy looked at the lieutenant, swallowing hard. "Do you really think this was the same person who . . . ?" She trailed off.

He nodded.

"Should we do anything . . . I mean, should we be taking some extra precautions or something?"

"Lock your doors and windows. Stay inside. Report anything strange. I'll have two men patrolling the area tonight and one stationed permanently on the street, so they'll be keeping an eye on the neighborhood. I doubt if anything will happen, but we'll be prepared if it does." He smiled kindly at her and Cathy found that more reassuring than any of his words.

McClure and the lieutenant left at the same time, and Cathy gave Jimmy's shoulder a final squeeze before walking home. She pressed through the remaining crowd, avoiding the gaze of the spectators, not answering any questions. Walking up her driveway, she saw for a second her father's face, peering out of the den window, before the curtains fell shut.

When she went inside, he was sitting in his chair pretending to be asleep.

Nineteen

Although it was Saturday and Al Goldstein did not have to work, he refused to accompany Cathy and Jimmy to the police station.

"If the lieutenant had wanted to talk to me," Al said, "he would have asked me to come by. He only asked for you and Jimmy."

Cathy stood uncomfortably in the middle of the Goldsteins' living room, not sure of how to respond. Unshaven, still wearing his dirty bathrobe, Jimmy's father looked like nothing so much as a derelict, although from what she could tell, he was suffering no ill effects from last night's drinking. His mind was alert, and no trace of a hangover showed on his face.

"Don't you think you should come along anyway?" Cathy asked.

"There's nothing I can tell him. I wasn't even here when it happened." He shook his head. "You're a big girl now. You don't need me to tag along. You two go on. I'll be here when you get back."

"Come on, Jimmy." She tried to keep the anger out of her voice, but the words came out sounding stern and cold. She turned around, walking out of the living room. Jimmy said nothing, following her outside and onto the sidewalk.

Her car was parked in the driveway of her house, and they walked down the street in silence.

Jimmy cleared his throat as they reached her driveway. "My dad said we can bury Dusty in the backyard," he said. "She liked to play there."

Cathy said nothing, did not trust herself to look at Jimmy. She seriously doubted whether the authorities would let the dog be buried in Jimmy's backyard. For one thing, it was illegal to bury an animal in a residential area, and after what had been done to Dusty, she wasn't sure the authorities would release the dog's body at all. She wouldn't be surprised if the city or the police or whoever had jurisdiction over these matters had already cremated the animal.

No, on second thought, they probably had not yet performed the autopsy.

She was sure Jimmy's father knew this already, and she wondered why he was leading his son on, allowing him these false hopes. Didn't he know that it would only hurt Jimmy more in the end? Didn't the man have any sense of decency or responsibility?

Obviously not, she thought. But that was to be expected. That was par for the course. Hell, he hadn't even seemed particularly upset by what had happened to his pet.

Or surprised.

Cathy felt the icy tingly fingers of fear caress the back of her neck. Was it possible that Mr. Goldstein had already known what had happened to Dusty when he had arrived home yesterday? Was it possible that he was involved with or responsible for the dog's death?

She pushed the thought out of her mind. Mr. Goldstein may not have liked Dusty, and he might be a slug, but he was not a killer.

"I've already picked a spot by the tree," Jimmy said. "I'm going to make a cross out of some wood we have in the back."

"She was a good dog," Cathy told him.

Jimmy nodded, swallowed. "Yeah," he said thickly.

They got into the car. Before starting the engine Cathy took from her purse the scrap of paper upon which she'd written the address of the police station.

She buckled her seatbelt, making sure that Jimmy did the same, before backing out onto the street.

They drove in silence.

It was an extraordinarily clear day, even for Phoenix. Snow-white clouds, like huge billowy tufts of cotton, drifted lazily across the clear desert sky, lending the blank blue an aura of depth. To the northeast, the graceful form of Camelback Mountain served as a scenic backdrop to the buildings of the city. Far off in the distance, blurred by shimmering heat waves even this early in the morning, the irregular, almost alien, shapes of the Superstition Mountains stood sentinel over the trailer-park town of Apache Junction.

It was a gorgeous day, the kind she usually reveled in, but today it seemed inappropriate, almost mocking. In her mind the gruesome picture of Dusty turned inside out just wouldn't go away.

An old woman, driving a gray Cadillac with Minnesota plates, pulled in front of her without signaling, and Cathy slammed on the brakes. One of the last snowbirds of the season, the old woman signaled left and turned right.

Cathy smiled at Jimmy and was encouraged to see a wan smile on his face.

"Old people," Cathy said.

Jimmy nodded. "None of 'em can drive."

Cathy turned right on Central, then glanced down at the address in her lap. She knew she'd passed by the police station before, but she'd never been there and couldn't remember exactly where it was located. They drove by a series of high-rise office buildings, byproducts of the redevelopment craze that had swept Phoenix in the late seventies, and Cathy slowed down. "Fifty-two eighty," she said. "Keep an eye out. I think it's on your side."

They passed a large park. "There it is!" Jimmy said.

The station was a tan two-story building with a small parking lot on one side and a law office on the other. Cathy recognized it now. Built in the low, squarish style favored by nearly all Southwestern architects until fairly recently, it looked oddly out of place against the backdrop of new mirrored glass structures along the street.

She pulled into the parking lot. There were plenty of marked spaces, but none of them seemed to be for visitor parking. They were either for official use only or for automobile inspections. She drove back onto the street and around the block before finally finding a parking spot across the street at the park.

They got out of the car. A group of brightly dressed kids skateboarded down the sidewalk, each trying to outdo the other in tricky maneuvers and flashy footwork. A cowboy-hatted old-timer walked slowly by, a gigantic wad of chaw in his cheek. Here and there, on benches, under bushes, homeless people slept in their coats.

There was a lull in traffic and they hurried across the street and into the station, where Cathy strode directly up to the uniformed officer at the desk. "We're here to see Lieutenant Grant," she said. She had meant for her voice to come out sounding confident and self-assured, but instead it sounded more like a timid squeak.

She did not like dealing with authority.

Miss Riley?

"Can I have your names, please?" the man asked.

"Cathy Riley and Jimmy Goldstein."

"And what's this about?"

"He asked us to come. We have an appointment."

The officer motioned toward a series of low padded benches against the wall. "Have a seat, then. I'll give him a ring. He'll be out as soon as he can."

They sat. The police station was quiet, not at all like she expected. The lobby was empty save for themselves and the desk sergeant, and there was none of the chaotic hubbub, the noisy crowds of crooks and crazies that television had led her to believe infested the interiors of all police stations. She looked around the room. On the wall above the sergeant's desk were photographs of uniformed officers, past police chiefs. On the opposite wall was a large pastel mural of Camelback Mountain, a small scattering of Utopian homes at its feet.

Jimmy tapped her shoulder, and she looked down at him.

"What do you think he wants to ask us?"

She shrugged. "I'm not sure. It's nothing to worry about, though."

He wiped his hands on his Levi's. "Actually, I'm a little nervous."

"So am I." She smiled. "But don't worry. I'll be right there with you."

"Maybe it's Samson and Halback," he said.

"What?"

"Those two guys that are after me. Maybe they're the ones who killed Dusty."

She shook her head. "I don't think so."

The desk sergeant walked over. "Lieutenant Grant's in his office. He asked me to take you there." He glanced around the empty lobby. "I think I can spare a moment," he said drily. "The crowd seems to be under control."

Cathy smiled.

The sergeant led the way through two sets of double doors and down a series of clean corridors. They stopped in front of a plain white door with the words "Lieutenant Allan Grant" embossed on a wooden plaque in its center. The sergeant knocked twice and pushed open the door. "Here they are."

"Thanks." The sergeant stepped back, and Allan motioned for them to come in and sit down.

Cathy looked around the room. The lieutenant's office was crowded and cluttered, but in a way that did not seem messy. On the top of his desk, a tape recorder, several law-enforcement manuals, stacks of official-looking documents, a newspaper, a copy of the magazine *Southwest Art,* and a stained coffee cup all vied for space. There was a full bookcase on the wall to the right of the door, and on the left wall were framed prints by Pena, R. C. Gorman, Dan Namingha, and other native American artists. Behind the lieutenant was a large window overlooking the street and the park.

"Sit down," Allan said, pointing toward two director's chairs in front of his desk. "We're going to have to make this quick."

Cathy looked at Jimmy, then took the chair closest to the wall. Jimmy settled into the other chair.

Allan picked up a folder from the pile of papers on his desk, opened it, and glanced at the contents. "This is the report from Dusty's autopsy," he said. "I just got it about an hour ago." He thought for a moment, then threw the folder back onto his desk, frowning. "I thought your father was going to come, too," he said to Jimmy.

Jimmy shook his head, looked toward Cathy for help.

"He couldn't make it," she explained, but even as she said the words, she found herself wondering *why* he hadn't wanted to come, why he had insisted on remaining at home.

Allan was silent, running a hand through his hair. He looked thoughtful.

Suspicious?

"Okay." He leaned forward. "First of all, do either of you know anyone who might have done this?"

Cathy shook her head, but she could feel her face reddening, could feel the flush of heat in her cheeks, could feel the beginning of perspiration on her forehead underneath her hair. She felt guilty, though she knew she shouldn't, felt as though she had done something wrong, though she knew she hadn't. "I can't think of anybody," she said aloud.

"I didn't think so. I just thought I'd ask—"

"I do!" Jimmy blurted out.

Allan's eyebrows shot up in surprise. "Who?"

"Tim Halback and Dan Samson."

The lieutenant frowned. "Who are Tim Halback and Dan Samson?"

"They go to my school. They're fifth-graders. They've been after me for almost a month now, but I always get away from them. They might have found out where I live and—"

Allan shook his head, smiling kindly. "This wasn't done by fifth-graders, Jimmy."

"Samson might have got his brother to do it. His brother—" He looked at Cathy, his face reddening. "His brother and his gang killed a baby."

"Killed a baby?" Allan's tone was serious, his eyes bored into Jimmy's. "When was this? And where?"

"I don't know when. It was a while ago. He's supposed to be in jail for it right now. But it was at the Safeway by my house." He looked at Cathy, then quickly looked away, leaning closer to Allan. "It was in the bathroom. They cut off the baby's . . ." He colored in embarrassment. ". . . you know."

Allan scowled. "I'll look into this. Nothing like that's happened in this district since I've been on the force, and I've been here for eight years, but I can't afford to ignore anything. I'll see what I can find, and I'll question this . . . Samson?"

"Tim Halback and Dan Samson. I don't know Samson's brother's name."

As Allan wrote down the names, a cloud of worry passed over Jimmy's face. Allan saw the boy's expression. "Don't worry," he said. "I'll keep your name out of this. They won't know it was you." He smiled at Jimmy, but his smile turned into a frown as he noticed the bruises on the boy's face. He reached over and gently turned Jimmy's cheek toward the light. "Did they do this to you?"

Jimmy shook his head.

"He got into a fight with another boy on the block," Cathy said.

"He's retarded, and he beat me up for no reason."

Allan threw his pen down on the desk. "It's not your week, is it?"

"I guess not."

Allan glanced at his watch. "I'm sorry," he said. "I don't mean to give you the bum's rush, but it's getting late and I have a conference coming up in a few minutes. Dusty's murder is part of the larger investigation now. I apologize for making you come all the way down here for this. I should have scheduled it for a different time, but this is sort of a last-minute meeting, and I didn't have time to get hold of you. I do have a few more questions to ask, more a formality than anything else, but I'll call and schedule an appointment. This time, I'll come by when it's convenient for you." He held up the piece of paper on which he'd written the names. "I'll look into these two also, but I'll be honest with you—I really don't think these boys killed Dusty. The dog was killed in a very sophisticated manner, by someone who knew a tremendous amount about canine biology."

Cathy clasped her hands nervously in her lap. "Do you have any clues at all?"

"I'd be lying if I said we did." He smiled, but his smile seemed a little forced. "That was probably the wrong thing to say. I'm sorry. I don't mean to frighten you. We're working on it, and we'll get the murderer eventually. He's going to slip up and make a mistake, and we'll be there when he does. But right now we're still on the ground floor of the investigation. We're concentrating a lot of manpower in your area, though, and I can tell you that if he tries anything anywhere near there, we'll nab him." He glanced again at his watch. "I'm sorry. I really do have to go. But before I do, I have to ask if there's anything you can recall that you didn't tell us yesterday. Anything at all."

Cathy had been wracking her brain all morning, trying to come up with some small detail she may have glossed over in her verbal report to the police or some item she may have noticed but simply blocked out of her mind. But there was nothing. She had seen no signs of forced entry, no fleeing suspects, nothing.

Only Dusty.

The jackrabbit.

She shook her head. "No."

Jimmy shook his head.

"I thought not. I just wanted to make sure. Thanks a lot for coming. And I'll look into Halback and Samson." Allan stood up. "I'll escort you out."

They walked down the hall, and Allan opened the door into the lobby. "We have your home and work phone numbers?"

Cathy nodded.

"All right. Thanks again. I'll let you know if we find something, and I'll check back with you in a few days to ask a few more questions." He patted Jimmy's shoulder. "Stay out of fights. And have your father give me a call. I'd like to talk to him too, okay?"

"Okay."

"I'll be in touch." Allan waved good-bye, closing the door behind him.

The two of them stood there for a moment. Cathy looked down at Jimmy. "You want to stop somewhere and get a donut or something?" she asked. "Or do you want to go home?"

"What about Dusty?" he asked. "When are we going to get her back?"

"I don't know. Your father will have to talk to them about that." She put an arm around him. "What do you want to do now?"

He shrugged. "I don't care."

"You want to get a donut? Or stop at McDonald's?"

"Sure," he said, but there was no enthusiasm in his voice.

"Okay. Let's get something to eat." She led the way back to the car.

Twenty

Like too many ex-hosts of children's television shows, Toymaker Tommy had ended up doing the rope dance, swinging from the rafters of his garage wearing a hemp necktie. The reasons for his suicide were no longer clear—if they ever had been—but Rina Ralston had refused to let her husband's memory die. With the diligence and single-mindedness of the truly devoted, she'd opened the Toymaker Tommy Toy Shop and, armed only with a small amount of capital and an obsessive, almost fanatic desire to succeed, had turned it into Scottsdale's trendiest toy store.

Ironically, her years of immersion in the business world had caused her to view cynically both her husband's legacy and his demise, although it was her handmade dolls, the oversized cloth depictions of characters her husband had played on his television show, that had sent the yuppies flocking to her store.

Rina drove down Camelback Road toward the setting sun, now a huge orange half dome at the edge of the desert horizon. As she did each day, she glanced admiringly out the windshield at some of the large homes on Camelback Mountain. In the near future, she hoped to be living in one of those homes herself.

Her eye was caught by a brown brick structure that looked like a medieval castle. The dream was not as unrealistic as she once would have thought. She had been hoarding profits over the past ten years, putting the money into T-bills, CDs, and other safe investments, while remaining in the small north Phoenix home she had shared with Toymaker Tommy. If sales continued the way they had been—and she had no reason to assume they would not—she figured she would have accumulated enough money within the next year to put a sizable down payment on her dream house.

Rina pulled to a stop at the intersection of Camelback and Central as the light turned red. The music on the radio seemed too loud, and she turned down the volume. She found herself glancing out both the driver and passenger windows. Although this was definitely not one of the better sections of town, she had never before felt nervous about stopping here. She had even eaten several times at a small hole-in-the-wall Mexican restaurant nearby. But with all the talk on the news about the murders the last few weeks, she had become increasingly cautious and increasingly paranoid. A bearded man walked across the crosswalk in front of her, and she quickly checked to make sure all of her car doors were locked.

As soon as the stoplight turned green, she took off.

There was only a hazy glow in the western sky when she pulled into her driveway ten minutes later. Rina turned off the ignition, grabbed her sack of incomplete dolls from the backseat, and got out of the car. It was dark on the patio, and she swore softly to herself. She'd just replaced the porch light a month ago, and the damn thing had burned out again. Couldn't they make anything right these days?

She pulled the key ring from her purse, sifting through the keys by touch until she found the one for the house. She opened the front door, flipping the light on in the living room as she walked inside and immediately closing the door behind her, locking it.

Sighing in disgust, she threw the sack of dolls on the couch and, still standing, pulled her shoes off, dropping them on the rug next to the coffee table. It had been a long day—too long—and before she did anything else she wanted to take a hot bath, soak for awhile, and rest.

She made her way through the house, turning the lights on as she walked. Living room. Bedroom. Hallway.

The light in the bathroom would not go on.

She flipped the switch on and off. Nothing. "Damn," she muttered. She stepped into the darkened room and stood on her tiptoes, reaching for the light fixture.

There was a low chuckle from the sewing room down the hall.

She quickly dropped to her flat feet, listening. The house was silent.

No, not quite silent.

She thought she heard a shuffle of footsteps in the sewing room.

Don't panic, Rina told herself. *Remain calm.*

The lights went off in the rest of the house.

Now she definitely heard it—a whispery shuffling, soft shoes moving quietly across a· floor. She tried to remain silent, but though she didn't scream, the intruder had to know she was there—in the still air, her ragged panicked breathing sounded like the amplified rasp of Darth Vader.

The noise came closer.

Her heart was pounding wildly. Should she try to sneak out or make a run for it?

She thought quickly. If she crept slowly out from the bathroom and he knew where she was, he could grab her immediately. On the other hand, if he wasn't sure of her whereabouts and she dashed out, she'd alert him to her presence and he'd come after her.

It was a split-second decision that she had to make, and she made it. Ten years in the business world had at least taught her to be decisive. She edged slowly out of the bathroom, as quietly as possible, moving down the hall away from the sewing room. Her breathing was still loud, but perhaps not as loud as she'd feared. She crept along the wall of the hallway, hoping there was nothing on the floor she could trip over.

Now she was rounding the corner into the living room. A not-quite-integrated amalgam of bluish streetlamp and refracted yellow porch light from the house next door shone through the window, partially illuminating the darkened room.

And then it came out of the corner, crawling on the floor, slinking like a giant cat. Only she could see a human head and hands and feet. There was a glint of knife steel in the refracted light.

Rina screamed and ran back the way she had come. It was not a coherent scream, not the "Help-call-the-police!" that she'd wanted, but it was loud, shrill, and uninhibited in the way that only a scream of terror could be, and it put across her message more forcefully than any words.

She ran unthinkingly down the hall into a room, shutting and locking the door behind her. It was several seconds before she realized that she'd run into the sewing room.

Where the first noises had come from.

Maybe there was more than one of them.

What if she were trapped in here with him?

Oh, my God, she thought, yanking at the doorknob. In one quick, amazingly coordinated motion, she had unlocked and pulled open the door and was back in the hall.

A hand grabbed her leg, and before she could kick free and get away, her skirt was ripped off. She fell forward onto the floor, hitting her chin hard against the wood. A strong dirty hand was clamped over her mouth.

The noise she heard before the knife silenced her permanently did not sound even remotely human.

Twenty-one

She was in the Lauter house. Katrina West's unpacked boxes were scattered about the floor. The walls were covered with huge splotches of dripping red blood. Before her stood David, and, next to David, skin turned inside out, teeth bared, posed in a pointer position, Dusty. A low growling noise was coming from the dead dog's throat. David took a step forward, and she saw that his zipper was down and his . . . thing . . . was hanging out. It was white and long and greasy, and he began fondling it as he moved toward her. It began to grow, becoming harder, thicker. "You want it," David said. "You know you want it."

Cathy awoke ready to scream, but she choked the scream off in her throat as the dark outlines of reality faded into existence around her. All of the covers had been kicked off her bed, and beneath her face, the pillow was damp with the sweat of fear. She sat up, heart still thudding loudly in her chest, and glanced at the clock on the nightstand next to the bed. Twelve o'clock.

She had only been asleep for two hours.

Six more hours to go.

Cathy sat up and slid her legs over the side of the

mattress, breathing deeply, trying to slow the racing of her blood. She reached down and pulled the blanket off the floor, wadding it up in her lap and clutching it tightly. It had been a long time since she'd had anything other than an occasional nightmare in which David played a role, but lately she'd been dreaming about him a lot.

Almost worse than the dream itself was the fact that she knew she would not be able to fall asleep again afterward. She would simply lie awake in bed, tossing and turning throughout the rest of the endless night, catching only little snatches of sleep here and there as the long hours dragged slowly toward dawn.

She stared at the negative silhouette of her bookshelf, light against the darkness, and listened to the silence. All of the televisions were turned off, and the only sound in the house was the faint electric hum of the refrigerator in the kitchen. There was no noise from her father's room. He was asleep. If he had been awake, she would have heard the relentless restless tapping of his crutches as he paced up and down the floor in front of his bed.

In the old days, she used to comfort him in his insomnia, and he used to keep her company after her dreams. They had been close then. Even after the accident they had been close. But something had happened to him, or at least to part of him—the important part of him. It had not been a sudden change or a transformation triggered by a single epiphanic incident. It had been instead a gradual descent, an erosion of his humanity.

She often thought that was the reason that Billy had moved so far away.

Now her father no longer even pretended to take an interest in her. When she had told him about Jimmy and Dusty last night, about the police, he had said only, "So that's why I got no dinner?"

She had been so angry with him for that remark that she had almost taken off right then, wanting at that moment nothing more than to drive around for several hours until he was either hungry enough to make himself something to eat or angry enough to have some type of fit. She wanted to punish him for his thoughtlessness and cruelty the way he punished her for her minor transgressions.

But, dutiful daughter that she was, she had instead gone into the kitchen to make him a hamburger.

Today they had ignored each other entirely, making a conscious effort to stay out of each other's way.

He had eaten dinner with his friends at the club.

Cathy ran a hand through her sleep-tousled hair and reached over to turn on the small lamp on the nightstand next to her bed. The circle of illumination thrown by the light made the corners of the room seem even darker, and she was reminded of Dusty.

The jackrabbit.

Now why had she thought of that again? She closed her eyes, trying to will the image out of her mind, but it would not go away.

The jackrabbit.

She had never told anyone about the jackrabbit. Not her parents, not her friends, not even Billy. After awhile, it had almost seemed as though it hadn't really happened, as though she had just dreamed it.

But she hadn't dreamed it. It had happened.

She'd been coming home from school, walking by herself after saying good-bye to Pam, and had come across David in the vacant lot at the end of the street. From the sidewalk, she'd seen him in the center of the lot, the top of his head visible above the wheatlike stalks of dried weeds, and she'd intended to pass on by and continue walking home, but he'd seen her as well and had called her over.

"Ca-athy!" His singsong voice.

She'd kept walking, quickening her steps.

"Cathy!" His serious voice.

She'd stopped walking.

"Cathy!"

Against her will, not wanting to obey him but not strong enough to disobey, she had threaded her way through the wall of weeds to where David stood in the middle of the lot.

Naked and carving up a jackrabbit with an X-Acto knife.

She'd remained unmoving at the edge of the small clearing, too frightened and confused to know what to do. The rabbit was on a low tree stump, dead and partially skinned, fur still clinging to its body in awkward red and brown clumps. David stood before it, X-Acto knife in hand. His pants, shirt, and underwear were folded neatly next to his shoes and socks off to the side of the clearing, and his nude body was spattered with so much blood it looked almost as though he had been skinned himself.

He had an erection.

She'd wanted to run, but David reached out and grabbed her arm, forcing her to stay. She could feel the slippery sticky warmth of the blood on his fingers. He was grinning, aware of her horrified repulsion and delighting in it. "If you tell Mom or Dad, I'll kill you." There was steel behind his smile.

Her nostrils had been filled with the putrid smell of animal blood and excrement, and she'd felt dizzy, almost as though she were about to pass out, but somehow, miraculously, she hadn't.

David laughed. He let go of her arm and, with bloody fingers, touched his penis, began rubbing it.

Cathy took off.

She'd run all the way down the street, not stopping until she'd reached home. David arrived home a half hour later, acting as though nothing was wrong, his skin and clothes spotless, explaining to his mother that he was late because he'd stopped off at the library on the way home.

He'd run away two years after that, a year after the accident.

Sitting on her bed, Cathy found herself wondering where David was now, what he was doing. Although she didn't believe in premonitions or psychic phenomena, she'd dreamed of him a lot lately, and she could not help feeling, in some dark irrational part of her mind, that maybe he had come back.

There was a light knock at the window.

Cathy jumped, startled, her heart leaping into her throat. Without thinking, she grabbed the edge of the curtains, pulling them open.

Randy West was standing outside, staring in at her, his face ghostlike in the reflected light from her room, darkness surrounding him. He was grinning hugely, saliva dripping in a single thread down his chin, and he continued to tap on the window with a square blunt finger.

She did not scream, though she came very close to it. She mustered what courage she could and pointed an authoritarian finger at him. "Go home!" she said firmly. "Randy, go home!"

He stared at her, grinning, continuing to tap against the glass.

"Get out of here!" She let the two halves of the curtain fall shut, and through the thin crack between them saw his bulky shadowed shape as he continued to stand in place, as he continued to tap against the window. She plugged her ears against the noise, told him again to leave. She waited, plugging her ears, staring at the curtains. Several minutes later, she saw him finally move away from the window and through the backyard.

Jesus.

She sat on the edge of the bed, trembling, feeling much more frightened, much more disturbed, than she had any right to be. Something about that child scared her. There was a strangeness about him, a wrongness, an abnormality at once subtler and much deeper than his obvious handicap.

Why was he out at this time of night? she wondered. And how had he gotten into her backyard?

Tomorrow she would have to go over to his house and talk to his mother. It was about time that someone did so. This morning, she had told Jimmy's father what

Randy had done to his son and had suggested that he talk to Mrs. West about it. He'd said that he would, but Cathy felt sure that he had only told her that to humor her, to get her to shut up and leave him alone. She knew that if she wanted anything done, if she wanted results, she would have to go over there and talk to Katrina herself. With the tight rein the woman kept on the boy and her almost fanatic insistence that he stay in the house, Cathy felt sure that she did not know he was wandering around in the middle of the night, sneaking into people's backyards and knocking on their windows. Once she did find out, she would no doubt put a quick stop to it.

The hour was getting late, or getting early, and Cathy went into the kitchen for a drink of water. When she came back, she locked her door, straightened out her blanket, and got into bed. She took a quick peek out the window and was relieved to see that the retarded boy was nowhere in sight. She closed her eyes, but as hard as she tried to pretend she was sleepy, she wasn't, and soon her eyes were again wide open, her mind wide awake.

Lying on her back, she stared up at the ceiling, able to make out whorled patterns in the white stucco above her. She found herself thinking, for some reason, of Lieutenant Grant. She was impressed with the respect he had shown Jimmy, with the way he had treated the boy. Most adults, particularly adults in positions of authority, seemed to talk down to kids, patronizing them, but he had shown an innate recognition of Jimmy's intelligence and dignity, and Cathy liked that.

He was also a very attractive man.

Attractive?

It had been a long time since she'd thought of anyone in that way, and even lying alone in the dark she felt embarrassed. This was stupid, she thought. She was too old for such schoolgirl childishness. But part of her enjoyed the feeling, enjoyed the light simple fantasy, and she found herself wondering if perhaps they had met in other circumstances, say in a class at college, whether they would have hit it off.

Cathy smiled at herself. She had never really been one for fantasizing about men, either men she knew or celebrities. Many women, she knew, daydreamed about sports figures or movie stars, or tried to imagine themselves in relationships with men they met and to whom they were attracted, but she had always considered that a useless waste of time. It had always seemed so silly and frivolous. Sure, if she saw a movie or read a book she would sometimes fleetingly wonder what her life would be like if she met this or that individual, but romantic daydreams had never seemed to her a valid form of mental entertainment. There were also not that many men she had met who really interested her. Even in college, surrounded by eligible males, she had not found anyone with whom she would have liked to have a relationship. Of course, a lot of that was her own doing. Emotionally, she'd always felt distanced from the men around her, uninterested in any sort of romantic involvement, although intellectually she realized that there were probably dozens of men she would or could like, if given a chance. She knew herself well, though—too well. She'd taken enough psych classes, read enough literature on the subject to be familiar with her behavior patterns. She knew the type of person she was, and she knew that she did not really have the confidence to put herself on the line, to get involved in a relationship.

Not that it had ever come up.

That was part of it. Although she had gone out several times, she had never actually had the opportunity to form a relationship with someone. She sometimes wondered why, but she wondered in a disinterested, almost thirdhand manner. It was not a question that plagued her, not something she cared about passionately. If she was not content with her life, she was not discontented, and she couldn't really ask for more than that.

So why was she thinking about this policeman?

She rolled over, closing her eyes, trying to blank out her mind. She had to stop herself from thinking about these things or she'd never fall asleep. She'd lie awake all night, the way she always did after having a nightmarc.

She concentrated on her breathing, forcing it into an even sleep rhythm, hoping it would fool her body into thinking that it was dozing. She thought of nothing, thought of blackness.

The last image in her mind before she fell asleep was the distorted face of Randy West, peering at her through the window, grinning.

Twenty-two

The randomness. That was one of the things that bothered him most about these murders. The chaos. Crimes of passion, bar shootings, murders for money, even gang killings—all of these had reasons for their occurrences. They were understandable and therefore solvable. But random murders, with a seemingly random selection of murder methods, were virtually impossible to pin down. With killings as perfectly executed as these, it would be by pure luck or chance that any of them were solved. Until they found either a witness to one of the crimes or mistakes made by the murderer, the investigation was for all intents and purposes dead in the water.

Allan looked down at the Miro book spread on the table before him. That's what he liked about art. Even in the most seemingly chaotic paintings, in the most arbitrary artworks, there was a purpose, an order, a method. There were reasons behind the randomness, a logic to the disorder. It was an organized chaos.

If only life imitated art.

The coroner had found other pinholes in Whitehead's body, holes that correspond exactly to lethal points in acupuncture diagrams and that overlapped the positions of almost all of the important nerves. The policeman's death had not been a quick one. Such precise positioning of pins and needles had taken a lot of time. And a lot of knowledge. Even working from diagrams, it had taken the coroner two days to document each of the 1,132 tiny holes in Whitehead's skin.

Allan closed the book, leaning back on the soft sofa and closing his eyes. There might be a method to this madness as well, but it was still madness, and he did not understand it.

They were assuming that Whitehead's murder was some sort of warning. Why else kill a cop? And why else painstakingly use hundreds of pins and needles to form such simplistic and meaningless patterns as tic-tac-toe games? The trivialization of Whitehead's death, the almost offhanded way the silly symbols were pinned onto his body could only be meant as an expression of contempt. It was, in the language of murder, a slap in the face, the taunting of a superior. *I can do this to him,* it said, *and I can just as easily do it to you.*

The murder of the Goldstein boy's dog could only be meant in the same way—a taunt, a demonstration that the murderer could do whatever he damn well pleased and there wasn't a single thing the police could do about it. To perform such an elaborate killing on an animal was an attempt at supreme humiliation.

Allan had attended three meetings this morning: one with Pynchon; one with his men; and one with representatives from the Glendale, Mesa, Tempe, and Scottsdale police departments. A lot had been hashed over, and rehashed ad nauseum, but the bottom line was that they were no closer now to closing in on a suspect than they had been a week ago. Because of the idiosyncratic grisliness of the crimes, they were working on the assumption that the murders were the work of an individual. That was frightening enough, but Allan suspected more and more that the murders were the work of a gang or cult of some sort. It was virtually impossible for a single person to execute so perfectly four wildly different murders without leaving some trace. The way he figured it, there had to be, at minimum, two people involved—one to perform the actual murder and one to mastermind the logistics, keep lookout, and tie up loose ends.

And that was truly terrifying.

Even more frightening than that was the possibility that Pynchon's half-baked theory might have some validity, that the killer might be a cop.

Or cops.

Allan opened his eyes and looked at the digital clock on the videotape recorder next to the TV. Five minutes to midnight. He should have been asleep hours ago. He had an early meeting in the morning, and he needed all the shut-eye he could get. He had been averaging only three hours of sleep a night. Tonight he had come home early, just after six, planning to hit the sack by eight and catch up on some much-needed rest, but his mind had kept him awake, going over every trivial detail, examining every possibility, reliving every mistake. He had gotten in bed just after eight and had lain there for what seemed like hours, tossing and turning. When he sat up to look at the clock, he had seen that it was only eight forty-five. That was when he had put on a robe and come out to the living room. If he wasn't going to sleep, at least he could make productive use of his time.

Now it was too late for sleep. Even if he did manage to doze off within the next hour, he still had to get up at five. That meant a maximum of four or five hours. He smiled. If he kept going at this rate, he'd get mono and end up lying in some hospital bed drinking juices and popping vitamins.

But who would he get mono from? He hadn't kissed anyone in . . . how long? Six months?

A policeman's lot is not a happy one, he thought wryly.

He was thankful for one thing, though: Aside from the dog, there had been no murders since Whitehead.

If the killer hadn't stopped, at least he had tapered off. And maybe something would turn up and they'd be able to nab him before he struck again.

He stood up and was walking into the kitchen to get a drink when he felt a chill pass through him. He looked at his bare arms and saw a field of goosebumps pop up. The hair on the back of his neck prickled.

He suddenly had the feeling that the weeklong dry spell had come to an end, that someone else had been murdered.

It was a powerful sensation, unlike anything he had ever experienced before, and if he hadn't been so tensed and stressed out lately he would have considered it a legitimate psychic experience. As it was, he remained rooted in place and stared at the phone, waiting for it to ring.

He must have stood there for five minutes, unmoving, knowing that the phone was going to ring, knowing that when he answered it he would hear the sound he wanted least of all to hear—Pynchon's gravelly voice telling him to get his butt in gear, there had been another one.

But the phone did not ring, and he drank some stale orange juice and returned to his bedroom, ready to give sleep another shot. There was nothing psychic about his intuition, he thought, nothing that some rest and relaxation wouldn't cure. But as hard as he tried to get rid of it, the feeling of dread did not go away; it stayed within his mind like an alcohol fog, coloring all of his thoughts, until, eventually, he fell asleep.

He was awakened at six by the phone.

The woman's body, clad only in yellow underwear, lay next to her open sewing machine. A thin line of black thread led from the needle of the machine to the woman's left hand, where her fingers had been sewn together. As Allan bent closer, he saw that her eyes had also been sewn shut, as had her mouth. A small knot tied in the thread protruded from her bottom lip. His gaze moved to the low shelf above the sewing machine, and here he saw a double-stacked row of mason jars filled with what was undoubtedly blood.

But where had the blood come from?

He looked more closely at the body, then turned away, swallowing the bile that rose in his throat. The woman's legs had been switched, as had her arms. Each of her limbs had been cleanly amputated and replaced with its complement. A quadruple stitching of black thread had been used to flawlessly sew the appendages back together. He turned toward Williams. "Her arms and legs have been switched."

Williams nodded. "It's like some fucking Nazi experiment."

"This had to have taken some time. He had to kill her, sever her arms and legs, drain the blood into those jars, sew the arms and legs back together, and then mop up the mess." He glanced down at his feet. "Look at the floor, not a spot of blood on it."

Williams nodded again.

"He was probably here for three to four hours tonight. I want this house dusted top to bottom. Unless he wore gloves, he's bound to have left at least one smudged print after spending that much time here. Look for fibers from material that might have come from clothing other than the old lady's, look for dirt from the bottom of his shoe. Look for anything that even seems like it might be out of place." He glanced again at the mason jars filled with blood. "I want this bastard."

"Yes, sir."

"Have men canvas the neighborhood as well. This is an older area; the residents have probably been here for a long time. Old people notice if someone new or unknown is hanging around. I want a description of anything even slightly unusual that has occurred within the past twenty-four hours."

"Got it."

Allan looked out the window of the sewing room at the backyard. Dawn was coming up over the horizon, shedding an orangish-white glow over the fruit trees and rosebushes. Uniformed officers were poking through the bushes with probers and going over the grass with metal detectors, looking for a weapon he knew they would not find. In the kitchen behind him, Lee was talking with Mary Hughes, the victim's sister and the one who had found the body.

"It's not in the same district," Williams said quietly. "You think this is a copycat or—"

"This is no copycat," Allan said grimly. "Not unless some of our local surgeons are moonlighting as psychotics. No copycat would be this detailed, would have this precision."

"Then he's moved."

Allan nodded dejectedly. "We've lost our only constant. I'd like to say we're up shit creek without a paddle, but we passed shit creek a week ago, and now we don't even have a boat." He walked through the house to the kitchen, where he stood for a moment by the front window, listening to Lee trying to calm the sister down and waiting for the coroner.

The phone rang in the living room, and Allan could tell from Dobrinin's tone of voice that it was Pynchon. He knew he should go in there and talk to the captain, but he really didn't feel like getting his ear bitten off right now. Outside, a tan county car pulled up to the curb and the coroner got out, lugging a briefcase filled with his equipment. Allan turned away from the window, ordered the two policemen who had just arrived in the kitchen to start dusting the door and window areas, and walked outside to meet the coroner. He led the older man around back to the rear entrance and the sewing room.

"Jesus," the coroner breathed as he walked through the door.

Allan pointed to the shelf above the sewing machine. "Eight jars filled with blood," he said. "We assume the rest of it has been mopped up. We're looking for a rag or towel, something that could give us a lead. If you can tell us, we'd like to know how the blood was removed from the body. Whether it was done before or after the amputations."

The photographer had already taken his photos, and Allan gave the coroner the go-ahead to examine the body. He watched as the coroner bent down and carefully probed, poked, and explored every inch of the old woman's flesh. Using small scissors he withdrew from his case, he cut off the woman's panties and pulled the thin material aside. He pointed a tiny flashlight between the woman's legs. "Her vagina has been sewn shut," he said. He moved the flashlight lower. "Her rectum is stitched together as well."

Allan grimaced. "Anything else you can tell us?"

The coroner looked up. "Not without a more comprehensive examination. It feels as though some of her organs have been rearranged—the area beneath her sternum is unnaturally distended—but I won't know for certain until I perform an autopsy. There are incisions made under her chin, to the sides of her vagina, and under her armpits, and I would guess right now that her blood was drained through these."

"How long would you estimate an operation like this would take?"

"The autopsy?"

"No. The murder."

The coroner shrugged. "Three to five hours, minimum, not allowing for cleanup."

"How long do you think she's been dead for?"

"The body's still a little warm, even without the full complement of blood. I would guess less than two hours."

"Williams!" Allan called.

The other officer looked up from where he was digging through a pile of laundry looking for blood-soaked towels or cleanup items.

"I want that net beefed up now. I want cars patrolling every street and alley within a five-mile radius, particularly the less-traveled routes." Allan spoke quickly. "If he's on foot, we might still be able to nab him."

"Gotcha." Williams hurried out the back door, already shouting to the men out front.

"You really think you might catch him?" the coroner asked.

Allan shook his head. "No. But I have to do something." His eyes were drawn again to the jars of blood on the shelf. "This bastard has got to be stopped." He looked down at the body, at the thin line of thread running from the sewing machine to the dead woman's hand. He felt useless, impotent, but he also felt angry, and after eight years as a cop he knew how to make that anger work for him. "Call your men," he told the coroner, and his voice was flat, emotionless. "Let's get that body down to the morgue."

Twenty-three

It was a terrible thing to admit, but the murders were the best thing to happen to Tom Houghton in the two years he'd worked for the *Arizona Republic*. He felt a little guilty that other people's deaths were advancing his own career, but his conscience did not keep him up at night. He was not responsible for any of the killings. Morrison, Welmers, Whitehead, and Ralston would have died with or without him. He simply wrote about them after the fact.

And, yes, he profited from it.

That was the news biz.

Houghton had come to Phoenix fresh out of college, with an impressive list of publications behind him. The editor of his university newspaper at UCLA, he had freelanced for *California* magazine and several local newspapers, and had had quite a few stories picked up by Associated Press. He had done his internship at the *Los Angeles Times* and had been lucky enough to have landed the police beat. Having received a lot of attention for a series of high-profile stories on a spectacular murder, Houghton had half hoped to land a position with the *Times* when he graduated, but the

paper had a policy of not hiring rookies—they wanted
reporters with more seasoning.

So he had gotten the job in Phoenix, where he expected to make a big splash and rake up some
credentials.

And where nothing had happened.

It was not really the fault of the *Republic*. His coworkers and editors were unfailingly cooperative, and
everyone treated him well. He'd asked for the police
beat and gotten it, but he might as well have asked
to cover Sun City or Leisure World. There were
crimes in Phoenix, but they were unfailingly routine,
invariably dull—fights in cowboy bars, random robber-
ies, traffic accidents, hunting mishaps. The big juicy
headline-grabbing stories? Nothing, nada, zip.
Houghton had had his share of front-page articles, but
in Arizona, where there were not just slow news days
but slow news months, that wasn't saying much. He
certainly had not had the type of story he wanted
or deserved.

Until now.

Houghton reread the article displayed before him
on the VDT—a piece on the simple precautions individuals could take to guard against becoming a murder
victim. There were no guarantees, but there were
some simple and obvious things people could do to
avoid being placed in a threatening situation. It was a
pretty good story, if he did say so himself. He scrolled
to the end of the article. He would never admit it to
another living soul, but the murderer was a real god-
send for him. He planned to hang on to this story and
make it pay off, milk it for all it was worth. Already
he had written profiles of each of the murder victims
and their families, had interviewed psychologists about
the probable mindset of the murderer, and had written
several articles based on the non-news updates dished
out daily by the police department.

While he might have been opportunistic, Houghton
was not a journalistic hack, interested solely in the

furthering of his own career, and he did worry about starting a panic. He wanted to make the people of the Valley cognizant of what was going on around them, but he did not want to frighten them unnecessarily.

In this case, though, perhaps it would be good to scare them. God knows, he was scared himself. Although he hadn't been allowed to view the bodies, he had received and recorded detailed descriptions from those who had. And he had seen the photos of Susan Welmers. The woman's body had been folded in half backwards, and the bones beneath her skin had somehow been manipulated so they were horrendously out of joint and in the wrong positions, pressing upward and outward at odd angles under her flesh. Her twisted spine looked like the work of a psychotic chiropractor with unlimited physical strength. Even the photos had made him gag and feel sick to his stomach, and he hadn't been able to look at them for any length of time.

Someone who could do that, Houghton thought, wasn't human. He was a monster, a fiend.

A fiend.

Houghton scrolled immediately back to his lead. He deleted a reference to "the murderer currently at large within the Valley," and replaced it with "the murderer referred to as the 'Phoenix Fiend.' " He glanced over what he'd written, saying it aloud.

"The Phoenix Fiend."

The name worked well within the sentence, and the alliteration was nice. It was catchy. He read the lead again, thinking. He knew it was risky coining his own phrase and quasi-attributing it to someone else in the way that he had, but it lent the name a certain authority and seemed less sensationalistic. *The Phoenix Fiend.* It was clever, and it just might catch on. If the right people read it—and he knew they would—he wouldn't be surprised to hear it used on the television news within a day or two, worked into the copy of rival newspapers.

It was tacky, he had to admit, but it was effective. And such informal handles for murderers were hardly unprecedented even in the legitimate press. They were not strictly the province of the *National Enquirer* and its ilk. Names like the "Zodiac Killer" were based on facts of the case, but other names such as the "Night Stalker," which was taken from a TV movie, had no such credentials. They were thought up by enterprising reporters.

Like himself.

Houghton wrote a quick note to the copy editor, suggesting that he use "The Phoenix Fiend" in a kicker, before saving his story and shutting off the VDT. He dropped the note on the copy editor's desk before leaving the newspaper office.

Outside, the night was warm, the heat of the day still lingering, though its source had long since descended below the horizon. Perhaps he was being tunnel visioned and was reading interpretations into things that weren't there, but it seemed to him that there were fewer people on the street than usual. Phoenix could by no stretch of the imagination be considered a "night" town, but there were usually more pedestrians and cars in the downtown area than this.

Maybe people *were* becoming too scared. Maybe it was wrong for him to contribute to that sense of fear by using such a horrific term as "fiend."

"Hey!"

Houghton jumped at the voice behind him, whirling to see Vern Rogers, one of his coreporters on the news desk come walking down the sidewalk toward him, arm raised in greeting.

"Shit," he said, as Rogers caught up to him. "You scared the hell out of me."

"It's those murders you're covering. You're bound to be tense working on a story like that." Rogers shook his head. "It's enough to scare the hell out of anybody."

"Yeah," Houghton admitted.

He'd keep the name, he thought.
The Phoenix Fiend.
It sounded good.
It fit.

Twenty-four

Allan stood up, folded his notebook, turned off his tape recorder, and shook Al Goldstein's hand, thanking the man for answering his questions. He smiled politely, though he did not feel like smiling. He had formed no opinion of Goldstein that first evening—indeed, things had been so hectic that the next day the only specific thing he could remember about the man was the fact that he had been drinking—but he had formed an opinion now.

And that opinion was not good.

Goldstein had agreed to let Allan come to his office and ask questions, and he had appeared to answer those questions honestly, unevasively, and satisfactorily, but there was something in the businessman's manner that Allan found not exactly suspicious but . . . false. Suspect. He was all smiles and consideration, he showed concern and outrage at the proper times, but there was something about his emotions that rang false, that seemed like an act.

He seemed to be hiding something.

Allan had sensed some of that when Cathy and Jimmy had been in his office. It had seemed unusual to him that a man would not accompany his son to the police station when it concerned the murder of the family pet, and when Cathy had apologized for Goldstein's not being there he had felt that, despite her bland words, she was resentful at having to cover for the man. Her tone of voice had implied that, in the great scheme of things, she thought him a step above scum.

He was inclined to agree with Cathy's judgement. Goldstein had the smug supercilious air of a born used-car salesman. He said all the right things at all the right times, but there was an underlying impression of mendacity in everything he did.

The man worried Allan. There was nothing real to be concerned about, nothing concrete, but the fact that Goldstein could in one sentence declare how shocked and upset he was at what had happened to his dog, and in the next sentence reveal that he was not shocked and upset at all, made Allan's police antennae go up.

When he got back to the station, he would run a discrete check on Mr. Al Goldstein.

And if anything unusual turned up, he would have the man placed under surveillance.

Goldstein walked Allan to the elevator, pressing the button for him.

"Thank you for your time," Allan said.

Goldstein smiled as the elevator doors opened. "No problem at all."

On his way down, Allan found himself wondering if Goldstein could possibly have the medical knowledge required to drain a body of blood.

Before returning to the station, Allan swung by the Ralston house, where a second search was now under way. Nothing had been found in the initial investigation of the premises, but the house had been sealed and the team was now going over everything with more advanced high-tech equipment and more thorough procedures.

He pulled in front of the house, in back of the other

parked police cars, and ducked under the yellow ribbon that blocked the driveway. Williams and Dobrinin were in the sewing room where the murder had occurred, Dobrinin examining the sewing machine and Williams cataloguing the contents of a small pink wastepaper basket near the door. Both men looked up as Allan entered, and he nodded his greeting. "Anything?"

Williams shook his head. "Goose egg."

Allan frowned, looking around the room. "Where's Lee?"

"Break."

"What do you mean, 'break?' This isn't a country club here. He can take his break when he gets back to the station. I want this site examined and analyzed yesterday. Where did he go?"

Dobrinin shrugged. "Burger King, I think. There's one around the corner. He was thirsty, and he obviously can't drink anything from here or he might fuck up the evidence."

"How long's he been gone?"

"I don't know."

Williams looked at his watch. "Shit, it's later than I thought. He's probably been gone thirty minutes already." He stood and glanced embarrassedly at Allan. "Sorry, sir. I didn't realize he'd been out for this long." He cleared his throat, looked at Dobrinin, turned back toward Allan. "Actually, he was going to pick up some Cokes for us, too."

"I don't mean to jump all over your ass," Allan said. "But we've got to get this finished up—" He broke off in mid-sentence as he saw Lee walking toward the house from the garage. He shot a glance toward Williams. "I thought you said he was at Burger King."

"I thought he was."

Lee opened the sewing room door and walked inside. He seemed surprised to see Allan, but it did not show in his voice. "Afternoon, Lieutenant."

"Where were you?" Allan asked.

"In the garage."

"Doing what?"

"Just seeing if there was anything we missed." He frowned, puzzled. "Why? Is something wrong?"

"You said you were going to Burger King."

"I changed my mind. I decided we could hit someplace on the way home and get something to drink. It's getting late, and I figured we'd better try to speed things up and get out of here."

"Why didn't you tell anyone?"

"I did. I guess they didn't hear me."

Allan stared at the young policeman, feeling strange inside. Maybe he was just being paranoid, but for a second time that day he got the impression that the man in front of him was not telling the whole truth.

He realized that Lee had been partnered with Bob Whitehead on the night Whitehead had disappeared.

What if our murderer's a cop?

"Go back to the station," Allan said. "I'll finish up here."

"What did I—"

"Go!" Allan ordered. "As of now, you are off this case. If you want to talk about it later, we can discuss the situation when I get back."

Lee stiffened. "I'm sorry," he said. "I was just finishing up what I'd started earlier. I didn't think—"

"That's right. You didn't think." Allan was aware that he was behaving in an unusually dictatorial, almost Pynchon-like manner, that all three men were staring at him in shocked disbelief, but he could not shake the feeling that Lee was hiding something. "I'll see you back at the station."

"Sir—" Williams began.

"Just shut up and get back to work. Let's finish up here."

Williams and Dobrinin returned to their respective duties while Lee headed down the driveway to his car, parked on the street. Allan watched him go, then walked out of the house and toward the garage.

Twenty-five

Halback and Samson had not been at school all week, and that worried Jimmy. He didn't know why they weren't here, he didn't know what they were doing, but whatever they were up to, he had a feeling it wasn't good. He knew they hadn't been arrested for killing Dusty. If they had, Lieutenant Grant would have called and told him. But he had not heard from the lieutenant at all, had not talked to him since he and Cathy had left the police station.

Jimmy stood next to the principal's office in his usual spot, watching as the other kids walked out of the gates to the school bus or headed down the street toward their homes. He saw other fifth-graders come out of their classes in the far building and he scanned the sea of faces expectantly, but the two heads he was searching for did not appear.

Where were they? What were they up to?

He was tempted to call Lieutenant Grant and ask him what had happened, but he was afraid to. The lieutenant seemed nice, but Jimmy knew that, no matter what they said, adults simply did not pay attention to kids. They did not take kids seriously.

Maybe he'd ask Cathy to call.

Jimmy had already asked his dad to call the police station and find out about Dusty, but his father kept putting it off. The grave had been dug in the backyard, at the foot of the tree near the fence, and Jimmy had constructed a headstone out of two boards upon which he'd written "DUSTY R.I.P." Everything was ready. But his dad would not make the call, claiming he didn't have enough time, pretending he had forgotten. Jimmy had a terrible feeling in his gut that his dad knew something that he did not, a secret he was keeping to himself, but he refused to let himself think about that or dwell on the subject. He tried to keep his thoughts optimistic and to look on the bright side of things. He'd had enough of darkness lately.

He had not seen either Randy West or his mother since the attack. Cathy had gone over to their house a few times to try to talk to Mrs. West about Randy, but no one had answered the door. They had been home, though. Jimmy was sure of it. He had seen no one leave or enter the house, but there had been lights in the windows. And he had heard noises at night.

Strange noises.

"BOO!"

Jimmy jumped at the sound of the voice and heard Paul laugh uproariously. Jimmy whirled around to face the smaller boy, who was standing next to the door of the office. "You scared the crap out of me!"

"What are you so worried about? Those guys aren't even here today."

"That's what I'm worried about." He turned again to watch the students leave the schoolyard, his eyes scanning the adjacent street and sidewalk, taking in the rows of tract homes, looking for any sign of the bullies. "You really are a jerk sometimes."

"Hey, I'm sorry. I didn't mean anything. I just saw you there and I couldn't resist it." Paul sounded hurt, and Jimmy immediately felt bad. Before all this started, he too would have jumped at the chance to scare a friend half to death. It wasn't Paul's fault that

Halback and Samson were after him and he was acting paranoid.

"No," Jimmy said. "I'm sorry. I didn't mean to get mad at you."

"I guess the war's still on, huh?"

Jimmy nodded. He picked up his books from the ground and moved out from behind the pillar, satisfied that the two older boys were not at school and were not waiting outside the gates to pounce on him. They might be lying in ambush someplace along the long route home, but they were not here, and for a little while at least he felt safe.

"Maybe the cops got 'em," Paul suggested. "Maybe they did kill your dog and the police caught 'em and now they're going to jail."

Jimmy looked at him. "You think that?"

"No. I was just trying to cheer you up."

"Thanks." Jimmy snorted. "You're a lot of help." He walked slowly out from the shadow of the office, past the multipurpose room, toward the playground and the exit. "If I can just make it to the summer, I'll be safe. They'll probably forget about me over the summer."

"Don't count on it," Paul said. "They don't live that far from you, and they're older, and their parents don't care what they do. They can come over to your house anytime they want and beat the shit out of you."

"What am I supposed to do then? Move to another city?"

Paul shrugged. "I don't know. I'm just glad they're not after me." The two boys walked through the open gate of the playground.

Jimmy looked over his shoulder, through the chain-link fence, at the school. From this vantage point, it looked like a prison, and to him that's exactly how it felt.

"Maybe you should take boxing lessons or something this summer," Paul suggested. "Then you could whip their asses."

"Yeah, right." Jimmy shook his head in resignation. He turned toward home. "I'll see you tomorrow."

"If you don't die first," Paul said. He grinned, moving in the opposite direction toward his own house. "Later."

"Later," Jimmy said. He walked slowly, staring at the ground before him. At least Paul didn't pressure him to talk about Dusty. He was grateful for that. He knew that the death of his dog was the number-one topic of conversation around school these days, and although he himself wouldn't talk about it, he could not help overhearing other kids' conversations. Many students, particularly girls, had been staying out of his way since it happened, careful not to get too close to him, as though they were afraid of him, and there were whispers among some of the students of monsters, witches, demons. No human could turn a dog inside out, they said.

It was just kid talk, Jimmy knew, but it scared him nonetheless. He couldn't help it. He didn't think anything supernatural had gotten Dusty, but he didn't really think Halback and Samson had done it, either. He didn't know who had committed the murder, and the not knowing scared him somehow. He wanted everything tied up and over with. He wanted the guy caught and put in jail.

Though he was walking down a residential neighborhood and there were kids and moms behind the closed curtains of the houses, the street was empty save for him.

He felt suddenly alone, vulnerable, and he quickened his step, trying not to think about Dusty, trying not to think about anything.

His father was home.

Walking up the street, Jimmy saw the Oldsmobile parked in the driveway and the front door of the house open. He wasn't sure if he should be happy or scared. His father so seldom came home from work early or on time these days that it was definitely out of the ordinary, perhaps even cause for concern, when he arrived at the house before Jimmy.

Maybe that woman's there, Jimmy thought.

But the woman had been by only twice since that first night, and she hadn't been by the past week at all.

Still, Jimmy made sure he loudly dropped his books, cleared his throat, and made plenty of warning noises before stepping up to the front door. He tried the screen, assuming it would be locked, and prepared to ring the doorbell, but to his surprise the screen was open. He stepped inside the house. "Dad?"

There was no answer, and Jimmy felt suddenly nervous. Neither Cathy nor the police had allowed him to see Dusty, but his mind had painted a detailed picture of what the dog must have looked like from the descriptions he'd heard. Now he imagined his dad in the same situation—posed behind a door, turned inside out, looking like some horrific slimy red mannequin. He stopped next to the couch, carefully putting his books down on the nearest cushion. Maybe he should go over and get Cathy, he thought.

No, he was being childish. Muscles tensed, he forced himself to move slowly forward, prepared to jump out of the way and dash out the front door if he saw anything unexpected. He peeked carefully around the corner of the living room into the kitchen.

His father was sitting at the table, staring out the window, a preoccupied look on his face, a cup of coffee in his hand. On the table before him was a huge Lego box: the medieval castle and battlements set with action figures.

The one Jimmy had asked for last Christmas but had not received.

"Dad?" he said nervously.

His father's gaze shifted into focus and he smiled. "How was school?"

"Fine," Jimmy said. He was not sure what to say. Something was obviously not right here, but he didn't know what it was or how to react to it.

"I called about Dusty," his father said. "They told

me they'd had her cremated. They said it was against the law for us to bury her here at home."

Was that all it was? Jimmy felt as if a weight had been lifted from his shoulders. The news was bad but was not the horror he'd feared. This, at least, had been expected. He was not sure what he'd thought had happened, but he'd known it was something unimaginably bad. He felt an emptiness inside him at the thought of Dusty being cremated alone, away from her family, but still he relaxed somewhat.

His father cleared his throat uncomfortably. "I, uh, bought you this today. I know you really wanted it."

Jimmy nodded gratefully, although he didn't feel grateful. He had wanted the Lego set for Christmas, and he supposed he still wanted it, or would want it under different circumstances, but it was such an inappropriate gift for this situation that at this moment it had all the appeal of flat Coke. "Thanks, Dad," he said.

His father said nothing but stood up and walked around the table to where Jimmy stood. For the first time in a long while, Jimmy noticed, he did not smell of beer and alcohol. He put his long arms awkwardly around his son, holding him, hugging him. It was a strange gesture, unnatural and stilted, given at the wrong time and probably for the wrong reasons, but Jimmy found himself hugging back. He closed his eyes tightly, trying to will the welling tears to stay in back of his eyelids, but they were soon rolling down his cheeks, and as he held his father tighter he began to sob aloud.

Twenty-six

After work, Cathy went with Ann to grab a bite to eat. Since both of them were poor and neither of them felt like eating junk food, they decided to go to Garcia's. Mexican food was both filling and fairly inexpensive. They could order something cheap and fill up on the free chips and salsa.

The restaurant was crowded, and they had to wait fifteen minutes amidst a group of humorless businessmen and happy loving couples before the high school hostess seated them at a small table in the center of the restaurant's main room. A Hispanic busboy immediately came by with a basket of tortilla chips and two small bowls of salsa.

"We came here on our date," Ann said, as the busboy poured their water.

Cathy smiled. "You should've told me. I don't want to bring back bad memories."

"Just slap me if I have any flashbacks."

Cathy dipped a chip into the salsa and bit into it. The red sauce was hot, and she was forced to take a long drink of water to cool the burning on her tongue. She looked around the room. At a table catty-corner from them were two young men in their early to mid-twenties wearing the red and yellow Sun Devil T-shirts that marked them as students of ASU. The one facing Cathy nodded at her and smiled, then leaned forward to say something to his friend. Cathy looked quickly away, focusing her attention on the basket of chips. She reached for the water and took a drink. "Those two guys are staring at us," she said.

Ann turned casually around, trying not to be too obvious. "They're cute," she said, again facing Cathy. "But they look sort of jockish."

Cathy glanced toward the other table. The young man held up a subtle hand in greeting. His friend turned around to smile at her. Blushing, Cathy bent to examine the menu.

Ann giggled. "The mating ritual of the American suburbanite."

"Very funny."

"Actually," Ann said, "physical appearance is the first thing people notice about each other. You can't base a relationship on physical attraction, but unless you're blind, you do see the person before you talk to them, before you get to know them. We like to think we're civilized and highly evolved, but when you come down to it, we're not that far removed from the animals."

"Cultural anthropology, right?"

Ann grinned. "You had that class too, huh?"

"It's required."

The waitress arrived to take their orders, and Cathy quickly scanned the menu while Ann ordered. She decided on a taco salad and a large iced tea. The waitress smiled at them, told them her name, picked up their menus, and left. Ann sprinkled some more salt on the tortilla chips and dipped a large chip into the salsa, using it like a shovel. "So how's your father these days?"

Cathy shrugged. "How else? Selfish, inconsiderate, unbearable. Same as always."

"Have you ever thought of moving out? Getting your own apartment?"

Cathy shook her head. "I can't just abandon him."

"That's no reason to live with abuse. You have rights, too. Tell him to shape up or you'll ship out."

Cathy smiled. "It's not that easy. Besides, he needs me. He needs me to help with difficult chores, he needs me to cook, he needs me to help him financially. He gets almost nothing from disability, you know."

"So get an apartment nearby. You could still help him out, you'd be close enough to dash home if an emergency arises, but you'd still have your own space."

"God knows I've thought about it often enough."

"Why not? No reason to be a martyr."

Cathy looked at Ann suspiciously. "Why all the sudden interest in helping me find my own apartment?"

"You caught me." Ann laughed. "I'm thinking of moving out myself, and I need a roommate. I certainly can't afford a place of my own. Not on what I make at the store."

Cathy was not only flattered, she was surprised. She glanced at the younger girl, biting into a tortilla chip, and she realized that she really would like to be Ann's roommate.

But could she, in good conscience, leave her father? She wasn't sure if she could, or if she should. He was cruel and thoughtless, but he was her father and she owed him something. "Let me think about it," she said, and she was amazed that she was brave enough to make even that commitment.

Ann nodded. "All right. It'll probably be a while anyway. I figure July, maybe August."

The waitress arrived a few moments later with their orders. "Be careful," she cautioned, placing the food before them. "The plates are hot."

"Could we have some more salsa?" Ann asked.

"Sure. Is there anything else I can get you?"

Ann shook her head. "Not right now."

The waitress left and Cathy glanced down at their meals. "We both ordered taco salads," she said. "How could our plates be hot?"

"Pavlovian reaction." Ann picked up her fork. "She probably says that every time she puts a plate on a table."

They ate in silence for a moment. The waitress returned with another small bowl of salsa, which Ann promptly poured onto her salad. "I still can't believe the murderer was on your street, a few houses down from you."

It was a subject Cathy had been avoiding, something she didn't feel comfortable talking about, and she found herself thinking, irrationally, of David. Nevertheless, she smiled gamely. "The 'Phoenix Fiend,'" she said.

"They have to call him something. How else are they going to sell papers, get good ratings?" Ann took a bite of her food. "I still can't believe it, though."

"I can't, either."

"Aren't you scared? I mean, they still haven't caught him. He could be lurking around your house right now, hiding in your backyard."

"Thanks a lot."

"Don't you ever think about that?"

"Of course I do. But the police have permanent patrols in our neighborhood, and I lock all of our doors and windows at night and try to be home before dark. What else can I do? I don't stick my head in the sand, but I try not to let it rule my life. If I spent every spare moment thinking about it, I'd be a nervous wreck. I'm scared enough as it is."

"I just wish they'd catch the guy. I'm scared too. And I'm worried about meeting new men. I'm sticking with guys I know for awhile. Who can tell about the men you meet? It's dangerous out there."

"Unless you're dating a cop."

"A cop? Who'd want to date a cop?"

Cathy said nothing.

"And no one knows what this psycho looks like. He could look just like an ordinary person. He could be anywhere."

"Thanks," Cathy said. "I still have to go to the store after this and pick up some groceries."

Ann laughed. "Eat fast," she told her.

They did eat fast, and though they had been only half serious, Cathy was thankful that summer was approaching and the days were getting longer. Still, by the time they got out of Garcia's it was dusk and the sun was already starting to go down. They said goodbye, walking to their respective cars. Cathy drove immediately to Bayless, where she bought enough groceries for the next few days.

When she arrived home, her father was nowhere to be found. She looked on the refrigerator and the kitchen table for a note of some sort but found nothing. Of course not. If, before, he would have not left a note out of thoughtlessness, now he would not do so deliberately, out of malice, in a perverse attempt to cause trouble for her. She put the sack of groceries she had been carrying on the counter next to the sink and went outside to get the other two sacks out of the car. She took the heaviest sack out of the backseat and bumped the car door shut with her rear end.

From across the street she heard screams. Although she couldn't be sure, the screaming voice sounded like that of Katrina West.

Probably yelling at Randy, she thought.

A week ago, before the attack on Jimmy, she would have been incensed at the sound of such shouting, furious at Katrina for being so cruel and abusive to her son.

Now she thought the boy probably deserved it.

She walked into the house, deposited the sack on the counter, and returned for the last load. Hefting the final sack with one hand and closing the car door with the other, she glanced across the street at the Lauter house.

The Lauter house.

It was strange how she still thought of the place as the Lauter house, even though it was now the West residence. Old habits die hard. She had called it the Lauter house for twenty years, and she would probably call it that for the rest of her life.

But perhaps she wasn't far wrong. Although the house had changed hands, it seemed to have retained much of its original character, and despite the new curtains and the trappings of modernity, the house remained unchanged in her mind. It might not be haunted in the traditional sense, but the house definitely seemed to attract the same sort of element.

The screaming had stopped, and Cathy carried the last bag of groceries into the house, putting it down on the table. She wondered where her father was. Probably at the club, she decided. He seldom went anywhere else these days.

On the way home from the store she had almost resigned herself to staying at home with her father, rationalizing her situation to herself, but now she felt justified in looking for a place of her own. She was getting pretty damn tired of the way he acted. She was getting pretty damn tired of being treated like dirt. She didn't expect him to show gratitude or express thanks; it was not in his nature. But she did expect a little common courtesy, and with these murders, it would have been only decent of him to inform her of where he was going. She might not get along with him, but she still worried about him. He didn't have to ask her permission for anything, but it would be nice if he at least told her of his plans.

She put away the groceries and went into the den, turning on the TV. The news was on, and once again the top local story was the search for the "Phoenix Fiend." Police, the newsman said, were concentrating their efforts in the east Valley. A woman in Mesa had been assaulted by a well-dressed middle-aged man in the parking lot of Fiesta Mall, and a child in Apache Junction was missing. There was really nothing to connect these two incidents to the Fiend, but the police could not afford to take chances at this point. A composite sketch of the man, taken from the assaulted woman's description, was shown and anyone having seen someone matching the description was urged to contact the Phoenix or Mesa police departments.

Cathy picked up the *TV Guide* from the coffee table. She didn't feel like watching the news right now. She'd catch the ten o'clock newscast instead. She glanced through the guide. *Singin' in the Rain* was on Channel 5, and she switched the channel. It was probably cut to shreds to make room for commercials, but a bad *Singin' in the Rain* was better than none at all and she settled down to watch it.

Her father came home an hour later, but though she called out to him, he went directly to his room without saying a word, shutting the door behind him.

She finished the movie, watched a rerun of the old *Bob Newhart Show*, watched the news, and went to bed herself.

She dreamed again of David.

In her nightmare, David was coming for her. She was thirteen again and alone in the house with him. He was in the hallway outside her bedroom. Through the crack in the bedroom doorway, she could see him pressing his hands against the zipper on his jeans. There was a bulge there, an elongated outline, and on his face was a thin sheen of perspiration. He saw her peeking through the crack, and she quickly closed the door.

"Come on!" he said, and his voice was almost a whine. "You'll like it! It'll be fun!"

She pressed her back against the door, holding it shut with all her strength, but he was stronger. The door inched inward.

And then she was in the bathroom, on the toilet, her dress and panties around her ankles. She was peeing, and the liquid spray made a musical tinkle as it splashed against the water in the bowl.

The door flew open, and David stood there with three of his friends, staring at her. He pointed, giggling, and she felt dirty, ashamed of herself, ashamed of being a girl. David and his friends broke into guffaws.

Cathy woke up sweating, her hands balled into fists, and it was a long time before she again fell asleep.

Twenty-seven

"Hello."

Cathy looked up from the counter where she'd been checking the new shelf list. Allan Grant stood before her, a friendly smile on his face.

"I didn't know you worked here," he said.

Cathy nodded silently, not sure of what to say. She could feel the warmth spreading up her cheeks.

"I come here all the time. I never noticed you before."

"I never noticed you either."

"It's always that way. Once you're aware of something you start seeing it everywhere. After I bought my car a few years back, I suddenly started noticing Broncos everywhere. It seemed like everybody was driving one. About six or seven years ago, I saw a painting of Dan Namingha's in an art magazine and I really liked it a lot. Then I discovered that his work was hanging in galleries all over Scottsdale and I just hadn't noticed." He shook his head. "I must have come in this store forty or fifty times. I probably even bought books from you. But I never saw you." He laughed easily. "I didn't mean that the way it sounded."

"It's okay," Cathy said. She tried to smile, but she knew the effort was not entirely successful. She felt nervous, certain that her face was an open book and that he could read everything on her mind. Her hands were shaking a little and she put them on the counter to steady them.

"Of course it may have been the circumstances."

She nodded dumbly. "Can I help you? What are you looking for?" She cringed inwardly. The transition had been too abrupt, too awkward. As always, her social backwardness was screwing everything up.

Allan did not seem to notice. "I'm just on my lunch break right now, and I thought I'd pop in and see if you have that new book on Expressionism. It's supposed to be really good." He looked at her questioningly. "Are you an art fan?"

"No," she admitted. "I really don't know much about it."

"One of the major drawbacks of the public school system."

"I went to Catholic school."

"Really? So did I. I wasn't Catholic, but they accepted anyone who passed the entrance exams, and my parents thought kids who went to parochial school had a better chance of getting into a good college." He smiled. "So I went to ASU, majored in criminal law, minored in art, and became a police detective."

"I went to ASU, too."

"It's a small world after all. What did you major in?"

"English." She smiled timidly. "So I became a sales clerk."

Allan laughed. It was a nice laugh, real and unforced, and Cathy relaxed a little.

"How's the investigation going?" she asked. "Are you any closer to finding the, uh, murderer?"

His voice took on a serious, almost grave tone, and his smile faded, the contours of his face reforming around a grimace. "I'm not supposed to say anything. I'm already in bad with my boss. But, to be honest, no, we're not any closer." Cathy was immediately sorry that she'd mentioned the subject. "Whoever this guy is, he's good. He's almost like something out of a Sherlock Holmes movie or a bad mystery novel. He just keeps sailing by us, leaving no clues, while we stumble around in the dark."

"The Phoenix Fiend."

"Please!" Allan said, covering his eyes in an exaggerated gesture. "I don't want to hear that phrase." He took his hand from his eyes. "That name drives me crazy. It makes me feel like I'm in a *National Enquirer* story." He smiled. "How's Jimmy? I called his house a few days ago, but no one answered. I was going to try back again. I wanted to report to him and check up on how he's doing."

"He's okay," Cathy admitted. "Much better than I would have thought. He was awfully close to Dusty."

"I thought he probably was."

"He's a brave little guy. A lot tougher than he should be at that age. He's had a pretty rough few years."

"Why? His father?"

Cathy examined Allan's face before answering. "Yes," she said carefully.

He looked like he wanted to say something else to her, to ask a question, but instead he said, "At least Jimmy has a friend like you. He's lucky there."

Cathy smiled gratefully, and this time the smile didn't seem strained at all. "I wanted to thank you for the way you treated him in your office. For the way you treated both of us, really. Adults don't seem to take kids seriously for some reason. I don't know why. Maybe they've forgotten what it was like to be that age. But kids don't like to be talked down to. They like to be treated as equals. You did that with Jimmy."

"Maybe you should've been a teacher."

Cathy shook her head. "Stand up in front of a whole class and talk for eight hours a day? I'm not that outgoing."

"You might surprise yourself." He looked at his watch. "I'm sorry. It's getting late, and I don't have that much time here. Things are really hectic right now. I have to be back at the station by one. Do you think you could tell me if that book's in yet?"

"Do you know the name of it?"

"No, I'm afraid I don't. But I know it has 'Expressionism' in the title."

Cathy looked at the shelf list before her and, seeing nothing, reached under the counter for the printout from their distributor. She scanned the title list and subject list. "There's one simply called *Expressionism*."

"That's it."

"It's supposed to be here," she said, "but I haven't seen it. I'll check in the back for you."

"Okay." Allan picked up an *Us* magazine and flipped it open while she hurried down the center aisle toward the stockroom.

"Cute guy," Ann commented as she passed by.

"Cop," Cathy said. She pushed open the stockroom door and walked down the length of the room to the nonfiction section. Some of the books were shelved alphabetically, but most were still in crates. "Damn," she muttered. Jeff was supposed to have unpacked these books two days ago.

"Now I understand the cop reference." Ann was leaning against the doorframe. She nodded knowingly.

"What cop reference?" Cathy scanned the shelved titles. *Expressionism*. It was there. She reached up and drew the book down.

"At dinner the other night. I said it wasn't safe to meet new men with the murderer running loose. You said it would be safe to meet a cop."

Cathy took a pen from her shirt pocket and made a checkmark next to the name of the book on the temporary inventory list hanging on a post of the bookshelf. "You record everything I say?"

"No, but that was interesting enough to remember. It's not a subject you often talk about. I wondered if there was something there." Ann put her hands on her hips in a pose of indignant outrage. There was a smile on her lips. "Why didn't you tell me you met someone?" she said teasingly. "I thought we were supposed to be friends."

"I didn't meet anyone. This is the lieutenant in charge of the case. I met him when Jimmy's dog got killed."

"But you're interested. Admit it."

"I'm not interested. I have to get out there. He's waiting." Cathy pressed past Ann and pushed open the door with her shoulder. Allan was still glancing through *Us*, turning the pages quickly, obviously finding nothing of interest in the magazine. "Here it is," she said, approaching the counter. She handed the book to Allan. "It's an expensive one, Lieutenant. Thirty-five dollars."

"That *is* expensive," he agreed. "But don't call me Lieutenant. You're at work here, I'm not. In my free time, I'm Allan."

"Okay," Cathy said, smiling. "You can look at it if you want, see if you're interested."

"Thanks." He placed the book carefully on the glass of the counter and opened it to the table of contents, perusing the names of chapters and subchapters, before moving onto the color prints in the text of the book. "You've never heard of Expressionism?" he asked.

"I didn't say that," Cathy said. "Of course I've heard of it. And I can probably recognize it. I just said I don't know a whole lot about art."

"I'm sorry. I didn't mean it like that."

"No, I'm sorry," Cathy said, blushing. She hadn't meant to come across so snobby, so pompous, and she felt embarrassed. Once again, she was doing everything wrong.

"Hi!"

Cathy looked up from the book to see Ann walking down the aisle toward the front counter. Against her will, she felt a sharp pang of jealousy as the younger

girl moved next to her. She was acutely aware of the
fact that Ann was not wearing a bra and that the
contours of her large breasts could be seen through
the thin material of her blouse. She was surprised at
herself, hardly able to believe her own reaction.

She might not want to admit it, but despite what
she'd told Ann, she was interested.

"Hi," Allan said.

Cathy's stomach knotted. Ann was going to charm
Allan the way she charmed everyone else.

"So you're the lieutenant Cathy's been talking
about." Ann smiled brightly, and Cathy stared at her,
horrified. This couldn't be happening. She stood
rooted to the spot, unable to react.

Allan looked surprised. "What?"

She wanted to sink into the floor and disappear. She
looked beseechingly at Ann, trying to tell her with her
eyes to shut up, trying to warn her not to say anything,
but Ann only smiled. "Oh, nothing," she said
innocently.

Cathy glared at her. Ann walked back up the aisle,
pretending that nothing had happened. Cathy dropped
her eyes, staring at the art book on the counter, too
embarrassed and too afraid to meet Allan's gaze. She
noticed that his hands had stalled and were not turning the pages, and she shut her eyes, willing this to be
a dream, willing it not to be real.

She swallowed, forcing herself to look up, prepared
to see confusion, scorn, even embarrassment in Allan's
face. She was not prepared for the expression of light
good humor she saw there. "Talking about me, huh?"
He laughed. "Well, since we're on the subject, what
are you doing for dinner tonight?"

This couldn't be happening either.

"Nothing," she found herself saying.

"Want to grab a bite to eat?"

She really needed time to prepare for this, to think
things out, to plan her reactions, to choose what she
was going to say, but she knew she could not. Mental

scenarios could be run and rerun, practiced and edited until they were perfect, but real life demanded quick choices, instant decisions.

She found herself nodding instinctively. "Sure," she said.

"All right, then. It's a date." Allan closed the book, pushing it toward her. "I have to go right now, but I want the book. Can you hold it for me?"

"No problem."

"Do you need my name or anything?"

"I know your name," Cathy said.

"Right." Allan shook his head, pointed to his forehead. "Alzheimer's. Should I pick you up here around seven?"

"I get off at five."

"I could meet you at your house."

"Okay." Cathy reached for a pen and scrap of paper.

"I already know your address," Allan said. "I took your report, remember?"

Cathy smiled. "Alzheimer's."

"Well, at least we have something in common." He looked at his watch. "Gotta go. I'll see you tonight."

"Okay."

"Good-bye," he said. "Cathy."

She watched as he walked out the door, aware that again she was blushing. He waved to her and she waved back.

Things had happened much too fast. She could not seem to catch her breath, and she was suddenly certain that she had made the wrong decision. She should not have agreed to go out with him tonight. She hardly knew the man. He was a police detective and had gone to Catholic school. That was about the extent of her knowledge of him.

He was a police detective.

A policeman.

That was the scary part. She had never felt comfortable around policemen, and although Allan didn't seem much like a cop, didn't seem like a cop at all, in fact, she knew she'd been stupid and rash to accept his invitation.

Miss Riley? I have some bad news.

She felt tense, and she walked around to the other side of the counter, trying to relax. What if they had nothing in common? What if it turned out they didn't even like each other?

Ann returned, creeping carefully up the aisle as though approaching a hungry lion. There was a look of polite contrition on her face, but underneath that Cathy could sense a feeling of pleased satisfaction. "I'm sorry," she said in a melodramatically small, sheepish little-girl voice.

Cathy looked at her. She wanted to be angry at Ann but found that she could not. She was, deep down, grateful to her friend, though it was not something she could admit to. Policeman or no, she liked Allan. "No, you're not," Cathy said.

Ann laughed. "Well, no, I'm not. I knew you weren't going to be assertive enough. You just needed a push, and I provided it. But I am sorry if you were uncomfortable. I didn't want to hurt you."

"I know." Cathy sighed. "So now I have a date tonight."

"I knew it!" Ann said excitedly. "I could tell!"

"I'm not sure I should go."

Ann was shocked. "Why not?"

"What'll I talk about? I don't even know this man. What if we have absolutely nothing in common?"

"You pays your money, you takes your chances," Ann said.

Cathy just looked at her.

"Look, there's always something to talk about on the first date. That's when you get to ask all the questions and find out about the guy's sordid past. It's sort of a screen test. If he passes, you go out again."

"What if I don't pass?"

Ann shook her head. "You have to think positively."

A customer walked into the store, a middle-aged woman looking for the latest Jackie Collins book, and Ann walked her over to the hardback fiction section. Cathy stayed at the front counter and tried to think positively. She liked Allan Grant, and she wanted him to like her, but she could not shake the nagging feeling that she had made a serious mistake.

Twenty-eight

Walking from the bookstore to his car, Allan was not exactly sure why he had asked out Cathy Riley. Particularly at this time. Yes, she was attractive and he wanted to get to know her better. She also had a shy, almost backward, quality that he found curiously refreshing after the shallow but socially sophisticated bimbos he'd dated in the past. But with these murders still unsolved and the killer still at large, he knew he would have virtually no free time to pursue a relationship. The odds were good that he would have to cancel at least half of the dates he made—something that was true for a cop even during normal times, but was doubly true when major crimes remained unsolved—and after being stood up three or four times, Cathy would understandably become frustrated with him and would never want to see him again. It had happened before, in considerably less stressful periods of his life.

But he still wanted to go out with her.

She was a strange one. No doubt about that. He had noticed in his office the other day that she seemed nervous and ill at ease while talking to him, that she seldom met his eyes, and that when she did she glanced immediately away. Just now, at the bookstore, she'd looked like she wanted to die when her friend came by.

Allan smiled. He liked her, though. Underneath that surface tenseness she seemed both interesting and intelligent. It might be quite a project to get her to open up and come out of her shell, but he had the feeling that it would be worth the effort.

As an added bonus, she appeared to be what his mother had euphemistically called a "nice girl." That was a rare find these days, particularly for a policeman. Cops didn't always hang out in the best circles, and the women they met and dated were often only a step above the women they arrested.

That was the reason the department had sponsored free VD/Herpes/AIDS tests last year.

And that was why he had immediately had himself tested.

He got into the car and drove back toward the station. Despite his reservations, he was not sorry that he had asked Cathy out. He was glad that he had. And he found himself thinking about her as he turned on the air conditioner and drove south toward downtown Phoenix.

The three Iwaspo church members stood before Allan, dressed entirely in black. Each of the old men had a long white beard and wore an identical white crucifix on a silver chain around his neck. Joseph, the group's designated speaker, had been talking nonstop for over a quarter of an hour, and though Allan had wanted to toss him and his cronies out of the station after the first minute, he had forced himself to keep up an objective demeanor, to maintain the bland expression on his face, and had let the Iwaspo put forth his bizarre theory. Joseph was earnest and obviously believed every word he said, but Allan found it hard to credit the word of a cult member whose religion was comprised of seven members who met in someone's garage each time there was a full moon.

Allan leaned back in his chair, his gaze flicking from

one old man to another. "So," he said. "You believe that these murders were committed by some sort of demon."

"We don't believe. We *know*. It was our ritual that inadvertently loosed Alsath upon the earth, which summoned him forth from Hell to perform his foul and unholy deeds."

The beeper sounded on Allan's watch, and he pressed the small button to shut it off. "Excuse me," he said. "I have to attend an important meeting. Thank you for sharing your information with me. Please leave your names, addresses, and phone numbers where you can be reached with the desk sergeant, and we'll contact you if any of this pans out." He stood up to go.

"You don't understand," Joseph said, obviously agitated. "Alsath is free, loosed upon the population of the earth to commit his blasphemies."

"Well he seems to be staying around the Phoenix area right now," Allan said. "So we should be able to find him."

"Are you mocking our beliefs?" Joseph asked.

All three men glared at him, and Allan could feel the strength of their convictions. He held up his hands in a gesture of appeasement. "No," he said. "I'm sorry if you got that impression. I apologize for offending you. But I'm really very busy today. Thank you for your time, effort, and concern. I promise you we will follow up on the information you have provided us."

Joseph nodded solemnly, apparently satisfied.

Allan opened the door of the interrogation room and led the three men to the front desk. "Officer Hall will give you a form to fill out and will be happy to assist you in any way he can." He shook each of the Iwaspos' hands while shooting Hall a "thank you" look over their heads. "I have to go."

Turning his back on the lobby, he strode through the door and made his way through the maze of corridors to the captain's office. Thank God for the old beeper routine. It was a trick he had learned as a rookie—pretending to have a prearranged appointment to get out of boring interviews that had gone on too long. It wasn't entirely a ruse in this instance. He really was supposed to meet with Pynchon to discuss the reports he and his team had submitted this morning, but he actually could have gone in at any time.

Allan sighed. It had already been a real shitter of a day, the only bright spot his lunchtime visit to the bookstore, and he had the feeling it wasn't going to get any better. Several of the newer recruits gave him strange looks as he passed them. It was a reaction he was beginning to get used to. Maybe it was the bizarreness of the murders or maybe it was something less definable, but most of the cops at the station, both those working on the case and those not, seemed to find the killings more than a little creepy. The usual joking, the usual gallows humor exhibited in the wake of most murders, was missing. No one in the station had even gotten together a pool, and Allan found this suspension of normal reactions almost as disturbing as the inability of his team to move visibly forward on the investigation.

He walked up to Pynchon's office and knocked loudly on the closed door.

"Come in!" the captain said.

Allan walked into the room, closing the door behind him.

Pynchon sat behind his desk, his bushy eyebrows beetled into a threatening scowl. He stood up, gathered together the reports on his desk, carefully paper-clipped them together, then threw the entire stack at the wall above Allan's head. Allan ducked, and the papers disbursed, fluttering harmlessly to the ground. "Assholes!" Pynchon bellowed. "Dickheads! What the fuck have you been doing since I've been out? This guy's making us look like a bunch of amateurs fresh out of clown college, and you're sitting on your asses, waiting for the goddamn key to the case to fall neatly into your goddamn laps. That's not the way it works!"

Allan bent to pick the scattered reports up off the carpet.

"Are you listening to me, Grant?"

Allan stood, facing the captain, leaving the reports on the floor. "Yes, sir."

Pynchon grabbed a newspaper off his desk. "Have you seen the *Republic* today?" Allan shook his head, and Pynchon tossed the paper at him. "Halfway down the page."

Allan glanced down at the newspaper, unfolding it as he did so. In the exact center of the front page, directly below a story about the latest economic forecast, was the kicker "Investigator Says," followed by the headline "Murderer Is Smarter Than Police." Allan looked up. "I—" he began.

"Did you say that?" Pynchon demanded.

"Well, yes, but—"

"No buts!" The captain glared at him. "I asked you not to be so cooperative with the press this time. At the very least, try not to undermine our efforts! We have enough problems as it is!"

"It's a free country. We have a free press."

"But you work for the PPD, not the *Arizona Republic*!" He reached forward and grabbed the paper out of Allan's hands. "I want you to call a press conference for tomorrow and invite all the local media. Make it for the morning so we'll be able to get it on the TV newscasts. You're going to put the best face possible on all this and give them a Pollyanna story that won't have us looking like such rubes. You got that? I'm taking a lot of shit from above for your big mouth, and I don't like it one damn bit." He shoved a fat finger in front of Allan's face. "And I'm going to be there at that conference too, to make sure you don't bend and spread 'em for the press. You understand?"

Allan's voice was soft and low. "Don't you think you're overreacting a bit here?" He stared defiantly at Pynchon but braced himself, awaiting the onslaught he knew would follow. To his surprise Pynchon backed up and moved behind his desk. The captain put both hands on the desktop, staring downward and breathing evenly, trying to calm himself.

"You're right," he said.

"What?"

"You're right. I'm sorry."

Allan stared at him in shock. In all his years on the force he had never heard of Pynchon apologizing before. To anyone. For anything.

"I know the kind of stress you're under," the captain said, looking up. "The kind of stress we're all under. We've only had one serial killer in the twenty years I've been captain, and he was captured while trying to stab his third victim. This time we already have four dead, one of them a cop, and the fucker's still at large."

"And a dog," Allan put in. "He's killed a pet dog."

"A pet." Pynchon straightened up, holding a hand against the small of his back, an expression of pain on his face. "What do you make of that? Killing animals?"

Allan said nothing, not knowing how to respond.

Pynchon was silent for a moment. "I also read your report on Lee, and I agree that there're no grounds to suspect him of any wrongdoing, but I want him off the team. Sometimes first hunches are the best, and sometimes you have to roll with them. I'm still not ruling out the idea that this killer's a cop, and until we can prove without a doubt that it's not, I want Lee close to home."

"There's not going to be any disciplinary action is there? His story did check out, and—"

"Nothing in his file, and an official apology if you fucked up. He'll just be temporarily reassigned."

Allan nodded. "I'll need a replacement, though."

"You'll get quite a few extra bodies. I'm calling for help on this one. The other Valley departments are already cooperating, but I want to put together a joint investigative team, put together the best minds in Mesa, Scottsdale, Chandler, Tempe, Glendale, and

Paradise Valley and see what we can come up with. This bastard's going to make a mistake sometime—he has to—and we have to be ready when he does.

"You and I are going to meet with representatives from the other departments tomorrow at eight. We'll go over strategies and tactics and try to do a little brainstorming. You have any ideas you want to bounce off me first?"

"Eight?" Allan said. "Isn't that when I'm supposed to have my press conference?"

Pynchon smiled, but there was little humor in it. "Get the hell out of here," he said. "I don't want to see your ugly goddamn face until tomorrow."

Allan left the captain's office, closing the door behind him.

Another meeting. He was getting sick and tired of meetings. So sick and tired that he sometimes wished he had not graduated to lieutenant. The pay was nice, and he was afforded a certain amount of autonomy in his investigations, but there was a lot of crap he had to put up with, a lot of useless rituals he had to go through, when he just wanted to get out there and do his job.

He walked by Communications, and Yvonne shook her head sympathetically. "Pynchon's really on the warpath today."

Allan smiled at her. "I survived." He ran a hand through his hair, grabbing a handful and holding up a large hank. "Still have my scalp." He continued down the hall, staring down at the squares of white tile beneath his feet. He heard snatches of conversation from the open doors of several offices as he passed by but paid them no heed. He wanted to fall into the old comfortable chair in his office for awhile and stop thinking, relax, rest.

"Allan!"

He looked up at the sound of Thomasson's voice. The beefy detective was hunched over his humming Underwood, obviously typing up some sort of report. He was wearing his battered straw cowboy hat and an incongruous blue business suit. "How do you spell 'salacious'?" he asked.

Allan shook his head. "I don't know. Look it up."

"You think you're the only one working around here? We just rounded up a nest of hookers over on Van Buren and I have, like, six days of paperwork in front of me."

"My heart bleeds for you."

"We picked up your sister there." Thomasson grinned. "She was on her knees, beggin' for my bonedaddy."

Ordinarily, Allan would have risen to the occasion and come up with a suitable retort, but he didn't feel much like joking right now. He waved a dismissive hand at Thomasson and walked into his own office next door.

"She was demanding dick!" Thomasson called out, trying to generate a reaction. "Calling for cock! Pleading for prick!"

Allan closed the door behind him and sat down at his desk. Before him was a list of several people he was supposed to call in conjunction with the investigation. He was already tired and he considered calling Cathy and canceling the date, but he decided not to. He might be beat, but he could legitimately make it tonight, and that might not be true at some future date.

He swiveled in his chair and looked across the street. The park looked green, fresh, and inviting, and he had a sudden urge to walk over there and just sit down on one of the benches and smell the flowers and look up at the sky. But he had no more time for aimless walks than he had for pointless fantasies.

He swiveled his chair back around, picked up the phone, and dialed the first number on the list.

Twenty-nine

Cathy took off fifteen minutes early at Ann's request. "It's a big day," Ann said. "Take some extra time to get ready."

"This isn't my first date," Cathy protested.

"But it's the first one in a long time."

Cathy smiled. "Yeah," she admitted. "It is."

Although Jeff was scheduled to start work at five, he conveniently came in fifteen minutes early, dressed entirely in black, his hair bleached blond. "How do you like it?" he asked, turning around. There was a strategically placed rip in the back of his jacket.

"Wonderful," Cathy said, rolling her eyes.

Ann shook her head. "In twenty years, you're going to look back at pictures of yourself and be ashamed of your own stupidity. Do you realize that?"

"You don't think this is the wave of the future?"

Ann pushed her glasses up the bridge of her nose. "It's already passé. Even in Phoenix."

"Oooooh." Jeff laughed. "You're so cool and hip."

Ann ignored him and went back to the invoices she'd been logging.

Cathy looked up at the clock on the back wall.

Four-forty. She cleared her throat. "I'm taking off," she said. "You two can handle it. Barry said he'd stop by after seven to go over the receipts and collect timecards."

"The big cheese," Jeff said. "Wait'll I tell him you skipped out on us." He grinned.

"Get out of here," Ann told her. "I'll handle this bozo."

"Thanks."

"We'll talk later. I want details."

"A date?" Jeff said. "Our Cathy's actually going on a date?"

"Shut up," Ann told him.

Cathy arrived home early, pulling into the driveway at the same time she ordinarily left the store. Jimmy was out front, as usual, but she explained that she had an important date, and he nodded and said he'd see her tomorrow, pedaling his bike back down the street toward his house.

She walked inside. Her father was sitting in the den, curtains drawn, watching TV. A game show was on, and though she knew he hated game shows, he was pretending to watch this one with interest, not taking his eyes from the screen even after she'd walked into the room. She knew he was purposely ignoring her, trying to goad her into anger, but she refused to take the bait. She lowered herself into the couch. "I have a date tonight," she said.

He did not respond.

"Did you hear what I just said?"

"I heard. What do you want me to do? Jump for joy? Kiss your feet?" He looked at her for the first time, his eyes cold and distant. He turned away. "I'm sorry. Have a good time. Enjoy yourself." The flat tone of his voice belied the sentiments expressed in his words.

"I thought you'd at least be interested. You're always harping about how I should go out more often."

"I am interested."

Did they try to get in your pants?

His attention returned to the game show. "What about dinner? What am I supposed to do? Starve?"

"I'll cook something. You can eat it now or heat it up later."

"Like what?"

"What do you want?"

"I don't know."

"A casserole?"

"I hate casseroles."

"How about a hamburger?"

There was an expression of supreme disgust on his face. "Don't you know how to cook any real food?"

"What is real food?"

"Anything."

She stood up. "I'm not going to put up with this. I have to get ready to go. He's going to pick me up at seven. Do you want me to make you something or not?"

"No."

"Fine." She stood up and started out of the room.

"Am I going to have to meet this asshole?"

Cathy did not answer him but continued down the hall to her bedroom. She closed and locked the door behind her.

Although she put on and took off four blouses, three pairs of pants, and two dresses before finally deciding on what to wear for her date, Cathy was still ready to go more than half an hour before Allan was scheduled to pick her up.

Stepping back from the mirror, she tried to look at herself objectively, to see herself the way Allan would see her. The results were not encouraging. Her nose was too flat. And her hair was dull, the cut boring. She stepped back even further. In the designer jeans she had chosen, her butt looked too big.

She suddenly wished she had picked out something different to wear, but if she made a switch now she would have to change her blouse as well and she did not have enough time to go through that again.

She sat in the den with her father, watching TV, waiting. She tried, initially, to engage him in conversation, to break his mood, but he was silent and stubborn and would not even look at her.

By the time Allan arrived, it was dusk, the sky a husky brownish-orange in the west. She saw his headlights against the curtains, twin white spots of illumination, and she stood up. "I'm going," she announced. Her father said nothing, and she turned her back on him as she left the room. She hurried outside, closing and locking the front door behind her before Allan had a chance to ring the doorbell and invite himself in.

Allan looked good. Almost too good. He was wearing expensive, slightly dressy clothes that made her feel embarrassingly underdressed, as though she should have chosen something more formal. Her hands were sweating, and she surreptitiously wiped them on the sides of her jeans before stretching one out to him.

Allan smiled at her appreciatively as he lightly shook her hand. "You look nice," he said.

He obviously meant it, and she reddened and looked down, painfully aware that she was unused to compliments and did not know how to respond to them. Allan smiled kindly, as if conscious of her discomfort, and walked over to his Bronco, opening the passenger door for her. She got in, and he shut it, walking around and getting in the driver's side. "Having second thoughts?" he asked, putting the key in the ignition and starting the car.

"No," Cathy lied.

He backed out of the driveway and started down the street toward Lincoln.

"Good."

Allan was an experienced conversationalist, his manner relaxed and natural, and the fear she'd had of spending a miserable evening in awkward uncomfortable silence soon evaporated. She had the feeling that even if she were as silent as a fence post, Allan would be able to keep the conversation going and make it seem as though it were the most ordinary situation in the world.

They drove out of her neighborhood and headed down Central, Allan talking as easily as if he'd known her forever, not asking questions about her, not talking about himself, but bringing up unrelated topics he felt might be of interest to both of them.

"Where are we going?" Cathy asked as he pulled onto McDowell, heading east.

"I thought we'd go out to Pinnacle Peak. You ever been there?"

She shook her head. "I've heard of it."

"I think you'll like it. It's a lot of fun. Particularly at this time of year. You can eat on the patio under the stars. They have a country band playing, and you can dance—"

"I don't like country music," she said. "And I don't dance."

Allan laughed. "Neither do I. But it's fun, in context." He turned on the radio. "What type of music do you like? Classical? Jazz?"

"Anything."

"No, it's up to you. I like almost everything. I have some tapes here if you want to look through them."

She found herself grateful for the deepening dusk. She had taken a music appreciation course in college and had enjoyed the classical music she'd been exposed to, but she'd never really followed through on her interest. Jazz was completely foreign to her, the music of another generation. She was obviously dealing with someone far more sophisticated than herself, and the thought scared her, made her feel nervous and under pressure, eroding the confidence she had begun to feel.

He would not let the subject die. "What do you listen to in your car?" he asked. His voice was easy and curious.

"I like The Beatles," she said.

"Who doesn't?" Eyes on the road, he reached into the space between their seats and pulled out what looked like a small briefcase. "Here. Dig through this, see what you can find. I know I have *Abbey Road* and *Rubber Soul* in there someplace."

She searched through his tapes, surprised to find amongst the classical and jazz cassettes music by artists she liked—The Beach Boys, Paul Simon, Joni Mitchell. She found *Rubber Soul* and inserted it in the cassette player, and the familiar sitar strains of "Norwegian Wood" wafted through the speakers, making her feel slightly less self-conscious.

Pinnacle Peak was located in the desert past Scottsdale, almost in Carefree. The drive was long, and though Cathy might earlier have been worried that the trip would be spent in silence, with only music to relieve the tension, she now had no such qualms, and as the lights of the last resorts receded behind them and the bumpy road moved into the darkness of the desert, she found herself loosening up.

They drove past Rawhide, a fake frontier town where stunt shows were performed for tourist families during the day and rowdy dances were held for local rednecks at night, and Allan told her about the time he had taken a date there—and lost her. "She wanted to dance," he said. "I didn't know how, so I just sat at the table and watched her out on the dance floor. I thought I saw her dancing with some goofy-looking guy in a black cowboy hat, but the next time I looked up she was gone. I waited and waited and waited, the band took a break, the dance floor emptied, but she never came back. I ended up eating dinner by myself at McDonald's and going home."

Cathy laughed. "Is that why we're not going to Rawhide?"

He smiled. "You got it."

Pinnacle Peak was at the top of a sandstone ridge and consisted of the restaurant and several small Western buildings. Allan pulled the Bronco in front of a hitching post and walked around to open Cathy's door. He reached for her hand, but she held back, and he politely and quickly withdrew. The air was filled with the smell of barbecued steak and the sound of fast country music, and they walked along the plank porch toward the swinging front doors.

A gun-holstered waitress led them through the restaurant to the patio outside. Here, in a barnlike bandshell, the band was playing, singing their version of "Whisky River." Huge steaks sizzled on a series of long barbecue grills flanking the bandstand. In the distance, Cathy could see the lights of the Valley, saguaro cacti silhouetted against the city backdrop.

They sat down at a table in the corner of the patio furthest from the band, and Cathy looked at the short menu given to them by the waitress, pretending to consider the choices though she was really searching for something to say. She sensed that it was her turn to initiate the conversation, but she couldn't think of what to talk about. It had been a long time since her last date, and she was out of practice. Even at her best, she had never been adept at the rituals of dating, and the lack of recent experience had made her woefully inadequate. As a student, her dates had been other students, and that had at least given them some common ground on which to proceed. But she was coming into this date cold. She knew nothing about Allan. Not really. She knew he was a cop, but that was a subject she wanted to stay away from if possible. She knew he liked art, but though she had taken an art appreciation course during her sophomore year in college and could probably fake her way through a conversation with a layman, she did not know enough to intelligently discuss the subject with someone knowledgeable.

Maybe this was a mistake, she thought. Then she looked up from the menu, saw his interested, caring face, and pushed the thought from her mind.

He folded his menu. "Have you decided?"

"Not yet."

"It's a tough decision: steak, steak, or steak."

"I think I'll take steak. Rare."

He smiled. "Wise decision." He picked up the wine

list, sandwiched between the napkin dispenser and the catsup. "Would you like some wine?"

She shook her head. "I don't drink."

He grinned. " 'Just Say No.' "

The band segued from "Bloody Mary Morning" into "On the Road Again," apparently in the midst of a Willie Nelson medley, and Cathy found herself unconsciously tapping her foot. She had never been a country music fan, but Allan was right. Here, under the stars, in the desert, looking down at the lights of the city, the music seemed somehow appropriate.

The waitress returned to take their orders and gather the menus. "Only one ground rule," Allan said once she'd left. "No shop talk. I don't want to talk about police work or murders or investigations or anything. Deal?"

Cathy nodded, smiling. "Deal. Although—"

"Oh, no," he groaned.

Cathy laughed.

They spent the meal talking mostly about books and movies. Cathy found him surprisingly well read and any stereotypes she'd held about illiterate policemen were quickly dispelled. She also found that they shared an affinity for old musicals and comedies, although he liked horror movies and she couldn't stand them. Despite Allan's ground rule, the talk did eventually turn to police work, and she found herself asking a lot of questions, eager to stamp out with knowledge her emotional biases.

Miss Riley?

She asked how the investigation into Dusty's death was going, and he explained that after the dog had been killed, they'd questioned everyone on the street but found no one who could remember seeing a stranger in the neighborhood.

"Speaking of strange," Cathy said. "Did you talk to Katrina West?"

Allan laughed. "She is a weird one. Wouldn't let us in the house, made us stand on the porch—"

"Did you see her son?"

He nodded. "That's the one who beat up Jimmy, right? From the way Jimmy described him, I expected him to be violent, but he seemed pretty passive."

"He is violent. She keeps him locked up most of the time and won't let him out of the house." She paused. "Which is fine with me."

He raised his eyebrows quizzically.

"Not because Randy's retarded," she explained. "It's just that . . . he scares me." She blushed, aware of how foolish that sounded. "The other night, he snuck into my backyard and was peeking into my window while I was asleep. He scared me to death. I tried to talk to his mother about it, but she won't even answer the door."

He frowned. "You want me to talk to her?"

"No," Cathy said. "That's not necessary. Not yet, at least."

"The Wests are weird," he said. "No doubt about that. But I don't think they had anything to do with Jimmy's dog, do you?"

She shook her head slowly. "No. Not really." She ate a bite of her steak, smiled. "When we were little, we used to think the house was haunted, the one the Wests are living in. A man killed his wife and then himself in the living room. No one's ever stayed there very long."

He grinned. "A haunted house, huh? Katrina West should fit right in." He took a slice of bread from the covered loaf in the basket between them and proceeded to butter it. "What do you make of Al Goldstein?"

"Why?"

He shrugged. "No reason. Humor me."

"I don't like him. I think he's a jerk."

Allan chuckled. "I had the same impression of him."

Cathy told him about the Goldsteins' bitter divorce, about the screaming fights they used to have, about the poor job Mr. Goldstein was now doing in his single-handed attempt to raise Jimmy, about what she considered the man's complete and utter selfishness.

"Did he seem upset to you at all when Dusty was killed?"

"No, he never did like that dog," she said. "Dusty was Jimmy's and Jimmy's alone."

Allan nodded, more to himself than in response to her statement. "That's what I thought."

The talk soon shifted to occupations, and Cathy was afraid that she was going to have to defend her decision to work in a bookstore, to justify her job, but Allan did not pressure her on that point. She did admit that although she enjoyed her work, the money left something to be desired, and that was something he said he could sympathize with. He told her that pay negotiations were coming up for police in the next few months.

"It gets frustrating sometimes, being a public servant," he said, downing the last of his iced tea. "A lot of people seem to be completely ignorant of the way government works. Our salaries are paid for by taxes, so people think we're getting a free ride. They resent it when we demand salaries commensurate with those in the private sector. They think we're leeching off their money. They don't realize that they pay the salaries of those in the private sector, too. When they plop down a buck fifty for a package of cake mix, they're actually paying about a quarter for the mix itself, a quarter for the advertising campaign, and a dollar to pay the salaries of the people who work for the company. Since those charges are hidden, people don't mind. But when it comes to paying that money in the form of a sales tax, they scream bloody murder. They'll pay more than what a product's worth to finance the company, but they object to an extra cent added on for our salaries." He smiled self-consciously. "Sorry. I didn't mean to get up on my soapbox here."

"Nothing to be sorry for."

"I just resent it when some rent-a-cop pulls down

twice as much as a real policeman for patrolling parties and guarding hotel lobbies, while we're out there getting shot at, killed, and abused for peanuts."

"You can always switch jobs."

"That's not the point. Someone would still have to fill my position, and that someone should be paid what he's worth. You know, if each person had to pay for his own private security force, his own library, his own street repairs, his own education, it would cost a hell of a lot more than he's shelling out in taxes."

Cathy laughed. "I'm convinced! I'm convinced!"

"Sorry," he apologized.

"So why are you a cop? I mean, you don't really seem the type."

"The type?"

"You know what I mean."

"You mean I don't fit your stereotype."

She colored, embarrassed. "Yeah, I guess that's what I mean. I'm sorry, I just—"

Allan smiled. "You've just seen too many movies."

"Maybe so." She was silent for a moment. "But why did you become a cop? You obviously have other interests. What made you go into this field?"

He shrugged. "I'm not sure. I've wondered myself sometimes."

"But you like your job."

"I'm not sure." He thought for a minute, then licked his lips. His eyes met hers. "You know, my first month on the force I rode with Jeff Herzog, an older policeman, and we were patrolling an area near the edge of the desert toward Sunnyslope when we saw an abandoned car off to the side of the road. We didn't really think anything of it, but when we saw it again the day after, we decided to investigate." He looked over his glass at her. "We found a dead body lying near a cottonwood tree just past the abandoned car. It was mid-August, the height of the monsoons, and he'd been there for awhile, and by the time we got close to him, we were both gagging from the smell. The guy was lying flat on his back in the sand, and his arms were frozen in a position above his chest, his hands pointing toward his head. There was a rifle nearby, a few feet in front of him. He'd tried to kill himself by putting the rifle in his mouth and pulling the trigger, and he'd blown a hole through his brain and out the back of his head." Allan licked his lips. "Only he hadn't died right away. He'd dropped the rifle and staggered backwards before falling onto the sand. His arms were frozen in that position because he'd been reaching for his head."

"My God," Cathy breathed.

Allan nodded. "The place was buzzing with flies. You could hear them, louder than cicadas. We radioed the call in and waited for the ambulance, and when it arrived, we put him on the stretcher. He was bloated, but his body was stiff as a board, and we picked him up by grabbing the front of his shirt and plopping him down. When we lifted him, there was blood and pieces of dried brain all over the sand, like brown glue. The flies . . . there were flies crawling all over the back of his head, in and out of the hole—that's where the buzzing was coming from. We put him in the ambulance and drove to the mortuary and brought him in, but the mortician saw the flies and told us to take him out. So we waited outside, on the doorstep, with this bloody corpse, until the mortician came out with a can of Raid. He spent about five minutes spraying it into the hole in the guy's head to kill the flies."

"Jesus." Cathy looked at Allan, trying to concentrate on his face, trying to blot out the images in her mind. The fact that he not only tolerated this sort of occupation but had actively sought it out should have scared her, but somehow it didn't.

"So you became a cop to stop things like that?" she said. "To stop violence? To catch the people who do it?"

Allan's mouth was about to say yes, but as he looked into her eyes, he seemed to change his mind. "I don't know," he said. "Maybe."

* * *

By the time Allan finally dropped her off at home, it was past midnight. Porch lights were on, house lights were off, and the only movement in the otherwise empty neighborhood was the slow steady crawl of a street sweeper several blocks south.

Allan got out of the car, ran around the front, and helped her out. Cathy bowed graciously. "Thank you, sir."

"Don't call me 'sir.' " Allan shivered in mock horror. "It makes me feel like I'm at work."

Cathy laughed. "I had a good time," she said.

"Me too."

There was an awkward silence, the first of the evening, and Cathy felt suddenly warm. This had always been the part of the date she dreaded most. No matter how the date went, the good-night kiss was always a part of the ritual, the token payment she must make for an evening's food and entertainment. This time, however, she did not feel the familiar sense of obligation, the expectancy of demand. Instead, she felt somewhat anxious, almost hopeful, as though she wanted to kiss him. But there was still an awkwardness, a nervousness, and she could tell from her sweaty palms that she was tense.

Allan must have sensed this, for he simply reached for her hand, held it and stroked it softly. "Things are kind of hectic right now," he said. "As I'm sure you know. I don't have a lot of free time. But if I do get a free night in the near future, I was wondering if you'd like to go out again."

Cathy was aware that her heart was pounding, almost loudly enough to be heard. Allan's fingers felt smooth and good on her hand. She did not trust herself to say anything, so she simply nodded.

Allan smiled and turned to go. "I'll call you sometime in the next few days," he said.

She reached out and grabbed his hand again, giving it a squeeze. "I'll be looking forward to it."

I'll be looking forward to it? Had she really said something that clichéd and that stupid? She had, but

Allan didn't seem to mind. He got into his Bronco, backed out of the driveway, and waved good-bye as he drove away.

She let herself into the house. Her father was asleep, and she tiptoed down the hall to her room so as not to disturb him. She looked at the window next to her bed, thought of Randy West, and pulled the curtains tight, making sure that there was not even a crack to peek through. She took off her clothes, slipped into her nightgown, and got into bed. The date had gone well, much better than she'd dared hope, and her head was filled with scenes from the evening that she was rerunning in the theater of her mind. She was still reliving the date when she fell asleep.

She dreamed of David.

He stood in the doorway, wearing nothing but a policeman's cap. Between his legs, sprouting directly from the thin tangle of pubic hair, was a worm. Pink and slimy, it wiggled randomly in the air. Then David caught sight of her and in that instant the worm curved in her direction. She could see its two hideous bulging eyes and, beneath them, a wickedly grinning mouth filled with razor-sharp teeth. She heard in the room the buzzing of flies, and when David opened his mouth, she could see through it to the hole in the back of his head.

She woke up sweating, and although she remembered the dream immediately upon waking in the morning, she could recall only vague images by breakfast, and by the time she got into the car to go to work, the dream had faded away completely.

Thirty

Katrina arrived home from work just after noon. The day was a scorcher, and rivulets of sweat cut through the light dusting of flour that covered her face and arms. She'd been up since two, baking since three, and she knew that Randy was probably starving by now.

Starving and roasting.

Why the hell had they moved to Phoenix?

She quickly unlocked the three deadbolts on the front door and let herself into the house. Sure enough, the air was stifling, unmoving, and overheated. She could hear Randy bellowing from the back room, his voice high, tinged with panic.

Although her muscles were sore, her brain dog-tired, she hurried down the hall. Slowly, cautiously, she pushed open the door to Randy's room. There was a loud crack as the soccer ball hit the wall.

"Randy!" she said sternly.

He whimpered contritely, and she pushed the door open all the way. He was on the bed, sitting up, the leash around his neck still secured to the bolt in the floor. He looked up at her with his sad, hurt eyes, and she immediately felt guilty for chastising him.

"Randy," she said, sitting down next to him and giving him a hug. "I'm sorry."

"Ma!" he cried. "Ma! Ma! Ma! Mamamamama-mamama!"

She held him close, and she found herself thinking about what had happened last week, about what she'd done. She closed her eyes against the memory. It had been wrong, and she'd known it had been wrong, but she'd had no other choice. Part of her thought she should be punished, wanted to be punished, but the stronger, more resolutely survivalist part of her was determined never to let anyone know what had happened.

She knew that if she were caught, Randy would be taken away from her and probably forced to live in an institution, and the thought that that might happen made her feel like crying. She held him tighter. He would never be able to survive something like that.

Neither would she.

Randy screamed in her ear, and as suddenly as it had come, her melancholy mood evaporated. He screamed again, and she laughed. He always knew how to cheer her up.

She gave his shoulder a squeeze. Beneath his shirt, she could feel hardness. Muscle. It was not something she had noticed before, and it made her feel strange and a little uncomfortable. He was growing up, she realized. It seemed like only yesterday that his body was soft, pliant, nothing but skin and babyfat. She squeezed harder. Definitely muscles. He was maturing.

Pretty soon she was going to have to start being careful.

She unhooked the leash from Randy's collar, then took the collar off as well. She ran a hand through his hair and smiled at him. He smiled back.

"Time to eat," she said. "Food. Lunch."

"Fa!" he cried. "Fa! Fa! Fa! Fa! Fa!"

"Yes, food. Come on." She led him to the kitchen, where she made him a peanut butter and jelly sandwich. She dropped the sandwich on the floor, pressing it down with her foot, the way he liked it, and he fell to his hands and knees, shoving his face against the food and pushing it into the corner before attacking it.

Katrina smiled indulgently as she watched him eat. She was standing in the doorway, and when she saw, out of the corner of her eye, a shadow pass in front of the closed curtains, she glanced back toward the living room. She waited, but the shadow did not reappear.

She looked around the room, her gaze taking in the unopened boxes stacked next to the brown thrift-store couch, the shadeless lamp on the TV tray table. She should feel embarrassed, Katrina knew. She should feel ashamed. But she didn't. Her house was ugly and she knew it was ugly, but she really didn't care. She was aware of the fact that other women made an effort to decorate their homes, trying their best to make their surroundings look nice. But she'd always found such action useless, the purposeful arrangement of items in a house a futile exercise. Here, as before, she'd simply left her belongings where the moving men had set them down.

Except in Randy's room.

Yes, she had made an effort to fix up Randy's room. A pleasant environment, though meaningless to her, was important to the development of a growing child. And she wanted her son to develop as normally as possible.

Katrina wiped the sweat off her forehead, and her fingers came back with wet white flour on them. She wiped her fingers on her pants. She'd had a lot of crappy jobs over the years, but working in a bakery had to be the worst. The hours were bad, the pay was shit. The people were assholes. Sometimes she thought she'd like to be a nurse again. It would be nice to have a real job, a job where she could actually do something, actually accomplish something.

But background checks were done on applicants for nursing positions. And in these computerized times, those checks were damn thorough. They'd find out immediately who she was, what she'd done.

She couldn't allow that.

Besides, with her headaches getting as bad as they were, she wasn't sure if she'd be able to successfully carry out her duties as a nurse. And she would not even attempt the job if she could not perform it successfully. She did have her pride.

"Fa!" Randy said. "Fa! Fa! Fa!"

She looked back toward the kitchen. Randy was already through eating. There was only a small wet spot on the floor where he'd licked up the excess food, and a light smearing of jelly around his mouth and nose. He stood up, and she got a washcloth from the sink to wipe off his face. "Let's get you cleaned up, and then we'll play," she said. "Okay?"

"Pa!" he said. "Pa! Papapapapa!"

She began to clean his face.

Thirty-one

The eight detectives sat around the long conference table slouched in their chairs, simultaneously stirring or drinking their cups of coffee, looking at the print-outs before them, and facing Allan at the head of the table.

"I know of nothing even remotely similar to this situation," Allan said. "Prolificacy such as this usually burns itself out. Patterns emerge quickly, murderers make mistakes, perps are caught. But that hasn't happened here." He took a deep breath. "I don't know, maybe it's time we changed our assumptions. Until now, we've been acting on the theory that these murders were committed by a single individual. But the dissimilarity of the killings, combined with the specialized expertise required for each one, suggest that maybe we should be thinking in terms of a gang. I don't think there's any question in anyone's mind that these killings are all related, but it's possible that there's a group of murderers out there, each of whose members possess a specific skill."

Pynchon, at the foot of the table, cleared his throat, hawking loudly. "I think Allan has a point. 'Phoenix Fiend' crap aside, there's no way in hell a single sicko could be doing all this and getting away with it without leaving so much as a smudged print behind. Not unless he's the Albert-fucking-Einstein of crime. And if he was, there'd be a record of him somewhere. Shit like this doesn't go unnoticed."

"But what kind of gang are we talking about?" asked Hank Reed, the detective on loan from Tempe. "Moonlighting surgeons? I mean, come on, street gangs don't usually go in for murders this complicated. This stuff's a little out of the league of your usual crackhead."

"No one said anything about crackheads or street gangs." Allan looked down at the papers before him. "Whether these murders are being committed by a single individual or a group of murderers, we're dealing with something extraordinary here. I don't think we should let our usual judgments or perceptions influence us. We're in uncharted territory, and the more we keep our wits about us, the less we rely on SOP, the more open we are to new ideas, the more chance we'll have of a breakthrough."

"Damn right," Pynchon said.

"But that still doesn't get us anywhere," said Reed.

"No," Allan admitted, "it doesn't. Right now, we're relegated to following up rumors by our usual streeters, fine-toothing the autopsy reports, doing background checks, and keeping a high profile so everyone knows we're out there. The canvassing in the crime areas has proved to be almost worthless, as has computer cross-referencing."

"But I still want to know why a murderer would go to this much trouble," Reed said. "What's the point?"

"There is no point," Pynchon replied. "The fucker's crazy."

"Then there must be some crazy reason for this. Otherwise, why make such an effort? Why not just kill the victims and leave it at that? It seems to me that if we could learn how this guy thinks, if we could get on his wavelength—"

The captain snorted. "You're thinking like a rational person. There are no reasons here. Insanity has no reason. There's not even a twisted logic in some of these minds. There's no logic at all."

"If the murderer was so crazy as to be incoherent, he would have screwed up somewhere along the line. We would have caught him by now."

"Obviously not," Pynchon said dryly. He stood. "I think we've chatted enough here, girls. We've said all we need to say and we're not going to learn any more by hashing over semantics. Like Allan said, we're batting oh-for-five. I want you to get your asses out there. I don't want our next clue to be a stiff. Let's try to nab this fucker—" he looked at Allan "—or these fuckers, before they hit again."

He walked out of the room.

The meeting was adjourned.

"Captain's pissed."

"No shit, Sherlock." Allan popped an aspirin and handed the bottle back to Yvonne before taking a sip from his coffee cup.

Thomasson grinned. "You don't seem like a ray of sunshine today yourself."

"What the hell do you expect? Not everyone gets to spend their time picking up prostitutes on street corners, you know."

Thomasson's smile shifted down to a frown. "Well, not all of us get a chance to save Western Civilization, either. Jesus, Allan, ease up."

"Ease up?"

"Yeah, ease up."

"Don't you pay attention to what goes on around you?"

"Yeah, but I don't take it personally. You're really letting this shit get to you."

"You're damn right I am. Did you see Bob's body? Did you see what was done to it?"

"You're right, Allan. You're right." Thomasson held up his hands in a gesture of surrender. He rolled his eyes at Yvonne and walked away, shaking his head.

Allan stood there for a moment, then looked down at the dispatcher. "Do you think I'm taking it too personally?"

"Yeah, but how could you not?"

"At least someone's in my corner." Allan picked up his sheaf of folders. "Thanks for the aspirin."

Yvonne smiled. "No problemo."

The temperature rose perceptibly as Allan walked back toward his office. One of the air conditioning units—the one servicing the entire east side of the building—had crapped out yesterday, and despite the fact that a team of repairmen had spent the morning atop a series of awkwardly placed ladders, the upper halves of their bodies buried in ceiling ducts, the problem still had not been solved.

Allan wiped the sweat from his forehead as he opened his office door. "Keep up the good work," he said sarcastically to the pair of legs protruding from a square in the hall ceiling.

The repairman did not reply.

Inside his office, the stale smell of leftover lunch—a Der Wienerschnitzel chili cheese dog and fries—permeated the closed room. He could still see the food lying half-eaten on top of the papers in the trash can as he walked past. Grimacing with disgust, he pulled some Kleenexes from the box on the shelf and draped them over the piece of hot dog and bun. He might have to smell the food, but he sure as hell didn't want to look at it.

He dropped into his chair and glanced down at the desk in front of him. On his desktop lay photos of the murders, graphic details blown up to eight-by-ten. The pictures had originally been arranged chronologically, by set, but he had lain them out in a different order, grouping them by aesthetic relationship. In black and white, blood did not look nearly so real, nearly as bad. Many of the shots were enlarged and cropped in such a way that they were completely disassociated from their original subjects and looked almost artistic. He would not even have known what some of them depicted had he not seen their real-life antecedents.

But he had seen.

And he did know.

He had arranged the photos the way he had because the thought had crossed his mind, more than once, that the killer was a deranged aesthete, some sort of perverse purist to whom murder was an art form and its victims his creations. It was a ludicrous thought, the stuff of B movies, but it kept returning, would not go away, and it seemed to him to make a type of illogical sense. Despite his rational and believable arguments that the murders had been committed by a group or gang, in his heart he did not believe it true. To him, there was only a single killer, a lone insane genius of death.

He leaned back in his chair and looked up at the small holes in the squares of the ceiling. He'd been living, sleeping, eating, breathing these murders for so damn long that it was no wonder he was beginning to turn the whole thing into a movie in his mind.

At least he was smart enough to feign rationality in front of his coworkers.

Allan's jaw hurt and a muscle in the back of his neck throbbed painfully. The aspirin still hadn't taken effect. He closed his eyes and tried to relax for a moment, tried to clear his mind, but found himself thinking about his dream of the night before. His dreams were almost always abstract, involving places that did not exist, people who never were. In the few dreams he remembered, he was always a confused spectator in a surrealistic universe, taking in what was happening around him, even taking part, but never understanding. He had not, to his knowledge, ever dreamed about someone he knew.

But last night he had dreamed about Cathy.

It was the first dream since Whitehead's murder that had not been a nightmare, and for that he was grateful. He and Cathy had been lost in a forest with night coming on and no one around for miles. Cathy had been scared at first, but it had been a peculiarly benign wilderness, a Walt Disney forest, the only animals small cute squirrels and cuddly bunnies, the vegetation soft and round and non-threatening. Even the darkness had been nice: a friendly black sky pointilistically dotted with millions of tiny blinking stars. Juvenile as it was, and embarrassed as he was to admit it, Cathy had spent a large part of the dream naked. He was not sure how or why—the details were fuzzy—but she had been forced to abandon her clothes, and they'd had to snuggle together for warmth. She was gorgeous nude—a brunette Botticelli Venus—and he could see her even now, her pale skin smooth and soft, her body perfectly proportioned. Her breasts had been small and pointed, with large nipples, and the sparse hair between her legs had been shaped in a perfect black triangle.

He found himself wondering what she really looked like naked.

Why was he thinking about Cathy when he was supposed to be concentrating on the murders?

Allan sighed, opening his eyes. He often thought of personal trivia when he was supposed to be paying attention to important business, and it was a habit—or character trait—that disturbed him. It seemed to him that he didn't have the concentration to do the sort of job he expected of himself. He found it impossible to concentrate solely on work when he was on duty, or to completely leave work behind when he was at home. The two always overlapped. That shouldn't be the case. On something like this, in particular, he should be able to put aside personal matters for at least the eight or ten hours he was on duty, to give that time completely to his work.

What the hell was wrong with him?

He sat up. This situation was taking its toll. He'd never felt as tense, insecure, and under pressure as he had these past few weeks. Ordinarily, he was an easygoing guy, fairly laid back, but lately he'd been short with his coworkers, impatient with strangers, a basic all-around prick.

The only person who seemed to be exempt from this behavior was Cathy. He felt relaxed with her, comfortable. Perhaps it was because she was out of the loop, not a cop, not someone involved in even the fringes of law enforcement. He didn't feel that she was judging him, second-guessing him, evaluating his handling of the case. She also seemed to be in even worse emotional shape than he was, and instead of feeling defensive with her, he felt protective toward her. And that was nice.

The phone rang and Allan jumped, startled. He knew that something had happened—something bad— while he'd been self-indulgently sitting here, and he instantly grabbed the receiver, hoping he'd be able to hear over the pounding of blood in his eardrums. *Please God,* he thought, *let it not be another one.* "Lieutenant Grant," he said.

"This is Dobrinin."

"What is it?" he asked. "What's happened?"

"Nothing." The policeman's voice was tired. "I'm just checking in."

Allan closed his eyes, leaning back in his chair, taking a deep grateful breath. "Good," he said, and the relief he felt was almost physical. "Good."

Thirty-two

The air was cool and wet, and at first Cathy's dream adjusted its specifics to accommodate the change in temperature—her romantic evening with Allan shifting its locale from Phoenix to Aspen, from summer to fall—but gradually the air became too cold, the dream broke apart, and she awoke.

On the grass.

In the backyard.

She blinked, closed her eyes, opened them again, hoping that this was still part of a dream, but underneath her head she felt not pillow cloth but wet ground, and when she opened her eyes again she saw blue sky instead of ceiling.

She sat up, her toes touching damp dirt, her fingers dewy grass stalks. Wetness had soaked through the thin material of her nightgown. The back door of the house was open, and she could clearly see a trail across the lawn where she had walked before lying down.

Sleepwalking.

The fear was almost overpowering. She quickly sprang to her feet and glanced around the yard, as if looking for someone, as if afraid of being caught. The

fear was tremendous, much worse than the simple terror of physical injury, because what she feared was
not outside herself but within. This was not something
she could hide from or escape from, this was a part
of her. And the most frightening aspect of it was that
it was something over which she had no control. Not
only could she not prevent it from occurring, she was
not even aware when it was occurring. Only after the
fact was she presented with an outline of the situation,
and then she was forced to guess or reconstruct what
had actually happened.

Why was she doing this? What in God's name was
wrong with her?

Cathy walked back across the yard to the door,
going inside and closing the door behind her. The
clock on the mantle said that it was six o'clock, and
the silence in the house told her that her father was
not yet awake. At least that was some consolation.
She prayed that he hadn't heard her sleepwalking in
the night.

She went into the kitchen, took a glass from the
cupboard, and filled it with water from the sink. Her
hand shook as she lifted the glass to her lips. She
looked at the black plastic kitchen radio. The thought
suddenly occurred to her that the sleepwalking had
begun at approximately the same time as the murders,
and she almost dropped the glass. She put the glass
down carefully on the counter next to the sink. That
was just stupid. It was a coincidence. The events were
entirely unrelated. She put both hands on the counter,
steadying herself. Now she was being crazy.

Wasn't she?

She looked down at her hands, saw dirt beneath her
fingernails. What had she been doing when the old
man had been killed? The first woman? Dusty? Everyone else? She'd been sleeping when some had taken
place, had been at work when the others had occurred.
The idea that she'd been sleeping when some of the
killings had taken place did not reassure her, but the
fact that she'd been at the store, had been seen by

other people, her presence verified, when some of the murders had happened made her feel better. She couldn't possibly be responsible for any of those deaths. And if she hadn't committed those murders, she hadn't committed any. They'd all been done by the same person.

But what if her memories of being at work were false memories? What if she'd really been somewhere else and just thought she remembered being at the store?

Now she was reaching, looking for a way to bend the facts to fit her theory. She obviously had some problems to work out, even after all these years, but she was not a murderer. She was not now and had never been a violent person. She never even had aggressive thoughts.

Really? a voice inside her said. She suddenly remembered an image from an old nightmare: herself, with a knife, slashing at a naked boy who looked remarkably like David.

Looked like David.

But was not.

She pushed the thought from her mind. She was just being stupid.

Crazy.

She did not have a violent bone in her body. There was no way she could ever harm or hurt another human being. She couldn't even bring herself to kill bugs—if she found spiders or beetles in the house she invariably scooped them up with a newspaper and threw them outside instead of smashing them or spraying them.

But the unease remained, and she walked back into her room troubled, leaving behind a trail of faint dewy footprints.

Thirty-three

"Pussy!"

"Oh, shit," Paul said under his breath. "Oh, shit."

Jimmy kept walking, not daring to turn around, pretending he hadn't heard anything.

"Hey, you! Pussy!"

Jimmy kept his eyes on the crosswalk up ahead. If he could just make it up to the edge of those yellow lines, to the curb where the old crossing guard sat in his sagging lawn chair, he'd be safe. Beyond the crosswalk was school. Sanctuary.

"What're we going to do?" Paul whispered, panicked. "They're going to get us."

"Walk fast," Jimmy told him. "And don't look back." His voice made him sound a lot cooler, a lot braver than he was. Inside, his heart was pounding crazily, and he could feel the trembling in his hands although the schoolbooks he was carrying weighed them down and kept them from visibly shaking. The kids in the crowd around them, behind them, were already whispering, talking, and he could hear the embarrassed excited giggles of some of the girls.

"Your ass is grass!"

There was the sound of sudden footsteps on the

sidewalk behind him, loud booted footsteps, running, accelerating.

Samson and Halback were going to jump him from behind.

Jimmy ran. Paul screamed, dropping his lunch sack, and ran too, following the two of them dashing past houses, dodging around groups of other students, trying desperately to reach the crossing guard and safety. Jimmy was already out of breath, and he could feel his muscles straining, his legs tiring. He was not used to exercise of any sort, but fear and adrenaline kept him moving at a speed that would have impressed even the athletes in his class.

Then he was pushed from behind and he dropped his books as he fell sprawling to the sidewalk. He was not quick or coordinated enough to put his arms out in front of him to cushion his fall, and his face hit the cement, upper and lower teeth slamming together with a loud bone crack that jarred his entire head. Hot blood gushed from his nose, flowing over his lips and chin.

Paul was still running. Through the blur of pain and even from this angle, Jimmy could see his friend's sneakered feet speeding toward the crossing guard at the end of the block.

A hard kick landed against Jimmy's right side, a powerful blow that sunk deep into his flesh and took all the breath from his body. He simultaneously doubled up in agony and rolled over to avoid the next kick, trying desperately to suck air back into his lungs. He couldn't breathe. Gulping and gasping like a beached fish, he squinted against the morning sun, expecting to see both Halback and Samson, but instead he saw only Halback glaring down at him.

"We told you we'd get you, pussy." The older boy smiled, a triumphant grin filled with malice. "This'll teach you not to fuck with us."

A crowd had gathered, and among the kids surrounding him Jimmy recognized Tina Papatos, Donna Tucker, and two other girls from his class. He would have expected to see sympathy in their faces, or at least understanding, but the girls were smiling and their smiles were derisive and he could see the scorn in their eyes. He wanted to be brave, wanted to suffer this humiliation with dignity if he could not escape or fight back, but hot tears of shame were already streaming down his face and he was crying.

"Ooooh," Halback whined in a mocking, affected voice. "Is little baby crying?" He bent down and grinned at Jimmy. "Is poor baby hurt?"

Jimmy tried to stop the tears but they kept coming. He heard a boy snicker. He heard Tina giggle.

"Get up," Halback said.

Jimmy remained unmoving, tasting blood, tasting tears.

"Come on, little girl."

Halback bent down again and was about to grab Jimmy's hair when a huge hand clamped over the bully's shoulder and an adult voice said, "What's going on here?"

Behind Halback, Jimmy saw the crossing guard, and he had never been so happy to see anyone in his life. Although the entire right side of his body hurt from being kicked, a deep pain that seemed to echo in each of his organs, Jimmy forced himself to sit up. He wiped a hand across his face, and it came back wet and red with blood.

How could they laugh at him when he was bleeding?

He scanned the crowd, but the circle of students had grown and he no longer saw the faces of his classmates. His entire head hurt, and when he wiped his face again, he felt strange bumps and swells. Pain flared in his jaw.

Where was Paul? Jimmy stood, wincing at the pain, trying to hold back the flood of new tears that was threatening to escape, and looked around, but his friend had not come back with the crossing guard.

Then he saw Paul, and a warm feeling of gratitude coursed through him. Paul was hurrying down the sidewalk toward him—bringing along Mr. Miller, the vice principal. He smiled through his pain. It was a brave thing that his friend had done. If, before, Paul had been in danger of being attacked by Halback and Samson by virtue of his association with Jimmy, he was now most definitely marked. He had taken action on his own. He had brought in adults. He had fought back to protect his friend. Jimmy had never felt prouder of anyone in his life. Paul had known the consequences of his action and he had done it anyway, and at that moment there was no one in the world whom Jimmy would have rather had as his best friend.

Paul's eyes widened when he saw Jimmy, saw the blood; guilt and hurt, and pain and anger all registering on his face.

Jimmy smiled. "I'm okay," he said, dabbing the blood from his mouth with the back of his hand. "I'm fine." His voice sounded raspy and shaky.

"What happened here?" Mr. Miller demanded.

"It's not school property," Halback said. "You can't do anything to me."

"You want to join your friend in a suspension?" the vice principal said.

"He was beating up this boy here," the crossing guard explained, nodding toward Jimmy.

Mr. Miller looked from Halback to Jimmy and back to Halback again. "I want to see both of you boys in my office," he said. He nodded toward Jimmy. "But first I want you to see the nurse."

"I'm fine," Jimmy repeated, although he felt far from fine.

"We'll let the nurse decide."

"I was a witness," Paul said. "I saw the whole thing."

"You'd better come, too, then," the vice principal told him.

"You're dead!" Halback yelled, pointing. "You're both dead!"

The crossing guard and Mr. Miller turned scowling faces toward Halback.

Paul flipped off the older boy behind the backs of the adults.

"I saw that!" Halback yelled. "I saw that! You're not getting away with it!"

Jimmy looked incredulously at his friend. Paul looked back at him and smiled. "I'm in it this far," he said. "Might as well go all the way."

"Might as well," Jimmy agreed. He wiped the blood from his nose, held up his own middle finger, and grinned.

Thirty-four

Jeff called in sick five minutes before he was scheduled to work, his whispered croak an obviously
feigned voice of illness, and Ann grimaced disgustedly
as she listened to Cathy's side of the conversation. She
was talking even before Cathy had hung up the phone.
"I told you, didn't I?"

"You're right."

"You want to bet he's at that concert tonight?"

"We both know he will be. But what do you want
to do? Tell Barry to fire him? Don't tell me you've
never called in sick when something important's
come up."

"I never have," Ann said defensively. "I've traded
hours, but I've never called in sick."

"Look, it's not that big a deal."

Ann ran a hand through her hair. "I just don't like
that guy. He annoys the hell out of me." She leaned
against the counter, sighing. "I'll stay, I guess. I'll just
postpone my date and—"

"Oh, no you won't," Cathy said.

"It's all right."

"No, it's not. I'll stay and close. I don't have any

plans tonight." She smiled shyly. "Besides, I may need you to return the favor one of these days."

"Our Cathy's finally entering the singles scene!"

"Very funny."

"Playing the dating game!"

"Knock it off."

Ann turned and looked up at the clock behind the counter. "Are you sure you don't need me?"

"I'm sure."

"Because if I'm not staying, I'd better get going."

"Get out of here, then."

The last hour and a half was slow. A few customers trickled in—a couple of lone browsers who read silently in the aisles, two busy yuppies who strode quickly to the books they wanted and bought them— but for the most part the store was dead. Cathy counted her change early, stacked the bills, and totaled the receipts. At five to nine, she switched the sign in the front window from "Open" to "Closed" and, before checking each aisle and clearing the store, locked the door so it could not be opened from the outside.

She turned off the back lights, leaving on only the fluorescent safeties, and the store's illumination was instantly halved. The cutting of the lights usually let stragglers know it was time to go, but, just to make sure, she walked past the magazines and around the front counter to double-check. She started, as always, with the west wall. The Biography/Nonfiction aisle was empty, as was the Religion/Philosophy aisle, but there was a lone man standing at the end of the Occult/New Age aisle, reading in the half-light.

She stared for a moment at the man.

Mr. Goldstein.

Cathy felt a chill pass through her. She had not seen Jimmy's father enter the store, and she had not left the front counter since Ann left. That meant that he had to have come in over two hours ago. Her mouth was suddenly dry. To her knowledge, Mr. Goldstein had never even been in the bookstore before.

What did he want?

And why wasn't he leaving?

Cathy cleared her throat loudly. "Excuse me," she said. "Mr. Goldstein? The store's closing now."

Jimmy's father looked up, but didn't seem to recognize her. He stared at her, through her, past her, then returned to the book he was reading.

Cathy swallowed hard, her heart pounding. There was no reason for her to be scared, there was nothing unusual here, not really, but she found herself already planning on what she would say to the police when she called and told them that a customer refused to leave the store. She found herself planning an escape route. Just in case.

Where did Jimmy think his dad was right now?

Cathy forced herself to move away, to pretend that nothing was wrong, to act as though she was efficiently in charge of the store and that all of this was routine. She continued on her rounds, checking the next aisle, the Fine Arts aisle. Empty. The Fiction aisle. Empty. The Children's aisle. Empty.

She realized as she looked down the empty last aisle of the store that she was alone in the building with Mr. Goldstein.

She stopped walking, stood there for a moment trying to force her staccato breaths into some semblance of a normal rhythm. Had she heard the man leave? She tried to convince herself that she had, tried to believe that he had left the store behind her back, but she didn't think it had happened. There had been no sound of footsteps on the floor, no jingling of the small Soleri bells attached to the door. She held her breath, listening, but the store was silent.

She was frightened. The idea that the man was still standing there, waiting at the far end of the aisle in the empty store, sent a wave of cold coursing through her.

This is stupid, she told herself. *Stop being a baby.*

You're not being a baby, another part of her said. *Run. Get out.*

She walked slowly toward the center row, forcing

her feet to move forward. Reaching the Occult/New Age aisle, she looked between the bookshelves, preparing herself for the worst. But it was empty.

Mr. Goldstein was gone.

The book he had been reading was shut and on the floor, and she hurried down the aisle to put it back on the shelf. She glanced at the title as she picked it up: *Witchcraft and Ritual Killings.*

Cathy quickly deposited the cash, checks, and receipts in the safe, turned off all of the safeties but the window night lights, and locked the door on her way out.

The parking lot, thankfully, was well lit and was still full—one of the advantages of being in a shopping center with a major grocery store. Around her, couples and families pushed shopping carts and opened car doors, and she felt a little better, a little less afraid.

On the way out to her car, she passed a red Corvette with normal plates parked in a blue-marked handicapped spot. A sticker on the back window of the sportscar read: "Clean & Sober Since 1989." Underneath that, someone had taped a sheet of white paper on which was written: "Asshole Since Birth."

Cathy had to smile. She too hated people who took advantage of handicapped spaces.

The note further bolstered her confidence, and by the time she reached her car, she had nearly forgotten about Mr. Goldstein standing in the dark at the end of the aisle, reading about ritual murders.

Nearly forgotten.

But not quite.

She checked her backseat to make sure it was empty before getting into the car, and, once inside, she quickly locked the door before putting on her seatbelt.

Halfway down Lincoln, Cathy saw the figure standing in the middle of the street. It turned awkwardly around, head moving as if searching for something. Suddenly caught in Cathy's headlights, the figure hurried over to the curb.

Cathy slowed her car.

Katrina West, wearing a tightly tied bathrobe and yellow crocheted slippers, her hair tangled and frazzled and sleep tousled, was standing on the corner, looking frantically left and right. She seemed at once panicked and confused.

Cathy pulled her car next to the curb, worried. This close, she could see traces of a white powder which looked like flour on the older woman's face. The powder accentuated wrinkles, made lines seem deeper than they were, etched an emotion of desperate worry onto the history of hardness that made up Katrina's features.

"Is everything okay?" Cathy asked.

"He's gone," Katrina said. Her eyes were wild, afraid. "I was sleeping and I forgot to lock the door and now he's gone."

"Who? Randy?"

"He's gone!"

"I'm sure he's—"

"It's my fault! It's all my fault!"

Cathy shifted the car into Park. "I'll help you look if you want—"

"No!" the woman said, and she backed away from the car as though it was a dangerous animal.

"I don't mind," Cathy said. "Really." She got out of the car and stepped around the hood onto the sidewalk.

"No!" Katrina grabbed Cathy's arm, squeezing, her fingernails biting into flesh. "I said no!"

Cathy pulled away, jerking back her arm, surprised and frightened by the vehement craziness of the woman's reaction. Blood welled immediately from twin trails of fingernail scratches on her skin. The thought came to her that Katrina was high, on drugs, and she quickly moved back behind the car for protection.

"Leave me alone!"

"Fine," Cathy said placatingly. "Okay." She got back into the car, closed the window, locked the door.

Katrina came running around to the driver's side,

knocking on the window. Protruding from the deep pocket in her bathrobe was the smooth wooden handle of a carving knife. "Don't tell anybody what happened!" she yelled. "You can't tell anybody what happened!"

Cathy put the car into gear and pulled away, watching in her rearview mirror as Katrina again wandered into the middle of the street, looking dazed and lost and frightened.

There was a dust storm that night, a towering wall of wind and sand that pushed east from the Papago reservation through Scottsdale and into Phoenix. Watching TV, Cathy saw the familiar warning band flash across the bottom of the screen: STRONG WIND WARNINGS ARE IN EFFECT FOR SOUTHERN GILA AND NORTHERN MARICOPA COUNTIES. She stood up and moved into the living room, peeking out the back windows. It was windy outside, the palm trees and oleanders swaying wildly back and forth, but the dust storm had not yet arrived. Hurrying out the back door, she dragged the barbecue off the patio and into the storage shed. She took off the seat cushions on the lawn chairs and brought them into the house.

She made it back inside just in time. Seconds after she closed the door, there was the familiar waterspray sound of dust granules hitting the window. She stood for a moment, unmoving. As children, she and David and Billy used to watch as the storms rolled across the flat desert toward them, a dark brown that blotted out the blue of the sky in the daytime, or a black mass that extinguished the stars at night. They had loved the storms. It had been fun to see their toys and bikes fly around at the mercy of the winds. It had been fun to hear the rough whispery sound of dust hitting the roof and windows while they remained safe and protected inside.

Now the sound did not seem quite so pleasant.

Cathy moved to the front of the house and looked through the window toward the Wests' home. She could see no lights through the blowing dust, and she wondered if Randy West was still lost, if his mother was still out looking for him. The thought of the two of them wandering about in the middle of the dust storm gave her the chills. In her mind she saw Randy, a thick squat shape moving slowly through the flying sand, being pursued by his screaming mother, her wild hair and bathrobe flapping in the wind.

Cathy let the drapes drop and concentrated on the television. The house was silent save for the TV—her father had long since gone to bed—and she turned up the volume, trying not to hear the sound of the howling storm outside.

Thirty-five

Allan sat with Dobrinin in the car outside Lee's house, feeling like a shit. They were across the street and down two driveways, in a nondescript rented white Toyota Celica, but their focus was on Lee's well-lit front windows.

Dobrinin was watching the house with binoculars.

Allan's coffee on the dashboard was starting to fog up the window and obscure their view, so he took down the styrofoam cup and sipped from it. He hated to be doing this. It made him feel so cheap and sleazy and so goddamn amateurish. Staking out a house from a car. It was something he'd seen in crummy movies and hour-long TV shows, but it was not something he had ever done himself, and he knew already that it was not something he enjoyed doing.

Particularly when it involved spying on a fellow cop.

It was Pynchon who had arranged the stakeout. The captain had temporarily reassigned Lee to traffic, had set him to work making out motorcycle assignments based on the city's most recent Traffic Safety Survey— a made-up job but one that carried enough authority not to be humiliating. Lee was a smart man, and Allan would have thought that he'd seen the farce for what

it was, but apparently he had not taken the reassign-
ment badly at all, had even seemed somewhat happy
to be doing the new work.

Then Yvonne had seen him using the traffic computer to obtain a woman's address.

She'd walked into the room while he'd been copying
information from the screen onto a yellow Post-it.
He'd quickly shoved the paper underneath one of the
printouts when he saw her, and she'd pretended she
hadn't noticed what he'd been doing. But she'd immediately told Pynchon.

Lee's attempt to cover up what he'd been writing
was so crude and so obvious that Allan doubted that
anything serious had been going down. Most likely,
he'd been attempting to track down the address of an
old flame, or to find out the name of a potential flame
based on a license number, but Pynchon said they
could not afford to take chances and had ordered
him tailed.

Now Allan felt like a traitor. It was his fault. He
had started this ball rolling. If he hadn't been so testy
and weirded out that day, if he had just talked things
over with Lee instead of jumping to conclusions and
leaping down the poor guy's throat, Lee never would
have been reassigned and never would have used the
traffic computer at all, let alone used it improperly.

On the other hand, what if Lee had been writing
down that address for another reason?

Dobrinin put down the binoculars, rubbed his eyes.
"Nothing happening. You want to watch for awhile?"

Allan shook his head.

"Suit yourself."

The two of them sat there, staring at the house, not
speaking, sipping their coffees.

Thirty-six

"Dalton says he lives somewhere here on this street."

Samson nodded.

"Teach that little shit to get me suspended."

The two of them stopped their bikes in the middle of the road and looked around. The neighborhood was quiet, the only sounds the muffled noise of cars on other streets, the low hum of rooftop air conditioning units, and the airplane buzz of cicadas in the trees. The day was hot, and if any kids lived here they were inside, watching TV, staying out of the heat. Halfway down the block, a middle-aged man with a potbelly and Bermuda shorts was washing his pickup.

Halback wiped the sweat from his forehead with a finger. "I say we ride up and down the street until we find the fucker. He'll have to come out sometime."

Samson said nothing. He knew Jimmy didn't have to come out at all, probably wouldn't come out if he saw them cruising by on their bikes, but the whole afternoon was ahead of them and anything was possible. Besides, he wanted to get that little son of a bitch, wanted to split his damn lip and break both of his arms. He wasn't sure why he wanted to hurt the kid so much, but there was something about the scrawny runt that just pissed him off. It was Dalton who had first told him what Jimmy had said, who had asked him to intervene in the interest of justice, but the moment Samson had set eyes on that weak little pussy he'd wanted to beat the crap out of him—and for reasons entirely unconnected with Dalton. For Jimmy was one of those natural victims, one of those people who begged by the way they walked, by the way they talked, by their very existence, to have the shit beat out of them. As his brother would have said, the kid was a born fruit, ripe for the plucking.

And Samson was a plucker.

"Which house you think is his?" Halback asked.

Samson glared at him. "How would I know?"

"Let's just cruise around, then."

"Sounds good."

They sped up the street in an unofficial race, pedaling furiously while trying to pretend they weren't. Samson reached the end of the block first, once again asserting his dominance. He sped around the corner and circled back around, sticking out his right foot and kicking over a plastic garbage can next to a driveway as he slowed to a halt. "Want to keep going or turn around? It's a pretty long street."

"Let's just cruise up and down 'til we see him."

"Look for a bike in the driveway," Samson suggested. "That might tell us where he lives."

"Good idea."

They continued up the street, past the next block, and the next. Ahead, on the left sidewalk, they saw a boy standing in one of the driveways. A squat kid with ugly mama's boy clothes who remained perfectly still and who appeared to be staring at them as they approached. Samson steered his bike toward the kid and sped up the driveway ramp and onto the sidewalk, his tires barely missing the boy's toes, but the kid remained unmoving.

Samson braked to a stop, skidded around. This close, he could see the thick slack features on the boy's face, could see the thin line of drool that stretched from his mouth to the collar of his orange shirt. "It's a retard!" he said.

Halback laughed, pulling his bike next to the boy. "Hey, retardo!"

The boy turned dully toward Halback, the thin spiderweb of drool stretching and breaking.

Samson grinned. "Maybe he knows where our friend lives. Shit, maybe he's his brother!"

Both of them laughed at that.

"Hey, retard!" Halback yelled.

The boy stared blankly past him.

"Retardo!"

No response.

Samson coasted his bike back down the driveway ramp. He spit on the boy as he rolled past. The saliva hit the kid's hair and hung there for a few seconds before falling down the back of his shirt.

"Hey!" Halback said. "Let's have a spitting contest! We can use him as our target. He's so covered with slobber anyway he won't even notice." He hawked a wad of phlegm and spat it through pursed lips at the boy. Greenish-white glop hit the kid on the chest.

Samson laughed, spit again into the boy's hair.

"Bulls-eye!" Halback yelled. He spit directly into the boy's face, hitting him on the nose.

Samson was about to top that with a well-placed shot to the eye when the boy's dull gaze turned slowly to look at him. The saliva dried in Samson's mouth and he swallowed instead of spitting, looking quickly away. There was something in the kid's face that gave him the creeps, that made goosebumps pop up on his arms. He shivered. He would never admit to such pussiness in front of Halback, but the retard scared him, and suddenly he wished they hadn't stopped here but had kept pedaling by.

Samson rolled his bike around the boy in a half circle until he was next to Halback. The retarded boy's head swiveled slowly. Saliva, both his and theirs, was dripping down his face and shirt, but he appeared not to notice. There was definitely something spooky about the boy, Samson thought. About his eyes. It was like someone else was looking out through those eyes, like there was a monster inside there that was only pretending to be a retard.

He felt cold. Whether to prove something to himself or save face in front of Halback, he forced himself to draw up a mouthful of saliva and, against his better judgement, spit in the retard's eye. The boy stared dully at him through the spit, unmoving.

"Fuck it," Samson said, hoping his voice sounded braver and more casual than he felt. "Let's hit the road."

"All right." Halback spit one last time, hitting the kid in the cheek.

"Let's cruise over to the park."

"I thought we were gonna look for the narc."

"He's not here, or if he is here, he's hiding." Samson made a U-turn in the middle of the street, hoping that it wasn't obvious to his friend that he just wanted to get off the damn street and away from that spooky ass kid.

"All right," Halback said reluctantly.

"He's gonna have to walk to school Monday. We'll just wait for him on the way and kick his ass then."

Halback brightened. "Yeah. Maybe we can make him eat dog shit."

"Sounds like a plan."

The two of them pedaled away, turning on Siesta and heading toward the park. Samson felt better as soon as they were off the street. Even riding away, he'd felt that the retard's eyes were on him, boring into his back, watching his every move, and he wasn't able to relax until they'd left the street behind.

The park was nearly empty. A couple of older kids were practicing batting in the baseball diamond and a Mexican family was having a barbecue picnic by one of the tables, but other than that the place was deserted. Even the old hippies who usually staked out a corner of the parking lot with their beat-up van were nowhere to be seen.

Samson and Halback rode their bikes over the low curb and sped down the dirt trail that other bikes had carved through the center of the grass. They topped the rise by the duck pond, then swerved left around the fence of the small maintenance yard until they were above the drainage ditch. They looked quickly around, to make sure they hadn't been spotted, then parked their bikes, hiding them in the bushes, and slid down the steep dirt embankment to the bottom of the ditch.

Before them, the ditch continued into what they called "the tunnel," an eight-foot-high storm drain that led underneath the street. Although they had been inside the tunnel many times, they had never found its end, never discovered the point at which it once again opened onto the world. They had walked it from inside, had tried to determine its path from above, but they could never find the corresponding exit ditch. The storm drain seemed to go under the street, wind beneath the houses across the way and continue on forever.

Now they stepped carefully over algae-covered rocks, jumping intermittent puddles, and marched into the tunnel. Inside, the storm drain smelled of sewage and alcohol, the dead air holding traces of old tobacco and older marijuana. It was dark—the light from the entrance penetrated only a few feet into the blackness, dying completely several steps in—but that didn't bother either of them. They'd been down here so often that they could navigate it easily even without a flashlight.

Samson led the way into the gloom, keeping one hand on the cool cement wall to retain his bearings. One time, he remembered, they'd come across a bum sleeping in here; he'd almost tripped over the old man in the darkness. They'd both been terrified at first, afraid they were going to be knifed or killed, but when they'd heard the man's weak whiny voice, heard his pitiful pleas, the fear had fled and they'd kicked his prone body hard, pretending it was an accident, the still silence of the tunnel echoing with the false sounds of their exaggerated apologies: "Sorry." "Excuse me." "So sorry."

Samson grinned. He continued forward, and his foot slipped in something squishy. He quickly pulled it out. "Shit!" he said.

"Smells like it," Halback agreed.

They rounded the first bend, and the white square of the outside world disappeared as the mouth of the tunnel was shielded from view.

Samson stopped, and a beat later Halback ran into him.

"Watch where you're going, damn it." Samson pushed his friend against the wall. "You got it?" he asked.

There was the sound of crinkling cellophane. A match was lit, unnaturally bright in the blackness, and Halback touched the small flame to the tip of a cigarette.

Samson smiled. He remembered the first time they had come down here to smoke. It had taken them nearly half an hour to make the decision to light the match, and by that time they had both been drenched with the sweat of tension. They had been afraid that the air of the tunnel contained some sort of flammable gas and that when they struck the match the whole place would explode and go up in flames. Looking back now, he couldn't remember why they had finally decided to light the match, and he thought that they had probably been mighty stupid and mighty lucky.

Halback shook out the match, dropped it in the low stream of water in the center of the tunnel floor, and puffed. The cigarette caught, the ashes glowed. Halback took a few more puffs before passing it to his friend.

They stood there like that for awhile, smoking in silence, Halback coughing every so often. The cigarette was almost out, down to a butt, when all of a sudden, Samson felt as though they were being watched, as though unseen eyes in the darkness were following their every move, unseen ears taking in every sound. For the second time that day, he felt scared, and he thought of the retarded kid. It seemed colder in the tunnel, and a chill passed through him.

From back the way they had come, he heard a low splash of shallow water.

"What was that?" he whispered.

"What?" Halback's voice, too loud, echoed in the tunnel.

"Shut up."

"Why are you whispering?" Halback's voice took on a mocking tone. "Are you turning pussy on me?"

"Shut the fuck up."

Halback was silent.

This time they both heard it. Wet footsteps, coming toward them in the darkness, splashing.

Samson reached out, took the matchbook from his friend, and lit a match. The orange glow illuminated their faces but little else. The surrounding darkness seemed somehow even darker. "Who's there?" Samson called out.

There was no answer, but the footsteps stopped.

Samson dropped the match and it hissed, dying, in the scummy water. "I don't like this," he said. "Let's get out of here."

"Okay," Halback agreed.

They started back the way they had come, hurrying, though pretending not to hurry. Their footsteps echoed in the tunnel. If they could just make it around the bend, Samson thought. If they could just see the entrance. In his mind he saw gang members. In his mind he saw—

—the retarded kid.

They were running now, tennis shoes splashing loudly in the sewer water as they desperately tried to reach the light. Samson put out his hand, touched the cold concrete. Directly in front of him, Halback screamed, and before he knew what he was doing, Samson stopped and jumped back. He heard a thumpcrack that turned instantly from clean and dry to wet and squishy, then the noise of Halback's body slumping, falling. There was a low splash as the body hit the thin layer of water on the floor of the tunnel.

Terrified, panicking, screaming at the top of his lungs, Samson tried to get away. He ran forward but immediately tripped over the still form of his friend and went sprawling into the slime. Underneath his screams and the furious beating of his heart, he heard a low chuckle.

The Fiend! he thought.

He tried to stand, tasted dirt and chemicals, algae and urine as he spit, and he promptly threw up. He was knocked over as something or someone rammed into his side, and he nearly choked on the vomit that was forced back into his throat. The attacker landed hard on Samson's chest, knees first, and suddenly it was impossible to breathe. He was choking, gagging, gasping for air. He kicked and punched but hit nothing. He jerked his head wildly from side to side. Through tear-stained eyes, he saw to his right the orange glow of the cigarette, somehow dry and miraculously still lit. The Fiend apparently saw it at the same time, for the pressure on his chest shifted, and now the cigarette was floating, growing, making a beeline for his face. He kicked, flailed, tried to roll over, tried to scream, but before he could move, the burning end of the cigarette had grown to fill the world and was being pressed into his right eye. He tried to close his eyes, tried to blink, but the heat shot straight to his brain and he felt the membrane of his eye melting, smelled above the stench of the sewage the roasting of his own flesh. His arms shot out, and his left hand connected with something warm and sticky.

Halback's head.

A fist punched Samson full in the face, followed by something harder. The cigarette moved to his other eye, burning through the gelatinous membrane, and then he was blind.

The sound that accompanied his death was laughter.

Thirty-seven

Another Pleasant Valley Sunday, Allan thought as he drove down the quiet street toward Cathy's. Around him, the houses looked like something out of a sixties TV show—nearly identical tract homes with cheerfully well-manicured lawns, morning papers lying perfectly placed on front stoops. The sky above was blue and cloudless, the street itself lined with recently trimmed trees. He hadn't noticed the Norman Rockwell wholesomeness of the street's appearance before, but when he thought of Cathy, it fit. This was exactly the sort of neighborhood in which he'd expect her to live.

She was waiting outside when he drove up, standing at the foot of the driveway, purse in hand, and she looked great. She was wearing a plain white blouse and jeans, and the simple outfit made her seem somehow both wholesome and sexy. She smiled and waved as he pulled up, and he found himself smiling as well.

He put the car into park and was planning to get out and open her door, but she climbed into the Bronco before he could even unbuckle his seatbelt.

"Let's go," she said.

"Don't I even get to come in and see your house?"

She shook her head and colored slightly, her fingers

nervously clasping and unclasping the purse in her lap. "Maybe some other time."

"Okay," he said, not wanting to push. He put the car into gear and pulled away from the curb. "I'd show you my apartment, but I'm bug-bombing it right now."

"Roaches?"

"Spiders. I saw one crawling on the ceiling yesterday. I hate the damn things, but I have a tough time killing them. I keep thinking of little spider wives and little spider children waiting for their father to come home after I've totaled him with a *Time* magazine. It's a lot easier to let the bug bomb do it. I don't feel so guilty."

"There's a metaphor in there somewhere. Or a moral."

"Typical English major."

Cathy laughed. "So where are we going?" she asked. "You still haven't told me."

"That's trust. You're willing to go out with me without even knowing our destination."

"You're a cop. I hope I can trust you."

He grinned. "We'll see."

They spent the morning at the Heard Museum, looking at the Indian art and artifacts. Cathy had been to the museum in third grade on a field trip, but had not been back since. Then it had been merely an excuse to leave school for awhile. This time, she got much more out of it. Allan was interested and genuinely enthusiastic about nearly everything they came across, and he proved to be knowledgeable not only about the more contemporary works but also about older pottery and baskets. As he elaborated on the paragraph descriptions displayed next to the exhibits, a small crowd gathered to listen. He stopped, embarrassed, when he noticed the people around him. He smiled sheepishly and took Cathy's hand, moving away.

"I feel like such a pompous jerk," he mumbled.

"Why? Knowledge is nothing to be ashamed of."

"Yeah, but nobody wants to stand there and listen to some amateur pontificate for ten minutes about Pagago pottery."

"If people didn't want to listen, they wouldn't," Cathy told him. "Besides, you weren't pontificating. You were just sharing information. I thought it was interesting."

"Really? Tell it to the tour guide." He nodded toward a stern-faced woman in a brown name-tagged jacket standing next to the door.

Cathy looked at the woman and started giggling, then looked back at Allan and he started giggling, then they were both laughing and couldn't stop, and they walked out of the room under the woman's scowling gaze.

It was lunch before the subject of murder came up. They had driven to Scottsdale and were eating lunch at the Sugar Bowl—banana splits—when a teenager at the next table over mentioned the "Phoenix Fiend." Cathy saw a cloud pass over Allan's features.

"It's your day off," she reminded him.

He nodded, but he seemed preoccupied throughout the rest of the meal.

Once outside again, standing under the desert sun in the blazing heat of midday, he excused himself and went to a pay phone to make a call. When he stepped out of the phone booth, his brow was less furrowed and he seemed a little less disturbed, but he was still not as relaxed as he had been during the morning.

"I should've worn my beeper," he said.

"No date would be complete without it."

He smiled apologetically. "Sorry."

"Don't be. I was just joking."

They walked slowly down Fifth Avenue toward the car. "It's been two weeks since the last killing," Allan said. "I know I should be grateful, but the waiting's almost worse. The murderer hasn't been caught, and you know damn well that he didn't just give up a life of crime to help homeless orphans. The only thing we can do, really, is wait until something new turns up or

the Fiend strikes again." He hit himself in the forehead with an open palm. " 'The Fiend.' Jesus, even
I'm saying it now."

Cathy smiled. "But what about the little girl?" she
asked.

"The one who's missing? Probably no connection.
Our murderer kills. He doesn't kidnap. Besides, it was
a rough domestic situation. There was a pretty heated
custody battle, and the husband didn't seem like a
good loser. It's not my case, but I have a hunch that
when they find the husband, they'll find the daughter."

"Oh."

He took her hand, squeezed it. "Come on," he said.
"Let's not talk about this anymore. Let's not ruin
the day."

"It's not ruined," Cathy said, and it wasn't. In fact,
she couldn't think of anything that could happen that
would ruin it. The morning had been perfect, and she
couldn't remember when she'd ever had a better time.
The longer she spent with Allan, the better she knew
him, the more she liked him.

But it was stronger than like, wasn't it?

She pushed the thought from her mind.

They spent the afternoon in Scottsdale, going
through small shops and galleries. Many of the gallery
owners knew Allan by name. He shrugged when she
asked him about it. "I guess I spend a lot of time
here," he admitted.

They ate dinner at Trader Vic's. From their booth,
Cathy could see the bar. She couldn't hear any of the
conversations, but from the expressions on the faces
of the well-dressed men and tight-skirted women she
could see how hard they were working to appear witty
and interesting.

Allan noticed her gaze, turned around to look himself. He shook his head. "It's tough to meet people,"
he said.

"Tell me about it."

"I've even sunk so low as to go on a blind date."

Cathy smiled.

"No, I'm serious."

"How did it work out?"

"It didn't. It wasn't a sitcom situation—she wasn't a beachball with Coke-bottle glasses or anything. She was fairly attractive and fairly intelligent. We just didn't hit it off."

"Why?"

"I don't know. Some people you like, some people you don't—"

"Don't give me that. Tell me what happened."

"I did. She's the one who dumped me at Rawhide."

Cathy laughed. "Sounds even worse than my blind dates."

"Dates? Plural?"

"Yes," she admitted. "Dates."

"I guess it's lucky we found each other, then, isn't it?"

Cathy looked down at her napkin. "I guess so," she said.

After dinner, they walked past the now-darkened shops on their way back to the car, the only people on an otherwise empty sidewalk. She could feel his hand against hers, his fingers intertwined with her own. It was a good feeling, warm and reassuring, and she gave his hand a small squeeze.

"I'm sorry I didn't invite you in this morning," she said. "But my father was home."

"I take it you two aren't exactly on the best of terms."

"No." She smiled sadly. "I don't have a very good relationship with my father."

Allan shrugged. "Who does? The last time I saw my dad was the night of my high school graduation. He was sitting in his chair in front of the television while my mom and I went to the ceremony. Hell, I don't even know where he's buried."

Cathy put a light hand on his arm. "That must be hard," she said.

Allan shrugged. "Not really. We were never close,

so when he died there was nothing for me to miss. My mom's still alive, though. She lives in California."

"Do you see her very often?"

"When I can. You know, holidays, birthdays, things like that. We talk quite a bit on the phone."

"Well, my father and I aren't quite that bad. Not yet, at least. But we're getting there."

"What about your mother?"

"She's dead. She was killed in a car accident."

"I'm sorry."

"Miss Riley?"

She looked up at the policeman in the doorway. His face was hard, devoid of all emotion, as though chiseled in granite. There was something in his eyes that scared her.

"Miss Riley?"

She nodded dumbly. The policeman's short gray hair stuck up in tiny bristles. Like the quills of a porcupine, she thought.

"I have some bad news. Your parents were in an automobile accident. I'm here to escort you and your brothers to St. Matthew's Hospital."

Cathy said nothing. They walked in silence for a few moments, holding hands. Above them the sky was black, moonless, the stars clustered so thick they looked like fine white gossamer clouds.

"What about your brother?" Allan asked. "Didn't you tell me that you had a brother?"

"Two. David and Billy. Billy moved to New York two years ago. We're still real close. David . . ." Her voice trailed off.

"What about David?"

She did not answer.

"You don't have to talk about it if you don't want to," he added quickly. He saw her hesitation. "But you can if you want. I'm here for you."

Cathy looked down at her shoes. "David was crazy," she said finally. "He was always strange, but it seemed to get worse as he got older. After my mother died . . . Well, he ran away from home about a year after the accident. You probably have a record of it somewhere. I think my father filled out a missing-person report, although I don't remember any police ever coming by. I'm not sure my father or Billy cared if he came back any more than I did."

Allan looked into her eyes, did not like what he saw there. "Did your brother try to . . . rape you?"

She shook her head. "No. Not really. He used to do some sick things, though. Once he charged his friends a nickel to watch me . . . you know, go to the bathroom." Cathy reddened but continued to talk on. "The lock on our bathroom door never worked, and David waited with his friends in his room until I'd gone in there. Then he threw open the door and said, 'There she is!' and all of them stared at me and laughed. For two years after that, until he left, I was afraid to go to the bathroom. I used to try putting a towel under the crack of the door to keep it closed. When I could, I used my parents' bathroom, which had a lock. I even went outside once, in the bushes." She shook her head. "God, I hated him."

"Did you ever tell your parents?"

She shook her head. "I never told them a lot of things." She licked her lips. "You know, for awhile, I even thought that he might be behind these murders."

Allan stiffened. "Why do you say that?"

She shrugged.

"Why didn't you tell me?"

"I thought about it, but it didn't really seem plausible. David was never a mental giant to begin with, and I don't think he'd be capable of committing a series of perfect murders. I figured it was probably my own paranoia, which I'm sure it is." She paused. "It's just that . . ."

"What?"

She told him about the jackrabbit.

Allan frowned, stopped walking. "I don't like this. I wish you'd told me sooner."

"I didn't think it was anything real. I mean . . . I

don't know what I thought. I guess I was scared. I didn't want to think it was David."

"I hope you're right, but this is something that needs to be followed up. Do you know if your brother ever killed any other animals?"

She shook her head.

"I'm going to check this out tomorrow."

"Tomorrow," she said. "Does that mean we can concentrate on other things tonight?"

He nodded. "Sure." He smiled, but his smile was not as loose as it had been, not as open, and she could see tension in the muscles of his face.

They started walking again. Rounding the corner, they passed another strolling couple, a pair of teenagers window-shopping in the dark. They reached the car, but instead of opening her door, Allan leaned against the side of the Bronco and drew Cathy to him. He felt her stiffen as he gently pulled her against him, and he stopped. "I'm sorry—" he began.

She kissed him.

It was an awkward kiss, a quick peck that only partially met his lips, but it was the sexiest kiss he'd ever received, and it gave him an immediate erection. He looked into her eyes, saw both nervousness and anticipation there, and he put his arms around her and slowly leaned forward, meeting her lips with his own. He gave her ample opportunity to stop, to pull away, but she did not, and he opened his mouth slightly, pressing his tongue between her lips. She opened her mouth wider to allow him entrance. She leaned against him.

And pulled back as if stung, jerking out of his arms.

She was staring at the bulge in his pants, and he stood away from the car and turned aside, embarrassed. He felt as though he should apologize, but he wasn't sure what for. "I, uh . . ."

Cathy shook her head quickly. "I'm sorry," she said. "It's my fault. I . . ." her voice trailed off.

They looked at each other, neither sure of what to say. Allan held her gaze, tried to surreptitiously press down on his erection, but Cathy saw the movement, her eyes darting down to his hand.

They both looked instantly away from each other, focusing on unrelated objects.

"We'd, uh, better get going back," Allan said. He unlocked her door, opened it, and walked around the front of the car. "It's getting late and I have to work tomorrow—"

"It's not you," she said.

He turned to look at her. "What?"

She licked her lips. "I just . . ." She couldn't finish the sentence.

"What is it?" He walked back around the Bronco to her side.

"I just . . . It's been awhile."

"I understand," Allan said. "It's okay."

"I really . . . I like you."

"I like you, too."

They drew together. He felt her press her body closer against him as they kissed, and he was embarrassed to find himself aroused again. This close, she was bound to notice, and he didn't know how she'd feel about it. He didn't want to scare her away.

But she wasn't scared away.

Her father was waiting for her when she came home, sitting in the kitchen, his crutches balanced on his lap. From the family room, Cathy heard the TV blaring loudly.

He glared up at her as she walked toward the sink. "So where the hell've you been?" he demanded.

She looked at him coolly. "Out."

"Don't you take that tone with me, young lady!" He tried to push himself to his feet, positioning his hands on the chair and table, but his crutches clattered to the floor and he slumped back down.

Cathy picked up the fallen crutches.

"I had to fix my own dinner," he said. "At least you could've told me where you were going. I waited and waited and when you didn't come I thought something might have happened to you. I almost called the police. You could've at least left a note."

Cathy felt immediately guilty. He was right. She should have told him where she was going. Even if they had been fighting, it was still thoughtless of her. She turned toward him, chastened. "I'm sorry," she said. "I didn't know we'd be gone this long. He asked me out, but—"

"He? The cop?"

Cathy nodded.

Her father grinned maliciously. "Did you—?"

"Don't even say it!"

Her father was still grinning, and he opened his mouth to respond, but before he could say anything Cathy strode out of the kitchen. The air in the house suddenly felt hot and stifling, and instead of going to her bedroom, she walked out of the house.

Outside, the night sky was clear and beautiful. She stood in the driveway for a moment, looking up at the heavens. The curve of the earth was reflected in the domed arc of the stars and constellations. There was still no moon, and the night behind the stars was black and blank.

"Da."

The sound was low, muffled, almost a mumble, but Cathy looked up immediately at the sound of the voice. The air seemed suddenly colder, and she rubbed her arms for warmth. The voice sounded as though it had come from across the street, but though she scanned the sidewalk and the lawns, she could see nothing. She squinted, trying to make out shapes in the shadows.

There.

A small figure was moving slowly against a backdrop of bushes in the Armstrongs' yard.

Cathy took two steps forward and stopped as the figure emerged into an area of grass illuminated by the streetlight.

It was Randy. He moved slowly but purposefully, as if aiming toward a specific destination but not caring when he reached it. He was wet, soaked, his clothes dripping, his short hair plastered to his head. In the dim yellowish glow of the streetlight, his body looked shiny, almost slimy.

Cathy stared across the street, looking more closely, and saw that the slick luminescent paleness of the boy's skin was augmented in several spots by equally shiny segments of blackness.

Oil? she thought, puzzled.

Blood?

Randy stopped walking and turned to look at her, as though somehow sensing her presence. Their eyes met, and Cathy glanced immediately away, afraid of the look she saw on his face, frightened by the perverse intelligence that seemed to radiate from his eyes in marked defiance to the rest of his features.

If the eyes are truly the windows of the soul, she thought, *then Randy's soul is damned.*

The expression on his face was one of pure evil.

She quickly turned around and hurried back into the house. Closing and locking the door behind her, she looked out the front window for the retarded boy, but there was no sign of him. The street was empty.

Shivering, she let the halves of the drapes fall and walked down the hall to her bedroom.

Thirty-eight

"Oh, God," Allan said. "Oh, Jesus."

The man on the lawn had exploded.

Allan took a deep breath. The man's chest and abdomen had burst, the skin ripping in jagged tears around several sets of irregular gaping holes. Reddish liquid was still bubbling in steady streams through the openings, fueled by the water pumped into the lifeless body through twin garden hoses shoved into the man's mouth and anus. Pieces of red and white flesh littered the lawn, clinging to plant stalks, caught on twigs, as the water filtered through the grass and overflowed onto the sidewalk.

The air smelled of excrement and urine, bile and blood.

Yellow cordoning ribbon was up, blocking off the house, but it wasn't really necessary. The body, or what remained of it, looked so gruesome and smelled so horribly that people were staying back of their own accord.

"Do we have a name?" Allan asked. "Statistics?"

"Harvard Brown," Dobrinin said. "Computer programmer. Apparently divorced. We're trying to reach his ex-wife now."

"Where's Pathology? I want a time of death."

"Pathologist's on his way. We already have the search net moving outward."

"Good." Allan looked down at the blood-tinted water pumping out of the dead man's body and grimaced. "Will somebody shut those damn hoses off!"

"The photographer isn't here yet!" Williams called from the front porch.

"I don't give a shit! He doesn't need to take pictures of the desecration of the corpse! Shut the damn hoses off!"

Allan watched as the streams of liquid slowed and died, the torn body sinking, collapsing in on itself. A portion of clean white intestine flopped out through the biggest hole, just above the man's crotch, flattening a shred of limp skin.

Allan looked up at the rising sun, then turned away and walked toward the house.

"We can rule out Lee," Pynchon said. "Not that I ever considered him a real suspect."

Allan stared at the captain, who was placing a red pin on the wall map at the location of Harvard Brown's residence. "What do you mean you never considered him a real suspect? You were the one who wanted him tailed."

"Just as a precaution."

"I think we owe him an apology. I mean, we fuck up his life and then discover we made a mistake? It's our fault this happened."

Pynchon waved his hand dismissively. "We didn't fuck up anyone's life. Hell, Lee probably didn't even know he was under surveillance."

"But he was. We tromped all over his rights in our desperate effort to find a suspect—"

"Knock off the holier-than-thou bleeding-heart crap. You're the one who started all this. You're the one who placed suspicion on him in the first place, so stop trying to make me feel guilty about it. It's over and done, we still have a killer to catch, it's time to move on."

"Well, I do feel guilty."

"Fine. Apologize. I just don't want to hear about it." Pynchon's finger traced an imaginary line on the map, connecting the red pins. "What about Goldstein? We getting anywhere on that?"

"I've questioned him twice. We've requisitioned his phone records." He shook his head. "The man's certainly no saint, but I don't think he's a murderer."

"Do we have enough circumstantial evidence to justify a warrant?"

Allan thought for a moment. "Not really. But I could probably arrange the information we do have in such a way that we could probably get one—depending on the judge."

"Do it."

"But I don't think he's guilty. He has a kid for one thing. A nice kid. I know him. Most serial killers don't have nice kids. And there's the timing of these murders. Most were committed after midnight. I doubt if Goldstein—"

Pynchon sighed. "The FBI's getting in on this, you know."

"Thank God."

"'Thank God'? They're coming because we screwed up. We look like dickheads of the first water here."

"But they have the resources and the experience to deal with something like this."

"So do we. This isn't fucking Podunk, Nebraska here. This is Phoenix, goddamn it. This is a major metropolitan police force. We should be able to clean up our own backyard."

Allan said nothing.

"Get out of here," Pynchon said. "And try to get a warrant for Goldstein. We have to do something."

Allan started to reply, then saw the expression on the captain's face and thought better of it. "Yes, sir," he said.

He headed back to his own office.

*   *   *

The murder made the national news.

Allan was resting on the couch, eyes closed against a headache, TV on as background noise, when he heard the name "Harvard Brown."

He immediately sat up, swinging his legs off the couch's armrest, and faced the television. A network correspondent, standing in front of Brown's house, a dramatic strip of yellow police ribbon visible through spaces in the crowd behind him, was describing the details of the murder, quoting liberally from an account given by one of the neighbors.

"It is believed by police that this is yet another in a series of killings by the so-called 'Phoenix Fiend,' who has been terrorizing this normally laid-back desert community for the past month with a series of grisly murders . . ."

Allan shook his head. Pynchon was not going to be happy. First local news, now national news, next tabloid fodder. The pressure was going to come down hard and heavy after this. Asses, as the captain said, were going to fry.

If people in the Valley had been worried before, Allan knew, they were going to be absolutely terrified now. There was something about seeing a story like this on national news that lent a validity to already existing fear, which somehow intensified the reality of a situation and made it seem even more serious than it was. The boiling down of complex facts into small soundbites always tended to multiply the importance of events. Hell, after watching the news, even he was half afraid that the murderer might show up on his doorstep tonight—and he'd been diligently searching for the fucker for nearly a month.

But for once the situation was not as bleak as the news made it sound. They finally had a lead. Footprints had been found this afternoon in dried mud near the body, and casts had been made and were being analyzed. The footprints were small, the size a dwarf or a small woman or child might make, and bore the pattern of a popular tennis shoe. Of course, footprints were not conclusive, were not easily identifiable, were not even very helpful in tracking down a suspect, but they were a start. Pynchon had decided to withhold the information from the press, wanting to work without interference, but Allan wondered now if that had not been a mistake. He thought it might help allay fears if people were at least told that "police are investigating new leads in the case."

He thought for a moment, then walked across the room and picked up the phone, dialing the station. Patty Thrall answered. "Pat," he said, "is the captain there?"

"We were just going to call you," the dispatcher said.

Allan frowned. "Why? What is it?"

Williams came on the line. "Allan? We've found two bodies. Boys."

Allan closed his eyes. "Where?"

"They're in a storm drain under Third, by the park. Bum found them."

"Oh, God."

"Looks bad. We won't be able to get a positive ID without lab assistance. Can you get out, meet us there?"

"I'll be there in ten. Call Pynchon."

"Will do."

Allan hung up. Three in one day. He grabbed his shoulder holster and tape recorder. He'd told Cathy that the waiting was bad?

The killing was worse.

The killing was much worse.

Thirty-nine

Katrina cried as she tied Randy to the post.

The garage was dark, the only illumination a dim dirty sunlight peeking through the grimy glass of the lone window. She was glad of the darkness, happy that it was hard to see. She did not enjoy punishing her son, and she did not want to watch his face as she administered the beating.

Why was God doing this to her?

Randy had been so good in Seattle. Until the end, at least. It had been years between . . . occurrences. And after Hank, after they had decided to move, after she had punished him, she had explained things to him. And he had seemed to understand.

Now they would have to move again.

"Ma!" Randy said.

Katrina tightened the twine, doubling, tripling the knot. She did not answer him, did not say anything. It was partly her fault, she knew. She should have been more careful, should have found some better restraints. He was good with his hands, clever that way, and she should have known that it would be only a matter of time before he mastered the lock.

She ripped the back of his shirt, then walked over

to the bench and picked up the gag. She tied it around his mouth. He struggled as she did so, but his arms and legs were effectively tied to the post and could not move more than a fraction of an inch. She stepped back and picked up the switch from the ground.

"Bad!" she said. The lash whipped across Randy's skin, leaving a long red mark. "Bad!"

He screamed, but the sound was muffled by the gag.

She hit him again, this time on the buttocks, putting all of her strength into the swing. "Bad!"

He struggled against his bonds, screaming beneath the gag.

Katrina was hardly able to see for the tears, but she continued to whip her son. Again.

And again.

And again.

"Bad!" she cried. "Bad! Bad! Bad!"

Forty

"This is a real good one," Jeff said excitedly. "It's called *Bloodletters and Badmen*. This is the one that has Albert Fish in it. He wasn't just a murderer, he was a cannibal, and he ate—"

"That's okay," Cathy said, putting the book back on the shelf. She should have known better than to ask Jeff about murders. She should have known better than to ask Jeff about anything at all. She glanced over at Ann, who was frowning at her, obviously worried.

She was worried herself. Ever since she'd seen the news last night and heard about the man who'd been killed with the hoses, she hadn't been able to get the thought of Randy West out of her mind. She kept seeing him creeping through the darkness toward home, wet with water and . . . what?

Blood?

Several times last night and this morning, she'd picked up the phone, intending to call Allan, but she hadn't been sure what to say. First her missing brother, now the mentally handicapped kid across the street? It sounded crazy. Allan wouldn't believe anything she said after this. Besides, in the cold light of reason the thought that a grown man had been murdered by a retarded child sounded not just far-fetched but idiotic.

She'd been distracted all day, though, unable to concentrate on work, absentmindedly shelving books in the wrong aisles, performing the same tasks several times. There was something strange and unnatural about Randy, something that bothered and frightened her, and that, at certain moments, did not make the idea that he had killed the man seem so implausible.

Made it, in fact, seem downright probable.

Randy had killed that man.

She looked at the shelf of books in front of her. Yes, she believed that. She had no evidence, nothing that would stand up in court, but she knew it was true. She felt it. It made no sense, not on any logical level, but it seemed right. In her gut it felt true.

That led to even more disturbing thoughts, though, didn't it?

Like the thought that he had committed the other murders as well.

"Are you okay?"

Startled, Cathy swung around to meet Ann's concerned gaze. She glanced down at the floor, unwilling to meet her friend's eyes, irrationally worried that her unspoken thoughts would be visible on her face for Ann to read. "Uh, yeah," she said. "I'm fine. Why?"

"You just seem . . . I don't know, a little preoccupied today."

"I'm fine."

"Yeah, she's finally getting some taste," Jeff said.

"That's what I'm worried about," Ann said. "When she starts finding things in common with you, there's definitely something wrong." She was joking, and her mouth was smiling, but her eyes were not.

"I'm fine," Cathy repeated. She moved past Ann and made her way toward the front counter.

Randy was waiting in her driveway when she got home.

Cathy almost decided to drive around the block, to keep driving until the retarded boy went home, however long it took. But she saw Katrina across the street, sitting in a chair on her front lawn, watching her son, and she decided to pull in.

Randy stepped aside as the Volkswagen bumped over the rounded curb and stopped in the center of the driveway. As usual, he was holding his soccer ball and he stared at her intently as she got out of the car, drool dripping down his chin.

"Ba?" the boy said. He looked at her with his dull brown eyes, his gaze never wavering, and she shivered. He held up the soccer ball in his hands, offering it to her, but she turned away.

"Randy!" Katrina called from across the street. "Don't bother our neighbor!"

The woman no doubt expected Cathy to say that he wasn't bothering her, that it was okay for him to be on her property, but it was not true and she could say no such thing. "Go home," Cathy said. She pointed across the street. "Go home."

Randy stared at her, unmoving, unblinking, and she had the distinct feeling that he was studying her. Goosebumps arose on her arms. She looked across the street at his mother for help, but the older woman had turned away and was ostensibly examining a bush at the far end of the yard.

"Go home!" Cathy said again, this time with more force, and finally the boy began to move off, walking in a slow, strangely loping manner. He continued to look back at her as he crossed the street.

Cathy pushed up the driver's seat and took from the back of the car the groceries she'd picked up on the way home. She walked around the small flower garden and went into the house without turning to look at either Randy or his mother. Her goosebumps had not disappeared.

"Father?" she called, closing the door behind her. She walked through the entryway.

Her father was sitting in the kitchen rather than the

family room, and he was staring upward at the ceiling, his head thrown back. The house was silent, the only sound her father's labored breathing. He looked old, tired, beaten, and for the first time in a long while, she felt real pity for him. Underneath the man he had become, she saw the father of her childhood; the strong, loving man who'd gone to her school plays and open houses, who'd brought her to church each Sunday.

"Father?" she said, placing the sack of groceries on the counter.

He did not answer.

"Father?" Worried that something was wrong, that he was having a heart attack or something, she pulled out a chair and sat down next to him. She took his hand, patting it. "Father?"

He looked at her, and for a second the expression in his eyes was one of caring and compassion. Then the years flooded into his gaze, his eyes hardening as he sat up straight. "What are you doing here?"

"What do you mean what am I doing here?"

"I thought you weren't coming home after work. I thought I was going to have to make my own dinner again."

"Of course not. I'm going to make dinner."

"That's a first."

Cathy took a deep breath, held it, counted to ten. She didn't want to fight with him today. She'd spent too much time yelling at him lately and then running out of the room. It was time for her to just swallow her pride and humor him. "Let's try to get along tonight, okay?"

He looked for a second as though he was about to say something, a nasty reply, a vicious retort, but he said nothing, and the thought came to her that maybe he was trying to compromise too, maybe he was trying not to argue with her.

"I'll start dinner," she said.

"What are we having?" His voice was belligerent again.

"What do you want?"

He reached for his crutches, stood. "I don't give a shit. It's up to you."

Cathy watched him hobble out of the kitchen and into the hall. A moment later, she heard him turn on the TV in the den. She had successfully averted a fight, but she had not succeeded in getting him to ease up on the unpleasantness. If this continued, she was going to be able to take Ann up on her roommate offer with no qualms or hesitation at all.

She stood up, walked over to the counter. She wished her mother were here.

Aside from her short discussion with Allan, Cathy had not thought of her mother in a long while, and she did not know if that was good or bad. It was an improvement, no doubt, over the days when she'd thought of nothing else, but she felt guilty that she had not been devoting enough of her thinking time to her mother's memory.

What kind of daughter was she?

She began unpacking the groceries—putting the milk in the refrigerator, the bread in the cupboard. She'd make homemade macaroni and cheese, she decided. It had always been one of her father's favorites, and he had claimed numerous times that he could eat it every day and not get tired of it. She took a package of elbow macaroni from the cupboard. He couldn't very well complain if she made macaroni and cheese for dinner.

But he would, she knew. He would.

After washing the dishes, Cathy joined her father in the den. Surprisingly, he had not complained about the meal, and he had actually acted somewhat civilly. He had even asked her if she would mind driving him to the club tomorrow. She had assured him that she would be happy to, and though they had not spoken much throughout the rest of the dinner, the mood had been relaxed, with none of the tenseness that had seemed to be present recently each time they were together.

Her father was already asleep in his chair, mouth open and snoring, and she didn't want to wake him. She sat down on the couch to watch TV. A news magazine show was on, and the slickly handsome reporter was interviewing a well-dressed middle-aged woman. "When did you first find out your daughter was special?" he asked.

The woman smiled. "We didn't discover her talent until she went to school. We had sent her, of course, to a private school, and as part of their curriculum they had played music to the children and had given them blocks and maracas and other, you know, percussive instruments to play along with the record. Well, when Suzie got home that night, she sat down at the piano and played 'Rubber Duckie.' She played it perfectly, note for note. My husband and I couldn't believe it."

The camera cut to another shot. A small girl, apparently retarded, was speeding through an intricate Rachmaninoff piece on the piano.

"We discovered that she could play anything. She could just hear something once and play it back perfectly."

The girl stopped playing, and her mother put on a record. Beethoven.

"She's never heard this one before."

The child listened, cocking her head. The mother lifted the needle, and when the music ended, the girl turned again to the piano and played it back without a hitch.

The camera focused on the reporter, now standing in front of a hospital. "It is believed that people who suffer from Savant Syndrome—idiot savants as they were once referred to—have what is roughly the equivalent of a short circuit in their brains. Doctors are still not entirely sure of the neurological basis for this phenomenon, but it appears to focus the brainpower or thought processes of the affected individual in a specific area of learning, to the exclusion of all others. Often, this means that the person can be a genius in a particular discipline while not being able to function socially, emotionally, or intellectually in any other way. Specifically, Savant Syndrome manifests itself in a spectacular ability to instantly reproduce, after a single exposure, a work of art, a piece of music, or an example of the discipline in which the savant has an aptitude.

"Dr. Margaret Harte, of the University of Maryland, has been studying children with Savant Syndrome since 1971."

Dr. Harte, a plain and slightly overweight woman on the far side of middle age, stood before a classroom of blank-faced boys and girls. "It is now possible, using a series of standardized tests, to determine whether an autistic child, or a child suffering from severe congenital learning disabilities, does indeed have Savant Syndrome. In addition to being worthwhile in and of itself for the insight it gives us into the workings of the human mind, this knowledge can also be used to bridge the communication gap between the child and society. Severely autistic children often live in a world of their own and are not cognizant of the real universe around them. If we can find a particular talent possessed by an afflicted child, we can use that as a means of breaking through to that child."

The camera focused on a young black boy with dull features and thick glasses, panning down to the child's short blunt fingers.

Cathy suddenly felt cold.

"Martin was born with Savant Syndrome," the reporter said in a voice-over. "His parents discovered early that he had a talent for art and enrolled him in Dr. Harte's program."

The boy was shown at an easel, fingers and paintbrush flying over the canvas as his eyes remained on a photograph of *Guernica* on the wall.

Cathy watched, holding her breath, the knot of fear that had been in her stomach all day growing larger. A perfect Picasso reproduction filled the screen.

The boy smiled simply, and Cathy got out of her seat, turning off the television. Her father continued to sleep, oblivious. She sat down shaking. She knew now how Randy had been able to kill, how he had been able to perform such brilliantly intricate acts of violence.

Randy West was an idiot savant.

His talent was murder.

Forty-one

Al Goldstein shut off the engine, turned off the head-lights, and stared through the car windshield at the darkened face of his house. He knew he was a little drunker than usual, but that didn't explain the dread he felt as he looked toward the blank black windows staring back at him.

He was frightened, he realized. It had been so long since he'd experienced fear—this sort of childish phys-ical fear—that it had taken him a moment to recognize the emotion.

He got out of the car and closed the door, holding onto the hood for support as he made his way toward the front porch. He thought of Dusty, and the thought made him uneasy.

He fumbled through his pockets for his keys, finally found them, and opened the front door. He'd ex-pected to see at the end of the hall the familiar blue light of the television glowing from Jimmy's doorway, but the inside of the house was completely dark. He felt the stirrings of the fear within him, but he forced those feelings aside as he staggered across the living room. "Jimmy?" he called.

There was no answer. The house was silent.

No, not quite silent.

There was a low mumbling coming from the back bedroom.

Al licked his lips, which were suddenly dry. His vodka headache had disappeared entirely, and he felt strangely clear headed. A voice at the back of his mind was telling him to call the police, dial 911, but he knew he'd feel foolish if it turned out to be nothing. Jimmy was probably just asleep in his bed and his timer had shut off the TV. Nothing strange, nothing mysterious, nothing out of the ordinary.

He reached over to flip on the hall light, but the switch clicked deadly. No light came on.

Jimmy, he suddenly remembered, had gone to his friend Paul's for dinner.

Jimmy wasn't home.

The mumbling grew louder.

Al started backing up. The taste of old liquor in his mouth seemed putrid, nauseating. He thought again of Dusty, turned inside out.

"Shit!" The heel of his shoe hit the radiator grill, and he stumbled, nearly falling backward.

From the darkness rushed a small dark figure.

A figure with a knife.

This time Al did fall backward. He scrambled to regain his footing, screaming in abject terror, but before he could stand, before he could move out of the way, he was knocked flat on the floor.

And then the figure was upon him.

Paul's mother dropped Jimmy off in front of the house.

"Are you sure you'll be okay?" she asked.

Jimmy nodded. "Yeah," he said through clenched teeth. "Thanks for the dinner." He winced. His jaw still hurt a little when he spoke.

Paul grinned at him from the back seat. "Maybe next time you can eat something besides soup!"

"Yeah."

"We'll see you later, then," Paul's mother said. "Good-bye, Jimmy."

"Bye!" Paul called.

Jimmy waved as the station wagon pulled away from the curb, turned around and drove off the way it had come. He watched the red taillights turn the corner and was about to walk up the driveway when he heard someone call his name.

"Jimmy!"

He looked up at the sound of the almost-familiar voice but saw no one. The sidewalk before him was deserted, as was the sidewalk on the other side of the street. At the end of the block, a red Camaro was turning right.

"Jimmy!"

The woman's voice was not shouting, was in fact barely loud enough for him to hear, and it was filled with a secretiveness that immediately put him on guard. He looked to the left, the direction from which the voice seemed to have come, and saw Mrs. West standing next to a tree on the small strip of grass that separated the sidewalk from the street. She beckoned him over. "Jimmy! Come here!"

A wave of cold washed over him. He shook his head no and started walking up the driveway.

"Jimmy! Come here for a moment. I need to talk to you. Please. I promise Randy won't hurt you."

He hesitated, looking around. He saw no sign of the retarded boy.

Mrs. West was now standing on the sidewalk. She was wearing a frumpy tan dress and was barefoot. Her mousy brown hair had been bobbypinned down, but heretical strands stuck out in a rough halo about her face. She looked worried, and though the coldness had not left him, he found himself walking across the cement toward her. "What?" he asked.

She grabbed his arm and pulled him next to the tree. Her ragged fingernails dug into his flesh, and he tried to worm his way out of her grasp, but she was stronger than he was.

"I just wanted to thank you for playing with Randy this morning," she said. "Six o'clock is a little early, but it's good for him to have a friend."

Jimmy looked at her, confused. "What?"

"Next time you want to play with him, though, please ask me first."

"I didn't—" Jimmy began.

Mrs. West smiled at him, but the smile was fake. "You'd better go now." She let go of his arm and pushed him lightly toward the driveway. "Randy had fun."

Jimmy hurried away, nearly sprinting up the driveway. What was all that about? He did not turn around, did not look back, but took the key from his pocket and opened the front door of the house, going quickly inside.

The smell nearly made him gag.

He pinched his nostrils shut with two fingers, looked around. Although his father's car was parked in the driveway, the house was dark and seemed to be empty.

Where was the smell coming from?

He flipped on the light switch. Nothing happened.

Something was wrong. He knew he should leave, get out of the house, go to Cathy's and call the police, but instead he stepped into the living room. "Dad?" he called. He walked slowly across the carpeted floor, peeked around the corner into the dark kitchen.

Empty.

"Dad?"

The fear was strong and growing stronger, but Jimmy moved across the living room to the hall. He was still plugging his nose, but now he could taste the smell, a thick, gagging, unpleasant taste that seemed to permeate the air. His hand felt for the hall light switch and found it, but the switch had already been turned on, although the hallway was completely dark.

"Dad?"

Jimmy stepped into the bathroom.

His father was propped up on the toilet, dead eyes staring at the flocked wallpaper on the wall opposite the sink, hands, bluish and dark, hanging limply at his sides. He was completely naked, and Jimmy saw almost immediately the bloody red gash where his penis had been. In the silence of the bathroom, the only sound was the quiet steady drip drip drip of blood into the toilet.

Jimmy screamed, a cry of loss and pain and terror, a sound of primal intensity, but he could not look away from the sight before him, could not make his feet take him out of the room, could not even make his head face another direction. His father stared straight ahead, bloodshot eyes unmoving, unseeing, and Jimmy saw that his penis had been inserted into his mouth. The portion protruding from between his lips looked strange and greasy, the thin coating of skin barely containing the wild redness within. Dangling from the crimson center was a white tube surrounded by several smaller veins.

Jimmy doubled over, able finally to move, and he jerked his head over the rim of the bathtub and threw up. He closed his eyes, hearing the sound of vomit splattering against porcelain, and in his mind it sounded like the dripping of blood into the toilet, magnified monstrously. He heaved again, continuing to throw up until the contents of his stomach had been emptied.

The police. He had to call the police and tell them what had happened.

He stood, wiping the vomit from his mouth with shaking hands.

From down at the end of the hall came a loud noise. A sharp thump that echoed against the walls and sounded like—

—a soccer ball.

The sound came again. Heart pounding, Jimmy quickly crawled into the bathtub. It stank sharply of vomit, but he held his nose, forcing himself to ignore the smell, and closed the shower curtain as quietly as possible.

The sound came again, closer, and now it could be felt, a vibration in the air, in the walls, in the floor that reverberated through the porcelain of the tub.

"Ba!"

The soccer ball hit the shower curtain and ripped three of the hooks from the transverse bar. The center section of the curtain collapsed around the ball, and through the newly created opening Jimmy saw Randy West, standing in the doorway. The retarded boy's hands and clothes were covered with drying blood, and he was grinning. There were flecks of blood on his teeth. He clapped his hands as he saw Jimmy and began bouncing up and down. "Pa!" he cried, walking into the bathroom. "Pa! Pa!"

Jimmy screamed and cried out instinctively for his father.

His father did not respond.

Forty-two

In the dream, David was advancing, one hand out-stretched, the other shoved down the front of his pants, fingers working furiously. There was an unpleasant smile on his face. "You'll like it," he said. "You know you will." And then he had reached her and his free hand grabbed her arm, squeezing tightly. She could feel his hot disgusting breath against her neck as he bent to kiss her. Her ears hurt. Sirens were approaching, coming closer and closer, the noise spiraling in intensity. He pulled his hand from his pants and began to unbutton them. Looking down, she could see the long outline between his legs. And now the sirens were right outside and the flashing red lights were shining through the sheer curtains, giving the living room the look of a hellish fun house.

Cathy awoke, and there really were sirens outside; her sleeping mind had incorporated them into her dream. The sirens wound down, died. Still half asleep, she pulled open her drapes. The window faced the backyard, but, looking sideways, she could make out the pulsing red of police lights flashing against a palm tree further up the street. She did not like the sight—the red palm tree—it frightened her for some reason, echoing in her mind, and she let the curtain fall, leaning back in bed and closing her eyes. Part of her wanted to get up and look out one of the front windows to see what was going on, but before she could make the decision to get out of bed she had again fallen asleep.

The police cars were still there in the morning.

In front of Jimmy's house.

Cathy, bending down to pick up the newspaper from the front stoop, dropped the paper as she saw the yellow ribbon wrapped around the trees and fence post of Jimmy's front yard, a semicircle of police cars in the street. Her bathrobe fell open as she stood and she did not even bother to pull it closed. "No," she whispered, her hand moving up to cover her mouth. "No."

She hurried back into the house, quickly pulled on jeans and a T-shirt, and ran barefoot down the sidewalk to Jimmy's house, where she was stopped at the barrier by a uniformed policeman. "I want to see Lieutenant Grant!" she demanded. "Let me speak to Lieutenant Grant!"

Through the Goldstein's front window, Cathy saw Allan talking to another uniformed policeman. She waved frantically in his direction until she got his attention. He looked up, catching sight of her flailing arms with his peripheral vision, and as soon as he saw her he said something to the policeman and hurried out of the room. He emerged a moment later from the front door.

"Let her through," he ordered the officer manning the barrier.

The policeman stepped aside, and Cathy slipped under the ribbon and ran across the lawn. She was crying, tears blurring her vision, and she felt grateful as Allan's strong arms encircled her shoulders. "What happened?" she asked.

"Al Goldstein's been murdered."

"Oh, my God."

"Jimmy's missing. We think he was abducted."

"Oh, God."

Allan peered into her eyes. "Not a word of this, okay? I'm not even supposed to be telling you."

"How did . . . ? Where . . . ?" She shook her head. It was suddenly hard to breathe, and she could not seem to catch her breath.

"We found Mr. Goldstein in the bathroom. It looks like Jimmy was hiding in the tub, and it looks like there was a struggle. We're combing the area right now."

"It was Randy!" Cathy said suddenly.

"What?"

Cathy looked toward the front door of the house. Two white-suited men were carrying out the body of Mr. Goldstein. She stared at the stretcher and the covered body of Jimmy's father. She could not really see anything through the translucent plastic, could not make out any details, but there were dark splotches shadowing the underside of the covering, and she knew that his death had been bloody. She felt lightheaded, almost dizzy, but she forced herself to remain calm, not to throw up. "I know who it is," she said. "I know who did it."

The worry on Allan's face changed into something else, something she did not recognize. "Who?"

"Randy."

"Randy?" He looked puzzled.

"Randy West."

"The retarded boy?"

"He's not retarded. He's an idiot savant. His talent is murder. He can—"

"Hold on there," Allan said. "Wait a minute."

"Allan!" a man called from the doorway. "Come here! I think we've got something!"

Cathy held his arm. "You have to listen to me. I saw him sneaking back home the other night. His mother never lets him out, but he was out then, and he was covered with water. And dark stuff that looked like blood." Her grip tightened. "That was the same night that the last murder occurred. He killed Jimmy's father, and he has Jimmy."

"Allan!"

Allan waved to the man in the doorway, then turned back toward Cathy. "We'll talk about this later. There's a lot going on here right now. I know you're upset—"

"That's not it!"

"Okay, okay. That's not it."

"Allan!" the man called.

"Coming!" He took Cathy's hands in his own. "I can't talk about this right now. I want you to go home, sit down, relax. I will be in touch as soon as we're through here, and then we'll discuss it."

"I don't want to discuss it! I just want you to go into the Wests' house and find Jimmy."

"We will," he said, and he gave her hands a squeeze. "We'll check it out. And we'll find him."

"Alive," she said. "Find him alive." She pulled away, no longer able to stop the tears from flowing and she did not look back as she crawled back under the cordoning ribbon and walked down the street toward home. She heard the man in the doorway call Allan's name again, heard Allan answer. She kept her eyes focused on the sidewalk in front of her. She did not want to look across the street and see the Wests' house. She forced herself to take small even steps, though she felt like running.

She reached her house, picked the paper up off the stoop, opened the front door and slowly closed it behind her. She put the paper down on the small table next to the door and walked into the kitchen.

"What is it?" her father asked.

Cathy sat down heavily in the chair. Suddenly she could not seem to think or concentrate on anything. It felt as though she was walking through water and as though the water had seeped into her brain. Everything was moving slowly. Even her thoughts seemed sluggish.

"What is it?" her father repeated. He actually

sounded concerned, and the expression on his face almost resembled worry.

"Mr. Goldstein's dead," she said dully. "He was murdered. Jimmy's disappeared."

She braced herself for a snide and vicious comment. A "Good." Or a "No great loss." She would not have been at all surprised to hear him say something like that. But he said nothing, only stared at her in silent shock. If there had been something other than shock on his face, if he had looked concerned, or at least sympathetic, she would have thrown her arms around him and hugged him and cried, cried for all she was worth, but as it was they continued to stare at each other, and it seemed to Cathy that the water around her was getting thicker and the pressure was too heavy to even allow her to move.

"Who found the body?" her father asked finally.

She realized she didn't know.

And she started to cry.

Forty-three

The last police car left just before eleven. Allan had stopped by on his way back to the station and had told her to meet him there at twelve, but Cathy was at the police station by eleven-thirty.

The desk sergeant brought her immediately to Allan's office.

He stood as she entered the room. He looked tired. Tired and stressed out. Naturally thin, he now seemed haggard, his cheeks sunken, his eyes bagged, grown a decade older in the last hour. She wanted to hug him, to hold him, to put her arms around him and feel his arms around her, but she knew that would be inappropriate. So she stood there dumbly, looking at him across the desk. She opened her mouth to talk, licked her lips instead. She found it suddenly hard to speak, to ask the question she had to ask. Her palms were sweating and she wiped them on her jeans. She cleared her throat. "Have you . . . found Jimmy?"

Allan shook his head, and her breath caught, though it was the answer she'd been expecting. "No," he said, "I have men out canvassing the neighborhood, and we're coordinating a Valley-wide manhunt. But . . ." His voice trailed off.

"Did you pick up Randy and his mother?"

"They weren't home."

"Did you search their house?"

"We had no warrant."

She stared at him. "So what? He did it."

"Cathy—"

"I know he did. Now he has Jimmy stashed somewhere and maybe he's already killed him because you didn't act soon enough. You know what an idiot savant is, right?"

Allan sighed tiredly. "Cathy," he said, "I have to ask you a few questions, okay?"

She frowned. "What kind of questions?"

He looked embarrassed. "Questions."

There was something in his tone of voice that put her on guard, that made her feel that all was not as it should be, but she forced herself to nod and pretend that everything was normal. "Sure," she said. Her hands were shaking as she sat down across from Allan, and she tried to disguise the fact by pressing them between her knees. She knew that she had done nothing wrong, but she suddenly felt as though she had been caught committing a crime.

Allan, too, seemed ill at ease, and he kept looking down, unable to meet her gaze for more than a few seconds at a time. "Now you don't have to answer any of these questions if you don't want to, but I have to ask them."

"Okay. Shoot."

"If you'd like to have a lawyer present—"

"What is this? *Dragnet*?" She smiled, but the smile was slightly strained. Her heart was pounding. "Are you reading me my Miranda rights? Am I a suspect here?"

"No, of course not. I just have a few things to ask you."

"Ask then."

He took a deep breath. "Where were you last night at approximately eight P.M.?"

"Watching TV."

"Can your father verify your whereabouts?"

She stared at him. "I thought I wasn't a suspect."

"Just answer the questions."

Cathy closed her mouth only when she realized that it was hanging open. She felt not only deeply offended but also angry. What the hell was going on here?

"It's routine," Allan said, as if reading her thoughts. He seemed almost patronizing. "When a person is murdered, we do a routine questioning of all family members and aquaintances of the victim. It's standard procedure. Most murders are committed by someone who knows the victim, and so we just automatically ask a few questions. Usually it's nothing, but sometimes we get—"

"You didn't ask me these kinds of questions after I found Dusty."

Allan shook his head. "Look, I'm sorry I—"

"Your boss thinks I'm guilty, is that it?"

"No, that's not what—"

"Then why are you questioning me instead of Katrina West?"

"We are going to talk to Mrs. West and her son, but right now no one's home and we don't know where she is. I have a man working on it."

"Get a search warrant!"

"We're going to."

"Now!"

"Listen to me," Allan said. "We have no proof that the boy has done anything. We have no indication that he might have or could have performed even a minor crime, let alone a murder. All I have to go on is your say-so. I'm going to check it out, but we're policemen here. There are rules and guidelines that we have to follow. We can't just arrest people because their neighbors don't like them. If we did that, we'd be spending all our time hauling in innocent—"

"Goddamn it!" Cathy yelled. "Jimmy could be dying right now! Wasting time on this shit could cost him his life!"

"This 'shit,'" Allan said evenly, "is the Constitution."

"Fuck you!" Cathy stood. "The next time you talk to me, I'm going to have a lawyer present."

"Fine. That's your right."

She glared at him. Her hands were shaking visibly, rattling her purse, but she did not try to hide it. "May I leave now?"

"Yes."

"Fine!" She turned to go.

"I want you to stay away from Mrs. West and her son, okay? There's probably nothing to what you say—"

"What do you think I'm going to do? Kill them?"

"No, that's not what I'm saying. I just don't want you to get hurt. I'm going to talk to—"

Cathy stalked out of the room, slamming the door behind her.

Outside the office, she leaned against the wall, trying to quell the trembling in her limbs. She was sweating. She knew she had blown any chance she'd had with Allan. She should have remained calm, not lost control. But, damn it, she had come here to talk about Randy and Jimmy and to get Allan to take some action—immediately, before it was too late—and he had started giving her the third degree.

She felt hurt and betrayed, naked and exposed, filled with both a defenseless vulnerability and a feeling close to the unique emptiness of sudden loss. She was angry, angry at Allan for doing what he was doing, for thinking what he was thinking, for making a mockery of her trust. But an irrational uncontrollable part of her also felt guilty.

A uniformed policeman walked by, looking at her, obviously prepared to offer assistance, but Cathy pushed herself away from the wall and hurried down the hallway toward the lobby and the exit. She was shaken and confused and above all she was scared—each time she thought of Randy her skin prickled. But it was obvious now that, Allan or no Allan, the police were just going to keep moving merrily along in their narrow tunnel-visioned direction, and that if Randy were going to be stopped, if Jimmy were going to be saved, it would have to be up to her.

She rushed through the sliding double doors into the hot afternoon sunshine, and though she was sweating, she felt cold. She felt very cold.

Allan stood as Cathy stormed out of his office. He considered following her, but gave up the idea immediately, sensing that she needed some breathing room.

He'd really screwed that one up.

He mentally kicked himself. Why the hell had he done that? How could he have been so stupidly insensitive? He'd thought that if he asked the questions it would be easier for her, but he realized now that it would have been better to let Dobrinin or someone else do the interviewing, someone who wasn't personally involved. Not only had he done some fancy tapdancing on top of his ethics here, he had also made things decidedly worse than they would have been had he simply stuck to procedure. What the hell was wrong with him?

He stared at the closed door. Part of him wanted to run after her right now, to tell her he was sorry, to take her with him to the Wests' house and break down the door and save Jimmy and be a hero, like a character in a comic book. But another, more rational, part of his mind told him that there would be time for reconciliation later. Right now, he had to coordinate the efforts to find Jimmy.

The real efforts.

The thought occurred to him that maybe he had been boorish on purpose, that subconsciously he had wanted her out of his hair, had wanted free reign to work on this murder without having to deal with personal matters at the same time and had pulled this stunt to free himself. When it came down to it, he hadn't really had to question her at all, had he? There was no reason to grill her. He didn't suspect her, didn't think she knew anything beyond what she'd told him.

But maybe he'd wanted to know for himself.

That was possible, and the thought made him uncomfortable.

He wondered if the computer had come up with anything yet on her brother David.

He closed his eyes, trying to defuse the headache he could feel building behind his forehead. Policemen were not trained to deal with situations that were not black and white, that did not have concrete answers. He could handle ambiguity in art, but in real life?

He found himself thinking about what Cathy had said, but the idea that the retarded boy had killed Al Goldstein, had kidnapped and killed Jimmy, and had performed all of the other murders was ludicrous.

He'd handled the situation poorly. No doubt about it. He should have been more sensitive, more aware of her feelings. And he had only compounded his initial stupidity by arguing with her and making her angry.

Where was she going now? Home? He didn't think so. She'd been awfully upset, awfully angry, and awfully determined. If she really believed that Jimmy was in danger, that he was still alive and about to be killed, it wasn't logical to expect that she would go home and spend the rest of the afternoon passively watching *Oprah*.

He shook his head. She wouldn't try anything on her own. She wasn't stupid enough to play Nancy Drew and go amateur sleuthing to try to dig up information on Randy West to corroborate her theory, was she?

Was she?

He was suddenly afraid that she might do something dangerous and he realized that in the midst of all this, despite everything that was going on, he was concerned most about her.

He was falling in love with her.

If he was not in love with her already.

That wasn't possible. He couldn't have fallen in love with her this quickly. He had only met her a few weeks ago. They had gone out only a few times.

It was possible, though. Love and friendship had no timetables. There was no set gestation period for emotions, no standard by which the growth of feelings could be measured.

But that wasn't the only reason he was so anxious about her, was it? That wasn't the real reason he was so concerned about her actions, so worried for her safety. No, there was something in her theory itself that stuck with him, that he couldn't just dismiss. On that gut level that all cops trusted, on that instinctive emotional level of subthought that led to more cracked cases than all of the computers and crime labs in the world combined, something in what she said spoke to him, something in her wild theory, ludicrous as it might be, rang true.

The small footprints in Harvard Brown's wet yard could have been made by a child.

The fingerprints on the jagged rock they'd found in the storm drain next to the boys could have been those of Randy West.

He rubbed his temples. Now he was being crazy. He had nothing to go on. There was not enough proof to justify taking any action against the Wests.

But if the boy really was the murderer, he couldn't afford not to take action.

He stared at the closed door. Despite all the bullshit he'd thrown at Cathy about procedure, it was still his call.

He thought for only a moment, then picked up the phone, flipped through the pages of his personal phone book, dialed.

Five minutes later, seconds after Allan had replaced the receiver in its cradle, Thomasson walked into the office without knocking and plopped himself down in one of the director's chairs. The lieutenant kicked his feet up on the opposite side of the desk. "There are few things more gruesome," he said, "than walking into a reeking bathroom and listening to some patrolman taking a monster shit."

Allan looked up from the desk and frowned.

"I was just in there. Did you ever notice how the bathroom on this floor always smells a lot worse than the ones on the other floors? I think it's probably the guy who's in there now."

"Why are you here?" Allan asked.

"I work here. Or did you forget already?"

"No, I mean why are you here? In this office? Can't you see I'm busy?"

"Pynchon said he wants you in his office. Immediately."

"Why didn't he call?"

"Who knows? Maybe he wanted me to check in with you. He asked me to work with you on the murder."

Allan stared at him. "You've been transferred to Homicide?"

"I'm on loan."

"Jesus," Allan said, running a hand through his hair.

"Hey," Thomasson said, "don't get your sphincter all clenched out of shape. I'm not here to horn in on your territory. You know I don't go in for this serious shit. Pynchon just thought you could use an extra body today. Besides, I think he's afraid you're getting a little too involved with your subject here." Thomasson leaned back in his chair, balancing on two legs, his feet against the edge of the desk. "If I recall correctly, I told you the same thing a week or two ago."

Allan stood. "Look, Hank, I'm onto something here. I don't have time to explain it to you right now, and I don't have time to chat with the captain. So just tell him I'm not here, I'm gone."

"I just got in, and you want me to cover for you already?"

"Hank, this is big." Allan's voice was serious.

Thomasson put all four legs of the chair back on the floor. He nodded, understanding. "Okay."

"After you talk to Pynchon, stay here. Dobrinin's in charge of the field operation and he should be checking in any time. Anything new, tell the captain and call me on my beeper. If nothing's turned up, tell him to stay out there until something does. Got it?"

"Got it." Thomasson shook his head. "But when this is over, I'm going to take those eight vacation days I have saved up and I'm going to California. I'm going to get me a beach baby and rent me a big old boat and do a little offshore drilling, if you know what I mean."

"You and me, both," Allan said. He grabbed his jacket from the coatrack and put it on as he hurried out the door.

Forty-four

Cathy walked up the driveway toward the Lauter house—for it was the Lauter house again, despite the new curtains, despite the new residents. It was once more the haunted house of her childhood, filled with terror and pain and death.

She approached the front door and the walk seemed to stretch out before her, unnaturally long, like a cheap special effect in a bad horror movie. Katrina West's car was gone, and the windows of the house were hidden behind drawn drapes. Cathy had no idea whether or not Randy was home. She did not know what she would do if he was. She did not know what she would do if he wasn't.

But she had to find Jimmy.

And, dead or alive, she knew he was inside the house.

She reached the front door, and she hesitated for only a second before ringing the doorbell and knocking loudly. She held her breath, but there was no answer from inside, no sound at all.

What if Randy had taken Jimmy someplace else?

She pushed the thought from her mind and reached out to try the doorknob. She pressed down on the thumb latch, but it would not move. The door was locked.

Undeterred, she walked through the side yard to the rear of the house. The back door was locked also, as she'd known it would be, but this was the door that David had used to sneak into the house, and if Katrina had not bothered to change the locks, the door could be forced open with just a quick hard shove on the knob.

Cathy glanced furtively around, listened once again for any sounds from within the house, then pressed hard on the knob.

The door rattled but did not open.

She tried again.

Nothing.

Maybe Katrina had changed the lock. Cathy licked her lips, wiped her sweaty palms on her pants and pushed again, this time putting all of her weight into the shove.

The door swung open with a low click.

Cathy was instantly on the alert. She stepped back, waited for a reaction from within, but there was no movement, only silence. She was aware, somewhere in the back of her mind, that she had just crossed the threshold from misdemeanor to felony, that trespassing had now become breaking and entering, but she did not care.

Slowly, quietly, carefully, she pushed open the door and stepped into the family room. The inside of the house was dark. All of the curtains were drawn, effectively shutting out the illumination of the afternoon sun. She swore at herself. She should have brought a flashlight. It was still not too late to go back home and pick one up, but she knew that if she did, she might not have the courage to return.

Her eyes were adjusting to the gloom. Around her, boxes were still piled high on top of one another, odds and ends were scattered over the floor in disarray. The house smelled vaguely of rotted food.

She was still not sure of her plan.

She knew she was right about Randy, but she had no proof. What could she do? Gather evidence? What evidence? Was it likely that he kept souvenirs of his murders around the house?

What if Randy were here? What if she met him? What then? Would she kill him? If she wanted, she could kill him without waiting for proof. She could trust her instincts and simply knife him while he slept or lure him outside and ram into him with the car. But she knew she would never be able to do that. As much as she hated and feared the boy, she could not bring herself to kill another human being.

She wondered if his mother were aware of what he had done.

She had to know.

Finding Jimmy was her first priority. Her only priority. Once she got him safely out of here, the police could take over. She would let them figure out everything else, let them do the rest.

She walked slowly forward, trying to make no sound, stepping around boxes, over sacks. The house seemed claustrophobic, the air thick and stifling. The rotting food smell was stronger, nauseatingly cloying, and she tried to hold her breath, inhaling and exhaling intermittently, breathing only through her mouth.

The idea that Randy might be here in the house somewhere, perhaps waiting in his room, holding his soccer ball and staring at the lonely picture of the dog in a snowstorm, terrified her. She was sweating. Fear was what she felt when she thought of Randy West. The fact that such a sophisticated evil could be concentrated in such a crude package scared her far more than anything she had ever seen in any of her nightmares.

She entered the hallway, and saw immediately that all of the doors were closed: the bedroom doors, the bathroom door. The hallway was even darker than the family room, and her muscles stiffened with tension. She should have brought a flashlight. And a weapon.

From behind the closed door to her left came a soft thumping sound, and she jumped as though it had been a gunshot. She froze in place, and the noise came again. It sounded as though someone within the room was throwing something against the wall. A ball?

Was Randy in there?

Thump.

Cathy licked her lips. She wished Allan were here. If he burst in right now, he would probably arrest her and throw her immediately in jail, but he would also find out what was behind the door and was causing the noise. It was a backward and old-fashioned thought, but she wanted a man to be there with her. She wanted to rely on someone else, to let someone else make decisions and take action so she wouldn't have to be so damned scared.

She could handle being arrested, she could handle jail. Jail was not what she was worried about. She had come in the house, knowingly committing a crime, because she knew that far worse crimes had been committed by Randy. She was not worried about breaking the rules of society, about being caught trespassing or breaking and entering. She was worried about something worse. Something much worse.

Dying.

Being murdered.

Thump.

"Randy?" she called softly.

There was no answer.

She tapped on the door. "Jimmy?" Heart pounding, she reached out to try the knob. She had not consciously decided whether or not to open the door, but she found herself acting instinctively. The yellow-gold metal knob was cold to her touch. She turned it slowly, half hoping that it was locked and would not budge, but it turned easily in her hand.

Thump.

She opened the door a crack but could see nothing save a bare wall and the headboard of a brass bed.

She steeled herself. She had gone this far; she might as well go all the way. Sucking in her breath and gathering her courage, Cathy pushed open the door.

She blinked, staring.

Spreadeagled on the king-sized bed in the center of the room, gagged and tied, was a naked man.

A naked man with an enormous erection.

She took an involuntary step backward, not screaming only through sheer force of will. It was not what she'd expected to see. She'd thought she'd find Jimmy. She had even been prepared for blood. But the sight that greeted her was entirely unexpected, so off the wall that it shocked her into startled confusion. Her first thought was that Randy, or maybe Randy and his mother together, was keeping this man prisoner, holding him captive for some unknown reason. He was filthy, only tendrils of dried sweat exposing white skin beneath the brown dirt. His blond hair was long and wild and uncombed. He was struggling against his bonds, and she could see reddened chafed skin at his wrists and ankles where the thick rope had rubbed against them.

But why would they keep someone a prisoner?

And why would he have an erection?

The bed was the only piece of furniture in the room, which was lit solely by the washed-out light that seeped through the nearly opaque curtains. Leaning against the wall opposite the foot of the bed was a thin riding crop. Next to the crop, on the bare floor, was a pair of stained white women's panties.

What the hell was going on here?

Cathy walked slowly forward into the room. She wanted to keep her eyes on the bound man's face, but her gaze kept straying to the enlarged organ between his legs. The huge penis frightened her. She licked her lips. "Hello," she said. She was not sure of what to say, not sure of what to do.

The man's eyes bulged hugely, and he began thrashing around in an even more frantic attempt to free himself from his bonds. Cathy stepped closer, keeping her gaze trained on his face. The gag in his mouth, she noticed, was soaked through with saliva. His chest was crusted with dried semen. She stopped a foot or so from the bed. She knew she should untie the man and free him, but something kept her from acting. She was scared, more so now than before she had entered the room. There was something wrong with this man. He was insane or epileptic or rabid or . . . something. The way he continued to strain against his bonds, the strength with which he strove to break the rope holding him was not natural. The entire situation here was decidedly unnatural, and her instincts told her to get the hell out and call Allan.

"Is Jimmy here?" she asked instead, timidly, stupidly.

The man responded by renewing his struggles. His erection bobbed up and down with each movement. Behind his gag, he roared.

Cathy stepped back from the bed. She looked up. Through a crack in the curtain, she caught a glimpse of red movement in the driveway outside.

Red.

The color of Katrina West's car.

Panic welled inside her. She ran out of the room and closed the door. Within the room, the man on the bed continued struggling. From beneath his gag sounded muffled cries of rage and frustration.

If she could just make it to the back door before Katrina made it to the front . . .

She heard the click of Katrina's key in the lock.

No time.

She tried the door across the hall, but it was locked. The knob would not turn. She swiveled around and reentered the bedroom. The naked man was still jerking about beneath his restraints. His erection was as large and hard as ever. Moving even before her brain had consciously made the decision to do so, Cathy pulled open the slatted accordion doors of the closet. It was empty save for a coiled rope and a mop, and she quickly slipped inside and closed the double doors after her. She slid down to a crouching position. She could see through the angled slats to the room beyond, and she tried to recall if she'd been able to see in the closet from the outside. She hadn't noticed. She reached up and tried to push the slats flat, but they wouldn't move and the effort was making far too much noise, so she crouched in a ball, remained immobile, and tried to stifle the noise of her breathing.

From somewhere in the front of the house, Cathy heard the muffled sound of Katrina's voice, followed by Randy's louder bray: "Ka! Ka! KaKaKaKaKa!" Her muscles grew even more tense. A bone in her ankle popped loudly. She closed her eyes for a second, tried to calm down, praying that she would not be discovered.

A few minutes later, as she'd feared, as she'd somehow known, Katrina walked into the room. Cathy adjusted the tilt of her head and peered through the slats of the closet door at the partially obstructed view that presented itself. Katrina stepped into the bedroom, closed the door behind her, and locked it. The older woman had come in alone, and Cathy's first thought was: Where was Randy? She had heard the two of them come in the house together, but now the boy was silent, not making any noise. Was he in his bedroom?

And where was Jimmy?

Katrina's footsteps were loud on the hard floor, and the thumping of the bed as the naked man jerked his body against his restraints had grown in intensity. Cathy took the opportunity to quickly and quietly adjust her position within the closet. She shifted to a kneeling position and balanced her weight on her knees and lower legs. Now she could see through the slats.

Katrina was standing near the side of the bed, hands on her hips, smiling at the naked man. There was something lascivious in the way she smiled, something expectant in the way she stood, and in a sudden flash of understanding, Cathy realized what the relationship was between these two. Her mouth grew dry.

Katrina kicked off her shoes. "I had a hard day, dear."

The man was still struggling wildly, jerking his body back and forth, up and down, causing the box springs of the bed to jump and fall loudly onto the frame. His erection alone remained unmoving, too stiff to be swayed, and it was now clear to Cathy that he struggled against his bonds not in an attempt to gain freedom but in an effort to satisfy his overpowering lust. His head rocked back and forth as he bounced, moving in some jerky alien rhythm.

"I'm coming," Katrina said. She laughed. Her laugh was rough and filled with no humor. "I'm coming." She unfastened her dress and carefully folded it, placing it on the floor. Her unhurried movements only served to further increase the frenzied movements of the man. She smiled to herself, as though fully aware of the effect on him and proud of it. She continued to undress slowly. Her panties and bra were large and simple, nurselike, an antiseptic industrial white, purchased for practicality rather than romance. She removed them both, and Cathy looked away, concentrating on the dark segments of slats rather than on the sight visible in the open sections between them. She was embarrassed at the sight of Katrina's large heavy breasts, her aggressively full thatch of pubic hair. Embarrassed and slightly intimidated. Katrina West was not, by any stretch of the imagination, an attractive woman, but there was a raw sexuality to her, a lustiness obvious in her bearing and being that made Cathy feel uncomfortably innocent and immature.

She forced herself to look again through the slats of the closet. Katrina was now climbing on the bed and straddling the man. She positioned herself above his stiff organ and reached for the ropes binding his wrists, untying first one hand, then the other. He continued to stare at some fixed point in the ceiling, and his head continued to rock back and forth in that strange rhythm, but his hands, supple and experienced, moved expertly over her body, touching, massaging, caressing; kneading her breasts, leaving the nipples hard before moving downward; following the contours of her stomach to the folds between her legs. The hands seemed to belong to someone else. Their touch was light and flexible, sophisticated, the movements sensuously poetic. Katrina leaned her head back and let out a sharp gasp of pleasure. Underneath her, the man's body began to move and undulate, awkward jerks transforming seamlessly into smooth fluidity. There was something right about the way he took possession of her body, something natural. This was what he had been made for, and his movements were those of an expert, each twitch of his body, each tiny motion designed to provide Katrina with maximum pleasure. As he grasped Katrina about the waist and thrust gracefully into her, he seemed like an entirely different man from the one Cathy had first stumbled upon.

Katrina screamed, a loud uninhibited animalistic cry of pleasure. She reached out and ripped the gag from the man's mouth. Even through the slats, Cathy could see the man's slack jaw, his thick protruding tongue.

He was mentally retarded.

Katrina screamed again, and the man screamed with her, a low guttural cry of primitive wordless ecstasy. The skin crawled on the back of Cathy's neck. She watched silently, growing increasingly horrified, increasingly frightened as realization dawned on her.

The man was Randy's father. And he, too, was a savant.

His talent was sex.

Cathy tried to move away from the door, to retreat further back into the closet without making any sound. She felt sick. She closed her eyes, tried to plug her ears, but she could still smell what was going on. The odor was almost overpowering, permeating the humid air of the enclosed room. The musky vaguely fishy fragrance of Katrina's arousal augmented by a sharper, more clearly defined scent, at once cleaner and more animalistic, that could only come from her husband.

Cathy tried not to breathe, tried to breathe through her mouth, but the smell was all pervasive, and she could taste it. She felt like throwing up, but she forced herself not to gag, not to react, not to do anything to give herself away.

Jimmy, she thought. Where was Jimmy?

She didn't know, and even if she did know, she wouldn't be able to do anything to help him.

Feeling scared and sick and frustratingly powerless, she crouched further back in the darkness of the closet and waited.

Forty-five

Dr. Frank Meredith's office was located in a tan fake-adobe medical complex at the trendy north end of Scottsdale. His suite was the farthest from the parking lot, across a sandy pseudo-desert courtyard, but Allan had no trouble finding it, and he stepped into the cool air-conditioned waiting room, grateful at last for some effective relief from the afternoon heat. He closed the door behind him. The room was decorated in light pastels and Southwest earthtones, tall cactus plants adorning the corners opposite the receptionist's window.

He stepped up to the frosted glass, rang the bell, and gave his name to the plump gray-haired woman at the desk.

"Dr. Meredith's been expecting you," she said. "Come on in, Lieutenant Grant."

The receptionist opened a door next to the front counter, and Allan walked back into an antiseptic white-walled hallway that branched in three directions and seemed to lead to a warren of equally white lab rooms. Through various open doors, he could see the amber-charactered screens of several computer terminals as well as the science-fiction forms of larger and more complicated high-tech neurological equipment.

"He's right back here," the receptionist said. "In his office." She walked up to and knocked on the first closed door in the nearest branch of hallway. The door was immediately opened by a tall robust man in his mid-fifties.

"Howdy," the doctor said. "Glad to meet you." He held out a big beefy hand, which Allan shook. Meredith's grip was firm and steady. He smiled at the receptionist. "Thanks, Gladys."

Were it not for the white lab coat that he wore, Allan would have pegged the doctor for a construction worker or a ranch hand of some kind. Meredith had none of the soft attributes traditionally associated with people who worked indoors. His complexion was tanned, his face sun lined, and his posture that of an athlete or outdoorsman. He towered nearly a head over Allan, and his strong voice carried more than a hint of East Texas.

"Come on in," the doctor said. "You want something to drink? Iced tea? Root beer? Water?"

Allan shook his head. "I'll only trouble you for a minute."

"Been thinking about what you asked me." Meredith walked around his desk, plopped down in a padded swivel seat, and motioned for Allan to sit down on the couch against the wall. "I knew the situation sounded familiar, so I made a few quick phone calls, did a little research." He put on a pair of wire-framed glasses and quickly leafed through a leather-bound book on his desk. He found the page he was looking for and loudly thumped his finger down at the top of a paragraph in the middle of the page. "Jorge Onofre. You're going to want to Xerox this."

"Why? Who's Jorge Onofre?"

"First, let me ask you what all this is about. This isn't entirely hypothetical, is it?"

Allan shifted in his seat. He felt awkward about

coming here already. The initial impulse to seek Meredith's advice had been transformed in his mind from a legitimate effort to explore a theory into a favor for Cathy, and sitting in this office, surrounded by hundreds of thousands of dollars worth of lab equipment, he felt embarrassed, felt as though the questions he had were frivolous and idiotic. He tried to think of a reply that would not make him sound like a complete and total boob. "It's part of an investigation," he said noncommittally.

"The Phoenix Fiend?"

"I'm not at liberty to say."

"It is, isn't it?" The doctor removed his glasses. "The reason I ask is because there's a case that occurred in Brazil in 1963 and is quite well documented that closely parallels your hypothetical situation. You asked me if it was possible for an individual suffering from Savant Syndrome to have a talent for murder. Technically, maybe. A savant, or what used to be called an idiot savant, is a person with severe mental handicaps who possesses one area of spectacular, often genius-level, intelligence. This area of intelligence, however, is confined to a rather limited range of skills, generally having to do with math, art, music, or mechanical dexterity. Mechanical dexterity might be the one here that is most applicable.

"Although we don't know for sure why savants are the way they are, the most accepted theory involves a dysfunction of the cerebral cortex. You see, savants are often born premature, their brains not fully formed at birth. In the normal brain, there is usually left-brain dominance. The left brain is in charge of the use of language and other abstract skills. The savant's talent is usually associated with the more mnemonic right-brain functions. Treffert, who is really the pioneer in this field today, postulates that when prenatal damage is done to the brain's left hemisphere, there is a consequent recruitment of right-brain neural cells. This means that the individual's particular genius, which normally would have remained untapped in the right regions of the brain, is somehow activated. Treffert also postulates that savants use a different memory circuit than do the rest of us, a circuit governed by the basal ganglia, which may grant them access to racial memory."

Meredith chuckled. "After *Rain Man* came out, people seemed to think that all savants were autistic. Actually, only fifty percent of savants suffer from autism—"

"That's fine, Doctor. But do you think it's possible for a savant to have a talent for murder?"

"Possible but not probable. There would seem to be far too many analytical skills involved in killing, particularly in carrying out sophisticated murders, for a savant to possess such a talent. The one constant all savants seem to have is that their thought processes are not subject to intellectual interpretation or associative thought." Meredith leaned back in his chair. "Then there is Jorge."

"What about Jorge?"

"Jorge was different. Technically, he did not suffer from Savant Syndrome. In fact, he exhibited several symptoms normally associated with Down's Syndrome and for all intents and purposes appeared to be severely mentally retarded, which meant that his IQ was considerably lower than that of most savants." Meredith leaned forward. "But he had a talent for murder. And he killed all of the residents of the village in which he lived."

Allan was stunned. "All of them?"

"All of them. He was found playing with the heads of his parents in the open square of the village, and around him were the bodies of the others, some sixty in all. They'd obviously been dragged there—the boy wasn't Bruce Lee or anything, he hadn't taken on the whole town at once—but he had killed each and every one of those people, and the amazing thing was that he had killed each of them in a different way. There was an old man who had been filleted, every bone taken out of his body, a young girl who had been flattened, looked like a steamroller had gone over her. The killings were all unique, and all wildly original. And bear in mind that this was a poor remote village. The weapons at this child's disposal were extremely limited and fairly primitive."

"How was this discovered?"

"A group of Peace Corps volunteers went to the village intending to teach the locals about modern farming techniques—the land was badly overused and unreplenished—and when they drove in on their Jeep, they saw Jorge and his kills. By that time, half of the bodies were already putrifying. They sped out of there and contacted the authorities."

"Did they have any problem capturing him?"

Meredith shook his head. "Apparently not. He was very docile, didn't even seem to know what was going on. As I said, he was severely mentally retarded."

Allan sat there for a moment, trying to sift through the information, trying to take it all in. Suddenly his questions didn't seem so frivolous. Suddenly Cathy's theory didn't seem so far-fetched. Suddenly Randy West seemed far more frightening. "If this boy wasn't a savant, what was he?" Allan asked. "Was this a disease or something?"

"We'll never know," Meredith said. "He killed himself a year later. He was institutionalized, kept in solitary, sedated and straitjacketed, but he somehow managed to dislocate his shoulder and twist the muscles of his neck, in such a way that when he threw himself down on the padded floor of his cell, his neck was broken immediately. It was not a suicide, at least not in the accepted sense. It was not the manifestation of a desire to die but more the manifestation of a desire to kill. The boy was acting not on the death impulse but on a killing impulse, and, lacking any other victims, he killed himself.

"You see, Jorge's mind ran along a very strict and very narrow path. All of the rational energy of his brain was directed toward murder, to the exclusion of everything else. It was much stronger than a compul-

sion, much more instinctive than an obsession. It was
more of a drive, a very strong overriding natural impulse. The tests they submitted him to—a battery of
psychological tests, very sophisticated and very comprehensive for that time—seemed to confirm this. The
tests were a complete and total failure in the traditional way, but they did reveal a fascinating—and
frightening—aspect of the boy's mental abilities. He
could turn almost anything into a weapon of murder."

Allan was becoming increasingly alarmed. "How
so?"

"For instance, Jorge was unable to eat with a fork.
He couldn't put on his clothes. He wasn't toilet
trained. But he could take, say, a plastic building
block, and use it to effectively force back the tongue
in the throat of a nurse—a little stunt he pulled on his
first day at the institution, before he was kept under
permanent restraint. Jorge was very definitely retarded, but his small-muscle coordination, when ap-
plied to killing, was absolutely phenomenal. The child
seemed to have an intuitive grasp of the lethal possibilities of each and every object with which he came
into contact. It was as though he sensed, as though
he innately understood, how everything—everything—
could be used to kill. I might add that an autopsy was
performed on the boy after his death, and a cystlike
structure was found in the third and lateral ventricles
of the left hemisphere of his brain. Similar but less
complex growths had been found in the brains of individuals suffering from Savant Syndrome, but this
structure was the largest and most complex of its kind
ever recorded. We think that this might have been
responsible for Jorge's remarkable abilities."

"My God," Allan said.

"Lieutenant Grant, is this about the Phoenix
Fiend?"

Allan thought for a moment, nodded. "Yes."

The doctor's face clouded over. "Is this a theory
you're working on, or do you have . . . a suspect?"

"I can't say right now."

"I would have contacted you earlier," Meredith said, "but I didn't know what was happening. If I'd known what was going on, I probably would have noticed parallels and would have come to you, on the off-chance that it might be of some help. But, to be honest, I wasn't really aware of what was happening with these murders." He smiled somewhat sheepishly. "I've been under a deadline, and I've been preparing for an upcoming conference and when I get really involved in a project, I tend to block out everything else. I just sleep, eat, and work. I lose track of time. Sometimes I don't even know what day it is."

Allan stood, held out his hand. "Well, thanks for your help now."

"If you need any additional assistance . . ."

"I may need an expert witness in a few weeks."

"I'm not an expert, but I can find you someone who is."

"Deal," Allan said. He started toward the door. "And thanks for your help."

Meredith accompanied him to the lobby. "There is a suspect, isn't there? You have someone in mind."

"Good-bye," Allan said. "Thanks again." He hurried across the fake desert courtyard through the heat toward his car.

Forty-six

Katrina pulled on her panties, feeling a delicious soreness between her legs. How was it that she had never grown tired of sex, even after all these years? That the malaise that seemed to have settled into the lives of so many people her age had never affected her?

Robert.

It had to be Robert.

She looked over at her husband on the bed, once again tied up. If anything, her sexual appetite had increased since those early days. She wanted it more often now, and she craved more variety.

And Robert provided it.

She remembered the first time she'd seen him, in the bathing room at Meadowview. Even heavily sedated, he'd had a powerful erection, and he'd been playing with himself while Otis washed him off.

It had been love at first sight.

She'd been vaguely aware that it was forbidden to have sex with a patient. She thought that it might even be illegal—she seemed to recall hearing about a doctor in another institution who'd supposedly done it with a catatonic woman and had been sentenced to prison—but the rules had never been specifically spelled out for her. What's more, she didn't care.

She'd wanted Robert.

She stood in the doorway of the bathing room, watching as he stroked his penis with his hand, completely ignoring Otis's ministrations. His gaze was dull, his mouth slack, he was drooling, but his hands had a life of their own and they massaged his organ tirelessly in a manner that was a revelation to her. She watched, fascinated, as his movements quickened, reached a peak. She saw him ejaculate and watched the orderly wash it off before she finally turned away.

She'd learned the patient's name from Otis, and several times during the following week she checked on him, making a special effort to learn in what ward he was located, when he ate, when he was exercised, when he was bathed. None of the other orderlies knew how long he'd been at Meadowview—he'd already been here when Jim Caldwell, the senior orderly, had started working—but it was clear that he was a lifer: he was severely mentally retarded and could not speak; he was apparently not able to recognize his doctor or regular orderlies, though he saw them each day; he was not even toilet trained.

She could have asked one of the administrators or a member of the medical staff more specific questions about him and about his condition, but she was afraid to. She did not want to draw attention to herself. Her interest in the patient was clearly not clinical or humanitarian.

Her interest was sexual.

That was one thing the other orderlies did talk about. Robert's tremendous sexual appetite. It was the reason he was either restrained or sedated at all times. Apparently, he had once attacked one of the other inmates, an aggressive woman whom even the biggest orderlies had had a difficult time subduing. After he'd finished with her, she had been silent, withdrawn, almost comatose and for several days afterward had had to take nourishment intravenously. He had very nearly raped her to death.

After that, he had been placed under constant medication, although even drugs were not able to entirely lessen his lust or dampen his desires. Emma Hall reported that one time she'd had to feed him and the restraints had been off, and he'd tried to assault her. She'd been assured that he'd been given enough sedatives to chill out even a head banger, but his erection had been as powerful as ever, and he'd tried to use it to rip through her uniform. Only the fact that Bill Colter had accompanied her to lock up and was right outside the door had saved her from being raped.

"That's the last time I dealt with him," she told Katrina. "I had myself transferred off that assignment. That guy scares the shit out of me."

"Now he's in semi-solitary," Otis said. "He still gets enough tranquilizers in his food to take out a mule, but it doesn't seem to affect him none. Hell, he doesn't even seem to notice. Since he can't poke someone else, he just beats off all day."

Sure enough, each time she peeked in on him, he was masturbating.

She watched him through the one-way glass.

She thought about him at night, alone.

Looking back, Katrina could not remember when the plan had formed in her mind and when she had finally made up her mind to go through with it. It seemed to her to be such a natural progression, such an obvious thing to do that she could not recall actually taking time to map out steps or strategies. And it had worked perfectly. She'd simply rearranged her schedule so that it would be convenient for her supervisor to assign her to work with Robert. She'd called in sick, gone home early, come in for partial workdays, manipulated her hours and shifts in order to be available for his feeding and bathing and toilet. She'd made it clear that she wouldn't mind the assignment—and she'd gotten it.

She remembered the first time she'd bathed him. He had wet himself, and she carefully removed his pants and used the wet washcloth to clean his penis. As always, he was hard, and she felt a shiver of excitement as she wiped his organ. It felt better than she'd imagined, spongier, with more warmth and life in it.

She had always been religious, and she found that she felt for Robert something close to what she felt for God: an awe, a respect, a love, a longing. She had been raised in the faith, and as a child the church had taken care of her between foster homes. The church had even helped her find the position at Meadowview when she'd needed a job.

Maybe she was crazy, but it had always seemed to her that she felt something more for God than did the people around her, the other people in the church. They all loved God—the priests, the parishioners, the volunteers—but for her it was not the same. What she felt for the Lord was not their kind of distanced, intellectual love. It was something she experienced in her soul, something deep, almost physical.

That was what she felt for Robert. When she watched him masturbating, his fingers expertly manipulating his organ so that he maintained an amazingly constant erection, her heart was filled with respect and reverence and an awed ecstasy. He was the most amazing human she had ever met, and though he seemed retarded, she knew that he was special, blessed by God, and that she could learn a lot from him.

She found herself spending more and more time with Robert, unable to stay away though she knew that she was jeopardizing her position with the institution. The other nurses and orderlies began talking. She received one warning from administration. Then another. She knew that her days at Meadowview were numbered, yet she knew that she would not be able to leave Robert.

In the end, it had been simple. She didn't give two

weeks' notice, she didn't fill anyone in on her plan. She just brought an extra coat to work one day and when her shift ended a little after midnight, she sedated Robert with a dose of Nembutal, freed him from his leg restraints, threw the coat over his straight-jacket, and walked out with him to the car. She was not questioned by Curtis Lowell, who waved her through the door, nor was her car stopped by Sonny Packard at the front gate, who nodded and smiled as she drove past.

It was a stupid plan, simple and without subtlety, and she supposed that was why it had worked. She left Robert in the car while she returned to her apartment and packed a suitcase, and then they were gone, driving west.

They'd consummated their love in a Motel 6 in Chicago.

Two days later, her credit cards were rejected by a Holiday Inn in Denver, and she knew that they were on to her. She sedated Robert with the extra drugs she'd brought, traded her old car in for a new used one, changed her name and hair color and headed toward Cheyenne.

And that was it. She'd never been caught, never been troubled by police.

She'd had to give up nursing, of course, and had been forced to take on menial jobs for menial pay, but it had been worth it. She and Robert had never been legally married—there was no way she could allow him outside unrestrained and unsedated—but they were married in the eyes of the Lord, in the only way that really mattered, and they enjoyed all of the fruits of a traditional marriage.

And sex that was far beyond anything found in a traditional marriage.

She smiled fondly at Robert as she finished putting on her housedress. She walked back across the room and kissed him on the forehead. His frantic struggling suddenly ceased, and he looked up at her with those big almond-shaped eyes that communicated so much more than any words could have. She heard his raspy breath beneath the gag and—

The sound of someone else breathing.

Katrina stiffened, listened, still heard the noise. She rushed over and grabbed the riding crop leaning against the wall. Her hands shook and, when she spoke, so did her voice. "Who's there?" she demanded.

There was no answer. Robert had started jerking about the bed again, and the noise effectively drowned out all other sounds.

The closet. Whatever it was, whoever it was, had to be in the closet.

Katrina rushed across the room, crop raised, taking the offensive. "Get out of there!" She jerked open the closet door.

And there was the bitch from across the street, crouched on her knees behind the slatted door.

Katrina stopped, stunned. She stood, staring at Cathy, caught completely off guard, but she did not lower the riding crop. "What are you doing here?" she screamed. "What the hell do you think you're doing here?"

Cathy stood, cringing, ready to ward off blows. "Nothing," she said in a small voice. "I wasn't—"

"You were spying on me!"

"No." Cathy shook her head. She was sweating, and droplets of perspiration dripped from her damp hair.

"Get out of there! Now!"

Cathy emerged from the closet. Her eyes flitted to Robert on the bed, and she seemed to straighten, gain strength. She turned to look at Katrina. "Where's Jimmy?" she asked.

Understanding dawned in the older woman's face. Her eyes widened, and she took a step back. "Randy," she whispered. "You want Randy."

"I want Jimmy. I know Randy's done something with him."

Katrina lowered the riding crop. She looked suddenly scared. "It's not what you think," she said, backing up. Her left hand found the knob and fumblingly opened the door. She stepped into the hallway.

Cathy followed, advancing. "Where's Jimmy?"

"Randy's a special boy—"

"He's a murderer."

"No!" Katrina shook her head violently, near tears. "He's not!"

"He is, and you know it. You've been protecting him."

"He doesn't know what he's doing."

"But you know," Cathy said. "Where's Jimmy?"

"He's special. He's—"

Behind Katrina, Randy stepped into the hallway. He was grinning hugely, his chin wet with saliva. There was blood on his face, on his shirt, in his hair. His hands were crimson. In one of them he held a hammer.

Cathy stopped, the words she was about to speak dying in her throat. She wanted to scream but could not. Jimmy was dead. If she had suspected it before, she was sure of it now. Randy had killed him in some unspeakable way and then had had his fun, playing in the blood. She stared at him, at his happy half-wit smile, and realized that her own chances of escaping alive from this house were slim to none.

Katrina saw the expression on Cathy's face and turned around, facing her son. She gasped when she saw the blood on Randy's hands, dropping her riding crop. "How did you get out? What did you—?" She jerked her head back toward Cathy. "I left him in his room! I locked him up—"

"Ha!" Randy said, triumphantly holding up the hammer. "Ha! Ha! Hahahaha!"

"Give that to me!" Katrina said sternly, swiveling around again, and the boy promptly handed the hammer over. She took it from his grasp and instinctively wiped the handle clean with the edge of her house-dress to remove any fingerprints. She blinked, as though suddenly unsure of where she was or what she was doing. She shook her head, then grabbed one of

Randy's hands and faced Cathy again. "You're not going to tell anyone, are you? He's not . . . He doesn't know what he does."

"Just let me out of here," Cathy said quietly. "Let me go."

Katrina's voice was tinged with panic. "Promise me you won't tell anybody. Randy's not a bad boy. He's just . . . special. He can't help himself. Promise me . . ."

"Let me go." Cathy addressed the words to Katrina, but her eyes remained fixed on Randy.

"No!" Katrina said suddenly, and there was strength in the word, conviction. Cathy realized that she should have run, should have forced her way out, that now the time for escape had passed. "You don't care about Randy. You don't care about my baby, my son. You're just going to tell the police."

"Yes!" Cathy said, and her own conviction surprised her. "He's dangerous, and I'm going to tell the police and I'm going to make sure something's done about him. He's a killer. I knew there was something wrong with the boy the first time I saw him, and now I know what. He's an idiot savant. You know what that is? He—"

"No!" Katrina screamed. She glared at Cathy. "He was just born different, like his daddy. Everyone thinks he's retarded, but he's not. The midwife told me he was retarded, but I knew she was wrong. I knew he was special even then. I knew he had his own talent, like his daddy. And when he killed his brother and he was only a year old, I knew what that talent was."

Cathy took a step back.

"Oh, it broke my heart. It did. I loved little Jason. He was my firstborn, and I loved him with all my soul. But somehow I knew even then that I loved Randy more. I was angry at Randy, but at the same time I was sort of proud of him, you know? He broke Jason's neck using the side of the crib, and it was so sad to see how he lay there with his little head all twisted off to the side and his eyes staring into space, but I couldn't help thinking that if God hadn't wanted this to happen, he wouldn't have made Randy this way. We might not understand it now, but it's all part of God's plan. Do you believe in God?"

Cathy did not answer.

"Do you believe in God?" Katrina demanded.

"Yes," Cathy said. "Yes." She was trying to think of a way to grab the hammer from Katrina's hand or to pick up the riding crop from the floor, but she could not see a way to do either without giving Katrina and Randy time to attack.

"God works in mysterious ways. I probably would have let you go home, if He hadn't sent Randy in here at just the right time. But He knew what you were planning, and He didn't want you to cause any harm to come to Randy."

"Ka!" Randy said. "Ka!"

"Yes," Katrina told him.

"If you don't let me out of here this minute, you're both going to be in even worse trouble than you are now," Cathy said.

"God has special plans for Randy. And for Robert. And for me."

Dimly, from far away, Cathy heard the sound of sirens. Katrina cocked her head, obviously hearing them too.

"I called the police," Cathy lied. "I called them when I saw you pull into the driveway." She tried to appear brave, on the offensive. "You can't get away now."

Katrina smiled. Her smile was nervous but genuine. "Neither can you," she said. Her voice once again sounded rational.

She let go of Randy's hand.

Cathy backed up. Randy was still grinning, and he scratched his forehead with a bloody finger, leaving a streak of pink sweat across his skin. He cackled loudly, obviously happy, obviously excited, and his laugh did not sound like the laugh of a retarded child. It seemed deeper, more adult, and consciously, definitely evil. He took a step forward.

"No," Cathy croaked.

Katrina put a loving hand on her son's shoulder, prodded him. "Randy," she said softly. "Kill her. Make her die."

Forty-seven

Allan pulled up in front of Cathy's house, parked the police cruiser. It was late afternoon, though it was impossible to tell from the sun, which still seemed to think it was around lunchtime and hovered only slightly west of center in the sky. Allan stepped out of the vehicle, the asphalt spongy beneath his feet, made soft by the heat of the day. He closed the door and looked over the white car roof toward Cathy's house. Her VW was in the driveway. At least she was home. He wasn't exactly sure what he was going to say to her, but he figured he'd start with an apology, tell her what Meredith had said, and then suggest that both of them take a little trip across the street to the West residence.

He walked around the hood of the car and glanced for the first time at the front door of the house, partially hidden by the Volkswagen. His heart leaped in his chest.

The front door was open.

So was the screen door.

He could hear the lightly rattling hum of the air conditioner on Cathy's roof.

"Cathy!" he called, yelling toward the house. He waited three seconds. "Cathy!" There was no response.

He didn't like this. He didn't like it at all.

Allan quickly backtracked to the car and opened the door, sitting down. He turned on his radio, picked up the mike. "Two-fifteen requesting backup," he said. There was a crackle of static, then Yvonne's acknowledgement. He wasn't sure what was happening, didn't want to waste manpower if he'd made a mistake, but he didn't want to be caught with too few people if something really had happened, so he tagged it as a "possible kidnapping" and asked for two black-and-whites, four uniforms.

He signed off, got out of the car, unholstered his gun and sped up the front walk.

He smelled it the second he walked in the door.

Violence. Blood.

Death.

He gagged, felt like throwing up, but instead of running outside, he forced himself to swallow the bile and continued into the house, hurrying. His heart was thumping crazily; it was hard to breathe. In his mind he saw Cathy lying on the dining room table next to a pile of skin, or sitting on the toilet, breasts lopped off and lying on the tile, and he cursed himself, wishing he'd listened to her, wishing he'd gone along with her, wishing he hadn't stood so hard and fast on his damn rules and procedures. He was being punished for his inflexibility, and now Cathy would be dead and he hadn't even told her . . . anything. How he felt. What she meant to him.

He swung into the doorway of the kitchen, automatically assuming the classic firing position, arms and pistol outstretched and ready.

And there was Cathy's father.

Allan took an involuntary step backward, the entire scene burning itself instantly into his brain. The blue Formica floor was covered with the crude chalk drawings of a child: crooked hopscotch squares, stick figures with out-of-proportion heads, tic-tac-toe fields. In the center of this lay the old man. He had been crucified, and his body was raised a few inches off the floor in irregular spots, balanced on crutches arranged in the shape of a cross.

Allan knew without being told that this was Cathy's father. He could see the resemblance despite the bald head, despite the parchment skin, and that similarity disturbed him. In his mind, he saw Cathy herself crucified, dead. He stared down at the unmoving body. Cathy's father had been gagged with a dish towel. A single bolt had been driven through the wide expanse of wrinkled forehead, and from the resultant hole blood dribbled feebly in a weak drying trickle. Another bolt had been driven through an arm, another through a kneecap, and blood had puddled and congealed beneath the body. It looked like the work of satanists, though Allan knew it had been Randy West, and the thought passed fleetingly through his mind that the boy was the antichrist.

And a little child shall lead them.

He forced himself to maintain his grip, to knock off the melodramatic horror-show crap. He had to think logically here, had to act intelligently. Already he could hear the sirens coming, and he still didn't know where Cathy was.

Gun drawn, calling her name, he quickly searched the rest of the house. The remaining rooms were empty and appeared to be completely untouched. He paused for a moment in the doorway of Cathy's room, feeling like a voyeur but still needing to see where she slept, where she lived. The room was pink and frilly and too cloyingly cute, the bedroom of a preteen girl. It was not at all what he had expected—only the small television and the well-stocked bookcase on the far wall fit his preconceived image—but he was surprised for only a second. Then he remembered what she had told him of her home life and what he knew of her past, and then he was walking back down the hall and through the laundry room to the garage. Here, too, everything seemed undisturbed.

He returned to the kitchen but did not yet holster his gun. He stepped over a chalk drawing of a stick-figured man, careful not to disturb any evidence, and once again he found himself staring at the body of Cathy's father. This close, he could see that the man had died terrified. His eyes were wide, the muscles of his lower face so contorted that Allan could tell he'd been screaming beneath the gag. He had wet himself and his bowels had evacuated, and the smell of his waste mingled sickeningly with that of the blood. He had died a pitiful and terrorized old man, and his death had been slow and agonizing.

Allan hoped to God that Cathy had not been here to see this.

But where was Cathy? She was not in the house or the garage or—

It suddenly came to him.

The Wests' house.

How could he have been so stupid? How in the hell could he have been so goddamned fucking stupid? He ran outside, yelling to the two officers who had arrived and were getting out of their car: "Montoya, come with me! Davis, call Homicide! I want Dobrinin, Thomasson, Williams, and whoever else is available over here now! Don't touch anything until Forensics arrives!"

He did not stop to see if they had understood him, did not look back to see if they were following his orders, but sprinted across the street and up the curb, pistol still in hand. He was panting, breathing hard not from exertion but from fear. He had the horrible feeling in his gut that his tardiness had cost Cathy her life, that she had been alive five minutes ago but was dead now and that she would still be living if he had been able to think more clearly on his feet.

He reached the front door and it was locked, and without thinking he broke it down, the panicked adrenaline coursing through his bloodstream giving him the strength of a television cop. "Cathy!" he called.

She was already screaming, though he had not heard the noise from outside. Her urgent cries were loud but breathy and grunted, the involuntary sounds of a person under attack.

He jumped the unpacked boxes on the floor, heading instinctively toward the darkened hallway, but saw movement out of the corner of his eyes and swiveled, pistol pointing, toward the dining room.

Cathy was on the floor, struggling. Her blouse had been ripped and one breast, ivory white with blood-red scratches, was exposed and pressed harshly against the carpet. A large chunk of torn hair was lying a foot or so from her head. Randy was on top of her, and though his hands were battering her body, easily by-passing and avoiding her attempts to ward off the attack, raining blows on her head, chest and abdomen, his face remained blankly impassive, his eyes looking nowhere, his mouth slack and open. The expression on his face was one of peaceful contentment, as though his head were entirely unaware of the violent chaos occurring below and being perpetrated by his body.

Katrina West was standing off to the side, next to the table, egging her son on. She was crouched in a posture of anticipation, and her mousy hair was hanging wildly about her face. "Kill her!" the woman said, and there was something like glee in her fanatic voice. "Kill her!"

"Stop!" Allan ordered. His pistol was trained on Randy, his hands were steady, and, child or no child, he would have fired had he been able to get a shot clear enough to ensure that Cathy would not be hit.

Randy looked up, surprised by the sound of Allan's voice, and immediately jerked Cathy's arm up and back. There was the sickening crack of crunching bone, and Cathy screamed in agony, a cry so atypically raw and loudly primal that it seemed dubbed, out of sync with her lips. The boy looked at Allan and grinned. It was a grin Allan would never forget, a malevolent smile of satisfied cunning, an intelligent evil suddenly overlayed on blankness, and it chilled him more than anything he had ever seen. Then it was gone, and in one smooth amazingly fluid motion the child was off Cathy and through the kitchen door.

The entire scene had lasted less than ten seconds, and Randy was gone by the time Montoya ran up behind Allan a beat later.

Allan knelt down next to Cathy. She was rolling on the floor, still screaming horribly, blood dripping down her face and flopping breast, her broken arm hanging limply at an unnaturally geometric angle. The boy had been playing with her, like a cat playing with a caught mouse before killing it, and Allan was grateful that he had arrived in time. A minute later and . . .

"He's in the garage!" Cathy screamed. "I saw him run into the garage!" She tried to point with her good arm through the kitchen door.

Allan glanced through the kitchen at the black rectangle of the open garage door on the other side of the small empty patio. "Are you all right?"

"Get him!" she cried.

Allan stood. "Watch her!" he ordered Montoya. He pointed toward Katrina, now huddled whimpering against the wall. "And watch her! Don't let her escape!"

He ran through the kitchen and out the door to the garage. He could hear more sirens from up the street, coming closer, and he wished he hadn't been so short-sighted as to come here alone in the first place. He'd been in a hurry, but he'd also had probable cause and he should have been prepared. If he'd had only three more men with him, they'd probably have that little fucker caught and cuffed by now.

He raced through the garage door.

Where he almost ran straight into Jimmy Goldstein. Jimmy was shirtless and shoeless, suspended by his feet from a rope tied to one of the crossbeams. He was not moving, and Allan thought at first that he was dead. His face and chest were swollen, puffy, blistered, the skin red and black and blue. About him, the garage floor was littered with nearly a dozen soccer balls, many of them smeared with blood.

Allan quickly scanned the darkened garage but saw no sign of Randy. There were some piled boxes near the big door and three metal garbage cans behind which the boy could conceivably be hiding, but other than that the garage was clean. Still holding his pistol, ready for an attack, he reached out, police training taking over, and grasped Jimmy's wrist, feeling for a pulse. It was there and surprisingly strong. Likewise the neck throb. Randy had been using the poor boy for target practice or something, but he had done no major damage. Obviously, he hadn't wanted to. Jimmy, for him, had been a toy, a playtime diversion.

There were footsteps behind him, running, and Allan whirled around, but it was only Montoya. Dobrinin was with him.

"Paramedics on their way," Montoya began. "We . . ." His voice trailed off when he saw Jimmy. "Jesus."

"He's alive," Allan said. "His pulse is steady, no bones broken, I think he's okay. Help me cut him down." He nodded toward Dobrinin. "Search the rest of the garage, see if you can find him. If not, spread out, move outside. I want him caught."

"Who?"

"The boy."

Dobrinin, gun drawn, was already sidling up to the garbage cans. "The boy?"

"Randy West. Our 'Fiend.' "

"It's a kid?"

Allan grabbed Jimmy around the midsection as Montoya loosened the knot around the boy's ankles. "I don't have time to explain, and you wouldn't believe me if I did. Just know that the kid's dangerous—

able and willing to use deadly force. He just killed a man across the street and injured these two here, and we have to find him now."

Still confused, Dobrinin swung around the side of the garbage cans in a firing position. "Nothing!" he called out. He moved quickly around the pile of boxes. "All clear!"

"Shit! He's outside, then. Get a team on it."

"What's this?" Dobrinin said from the far side of the garage.

"What?"

"Some type of metal gadget."

"Look at it later! I want a team out there now!" Allan grunted as Jimmy's full weight slid into his hands. He placed the boy carefully on the floor. Jimmy remained unmoving, eyes closed.

Dobrinin ran out the door. "I'll get the paramedics in here!" Montoya said, hurrying out after him.

Allan knelt by Jimmy's side, trying to revive him. From within the house, he could hear Cathy's screams and the unintelligible but recognizable sounds of orders and responses, investigation hierarchy swinging automatically into action. Outside, more sirens were arriving and he could hear the mumbled undertow of beginning crowd noises.

A few moments later, the big garage door was opened and as Allan stood, two white-suited paramedics came in carrying a stretcher and emergency medical paraphernalia. Twin ambulances were backed up in the driveway. Cordoning ribbon was already being strung up around the house and around Cathy's house across the street. Six police cars were parked catty-corner on the street and uniformed officers were trying to move back the gathering crowd.

"We'll take over from here," one of the paramedics said, crouching down and taking Jimmy's wrist in his hand. The other paramedic unfolded the stretcher and placed it on the opposite side of the boy.

"Thanks." Allan nodded. "I've been trying to revive him, but he hasn't come to—"

The first paramedic carefully felt Jimmy's swollen purple-red chest. "I think he'll be okay. He probably has a slight concussion, but it isn't a coma or anything. He'll snap out of it."

"Thank God." Allan left the paramedics to their work and hurried back into the house. Cathy was already loaded onto a stretcher and was being strapped in. She seemed a lot calmer. Her arm had been laid atop her chest, but it was still twisted at an angle that was painful even to look at, and he realized that she must have been given a tranquilizer. "How do you feel?" he asked her.

"Did you get him?" Her voice was slow and slightly slurred.

"Not yct."

"Get him!" She tried to sit up, but couldn't and fell heavily back down. She closed her eyes, opened them. "The bedroom," she said.

"What?"

"Jesus!" Thomasson called from somewhere down the hall. "Allan! Get over here!"

Allan took Cathy's good hand in his, squeezed it. "Are you going to be all right?"

She nodded tiredly, closing her eyes again.

He gave her a quick kiss on the forehead. "They're going to take you to the hospital. I'll be over as soon as I'm through here."

"My father," she said thickly. "Tell my father."

"Ycah," he said as two paramedics picked up the stretcher. He patted her head and started toward the hallway, where a slack-jawed Thomasson was emerging from the darkness, then thought the better of it, turned around and kissed her lightly on the lips. "I love you," he said.

But she was already out and didn't respond as the paramedics carried her through the entryway and out the door.

"Allan," Thomasson said. His voice was low, unnaturally subdued. "I don't know what the hell this is in here, but you've got to see it."

"Wait a minute." Allan held up a hand. "Montoya!" he called.

The uniformed policeman stuck his head around the corner of the kitchen.

"Where's Mrs. West, the woman I told you to watch?"

"Still here. She's not talking."

"Read her and book her."

"For what?"

"Obstruction, harboring, we'll figure the rest out later."

"Allan!" Thomasson yelled.

Allan turned around. "What?"

"Get in here!"

Allan followed the other lieutenant down the hallway and into one of the bedrooms. In a room devoid of furniture save for a brass bed, a nude man was bound and gagged, tied to the bedposts. Between his legs was a huge erection. Allan stood unmoving just inside the doorway. "What the hell is this?"

"You tell me."

"Get the woman in here. I want some questions answered, and I want them answered now." He stared at the naked man as Thomasson hurried off to get Katrina West. The man jerked and bucked on the bed, causing the barred headboard to smack rhythmically against the wall. The man's face was straight out of Munch: gaunt and white, haunted, all sunken cheeks and overlarge eyes. There was something about his expression or the set of his features that didn't seem quite right, though, and Allan stepped forward and removed the gag from the man's mouth.

The man bellowed loudly, a cry not of rage or pain or joy or sorrow, but an attempt to communicate.

The man was retarded.

Allan stepped back instead of untying the man's arms and legs as he had intended. He understood now. He saw what was going on here, and it scared the hell out of him.

"Leave Robert alone!" Katrina West screamed from behind him.

Allan turned around to see the woman, handcuffed, held in place by Thomasson. "Who is this man?" he asked. "And why is he tied up?"

"Leave him alone!"

"Are you going to tell me who he is?"

"I want a lawyer!"

"I'm going to untie him."

"Leave Robert alone!"

"Why?"

"He's my husband!" She glared at Allan. "I'm not saying anything else without a lawyer."

"Where's Randy?"

"I don't know."

"Is this Randy's father?"

"I want a lawyer!"

Thomasson shook his head, renewed his grip on Katrina's upper arm. "You're not gonna get anything out of this broad. She's crazy as a damn bedbug."

"I know my rights!"

"Allan!" Montoya called from the front of the house.

"Take her out of here," Allan said disgustedly. "Call the PD. And call County." He gestured toward the bed. "Have someone pick this guy up." He ran a quick hand through his hair. "We also need more backup. We have to get a search started out there before it's too late. Has anyone called Pynchon?"

"He's on his way," Thomasson said.

"We're not leaving this house until we've gone over every inch of it."

"Allan!" Montoya called.

"Coming!" He pushed past Thomasson and Katrina West, moving back into the living room.

Montoya ushered him through the kitchen and out to the garage. "Before things get too crazy, you gotta see this. Remember the gadget Dobrinin found in the garage?"

"Yeah." Allan followed the patrolman inside. The big garage door was still open. Both ambulances were already gone, though Allan hadn't heard the sirens, and a photographer was already taking pictures of Jimmy's rope and the bloody soccer balls. Outside, a large crowd had gathered.

"Shut the door," Allan ordered.

A patrolman he didn't know hurried to carry out the order.

"Look." Montoya pointed.

On a broken table against the wall lay pieces of metal: small machine, tool and hardware parts obviously scavenged from around the house or neighborhood. Scattered on top of the rough unfinished wood were nuts and bolts, springs and washers, screwdrivers, hacksaw blades and wire cutters.

"Jesus," Allan said. "Look at this." He pointed toward a small contraption sitting at the far end of the table. The device appeared to be constructed primarily from bits and pieces of old toys, but Allan knew immediately that it was no toy. Wicked-looking blades, apparently hand-sharpened from scraps of discarded sheet metal stuck out in all directions. "He made this?"

"I don't know. What is it?"

Allan moved slowly around the side of the workbench, carefully examining the device without touching it. He shook his head, amazed. "I can't believe this."

"What do you think it is?"

"Stand back." He scanned the garage, his eyes alighting on a broom. He picked it up, holding it backward, by the bristles, using the rounded end of the handle to prod the device.

The contraption jumped and snapped like a set-off mousetrap, the sheet-metal blades whirling. A set of sturdier garden-shear blades whipped out on a crude extension to stab the air in front of the device.

"Shit!" Montoya cried, jumping back.

Allan stared at the now-unmoving object, too

stunned to respond. Meredith had said that Jorge, the boy from Brazil, had been able to instantly determine the lethal applications of any object, but the doctor had not mentioned anything about the ability to construct special instruments of death, to build complex mechanical objects specifically designed to kill. He felt a chill pass through him.

Obviously, the doctor had not known about this ability. This was something new.

He found himself wondering what else the doctor might not know about, and he felt more powerless, more impotent, less in control than he had before they'd discovered the identity of the killer.

His gaze remained fixed on the multibladed object on the edge of the table. The metal gleamed. What if Randy had built more of these things? What if he'd left them around the neighborhood or around this section of the city and they were waiting like time bombs to go off?

He pushed the thought to the back of his mind, tried not to think about it. There was too much going on. Things were too hectic; he had too many other things to worry about without fretting over what-ifs and might-bes.

But the thought wouldn't go away.

His head was beginning to pound.

"Shit," Montoya repeated. He approached the device with trepidation, tentatively touched a blade with the barrel of his pistol. Nothing happened. The patrolman looked up at Allan. "Your kid built this?"

"I think so."

"What is he?" Montoya demanded.

Allan shook his head. "I don't know."

The sidewalk in front of the station was crowded with reporters—locals, nationals, radio, TV, print. Well-dressed men and well-coiffed women vied for prime position on the low steps, posing in front of their cameramen. A convoy of logo-sporting vans with open doors and attached snakes of cable was parked in the street, and in front of the first van two uniforms were arguing with a group of men in business suits, obviously trying to explain that a press pass did not invalidate a "No Stopping Any Time" sign.

Allan drove around the mess and tried to sneak through the back gate into the motor pool lot, but even here three enterprising reporters were already waiting. They came hurrying after his car as he pulled in, fingers expertly working tape recorder buttons as they ran.

Allan stepped out of the car just as the reporters reached him. How did they get their information so damn fast?

"Lieutenant Grant!"

"Lieutenant Grant!"

"Lieutenant Grant!"

He was holding up his hands for quiet, intending to give the reporters a generic "We'll-let-you-know-as-soon-as-we-find-out-the-details" statement, when he saw Pynchon throw open the station door and storm out onto the pavement.

"Grant!" the captain roared.

"Excuse me," Allan told the reporters. He pushed his way through the mini-mob, and walked over to where Pynchon stood fuming.

"Shut the hell up and don't tell them a damn thing," the captain said. He ushered Allan through the door and into the station.

"I wasn't going to."

"Make sure you don't," the captain told him. "We're going to have to be very careful of what we say from here on in. No matter how you cut it, this is going to end up being an embarrassment to the department and making us look bad. Our mass murderer, our cop killer, our 'Phoenix Fiend' turns out to be a retarded kid. Jesus, do you know what kind of field day the press is going to have with that? We're going to come out looking like a bunch of Keystone Kops."

He led Allan down the hallway toward his office.

"I have Holman working on a press release right now. That's going to be our only statement until we figure out what to say. We're going to have to map out a full PR approach on this before we confront the media."

"Talk to Dr. Frank Meredith over at the Maricopa Clinic for Neurological Studies. Meredith has some information that'll curl your hair. People get ahold of some of that stuff, and we'll start looking a hell of a lot better. I think Meredith can really make it clear what we're up against."

"How much does this Meredith know about the situation? Should we have him here now? Should we be using him for a resource?"

"Probably," Allan admitted.

"Goddamn it then, get on the ball! I don't want this thing botched any more than it already has been."

"Look, I just got in. Stop bitching at me, for Christ's sake. You saw what it was like at that house. What the hell do you expect?"

Pynchon put an awkward hand on Allan's shoulder. "You're right," he said. "I'm sorry."

Allan shrugged the hand away. "No news yet?"

"Nothing."

"How's Cathy?"

"She's fine, the kid's okay, the mother's in custody, the father—or whatever the hell he is—is in County Psych."

The two men walked into Pynchon's office. The captain flipped on the lights and Allan sat gratefully down in a chair. He shook his head, sighing. "I feel like I'm in a damn movie."

"Who doesn't?" Pynchon said. "This isn't real life. This is a fucking horror flick. I'm not even sure what we should be doing here. We're hunting down a grade-school kid? Do I give shoot-to-kill orders? What kind of lawsuits are we going to run into if I do that? What's going to happen if I don't?"

"You put guards in the hospital, didn't you?"

Pynchon waved his hand dismissively. "Guards outside both the woman's door and the kid's. We took 'em to Memorial. That hospital's got a better security system than the White House."

Allan relaxed a little. "So what's the plan?"

"I've called a meeting in forty-five minutes. Everyone except the men out searching and a bare-bones regular shift. I want you to tell them where we stand, what we're up against. This is so far out in left field that it's hard for people to comprehend. Hell, before I got to that fucking spook house I didn't even really understand what we're up against. I kept asking myself how Whitehead could have let himself be taken down by a kid. 'Let himself.' Like his death was his own fault because he'd been murdered by a child. But when I got there, when I saw his mom and dad, I realized that this wasn't just a 'kid.' What we're dealing with here is a monster. A fucking real-life Freddy or something. That's what you have to get across. Make them realize what we're dealing with. We can't be thinking like that if we're going to capture him before he strikes again."

"We'd better catch him fast," Allan said.

Pynchon nodded. "I know."

"I'm worried about those little traps or whatever the hell they are. What if there are more of them? What if he's planning to use them?"

The captain sighed. "What I'm worried about is that he may be able to think in terms larger than a single murder. He may be able to map out plans for multiple murders. He may be able to lay out a coherent long-term strategy."

"Which means that—"

"We're fucked," Pynchon said. He coughed. "Did you happen to ask Meredith about that?"

"Not yet."

"Ask him."

Allan nodded.

Pynchon removed a key ring from his desk drawer, stood, pocketed it. "I'm going to Forensics. Want to come?"

"No." Allan stood as well. "I need a few minutes alone. And I'd like to call the hospital."

"Cathy?"

Allan nodded, slightly embarrassed.

"Is this woman a girlfriend or something?"

Allan shifted uncomfortably. "I don't know," he said. "Sort of. Yeah. I guess."

"Are you going to be able to handle this?"

"Sure, no problem. You know me."

"She's pretty," Pynchon said. He looked at his wall clock. "Time's ticking. I gotta get going. See you in the squad room. Half hour."

Allan nodded. "I'll be there." He followed the captain out of the office, then headed back down the hall toward the rear of the building and his own office. The hallway was practically deserted. The only officers he saw, two young recruits in the break room, were speaking lowly, almost conspiratorially. The station seemed like a fortress under siege, and he felt like he was walking through the back rooms while everyone else was out front manning the barricades.

Allan stepped into his office, turned on the light. He was exhausted, his brain throbbing painfully. He could not remember ever feeling this flat-out tired. Although he hadn't eaten since breakfast and his empty stomach was rumbling, food did not sound good to him. The only thing that sounded good right now was sleep, crawling into his own bed, snuggling under his own blanket, resting his head on his own soft pillow, and closing his eyes and not waking up for a long, long time.

He collapsed into his chair. He finished off the flat warm Diet Coke that had been sitting on his desk since this morning, but he was so tired that even caffeine couldn't perk him up. He tossed the empty can into the trash. His headache ran so deep that six Tylenols had still not made a dent in its strength.

He stared through his window at the orange sunset sky outside. The machinery was in motion now, Pynchon was running the train; he could probably catch ten minutes of quick shut-eye before the meeting.

But no. He had to prepare. He had to think of what he was going to say. A team was already out there, and though they were searching in twos, there was still a possibility that if they found the boy one of them might be injured. Or killed. He owed it to them not to succumb to his own softness. He owed it to them to give them the best that he could.

But was his best good enough? He wasn't sure. And right now he was too exhausted to worry about it.

He picked up the phone, dialed Memorial Hospital.

The entire squad room was filled, all of the chairs taken, every inch of wall space blocked. People were funnelled out through the door into the hallway. It was the first time since he'd joined the force that Allan had seen all officers from all shifts gathered together while on duty, and the sight was rather sobering.

One kid had been able to outthink and elude all of this?

It was a truly terrifying thought.

He stared out at the crowd, his eye drawn instinctively to the small islands of civvies within the sea of blue. For some reason, the faces of the individuals not in uniform seemed clearer, more distinctive to him than those surrounding them. He caught Pynchon's eye, saw the captain nod, and held up his hands for silence. The murmur of voices quieted and died.

"You all know why we're here," Allan said. "And I'm sure you've all heard at least one version of what went down. But I'm here to tell you what really happened. So you'll know what you're dealing with."

He explained everything from the beginning, speaking slowly and clearly, leaving nothing out. He did not mention his relationship with Cathy, but he did relate how she had first come up with the savant theory and how he had decided to check it out.

"The most important thing to remember," he said, "is the fact that we are not dealing with a regular child here. We are not even dealing with a regular human being. What we have here, in the body of a boy, is a mind so brilliant, so sick, so amoral, so . . . evil, that it has been able to devise and carry out at least eight murders—unique, original, torturous murders—under our very noses, including one of a fellow officer. And with all of our technological tools, all of our psychological knowledge, all of our experience and training and resources, we have not been able to catch him. Randy West is dangerous. I cannot stress that enough. He has the ability to turn anything into a weapon. Anything. We have no way of predicting his behavior, we have no way of knowing how he thinks. He has no M.O., no pattern. We do not know how he will react when cornered, what he will try to do, what he is able to do."

Pynchon stood. "What Lieutenant Grant is trying to say is don't try to outthink this kid. You can't. And don't consider that some sort of challenge. If you do, you're likely to end up on a slab. The only advantages we have here are numbers and firepower. Use them. I want you to comb the damn city, find that kid and take him in. If you can't take him in, take him down."

Allan nodded. "He's small, he's on foot, and he was at his house at about four o'clock this afternoon. So we're spreading out in a circle. He's small enough to hide anywhere, but we're hoping he's aware of the fact that we're after him and he's panicking, running. We'll see. But we'd better get out there now and we'd better get busy before he has a chance to think things over."

"Team assignments are posted on the board," Pynchon said. "Clerical and non-safety personnel will continue to perform regular duties on regular shift schedules. Everyone else will be getting hazard and overtime pay." He looked at Allan, who nodded. "Let's get busy."

"And, hey," Allan said. "Let's be careful out there."

Most of the older officers chuckled, but a young policeman standing in front of him looked puzzled.

Allan smiled at the rookie. "Old joke," he said.

The meeting broke up, the assembled individuals filtering quietly out into the hall, and Allan hurried to Dispatching to check in with Williams, Dobrinin and Thomasson, who were on remote hookup, but none of the three team leaders had seen or heard a thing.

It was eight o'clock.

Forty-eight

The first device went off at nine-thirty.
The second at ten.

Forty-nine

John Boyd had never covered anything like this, and he was not quite sure how to act. Usually, on camera, he smiled personably and delivered his report in a friendly, reassuring, slightly condescending manner, following the advice of one of his old college professors and talking to the camera as though it were a confused idiot child. But that did not seem appropriate in this instance; in fact, it would probably come across as downright ghoulish. The subject here was sensitive. It had to be handled with kid gloves. He didn't want to upset or offend people.

At the same time, this story was big, and he knew that it was spectacular enough to gain national attention. If he did a creditable job here tonight, the network might use him as a stringer on this story instead of assigning it to one of their usual correspondents. With the current budget constraints in the network's news division, there seemed to be a trend toward using stories by regional affiliate reporters, and that was definitely a factor in his favor. If he didn't completely screw this up, there was a good chance that the "Phoenix Fiend" would be his beat.

And this was the sort of story that could make a career.

It was a measure of the power of television and its dominance over print that after tonight, if all went well, he would be automatically identified with the "Phoenix Fiend," while the *Republic* reporter who had coined the phrase would languish in obscurity, watching from the sidelines as his moniker gained national prominence.

But what the hell. That was the news biz.

John adjusted his tie, followed Rudy's instructions as the cameraman tried to frame a shot, and tried not to think of the carnage behind him. For the past twenty minutes, Rudy had been videotaping the covered bodies and the metal contraption that had sliced through the victims' midsections as they'd walked out of the movie theater, attempting to capture the horror of the scene in a way that would not be offensive to a family viewing audience, but John had seen the bodies just once and had immediately turned away. He had never seen anything so horrible before, and the sight made his stomach churn nauseatingly. In that brief glimpse, he had seen holes of blood tunneled through casual clothes, pastel-colored entrails lining the holes' parameters. It was not something he would ever forget, and the idea that the scene remained unchanged behind him, that if he turned around he would see the same two bodies in the same positions, the wicked-looking metal object between them, gave him the willies. He had to fight the urge to run.

He tried to think of something else.

He closed his eyes for a second, and then Sam the sound man was thrusting a headset into his hands. "They want a newsbreak," Sam said. "We're going to interrupt the beauty pageant."

John felt the fear slide away, replaced by the more familiar and calming influences of opportunity and ambition. Interrupting the beauty pageant? This was big.

This was *it*.

Gina handed him a mirror, puffed his hair, sprayed it into place.

"We're on in five," Sam said, handing him a microphone and moving quickly into the van.

Rudy, his shot framed, gave the high sign, turned on the lights.

To smile or not to smile?

"Three," Sam said. "Two. One."

John took a deep breath, nodded, looked into the camera. He did not smile, but he did not frown. His expression was objective, detached. Professional.

"This is John Boyd with Channel Four Action News," he said. "A man and a woman were killed on First Street tonight as they . . ."

Fifty

It looked like a scene from a movie.

Two lanes were already blocked off; a detour set up; and policemen, reporters, and photographers for both were milling about the cleared section of street. In the center of the cordoned area, three bodies were lying on the pavement, their unmoving forms marking the points of a rough triangle. The bodies—two women and a preteen boy—were being ignored, and the exaggerated way in which their limbs were spread out made them look like dummies or in-place extras. The entire scene, in fact, reminded Allan of a movie shoot: the small clusters of quietly milling people, the cameras, the bright temp lights.

Except that the blood was real.

And the small irregularly shaped metal object in the center of the street was not a special effect.

If possible, the horror here was even worse than that on First Street, despite the distancing air of unreality. The other two bodies had been eviscerated, but that was nothing that had not been seen before.

This was different.

Allan's gaze lingered on the young boy. He was repulsed but unable to look away. The front of the child's body had been sheared off, the face and chest and genitals and legs neatly sliced in such a way that their severence had not affected any major veins or arteries, had not caused a gush of blood. There was only a puffy layer of red topped by a thick clearish yellowish liquid on the perfectly flat surface of the body.

The two women had been killed the same way, and the faces and fronts of all three victims lay in crumpled heaps on the asphalt.

There had been witnesses for the incident on First, but there had been no witnesses here. A busboy and his friend had found the bodies immediately after the trap had done its work, had almost run over the bodies still twitching spasmodically on the ground, but they had not seen the device in action. They had not even noticed it at first, it had been so small and unobtrusive.

Then they had seen the nails.

And the blades.

Allan walked over to the object. It looked like a cross between a hand mixer and a Slinky. Although changing the air filter in his car and setting the timer on his VCR was about as deep as his mechanical knowledge went, even he could see the brilliance in this design, and he marveled at the mind that could produce such a uniquely effective killing machine.

A chill passed through him. The more he saw of Randy's handiwork, the more frightened he became of the boy.

"After the regular tests are done," Allan said, "I want the guys in the lab to examine this thing and find out how it works, why it works, whether it has a timer, whether it can be used more than once, and what it's similar to."

Montoya nodded, jotted down a sentence in his notebook.

"Is there any way to tell how long this has been left here? How long it sat before it went off? Randy was off and running as soon as he saw me in the house. I find it hard to believe that he had time to pick up two of these things, lug them around, and then deposit one of them on First Street and one of them over here. I also don't think he's stupid enough to leave a trail this obvious. These may be decoys. I want to know if these devices were put here a while ago, or if they actually do chart the direction of his movements. Get someone on it now."

"You got it," Montoya said.

Pynchon arrived a few minutes later, and Allan walked across the asphalt to meet him. He talked for a few moments with the captain, explaining what had happened, what was known. Pynchon said he'd take over the on-site, and Allan acquiesced. He wandered about by himself, trying to stay out of the captain's way. The two of them had opposite investigational and command styles, and Allan knew from experience that it was best to let Pynchon have his way and then take over when the captain left. It served no purpose to waste time with meaningless procedural confrontations.

Allan walked past the bodies on the sidewalk, noted the blackness of the drying blood in the glare of the photographic flashes. He felt nervous, tense, ill at ease, and not just from the murders, not just from the fact that Randy was still out there somewhere. His uneasiness was more personal, but he could not quite articulate it, could not quite bring it to the forefront of his consciousness, and that nagged him, disturbing him even more. He walked around the border of yellow tape, ignored the gawkers who addressed questions to him. Then he walked by the hood of the patrol car that had been serving as the base of operations for this site, and amidst the cups of coffee and still cameras he saw a map of Phoenix with both of tonight's murder locations marked with a red "X."

He suddenly understood what had been bothering him.

This location was closer than the last to the hospital where Cathy had been brought.

He shook his head, looked away. It was entirely illogical. There was no way Randy could know where she was. He'd been long gone before the ambulance had arrived to pick her up. Even if he had been hiding someplace and had seen the ambulance, his reasoning abilities were not sophisticated enough to figure out that she was being taken to a hospital. And even if he had somehow understood that she was being taken to a hospital, there was no way for him to know which hospital. And even if, by some miracle, he did learn which hospital she had been taken to and then somehow found a way to get there, there was no way he could ever get past the guards and the surveillance equipment to her room on the third floor.

And yet . . .

And yet Allan was worried, nervous. Randy had already done the impossible. Several times. Many times. Knowing things he should not have known, doing things he should not be able to do, successfully killing God knew how many people in unfailingly unique and gruesome ways.

He didn't want the boy anywhere near Cathy.

Allan looked away from Pynchon and the other policemen, down the empty street, all de Chirico angles and shadows. It was probably only his own paranoia projected outward, but everything tonight seemed filled with an aura of menace, even the star-filled sky seemed threatening. He felt the urge—no, the need—to visit Cathy, to reassure himself that she was all right. He turned back toward the investigators. The situation here was under control, the preliminary investigation nearly wrapped up. There was nothing he could do besides oversee the work of people who already knew their jobs.

And Pynchon was already doing that.

He hurried back to where the captain was ordering a rookie to once again dust for fingerprints on the lower edge of a shop door adjacent to the sidewalk.

"I'm going to take five and head over to the hospital," Allan said. "I'll meet you back at the station."

"Going to check on your girlfriend?"

"Yes," Allan said.

"All right. But get your ass back ASAP. We need you out here. This is going to be a long fucking night for all of us."

"Yeah." Allan waved goodbye as he ran across the street. He got in the car, started the engine, and backed up.

He should have felt better now that he was going to the hospital, he knew. He should have breathed easier.

But he didn't; he wasn't. The tightness in his chest grew, and he flipped on his lights and siren and floored the gas pedal as he sped down the street toward the hospital.

Fifty-one

Cathy sat up in bed. She had not been in a hospital since having her tonsils out as a child, and the feeling was strange, disorienting. She remembered the hospital as being huge, labyrinthian, with miles of twisting hallways and rooms filled with monstrous machines, but it seemed far smaller, far less frightening than she remembered, closer to the friendly organized medical centers shown on television than the sterile hell of the hospital in her memory. Most of the nurses were approximately her own age.

She shifted her position in the bed, or tried to, but her body did not respond the way it should—she could not move her right arm and that entire side of her torso was numb—and despite her efforts the attempt was only a partial success.

With a grunt, she rested her back against the propped-up pillow. The physical pain she'd experienced earlier had been tranquilized into nothing, but her partial incapacitation served to keep its flame alive and burning brightly in her mind. Not that it would ever flicker out. That feeling of agony she'd experienced as Randy jerked her arm backward, twisting it in a direction it was not supposed to go, would stay with her forever. She had been so certain that she was going to die, her adrenaline had been running at such a fever pitch, that her senses had been heightened and each second of that hellish encounter had been recorded with photographic clarity and permanently etched on her brain. She could recall perfectly how she'd thought that he'd ripped her arm completely from its socket, how the pain had been so great that she'd nearly passed out. She could still see him sitting atop her, could still feel his little fists expertly avoiding her own thrashing attempts at self-defense and punching her body in all of its most vulnerable spots. She'd been able to smell and feel the sticky drying blood on him, and flecks of spittle, threads of drool, had landed on her face, making her feel like throwing up. He had been like a demon from hell, unnaturally strong, unimaginably intuitive, and the terror, despair, and hopelessness she'd felt in those endless horrifying moments left an emotional imprint she would carry with her always.

Randy West, she thought, was evil. Not misguided, not misunderstood, not sick, not disturbed, but evil. She recalled his idiot eyes staring blankly into space, his mouth crowing in animal triumph, as his hands expertly yanked her bones out of their sockets, and she shivered.

It frightened her to think about the boy, and she wished someone were here with her. Allan. Her father.

Her father.

Had someone told him what had happened? She sat up in bed. Earlier, she recalled, when she'd still been under the influence of the tranquilizers and the anesthesia, the doctor had come in and told her that reporters had been clamoring for an interview all evening and that he'd informed them that she wouldn't be strong enough to face them for a few days. He'd said that the requests to see her had continued, however, and he'd asked her permission to fend off questions concerning her physical condition, saying that he wouldn't discuss her attack at all but would stick strictly to the subject of injuries. Groggily, she'd said okay.

Later, she'd had a nurse call the bookstore and tell them that she wouldn't be at work tomorrow. Or the next day. Or possibly the rest of the week. She remembered thinking it strange, surrealistic almost, that outside the boundaries of her life, the real world was going on as normal. Jeff would come to work wearing weird clothes in the morning; Ann would prepare for her finals during breaks between customers.

The nurse had made the call and had talked to Ann, who'd demanded that she be allowed to speak to Cathy. Cathy had still felt a little out of it, but she'd talked to Ann, calmed her down, given her a short version of the events, sworn that she was okay. Ann had wanted to rush right over, but Cathy told her that visiting hours were not until morning and that she should wait until then. She didn't really know when visiting hours were, but she really had felt tired and hadn't felt like seeing anyone right then.

But no one had mentioned her father.

And where was Allan?

There was a noise in the hallway outside her room and she jumped, startled.

It was only an orderly, walking by with a row of clear glasses on a steel tray. She told herself to relax, calm down. Allan was probably doing police business, booking Randy and his mother, trying to tie up all of the loose ends involved in this case. Her father was probably in the waiting room. He'd probably come by while she was out of it and she just didn't remember.

She looked across the empty bed in the darkened other half of the room. Through the window, she could see the skyline of Phoenix, the hulking shape of South Mountain and its blinking red-lighted arials in the background. Twin villages of rectangular glass high-rises, symbols of the new Southwest, clustered around Central Avenue and the state capitol, rising up like multicolored alien intruders from the otherwise single-story cityscape. Above Phoenix, the night sky was clear and black, peppered with stars, taking up three-fourths of her window space, and just looking at it made her feel better.

What about Jimmy? she wondered. Had the police found him? Somehow, she thought that they had. It was not a question that bothered her, not something she was worried about, and she assumed that she'd heard he was all right while still under the influence of the painkillers.

She closed her eyes for a second. Everything seemed so confused, so disjointed, so out of sync.

Was this what it was like to be on drugs?

There were footsteps in the hall outside, men's voices talking low, and then Allan was walking into the room. He looked worried and worn out, and though that was to be expected, there was something else in his expression, in his manner, that she could not quite identify and that put her on edge.

Allan smiled at her. The smile was genuine, but the worried crease in his forehead remained. "How are you?" he asked.

She smiled wanly, tried to lift her cast. "I've been better." She cleared her throat. "How's Jimmy?"

"He's coming along. He's in shock, but the injuries are mostly superficial. There are no broken bones or anything. I imagine you'll be able to see him tomorrow."

"Where did you find him?"

"What? Oh, I forgot. You were gone by then. We found him in the garage. Randy had tied him up, hung him from a beam and was using him for . . . target practice, I guess. He'd been throwing soccer balls at him."

Cathy sucked in her breath.

"He's okay, really. He'll be up and about in no time."

"Have you . . . ?" Cathy's voice trailed off.

"Caught him?" Allan said gently. "No. But it's only a matter of time." He sat down on the chair next to the bed and put his hand on hers. "I didn't have time before, but I wanted to apologize. I was wrong. I should have listened to you. I—"

"Shhhh." She used her left hand to put a finger over his lips. "It's all over with."

He nodded, but there was still something in his expression that bothered her, a cautious, almost secretive look, as though . . . As though he was keeping something from her.

The rhythm of her heart shifted, and all of the saliva suddenly fled her mouth.

She took a deep breath. "Where's my father?" she asked. "Why hasn't he come to see me?" She saw the expression on Allan's face and felt a sinking feeling in the pit of her stomach. "He's dead. Oh, my God. He's dead."

Allan looked away, stared at his shoes, said nothing.

"He's dead, isn't he?"

"Cathy, I don't think you should be—"

She pulled her hand away from his. "At least have enough respect for me to tell me the truth."

Allan thought for a moment, looked at her, and took a deep breath. There was pain in his features, sympathy in his eyes. "Yes," he admitted. "Your father is dead."

"Oh, Jesus," Cathy said. "Oh, Jesus." She'd been prepared, she'd known what to expect, but the confirmation still made her feel as though a hole had been punched into her, instantly letting out all of the air in her lungs, all of the strength in her system, all of the emotions in her heart, all of the thoughts in her mind. She slumped back on the pillow, drained and empty and numb. Allan reached for her hand, tried to say something, but she dazedly shook her head, waved him away.

She had not liked her father for a long time, had sometimes hated him, but she had never wished him dead. Never. Now she didn't know how she felt about him. She didn't know how she felt about anything. The thoughts in her mind were confused and out of sequence, and whatever emotions she was supposed to experience were buried beneath a blanket of numbness. She wished she'd had an opportunity to at least work out her feelings before this had happened. She wished she had been able to prepare herself somehow, to talk with her father, to sort things out. Now it was too late. He was gone.

"Cathy, I—"

"Go," she said, shaking her head. "Leave."

"I'm sorry—"

"Please. I just want to be alone right now." She closed her eyes, pulled the sheet up above her chin, as though merely speaking a sentence of that length had taken a lot of the strength and will out of her.

"I have to tell the doctor that I told you. He asked me not to and said that it would upset you, but . . ." His voice trailed off.

Cathy did not respond. She rolled over, faced the empty bed and the window, pulled the sheet higher.

Allan touched her lightly on the top of the head. "Cathy?"

"Go away."

"I'll be back later," he said.

He turned around in the doorway, looked at her, was about to say something else, then thought the better of it and hurried down the hall.

Fifty-two

He was in the hospital and he knew he was in the hospital, but part of Jimmy could not believe it. The scene around him seemed distanced, removed from himself, as though he were watching it on TV or imagining it in his mind.

There was no disorientation. He knew exactly where he was. He had awakened several times along the way—in the ambulance, in the examination room—and though his bouts of consciousness had been brief, the images retained by his mind were vivid and coherent. He had a pretty good idea of what had happened to him.

But it was still hard to believe.

He tried to swallow, but his mouth was dry and he could only cough. The cough stuck in his throat, and he felt like throwing up. He reached over to the tray next to his bed, where he could see a plastic cup of clear water. He grasped the cup and put it to his lips, swallowing gratefully, the cool soothing liquid dispelling his desire to vomit.

He put the cup back, took a deep breath. What surprised him most was that he was alive. After what had happened, he thought that he'd be dead.

Dead.

Like his dad.

Jimmy suddenly remembered his dad seated on the toilet, his eyes open—

Cut his dick clean off.

—the sound of blood drip drip dripping into the water.

He felt like throwing up again, and he quickly looked around the room. His eyes alighted on his mom, sleeping in a chair on the opposite side of his bed. He had not noticed before that his mom was here, and her mere presence immediately made him feel better. His mom used to sleep in a chair by his bed when he was little, when he was sick and he had a fever. She would watch him while he slept, wiping the sweat from his forehead, periodically waking him up to have his temperature taken or to take a cold bath, and he would always feel safe knowing that she was around, knowing that she was taking care of him. He felt safe now, too, for the first time in a long while, and though part of him wanted to wake up his mom and hug her and tell her what had happened to him and let her comfort him, another part, a newer part, wanted to be alone and decided to let her sleep.

He closed his eyes. He didn't feel as sad as he should. He wasn't crying and he didn't feel like crying.

But he'd loved his dad. Despite everything, he had still loved his dad.

Hadn't he?

He lay unmoving on the bed, eyes closed. He wanted to think about his dad, wanted to go over in his mind all of the things the two of them had done together, wanted to remember the good times they had shared, but he could not get out of his brain the image of his dad on the toilet, bluish hands hanging limply at his sides, bloodshot eyes open, bloody penis in his mouth, dripping gash between his legs. When he tried to think of his dad at home, making breakfast, mowing the lawn, getting ready for work, the picture would not come. Like a broken television set, his mind remained on a single channel, and the harder he tried to remember his dad alive, the more vivid became the memory of his death.

"No!" Jimmy yelled, angry, frustrated, trying to force the image out of his mind.

His mom awoke instantly and quickly sprang up from her seat to sit next to him on the bed. She took his hands in hers.

"No!" Jimmy yelled.

"It's okay," she said soothingly. "Everything's all right."

She took him in her arms and held him, and though he opened his eyes and hugged her back, hard, he still saw in his mind his murdered father. He squeezed her tightly. He wanted to tell his mom what had happened, wanted to tell her what he had seen, wanted her to understand everything he had been through, but before he could even say a word to her he was crying.

Fifty-three

Ellen Brigham had been on duty since nine in the morning, and she was beat. Wanda, as usual, had been late for her shift, and Ellen had had to cover for her. Then Barbara had called in sick, and Sam had recruited her to handle Admissions until a substitute could be found for the night.

That had been two hours ago.

General Admissions wasn't bad—at least it wasn't Emergency—but she'd been in the hospital for so long today that she felt like a damn patient. And with all of the cops hovering around the building, the place felt more like a police station than a hospital.

To top it all off, she was supposed to go out dancing with Hank tonight, and she'd had to keep calling him at home with revised estimates of her time of arrival. Now it looked as though she was going to have to call him yet again and cancel out entirely.

Which might have been one reason why she didn't see the retarded boy walk through the double doors into the lobby and then past the line of waiting patients into the restricted hallway beyond.

Elvin Brown hummed to himself as he mopped the

white linoleum of the first-floor stockroom. He always
hummed while he worked. Hell, sometimes he even
hummed songs he didn't like. Yesterday he'd caught
himself mopping to the rhythm of that old white-bread
Captain and Tennille piece of crap, "Love Will Keep
Us Together," one of the true pukers of all time.

But he liked to hear music while he worked, and if
there was no radio on, he automatically supplied the
tune himself. He couldn't help it, and, for better or
worse, his brain was like a real radio station—some
of the songs in there were classics, some of them stunk
to high heaven.

Today he was going through the Stevie Wonder
hit parade.

Good stuff.

He reached the end of the dispensary and sat down
for a moment to rest on the small two-step ladder
provided for the shorter nurses and doctors. The
building was air conditioned, but when he was mopping or sweeping in little closed back rooms like this,
he always ended up sweating like a pig. It was probably psychological, but it never felt to him like the
cooled air reached far enough back in these non-
public areas of the building.

He picked up his sports bottle from where he'd
placed it on the floor, uncapped the small drinking
tube, and sucked down a big gulp of water. He wiped
the sweat from his forehead, swirled the water around
in his mouth before swallowing it. He'd just bought
the bottle two days ago, and it still tasted new. He
closed his eyes, savoring the flavor. His wife, he knew,
would object to such a taste, would clean and scrub
the plastic until there was no trace of anything left in
the container, but to him it brought back memories.
Good memories. It reminded him of the taste of summer water from a hose, where the blank taste of the
cool liquid was lightly overlayed with a subtle hint of
rubber. And that reminded him of childhood. And
that made him feel good.

He opened his eyes.

And there was a kid standing in the doorway.

Elvin damn near jumped. He put down the bottle, stood. He wasn't a nervous guy, not a jittery sort by any stretch of the imagination, but something in the way the kid had just suddenly appeared spooked him. He laughed, trying to make a joke out of it. "You startled me, sport. Didn't see you there."

The kid said nothing.

Elvin looked at the boy more carefully. He looked like a retard, Elvin thought, looked like he'd probably snuck down from the fourth floor where they kept the "special" kids. But there was another quality to this one too. An element of wrongness, a feeling that Elvin couldn't quite place but that he definitely didn't like.

He smiled at the kid, though the smile didn't come natural like it usually did and it felt funny on his face. "You know this is off limits to patients," he said. "You'd best be movin' along if you don't want to get into no trouble."

Then the kid grinned at him, and, Jesus, there was something in that grin that made him want to pee his pants. A field of solid cold goosebumps ran down his back. It was crazy, but looking at that little boy he felt the same way he had last December when a group of skinheads had surrounded him in the parking lot of the mall, before the chance arrival of a stray police car had scared them away.

The kid's eyes darted around the room, taking in the shelves of bottles and phials, the rows of boxed supplies and new equipment, and for a brief second, Elvin thought, he didn't look so retarded. He looked . . . not intelligent exactly, but . . . crafty. Like the look a not-quite-tamed dog got when it knew it could do something wild and get away with it. Only this look was a lot deeper, a lot more serious, and a lot scarier.

"You'd better go now," Elvin said, walking toward the boy, and he tried to make his voice sound as authoritative as possible. "They'll be looking for you."

The kid stared at him, looked him up and down,

then kicked him hard in the left knee, connecting with what had to be the leg's equivalent of the funny bone. Elvin went down, his suddenly useless knee a whirling spiral of agony. Before he could even raise himself up off the floor, the boy had grabbed a spray bottle of some chemical and squirted the mixture into Elvin's eyes.

The pain was immediate and overwhelming. The world disappeared in a blurry stabbing spasm of anguish, and Elvin felt his eyeballs burn and begin to dissolve, the outer covering thinning and disappearing as viscous juices oozed out, the sensation shooting straight into his screaming brain.

In the universe beyond his own pain, he heard a clatter of metal, a rattle of glass.

And then the boy jumped hard onto his back and snapped his spine.

Fifty-four

The lights flickered, dimmed, brightened as backup generators kicked into gear, then finally blacked out entirely.

Dobrinin stood up and flipped on his flashlight. He wished he hadn't let Montoya take ten for a coffee break. He'd feel a hell of a lot better right now if there were two of them staked out in front of this babe's room.

But how was he supposed to know that the retard would find his way to the hospital?

He glanced at his watch, the digital letters easy to read in the darkness. The security man had said Randy was on the second floor three minutes ago. Allan, Pynchon, and a whole shitload of backup should be arriving within the next five minutes. It would probably take the damn kid longer than that to—

There was the sound of a door clicking closed at the far end of the hall.

And shuffling tennis-shoe footsteps.

Dobrinin tensed, switched the flashlight to his left hand, unholstered his gun. His hands were sweaty. "Who is it?" he called. He pointed the flashlight toward the sound. He could see the precise borders of the beam in the blackness.

And there was the kid.

A chill passed through Dobrinin as his flashlight played across the unmoving form of the boy. Short and squat, he looked more like a midget than a child.

A malevolent midget.

An evil midget.

Dobrinin's bladder suddenly felt full, the muscles in his crotch too weak to control, and he knew he was going to piss his pants. He'd never been this scared in his entire life, and for the first time he wished that he'd followed his old man's advice and gone to pharmacy school. Pharmacists didn't get killed while doing their job; they did their day's work, went home, and had a peaceful night's sleep.

That was stupid. He wasn't a pharmacist. He was a cop. He had always wanted to be a cop and now he was, and now that the shit had come down he was turning pussy. He tried to steel himself, tried to will himself not to be frightened. The kid wasn't a Superman. He might be a genius, but he was still just a child: shorter, smaller, and weaker than he himself was.

The element of surprise, Dobrinin thought. That was what the kid had in his favor. That was the reason he'd been able to do what he had. No one had been expecting him. No one had been prepared for him. That's all there was to it.

Dobrinin stared at the boy. He tried to be brave, tried to think logically of all the points on his side of the scale, but his resolve fled quickly. The child did look evil. There was something in the kid's face, particularly, that he didn't like. A blankness. A complete absence of expression that went far beyond anything he had seen on even the most severely retarded individual.

Then Randy's expression changed. The slack jaw closed, mouth muscles moving upward in an idiot grin, a strange light sparking in the drooping almond eyes.

He began loping down the hall toward Dobrinin in a weird, angled, awkward half-run, swinging his thick arms in an unnatural rhythm that threw grotesque shifting shadows on the walls and ceiling.

Dobrinin pointed his pistol, shot, but his flashlight arm had dropped and the bullet went high.

And then the boy was on him.

The scalpel that slashed open his eyeballs looked shiny even in the dark.

Fifty-five

At twelve o'clock, a nurse had come in to turn off the lights and the television. Although Cathy's eyes were closed in an effort to fall asleep, she was still wide awake, her overactive mind unable to slow down after the horrible events of the day. She wanted the lights to remain on, she wanted the TV to remain on, but for some reason she said nothing while the nurse performed her curfew duties. She pretended to be asleep, not stirring even when the nurse pulled the blanket up around her chin.

When she opened her eyes a few moments later, the room was dark. She knew that a policeman was stationed just outside her door to protect her, but she still didn't feel very safe. She closed her eyes again, tried not to think about her father.

She had finally succeeded in falling asleep when she was awakened by the sound of gunfire. Or rather the sound of a shot. A single shot that echoed and reverberated through the building with the force of a cannon. She sat up in bed, instantly wide awake, and noticed immediately that no lights were on. No light was even creeping under the door.

Through the window, the other wing of the hospital was visible, and it, too, was shrouded in darkness.

The power was off.

From the hallway came a strangled scream.

She held her breath, her heart feeling too large in her chest. Then she heard another sound.

A sound that made her blood run cold.

"Ba! Ba! Babababa!"

Randy.

Cathy froze, suddenly unable to move. She knew she should get out of bed, try to get away, but her brain seemed to have temporarily lost contact with her muscles. Randy's voice had come from a ways down the hall, but she could tell that he was close. Somehow, he had found her here, tracked her down. He was going to finish what he had started. He was going to kill her.

The door was closed but she did not know if it was locked and, heart pounding crazily, she slipped quietly out of bed and across the room to the door. She was hoping unreasonably for a big deadbolt or something, but there was only a regular doorknob lock. She held the knob with the elbow crook of her broken arm, turned the lock with her good hand, and backed away from the door. There had been only a small barely audible click, nothing he could have heard, and she prayed that he did not know where she was, was randomly searching and would skip her door entirely.

But she had to be prepared.

She hurried quietly back to her bed. She tried to push it over, planning to use it as a sort of wall or barricade to hide behind in case he did get in somehow, but with only the one good arm she could not even get it to roll, much less tip over. Praying that the locked door would hold him until help could arrive, she picked up the phone, intending to quickly and quietly call hospital security. She dialed "O" for the operator, winced at how loud the beep sounded in her ear. The phone rang once. Twice. Thrice.

And then the doorknob rattled and began to turn. It hadn't locked!

She looked desperately around the room for a weapon of some sort, hoping against reason that there was an extra scalpel or syringe lying on the metal tray adjoining her bed, but of course there was nothing.

And then the door swung open and he was standing in the doorway, backlit by the dim refracted glow of a downed flashlight, and he was laughing, that frighteningly deliberate adult laugh she had heard before in the hallway of his house. Her legs felt rubbery, as weak as her broken arm. The sight of that short squat silhouette triggered some sort of mnemonic reaction within her. There was no way for her to escape, and there was nothing she could do about it.

Something hardened within her. She couldn't give in. She had to at least try to fight him. She ducked behind the bed, hoping that he hadn't seen her in that first second, that his eyes were still adjusting from the soft light of the hallway to the total darkness of the room.

Through the space under the bed, she could see his feet and the lower portion of his body.

"Ka!" he cried. "Ka! Ka! Kakaka!"

He took a step forward.

She reached up. On the nightstand next to her bed was a flower vase left over from the previous occupant, and with her good arm she grabbed the vase by the thin neck, smacking it against the floor. She'd wanted it to break cleanly enough to be used as a weapon, the way she'd seen Coke bottles break for people in movies, but instead of cracking along a sharp jagged edge, the vase shattered into dozens of small shards too small to be used for anything at all.

She began crying, unable to stop the tears of fear and frustration from streaming down her unwilling cheeks, but she crawled backward across the floor toward the next bed.

"Ka!" Randy repeated happily. "Kakakaka!"

He dropped to his knees, bent over, peered at her through the space underneath her bed, and grinned.

Fifty-six

Jimmy, too, was awakened by the shot. He, too, noticed immediately that the hospital was dark.

He, too, heard Randy's cry.

Jimmy glanced over at the chair next to his bed, but it was empty. His mom was gone.

He felt an instant of panic. Where was she? Was she out there in the hospital somewhere? Near . . . him?

He kicked the covers off his bed. He was more afraid now than he had been even when hiding from Randy in the shower. He knew what Randy was capable of doing.

But he was also tougher now than he had been before. He was stronger.

He swung his feet off the bed, tried to stand and almost collapsed. He held himself up with his arms, balancing one hand on the mattress, one on the nightstand, and waited for a few seconds until he regained his equilibrium. He took a tentative step forward, grimacing. It hurt to walk. His ankles were weak and painfully sore; he could still feel the pressure of the rope around them. His head was pounding as well; all of the painkillers they had pumped into him had not been able to entirely quell the thumping in his skull, although the sensation was now closer to a dull ache than to the previously sharp stabbing.

He opened the door to his room, holding onto the knob for support, and stepped into the hallway. The corridor was dark, pitch black save for the single yellow beam of a grounded flashlight fanning outward halfway down the corridor. His eyes followed the path of the flashlight, and he leaned, almost fell, against the wall as he saw what was revealed in the dissipating illumination.

The corridor was covered with broken equipment and unmoving bodies.

He closed his eyes, opened them, but the nightmare scene was still there. Close in, near his end of the hallway, lay a tangle of metal hospital equipment, what looked like a broken stretcher, and two crumpled human forms. One of the figures, a woman, wearing nothing but the remains of a ripped hospital gown, was staring at him with dead eyes, a sharp pole of metal emerging from her cheek. Further down the hall, lying next to the flashlight, he could make out what appeared to be a downed policeman. Everywhere blood, a shocking amount of it, had splashed onto the walls and pooled into wide puddles on the floor.

He'd been here. Randy. He'd been here.

Jimmy forced himself to walk forward, stepping gingerly around as much of the blood as possible. It could not be avoided completely, though, and several times he heard a soft squish as his foot came down, felt stickiness as he lifted it up once again.

He reached the flashlight, picked it up, shone it about the corridor. The carnage wasn't nearly as pervasive as he'd originally thought. The flashlight beam had somehow illuminated the worst of the destruction, carving a path through the blackness that hit both bodies and the machine mess near his room, but he could see now that most of the corridor was clear, untouched.

He wondered if there were other patients behind

the other doors off the hallway. If there were, they were obviously bedridden and could not get out to see what had happened. Otherwise, they too would have come out when they heard the shot.

Unless they were dead.

He had to get off the floor, find a doctor, find a nurse, call the police.

There was a scream from behind the closed door of the next room down and to the left. A scream that was at once familiar in the specifics of its voice and totally alien in the terrified hopelessness of its pitch. He stopped walking, his heart lurching in his chest. Cathy. It was Cathy.

She was in the room and Randy was in there with her.

Panicked, he looked down. On the floor at his feet, still clutched in the outstretched hand of the dead cop, was a revolver. Jimmy bent down, his knees cracking loudly in the silent corridor, and placed the flashlight on the ground. He did not want to touch a dead body, not even a hand, not even a finger, but Cathy was in danger, was being attacked, was probably going to be killed and he was the only one who had even half a hope in hell of doing anything to save her. He quickly reached out, grabbed the muzzle of the revolver and pulled, but the policeman's finger was still caught on the trigger and would not be dislodged. Jimmy grimaced distastefully and, holding the muzzle with one hand, used his other hand to straighten the dead policeman's finger and push it out of the trigger catch. The man's skin was still warm, but the hand and finger felt heavy, strange, and Jimmy stood immediately after pulling free the gun, nearly jumping back from the body.

He took a deep breath. He had never fired a gun in his life, had only seen it on TV and in the movies, but he thought he had a fairly good idea of how to work the weapon. Using both hands, he held the revolver out in front of him.

Cathy screamed again (had she ever stopped

screaming? He hadn't noticed), and he used a finger
to cock the hammer back. It was heavier than he
thought and harder to pull than it looked on TV, but
it caught, and then his finger was on the trigger and
he was walking forward.

His hands were shaking before he reached the door,
as much from the weight of the gun as from fear, but
he managed to keep the revolver pointed in front of
him, and he kicked the door with his foot. He had not
thought that the door might be locked, that it might
just be closed, that his kick might bounce off unmoving wood, but the thought occurred to him now, at
the last minute, when it was too late for him to do
anything about it. Fortunately the door had been partially open to begin with, and it swung inward with
his kick. It did not swing far enough, however, did not
fly forward and smack the wall with a crash the way
doors did when kicked by cops. It simply pushed halfway open then began to close again.

Still holding the gun in front of him, Jimmy turned
his body to the side, pushed open the door with his
shoulder and burst into the room.

Randy was standing next to the first bed, staring at
him, smiling.

Holding a scalpel.

Jimmy's first thought was that he had made a mistake, a huge mistake, that Cathy was not here at all.
The room was lighter than the corridor, semilit by the
light of the world outside the window, and after the
blackness of the corridor he could see fairly well.

But he did not see Cathy.

He had heard her screams, had heard the terror in
her hoarse high-pitched shrieks, but now there was
only Randy, alone in the room and waiting for him.
He was about to run, about to turn and take off down
the hallway to try to find a stairway, but then he heard
a muffled snuffling hiccupped cry from somewhere
past the first bed, and he knew that Cathy was here.

"Pa!" Randy said. "Pa! Pa!" He began to advance

on Jimmy, holding the scalpel at a level just above his head.

Staring into the familiar blankness of that retarded face, seeing the same look of expectant joy that he'd seen upside down in the garage, Jimmy was filled with rage, with hate, and with an adrenaline rush of courage.

Arms shaking, he fired.

The bullet hit. Amazingly, it hit. The recoil knocked him back, made him drop the gun, diverted the focus of his eyes for a second, but when he looked again at Randy, he saw that the boy was sitting on the ground and that he had dropped the scalpel. The sharp instrument lay on the floor halfway between the two of them.

Jimmy rushed forward and grabbed the scalpel to make sure that Randy could not pick it up again. He backed away, toward the spot where he'd dropped the gun, keeping his eyes on the other boy. He could not see any blood on Randy's shirt or pants, on his arms or his head, and he wondered if he hadn't missed him after all, if the sound of the shot hadn't just scared Randy into dropping the scalpel and falling down.

Then Randy stood, and Jimmy saw the dark stain snaking down the underside of the boy's hand. He had shot off one of Randy's fingers.

Randy laughed, his normal, natural evil adult laugh, and Jimmy realized with horror that the boy did not realize that one of his fingers was gone. He did not feel any pain.

"Pa! Pa! Pa!" Randy said. He reached down, pretending to pick up a soccer ball and throw it at Jimmy's head.

"Get out!" Cathy cried from behind the bed. "Jimmy! Go get help!"

Randy continued to laugh.

The combination of Cathy's terrified voice and Randy's familiar reactions caused something in Jimmy to snap. He looked at the retarded boy, and he suddenly wanted to kill him, to make sure once and for all that he would never be able to hurt anyone ever again. "Fucker!" he cried. He advanced on Randy. There was hate in his eyes as he walked toward the boy, slashing the air with the scalpel. "Fucker!"

"No!" Cathy screamed. "Jimmy!"

Randy ran forward, laughed, cawed, and stepped easily aside, avoiding Jimmy's attempted swipe. He kicked Jimmy hard in the back, sending him flying chin-first into the floor, then leaped onto his back and grabbed a handful of his hair, jerking up his head.

Jimmy felt a whipcrack of excruciating pain flash through his back and neck, superceding the dulled agony that had been there before.

Then he felt his hair yanked, his head jerked back, and then he was out.

Fifty-seven

Cathy crouched behind the bed, despair nearly overwhelming her as she watched Jimmy's head fall limply to the floor. It was hopeless. She might have given up there and then, might have sat and waited for Randy to come, for it all to be over, but instead of twisting Jimmy's neck, breaking his spine or in some other way killing him, Randy stood and moved away from Jimmy's unconscious body. He walked over to where the scalpel lay and, chuckling, picked it up. She held her breath, but instead of moving back toward Jimmy and carving him up, the savant turned once again toward herself.

He might kill Jimmy later, but for now he was going to let the boy live.

He wanted to play with him some more.

That gave her the resolve to stay alive, to keep fighting.

"Da!" Randy called.

How long had this been going on? Three minutes? Five? Ten? It seemed like an hour. If she could just stall, if she could just manage to keep Jimmy and herself alive for a little while longer, help would probably come. Someone somewhere in the building must have noticed that the power was out, must have noticed that something was wrong, must have called the police. It was only a matter of time before the troops came to save the day.

"Da!"

If she could just keep the monster at bay until then.

Her head seemed to have cleared, her brain receiving its second wind or the mental equivalent. The muddled fogginess that had impaired her thought processes until now was gone, replaced by a calm rationality. She was still crying, still terrified, but a part of her brain was thinking clearly, overriding the irrational impulses of her instinct. It felt almost as though she were a spectator, a visitor in her own mind, a third party watching the movements of her body but not participating, and she wondered if she were in shock.

She rose to her knees. On the nightstand next to her was the telephone on which she'd tried to call for help. Now she yanked out the receiver, hefted it in her hand. The object was light but solid and could be used as a weapon. If she had to, if she got the chance, she could bludgeon him with it.

She began crawling toward the window, away from the door, away from Randy.

Like the lights, the air conditioner was out, and the room was hot, the air still and dead and humid. Cathy found herself wondering what had happened to the rooms with life-support machines, with emergency medical equipment. She assumed that the hospital had backup generators and that those areas of the hospital took precedence over all others when a blackout occurred, but she could not help wondering if somehow Randy had done something to the backup generators too.

How many people were dead? How many people in the building had Randy killed?

Randy rounded the corner of her bed just as she reached the next bed over. Her grip on the phone receiver tightened. The plastic felt slippery in her sweaty hand.

Then Randy lunged for her.

She had time only to stand, leap on top of the bed, and roll over the other side of the plastic-covered mattress. She felt searing pain in her right foot, on the underside of her arch, and then warm wetness was coating her toes. He had slashed open her foot.

She was on the floor and screaming, the calm reason of a few moments before fled and gone. She tried to stand, tried to crawl, tried to roll away, but no matter how she turned, what she did, she could feel the pressure on her foot and the sudden stabbing pain that overwhelmed her senses and threatened to knock her out.

Randy crowed triumphantly. He too jumped on top of the bed, but when he leaned over the side, scalpel in hand, to see where she was, she forced herself up and used the phone receiver to smack the side of his head. The plastic connected with bone with a satisfying crunch and blood welled from a smashed sunken section of skin above the boy's ear.

She did not wait to see if he was knocked out, if he dropped the scalpel, if he backtracked or came at her. She forced herself to crawl backward toward the window of the room, ignoring the bleeding agony of her slashed foot and the throbbing pain of her broken arm.

The retarded boy toppled over the side of the bed, landing hard on the spot where she had been only seconds before. He continued forward on bended knees, still grinning, his eyes still trained on her face, his hand still clutching the scalpel.

"Da Da Da Da! Dadadadada!"

More than anything, she wanted him to shut up. It was his cries that were driving her crazy, that were making her head pound so. She wanted to scream at him to stop it, but her mind did not have the luxury of coordinating speech, and the desire to yell at him remained a vague impetus at the back of her mind as she crab-crawled toward the window.

He followed her, yelling, laughing, and then they

were there. Cathy looked toward the half-open door at the far end of the room, hoping against hope that she would see lights come on, that she would hear the footsteps of authority, that Allan would rush through the door and kick Randy away from her and save her. But the parallelogram of blackness behind the doorway remained, and she realized that this was it. No one was coming and she could go no further, she could stall no more. Time had run out.

She backed against the wall directly below the window and slumped into a sitting position. She felt weak, and she wondered how much blood she had lost. Randy knelt next to her, and she did not even have the strength or will to put up her hands in defense.

He flicked the scalpel and cut off the tip of her left ear.

He began laughing uproariously.

The rage exploded within her. Rage at Randy, at what he had done to Jimmy, to her father, to her, to everyone else; rage at fate, at the world, at everything that could have and should have been nice but had somehow turned out so desperately wrong. The pain, the hate, the frustration coalesced into a single burning core of anger that filled her with strength and instantly displaced the weakness and fear.

Using the wall against her back for support, she kicked out. Both feet connected with Randy's midsection, and with a harsh involuntary intake of air he fell backward, knocking his head against the floor. The pain of her slashed foot was screaming torturously in the nerve centers of her brain, but she ignored it and rose to her feet and kicked Randy hard in the face. She was still clutching the sweaty receiver, and she brought it down on his forehead, feeling a grim satisfaction as she watched the blood sweep over his eyes and down the sides of his cheeks.

She wanted him to cry, to feel the same pain, the same desperate fear that she and everyone else had felt, but there was no satisfaction to be had there. He continued to laugh, as though he were entirely unaware of the fact that he had been seriously injured, and the blank expression in his eyes told her that even if he had been aware of his injuries, his brain would not have been able to make the causal connection between what he had done and what was now happening to him.

He reached for the scalpel, and again she hit him hard across the face. As blood filled the gaps between his grinning teeth, she thought that he looked as though he was enjoying this, and in a frightening flash of insight she realized that he was enjoying it, that he enjoyed any and all violence—even if it was directed against himself.

She backed away from him, and he jumped to his feet and threw himself at her midsection. She screamed as one fist punched her right breast, the other her stomach. She grabbed him, held his arms, and picked him up by the wrists. He twisted and squirmed in her grasp, his foot connected with her soft stomach, with her softer vagina, but she willed herself not to let go, ignoring the pain, twisting around until his head was against the window, his legs pinned to the wall.

He tried once again to buck out of her grip, but she pushed him hard against the window, throwing all of her weight against him, and a section of glass smashed, broke, cutting the back and left side of his head. Cool night air streamed through the hole in the window. She smelled his blood and his breath, strong and rotten and overpowering against the subtle nicer night smells of the city.

From the parking lot below she heard the sounds of engines and brakes, squealing tires and slamming doors. The sounds were muffled, indistinct, as though coming from underwater. She moved her head next to his and looked down through the window. The police were here. Finally. All she had to do now was hold him and wait until they could get inside and get upstairs. She stared at Randy. He was remarkably light, and for the first time since she had first met him, she realized how young he was. He was just a child. Part of her felt sorry for him. It was as if, at that moment, she could see a normal boy inside the savant, as if there were two beings existing in the same body and she saw for a second the one who had been supplanted.

Then he flung his head backward into the broken window and with a shocking crash of glass knocked out an even bigger opening. Jagged shards ripped the soft skin of his cheeks, causing multiple welling rivulets of blood to pour down his forehead, nose, cheeks, and chin, adding new currents to the streams that were already there, but he was oblivious to the pain and he smoothly grabbed one teetering icicle of glass with his teeth and quickly whipped his head forward. The pointed piece of glass barely missed her throat, and then his head was shifting, compensating, adjusting, maneuvering in an attempt to make sure the next strike was fatal. His head darted forward, and with an animalistic scream of self-preservation she pushed outward and let go, throwing him out of the window. He yelled as he plunged toward the parking lot below, but it was not a cry of fear, it was not a cry of defiance, it was merely his usual attempt at speech: "Ka! Kakakakakakak—"

The cry was shut off in midsound as his body hit the pavement.

Cathy staggered back from the window, looking at her hands, apologizing for her actions though there was no one in authority to hear her. "I didn't mean to do it. It was an accident. He was trying to kill me . . ."

The left side of her head felt cold, and she put a hand there to warm it up, but she felt only stickiness, and she realized that everything sounded muffled because the blood from her cut ear was flowing into the ear's opening.

Was Randy really dead?

Maybe he couldn't be killed. Maybe he had fallen and bounced to his feet and was now racing back up the stairs to get her, yelling at the top of his lungs: "Dadadada!"

She forced herself to step next to the window and look down. In the parking lot below, she could see the white roofs of the just-arrived police cars, parked at random angles in front of the building. Lights were flashing on several of the cars, but there were no sirens, and the dizzying whirl of red and blue in the relative silence gave the entire scene a psychedelic surrealistic air. The policemen themselves had been about to rush inside the hospital and were spread out between the cars, moving toward the front entrance, but now they stopped in midstream and altered their course, converging on the small still body on the ground, drawn like ants to sugar. She could see clearly the pale tops of heads, framed by indistinct blue-black uniforms in the semidarkness.

She stared at the unmoving form of Randy West, the center of all the activity, and she watched as the density of the gathering crowd grew, the pale heads funnelling between the cars and cramming closer together.

He looked small from this angle. Small and amazingly normal.

One by one, as if on cue, the policemen began to look up. Heads would swivel for a moment, searching, then catch sight of her in the window and freeze. She could not see their faces, could not see their eyes, but she had the distinct impression that they were staring at her as she stared at them, and it suddenly seemed to her that the flashing red and blue lights had increased in intensity.

Amongst the upturned faces, Allan's stood out, his features obvious to her even from this height, even in this light. His head seemed more rigid than the others, and it did not move as he stared up at her through the broken window. The sound of voices reached her, and she saw some policemen kneel over the boy's body, saw others hurry to meet the doctors and nurses who had begun to come out of the hospital, but she continued to stare at Allan. His gaze made her uncomfortable. She felt hot, slightly nauseous, and she backed away from the window into the safe darkness of the room. She moved past both beds, then sat down hard on the floor next to Jimmy.

He was conscious, awake, and she found that she was not surprised.

"We did it," he said, his voice a cracked whisper.

She nodded, took his hand in hers.

He smiled at her, she smiled back, and then she began to cry.

Epilogue

Cathy turned off the faucet, rolled up the hose, and stared for a moment at her chrysanthemums, admiring their bright colors, noting the new buds that were peeking out even this late in the season. The flowers made her feel good and served to remind her that not everything in the world, not even everything in her life, revolved around human beings and their actions.

She found that thought comforting somehow.

There was a weed growing next to one of the chrysanthemums, a refugee from the lawn, and she bent down and plucked it out.

She found herself wondering again what David was doing. Where he was. Who he was. Had he gone to college? Did he have a job? Was he married? She realized that she did not know what he looked like as an adult.

Did she really want to know what David was like now? No. Not really. But the fact that she could actually think about him, could wonder about him without immediately and instinctively pushing the thought from her mind, meant that she was getting stronger, that she was finally putting her past behind her. In all these years, she had never allowed herself to think about her brother in anything but the past tense, and when she thought of him at all it had always been dispassionately, the way one would think of a cartoon character or an inanimate object.

She had hated David and she still hated David, but she was no longer afraid of him. She was no longer afraid of her hate, either. To acknowledge the emotion felt good, to be free to experience it felt better, but she knew too that her hatred would fade. It simply wasn't worth the effort of maintaining it. What had happened was over and done with—it was time to move on.

She walked up the porch steps and into the house, closing the door behind her. The house seemed empty with her father gone, much emptier than she would have thought, and while she had considered selling it, had even discussed the matter with Billy at the funeral, she had eventually decided against it. She had rearranged the furnishings, thrown some things away, bought new items in an attempt to make the house more hers, less her father's, but she found that, right now at least, she still needed this link with the past, she still needed the stability and familiarity provided by her old home.

She walked into the kitchen to get a drink of water. This room, however, was totally different, completely remodeled. The kitchen had been cleaned up by the time she had come and seen it, but she had still known what had happened here, and whenever she'd walked into the room she could not help thinking of her father, dead, crucified on the floor.

She had spent a week at Ann's while Allan oversaw the remodeling. Then and only then had she been able to return.

There had been a lot of other changes during the past few months as well.

For one, the Lauter house was no more. It was gone. The building was still there, vacant and for sale, but it was no longer the Lauter house.

It was the West house.

For now and forever, the residence would be known as the West house.

And it would probably remain on the market for a long, long time.

She did not know what was happening with Katrina West and her . . . husband. She did not want to know. She had purposely avoided reading the newspaper for the past two months, and if a news story came on TV that seemed even remotely connected with the case, she quickly switched the channel. Allan would have been happy to tell her how things were progressing, but he did not volunteer any information and she did not ask. It would have been wrong to say that she was not interested in what happened to Randy's mother and father. She was interested. She just did not want to know.

She wondered if Jimmy felt the same way. She had not really talked to Jimmy since that day, not talked seriously or in depth, and the few times that they had seen each other, the conversation had seemed a little stilted, a trifle awkward. They'd been like old friends who hadn't seen each other in years and who no longer had anything in common.

But she still felt close to Jimmy, still cared about him and always would.

He was now living with his mother in Glendale. They'd decided to sell the house, sell it furnished, and, according to his mother, Jimmy had not taken anything with him. Not clothes. Not toys. Nothing. He wanted nothing that reminded him of the past.

Out of everyone, it was Jimmy she felt for the most. She knew how hard it was going to be for the boy. It would be years, perhaps a lifetime, before he'd be able to put all of this behind him. Like her, he was undergoing therapy, seeing a psychiatrist twice a week, but she knew that that was not always enough. There were a lot of things she wanted to tell him, a lot of advice she wanted to give him, but she knew that it was probably better if she kept her distance at this point. He would have to heal on his own.

She wondered if, in time, his memory of her would be buried, consigned to the black years that he would associate with this time period and blocked out of his consciousness.

Probably.

But that was okay. As long as he turned out healthy and happy and whole. That's what was important.

The phone rang, and Cathy went into the living room to answer it. It was Ann. She was moving tomorrow and wanted to remind Cathy to remind Allan to rent a truck. Originally, Cathy had offered to let Ann move in with her, to stay in the house and pay only minimal, token rent, but Ann, smiling, had suggested that Cathy offer Allan the same deal if she really wanted a roommate.

Cathy had blushed but had not disagreed.

Allan had been great. Through it all, Allan had been great. He had been there for her whenever she needed him, had protected her from the media, had helped her deal with the insurance companies and the lawyers. He had also used some of his vacation time to be with her, and while they were not living together, not roommates yet, they were the closest thing to it.

She glanced up at the clock. Four-thirty. He was coming over today after he got off, around six, and she'd promised to cook dinner. He'd asked for hamburgers, but she'd told him that he got enough cholesterol and that she was not going to contribute to potential health problems.

She told him she'd make chicken fajitas.

Allan arrived early, about five forty-five, and she let him sit in the kitchen while she cooked. She liked to have him around. She enjoyed being with him.

"So, are you staying over tonight?" she asked.

"Do you want me to?"

She nodded.

He grinned and took a sip of his Diet Coke. "I just happen to have tomorrow's clothes in the backseat of the car. What a coincidence."

"You think you're tricky, don't you?"

He laughed. "When you've got it, use it."

After dinner, Allan brought his clothes in from the car and they watched an old Humphrey Bogart movie on cable. Her father had liked Humphrey Bogart. It was one of the few things they'd agreed upon near the end, and as the evening wore on, Cathy became quieter and quieter, more depressed. After the movie, Allan turned off the TV.

"Are you all right?" he asked.

She nodded. "I was just thinking about my father."

He held her, saying nothing. There was nothing to say. They'd been through this before, and it was not something that could be resolved with words. It was just something that had to pass.

Cathy squeezed his hand and tried to smile, but her eyes were misty. She thought of all the times she had sat in this room with her father, and in her mind he was not the mean and misogynistic old man she had been living with for the past ten years but a whole and vital middle-aged parent. He was the loving, caring father she had grown up with, a man ready and willing to take on the world, a man who loved his family and protected it at all costs against all comers. And she wept for the death of that man, though he had really died long ago.

She wiped her eyes. "Don't leave me," she pleaded.

"Never," he said.

And he held her close as she cried for her father, for her mother, for her brother, and for everything she had lost.

And when she had finished crying and the tears had dried, Allan was still there.

ABOUT THE AUTHOR

Born in Arizona shortly after his mother attended the world premiere of *Psycho,* **Bentley Little** is the Bram Stoker Award-winning author of fifteen previous novels and *The Collection,* a book of short stories. He has worked as a technical writer, reporter/photographer, library assistant, sales clerk, phonebook deliveryman, video arcade attendant, newspaper deliveryman, furniture mover, and rodeo gatekeeper. The son of a Russian artist and an American educator, he and his Chinese wife were married by the justice of the peace in Tombstone, Arizona.

Penguin Group (USA) Online

What will you be reading tomorrow?

Tom Clancy, Patricia Cornwell, W.E.B. Griffin,
Nora Roberts, William Gibson, Robin Cook,
Brian Jacques, Catherine Coulter, Stephen King,
Dean Koontz, Ken Follett, Clive Cussler,
Eric Jerome Dickey, John Sandford,
Terry McMillan, Sue Monk Kidd, Amy Tan,
John Berendt...

You'll find them all at
penguin.com

*Read excerpts and newsletters,
find tour schedules and reading group guides,
and enter contests.*

Subscribe to Penguin Group (USA) newsletters
and get an exclusive inside look
at exciting new titles and the authors you love
long before everyone else does.

PENGUIN GROUP (USA)
us.penguingroup.com